MIND GAMES

CAROLYN CRANE

Ballantine / Del Rey
Presidio Press
One World / Spectra

ISBN 978-0-553-59261-0

U.S.A. $7.99 CANADA $10.99

5 0 7 9 9

S EAN

A Secret Cabal

Packard sets out wineglasses, and soon Shelby and Helmut arrive bearing plates piled with skewers of colorful vegetables and fat scallops.

Packard opens a bottle. "Ouzo okay?" He seems to be addressing me.

"For what?"

Packard gives me a stern look. "We're celebrating."

Shelby scoots a chair up next to mine and raises her glass. "I will toast to you, Justine," she says. "May the targets never see you coming." We laugh and clink and make more toasts. I've never belonged to a squad or a club, especially not a secret one like this.

As we dig into our food, I have this crazy sensation that I'm finally home. I smile at the thought. And then I chuckle. And then we all just burst out laughing.

It's exhilarating, just laughing around the table. I have this brief sense of us as supervillains from a B-rate thriller. Except we're more like crime fighters—if there were crime fighters who got their superpowers from being really neurotic, and used them as part of a bizarre and marginally ethical program of criminal rehabilitation.

I gaze across the table and catch Packard staring at me, eyes sparkling in the candlelight. . . .

MIND GAMES

CAROLYN CRANE

SPECTRA
25 YEARS

BALLANTINE BOOKS • NEW YORK

A Spectra Mass Market Original

Copyright © 2010 by Carolyn Crooke

All rights reserved.

Published in the United States by Spectra, an imprint of The Random House Publishing Group, a division of Random House, Inc., New York.

SPECTRA and the portrayal of a boxed "s" are trademarks of Random House, Inc.

ISBN 978-0-553-59261-0

Printed in the United States of America

www.ballantinebooks.com

9 8 7 6 5 4 3 2 1

For Mark

Acknowledgments

First and foremost, I would like to thank my teacher, Ian Leask, for giving me so much of his wisdom on how to actually write a novel. I also owe a huge debt of gratitude to Elizabeth Jarrett Andrew, Marcia Peck, and Teresa Whitman for their tireless readings and brilliant feedback on this manuscript throughout the long haul.

Special thanks to my agent, Cameron McClure, for jumping on this book—and for her strong vision and refusal to settle for easy fixes. I'm grateful also to Juliet Ulman for fighting to buy this novel, and to my wonderful editor, Anne Groell, whose insights and ideas greatly strengthened this text. In fact, I feel lucky to be partnered with all the folks at Spectra—I am honored and blown away by the quality and professionalism of your copy edits, cover art, and support.

So many people have been allies on my adventure through the writing wilderness: my Tertulia pals, the folks in the English Literature and Creative Writing programs at the University of Minnesota, Ian's group of scribblers, and all my writing groups ever.

I'm also eternally grateful to my many blogger pals, whose smart, lively discussions continually deepen my love and understanding of this genre.

Heartfelt thanks to my mom and dad and sisters for all their love and support through the years and a home full of books.

Finally, and most important, I want to thank my husband, Mark—the love of my life, and the greatest manuscript critiquer, creative partner, friend, and helpmeet a girl could ever have.

Chapter One

FROM WHERE WE SIT I have the perfect view of Shady Ben Foley, dining on the other side of the lavishly decorated Mongolian restaurant. He's with an innocent-looking young couple—a pretty girl with dark ringlets and a wholesome blond country-boy fellow. Do they not get what he is?

The last time I saw Foley was maybe fifteen years ago—I was a teen and he was a middle-aged man in drawstring pants, mowing his lawn and ripping off my family. He's grown paler and thicker, but I recognized his sharp little nose and peering eyes the instant I saw him out on the street.

My boyfriend, Cubby, pulls a hunk of meat off his skewer. He's been a good sport, letting me drag him here to basically stalk a man. He smiles, all dimples and short blond curls. "Kebabs is a weird food," he says.

"Definitely."

Cubby glances over his shoulder. "Maybe he's reformed."

"A man like Foley doesn't reform." I glare across the room; judging from his victims' body language, Shady Ben has maneuvered himself into a power position. Con men are experts at that. "I have to warn them."

And this is when I feel it—the sensation of prickles raining over my scalp, followed by a suspicious twinge in my head. *No!* I think. *Please let it not be happening right now!*

"Justine, is something wrong?"

I put down my napkin. "I have to say something."

"It's not your job to save them," he says.

"But I have to try."

A wave of wooziness suggests my blood pressure's dropping. *It really is happening,* I think with some shock. My condition, known as "vein star syndrome," is the proverbial ticking time bomb in the head. Once you're past the point of vascular rupture, no medical attention can save you.

This strange clarity comes over me and I decide not to tell Cubby. If these really are my last minutes, I want to spend them warning these two innocent people, like I wished somebody had warned my family.

I stand and stroll deliberately across the expanse of candlelit tables and Oriental rugs. Hopefully it's not too late.

Time slows as I round one table and then the next. Details take on a dreamlike aura: the snake charmer music, the scents of curry and cinnamon, the painted horse heads and bejeweled scabbards along the walls.

I come up behind the empty fourth chair at their table, gripping the back for support.

"Ben Foley," I say. "Remember me? Justine? From Pembroke Pines?" I can practically feel the blood cascading through my head.

Foley gives me this blank look, then exchanges bewildered glances with his young friends.

"Don't act like it's not you." I take a centering breath to slow my heart rate, thereby extending my precious minutes of consciousness. That's the sort of thing Mom would've suggested.

"I'm sorry," he says. "I'm not Ben Foley."

I turn to Foley's companions who regard me with suspicion.

"Around fifteen years ago, your pal here"—I enunciate his name with *oomph*—"Mr. *Ben Foley*, swindled my dad. He gained his trust, then robbed him. Whatever you have going with him, stop it. Don't trust him."

Shady Ben has been shaking his head vigorously this whole time. "I'm sorry. You have the wrong guy."

"I don't have the wrong guy." The pinpoint sensation at the crown of my head increases. How much time do I have? Ringlets Girl shifts nearer to Foley, as if to protect him. Can she not see I'm trying to help her?

"My name is David DelFino," Foley says. "You want to see my driver's license?"

"As if that would prove anything."

They all seem to be focusing on something behind me, and I turn to see a tall, strikingly handsome man approach. There's a molten quality to his movements, like a leopard walking loose. His hair, the brownish red of an old penny, curls down over his ears, but the oddest thing is the look he gives me.

I'm medium-pretty, and this is not a look you give a medium-pretty girl. It's almost like he *beholds* me, full of awe—as if there's something miraculous about my appearance. What does he see? I've heard of people looking beatific in their last moments of life—is that it? My pulse elevates; the *whooshing* in my ears is nearly deafening.

But then again, nobody else seems to think I look beatific. I decide he must have a highcap mutation of some sort. He's a highcap telepath or maybe a highcap medical intuitionist who sees what's happening—not like that could help me now. Cubby doesn't believe in highcaps, but I do. I just wouldn't trust one.

Briefly the man tears his attention away from me and addresses the table. "Everything okay here?" He's the manager, maybe the owner.

"Case of mistaken identity," Foley crows.

My entire scalp tingles. "Save yourselves," I tell Foley's victims. Surely I read the situation right; surely they're victims. I turn back to the restaurateur, whom I still appear to have in my thrall. "Don't worry; I won't bother anyone anymore."

I make my way back across the dining room to Cubby, who smiles up at me. "How'd it go?"

I take my seat, wondering if my field of vision is dimming, or if it's just the candlelight. I feel like I should say some last words to Cubby, but we've been dating for only two months. Though I really, really liked him.

"Oh, no. You have that look on your face," he says.

"What look?"

His shoulders slump. "Please tell me you're not obsessing about that bursting vein thing again. You are, aren't you?" Cubby sighs. "We just went through one of these this morning."

I feel like I might cry. "This is different. There's this pinpoint sensation . . ."

"It's always different," Cubby says. Cubby's led a charmed life, and when you meet him, you understand that he will continue to lead a charmed life. His luck and good looks and carefree happiness are like forces of nature.

"It's really happening," I whisper.

"Okay, well . . . Justine . . ." He gazes at me solemnly. "Do you think you might have time for dessert before you depart for the hereafter? The chocolate fondue looks excellent."

I exhale indignantly. "You know, even hypochondriacs die of horrible diseases. Sometimes they even die of the horrible diseases they fear the most."

Cubby's expression darkens. He knows who I'm talking about—my mom, dying of vein star syndrome after years of not being believed. I put my hand to my head where the tingles are strongest.

"It's anxiety, Justine. Think about it—you were just in a stressful situation. And wouldn't you have collapsed by now if a vein actually had ruptured?"

"Maybe it's a tiny rupture."

Cubby just stares at me. Then our waitress appears and he turns to quiz her on the fondue, as though I've been prattling on about nothing.

There are four stages my boyfriends—really, all my friends—go through: concern, ridicule, disdain, and finally flight. Cubby, I realize with a sick heart, has just graduated to disdain. I touch my head. Actually, the pinpoint sensation has lessened. The tingles linger, but yes, it could be anxiety.

The waitress describes the meltiness of the chocolate, eyes shining. Like most waitresses, she's charmed and excited to be waiting on Cubby. For the trillionth time I wish I could be free of fear, even for just one day.

Why can't I be normal?

I have many pathetic pastimes. One of them is what I call an aspirational shopping trip, where I'll go to this exclusive coat store and find the most beautiful coat to try on and walk around in, relishing its snuggly, elegant construction. Thanks to my low retail wages and my sky-high medical debt, of course, I can never actually have such a coat.

I can never actually have Cubby, either—he's an aspirational boyfriend. Because soon the episodes of health anxiety, the panicked phone calls, and the midnight treks to the ER will outweigh whatever he sees in me. And now I've ruined our night out, which was supposed to be a celebration for his being named top salesperson at InfiniVector Systems. He sold the most business operations and assets integration software of anybody in the entire company.

He excuses himself for the rest room and I take the opportunity to go up to the bar to pay the bill. It's the least I can do—not that I can afford it. I'm praying my card clears when Shady Ben Foley sidles up next to me and loudly requests another round for his table. The bartender turns to his wall of bottles and Shady Ben turns to me, drawing in a breath like he's inhaling my scent.

"Greedy, stupid, and paranoid, with two suitcases full of undocumented cash," he hisses. "Forgot what a perfect mark your pop was. Probably my easiest ever."

I stare, shocked, as he exhales oniony breath. Then he slides his fat tongue up over his lip, revealing its slimy underbelly, adding grossness to insult.

My heart races, and my head tingles dangerously. But I straighten up and smile, like he's this buffoon. If there's one thing I'm good at, it's hiding fear and horror. I spend my whole life hiding fear and horror.

"There were ten suitcases of cash," I lie. "You didn't know because you're an idiot."

The deadish way he peers at me gives me chills; I want desperately to escape. The bartender starts placing drinks on a tray.

I smile and continue. "We hardly even missed the two." Another lie. The truth is that Foley's scam helped to destroy what was left of our family.

A hand on Foley's shoulder; it's the handsome restaurateur. "Those drinks for you?" He doesn't wait for Foley's answer. "I'll have Chuck bring them out to your table. On the house. Sorry about all this." He gestures toward me. Me!

With an oily smile, Foley pushes off the bar.

"I wasn't bothering him," I protest. "He came up to me."

"I know," the restaurateur says, watching Foley cross the large, dim dining room. "I know." Some men are handsome in a sculptural, symmetrical way, but the restaurateur's good looks come from imperfection:

bumpy, maybe once-broken nose, crudely shaped lips, a sort of rough-and-tumble allure you can feel sure as gravity. "Forget him." He draws closer, and I become acutely aware of my pulse pounding. "I want to talk about what I can do for you, and what you can do for me."

"I'm fine, thanks," I say. "My boyfriend and I are just finishing up."

"You're fine?" He looks at me hard—looks into me, it seems. "What about the vein star problem?"

How does he know? "What about it?" I ask.

He smiles, all radiant self-possession. "I'm the one who can cure you."

"Cure me of what? Anxiety or vein star syndrome?"

"Both. I can give you your life back."

I regard him carefully. He has to be a highcap. My guess is he read my thoughts back there and wants to con me. Still, I have to ask. "What's the something I do for you?"

"You'd work for me."

"Doing what?"

"Does it matter? Is there anything you wouldn't do to be free?"

I know a Faustian proposition when I hear one. "A lot of things. I'm not that desperate."

"You were desperate ten minutes ago. You'll be desperate again." He fixes on my eyes. Slow smile. He's like this handsome maniac.

"I'm used to desperate, buddy. Desperate's my factory default. But thanks anyway."

I return to our table to find Cubby digging into dessert. He protests about my paying, of course.

I say, "You paid for the last ten meals and I can't buy you one congratulatory dinner?"

He tilts his head. "Thanks, Justine."

"Well, congratulations to you, Cubby." I don't tell him about the drama up at the bar; it'll just remind him how messed up I am. I glare over at Foley and his victims.

"It was kind of you to stick your neck out when it wasn't even your problem."

Crime is everybody's problem; that's what I'm thinking. I spear a nutty, gooey cluster with my fondue fork and dip it into the melted chocolate. "Mongolian Fondue," I say. "Very authentic."

Cubby beams at me like I said something clever. He always thinks I'm cleverer than I am.

Chapter Two

WE'RE STUCK IN TRAFFIC soon after we turn onto the lakefront. Up ahead you can see the Midcity police walking between cars, checking in windows. Flashlight beams flit like bright bugs over the boulders piled along the shore.

"Jailbreak," Cubby says. "I bet you anything. They'll never find him here."

I nod. Lake Michigan on one side, warehouse ruins and half-built condos on the other. It's a wonderland of hiding places.

"You don't hear about constant jailbreaks in other major metropolitan areas," he says. "No wonder crime's out of control. If they can't even keep the perps locked up . . ." He points at me. "And don't say it's all because of the highcaps."

"Okay."

"You were thinking it."

"Lots of people are thinking it."

Cubby looks away. He's one of the few people left in Midcity—besides the authorities, of course—who still maintain that believing in highcaps is like believing in UFOs and Elvis sightings. "Even physics professors are susceptible to mass hysteria," he says.

"Did you hear me mention the physics professors?"

"No. But you were about to mention them."

He's right—I was. Two physics professors witnessed last month's brick attack, and they've been going on all the news shows saying that the brick's zigzag trajectory defied the laws of physics, and that there's no way it was propelled by a high-powered slingshot like the authorities claim. They didn't come out and say it was highcaps, but that was the implication.

The crime wave makes me sad and angry, and every year it gets worse. Now, thanks to our new serial killer, the Brick Slinger, the playgrounds and ballparks are empty even though it's the height of summer, and people scurry from cars to houses to cars, many of them wearing helmets and hardhats, even when it's ninety degrees. Midcity used to be a happy city. And in spite of our decaying industry and schools, we managed to stay average in most every measure—people were really proud of that. Now they live in fear.

I know all about fear. And nobody deserves to live that way.

"Chief Otto Sanchez is going to turn this around," I say.

"You put way too much faith in that man."

"Just wait, you'll see. He different and he *cares*. You can tell."

Cubby lowers our windows. "He's the same as the rest." The warm breeze off the lake smells faintly of rotting fish.

I give an annoyed little grunt. It's not like I know Otto Sanchez personally, but I have this deep trust in his goodness, his arrow-straight strength. Even seeing photos of him makes me feel warm inside. He's the man who will turn this city around—I'm sure of it. From time to time he also stars in various fantasies of mine, though these have little to do with law and order.

I turn to smile at the officer who comes up to my

window. He swings his flashlight beam around on Cubby's backseat.

The Brick Slinger is a telekinetic, of course—the most common kind of highcap. Telekinetics are believed to be responsible for a lot of the burglaries and pickpocketings, though highcap telepaths and precogs reportedly cause their share of mayhem. Some people blame the highcap mutations on the sludgy Midcity River. That's a little comic-booky for me, but who knows?

As soon as the cops turn to the car behind us, Cubby rolls the windows back up. "We'll be here forever," he says. And he looks over at me with a suggestive smile.

"Right here? I'm not so sure, Cub." I'm still off-balance from the restaurant situation.

"I understand," he says. He reaches over and places a heavy hand on my knee.

"Cubby—"

He creeps it up teasingly. His hand is smooth except where the weightlifting calluses scratch my tender skin. His hand makes my whole thigh feel alive. I inhale softly.

He says, "Are you sure?"

I'm feeling a lot less sure as his fingers slide up under the hem of my skirt.

"Because if you're not *really* sure . . ."

I give him a saucy look. "That's a winning salesperson's pitch? *If you're not really sure?*"

He moves his hand again: a squeeze, a shift. "I'm just setting the stage for my pitch." The hungry way he looks at me makes my blood race. He moves his hand closer. I find I'm feeling better. He leans over and kisses me, tasting like Mongolian barbeque, pressing his fingers to my panties in the perfect spot. I inhale sharply. He is a connoisseur of perfect spots, and I am a connoisseur of him and his perfect life.

"Let's do it right here," he says.

"Cuthbert Montgomery!" I scold. "We're in a traffic jam!"

"The windows are shaded."

"Not *that* shaded."

"Come on," he cajoles.

"Car sex in public? You've got to be kidding."

"You are such a square."

He's close. I'm *trying* to be a square.

Saved by the honks. The line is finally creeping.

"Patience is a virtue," I say, adjusting my skirt. He puts the car into gear and I sit back.

I was always the kid who followed the rules, cut perfectly in the lines—not because I was normal, but because I came from the town's weird family. People who grew up normal think it's something to be rejected. They're wrong. Normal is a precious kind of freedom, and if you don't have it, it's all you ever want.

Two hours later we're sitting across from each other in Cubby's luxurious whirlpool bath, accommodating each other's shins and feet and discussing the merits of standing sex, which we just had. I liked it, though my standing leg got tired. Cubby had to bend his knees a bit, but it gave his quads quite a workout. We'd moved to the couch partway through.

"You know what this whole thing means, of course."

"The standing?" I ask.

"Winning the top salesperson. The trip. It means we're going to Belize in December."

"You're asking me to go?" I'm stunned. It's seven months away. I can't believe he's asking me something so far in the future.

"Yeah, I'm asking."

"Then I'd love to go with you. I would love that."

"Clear your calendar."

"God, how exciting. I've only ever been to Canada."

"Belize is no Canada, baby."

"I bet." I rest my head on Cubby's knee, trying not to picture dirt-floor clinics and bright tropical bugs darting across rusty surgical instruments. "I bet."

I wake up alone in Cubby's king-size bed after a nearly sleepless night. A note on his pillow: *Off at b-ball*. His Saturday game. Out the window, the sky is a brilliant blue over the smokestacks and less fancy neighborhoods north of the river. Mongolian Delites is over there somewhere. And I know that if I were to clamber over the bedside table and press my cheek to the window, I'd see a slice of Lake Michigan. We joke that that qualifies Cubby's condo as lake view.

I plop my head back down. I'd woken in the middle of the night, panicked that the extreme anxiety I experienced at the restaurant might have triggered a slow leak. Anxiety worsens vein star syndrome, so you get anxiety about anxiety. I sneaked into Cubby's home office and went online and discovered the following horrible news on veinstar.org: a new MD forum posting refers to "persistent" tingling. My tingling is persistent—persistently intermittent. That's a kind of persistence. After that I'd just crept around the dark condo in various states of panic.

This morning, of course, I'm fine. It's easy to see, in hindsight, that you were being a crazed hypochondriac, but when you're in it, it seems so real.

I pull the covers over me, wondering what it would be like to be Cubby. Cubby has faith in life the way you might have faith in a five-star hotel: it's a world of sunny swimming pools, plush towels, and capable people at the front desk, and your happiness is the number-one priority. I want more than anything to live in Cubby's safe hotel. To go through one day without health fears. One day.

An hour later I'm all ready for work in a pink tank top and nubby white skirt I'd stashed at Cubby's, and I'm down on the river promenade buying a tall, extra-strong coffee from an elderly vendor. The city paid all kinds of money to make the promenade pretty, but thanks to the rumors about telekinetic pickpockets and mind-control muggers, it's deserted. And, of course, the Brick Slinger doesn't help. I don't care; I refuse to let the crime wave dictate my movements. Though I do keep my cash pinned to the inside of my purse.

I arrive at Le Toile Boutique, the fancy dress store I manage, right on time. Marnie and Sally, my favorite underlings, are unpacking scarves from China. The scarves have tiny, angry-looking faces on them, and the girls joke about Le Toile's owner being drunk when she ordered them. I lean on the glass counter watching the upscale shoppers rifle through the racks of dresses. A few of them wear steel-reinforced safari hats in pink or beige, the latest in protective headwear. We tend to get a lot of the horsey set in from suburbs like Ellsworth Heights, though I don't know where they got "heights," since the land here is flat for miles.

My thoughts keep going back to the restaurateur. How could he tell about the vein star? Surely he was just a highcap telepath, reading my health anxiety. That's all.

I sigh. I can still picture my mother at the kitchen table in front of her medicines and vitamins. *Never take aspirin for a pinprick headache,* she'd tell my brother and me, *because that's an indicator of vein star syndrome, and the anticoagulant effects of aspirin will only speed the bleedout.*

The doctors and most everybody else thought she was an alarmist—until she died of a ruptured vein star. I was thirteen. I went through the years after that in a haze. I get this pang, thinking back on it, wishing I could have been there for her. I can only imagine how alone and scared she felt.

Dad had health issues, too, though his tastes ran more to a widespread Ebola outbreak. We had a stash of level-four respirators, a year's supply of food and water, and the weaponry to defend it. After Mom died, Dad got even more into protecting us. That's where Shady Ben Foley and the land came in. Freshwater stream. Defensible elevation. After Foley was through with us, we were so poor we had to eat up all the food we'd hoarded.

Dad became reclusive after that. He worked as a programmer, rarely emerging from his bedroom. My older brother moved to Brazil, and as soon as I finished high school, I moved from our rural town to bustling Midcity. I bleached my dark hair blonde, got a job at fancy Le Toile, and started a new life on the sunny side of the street. I thought I'd be free from the family legacy of fear, but it followed me—my very own portable prison.

I try to convince myself that the restaurateur didn't really see anything wrong with me—he read my fear of vein stars, that's all. But what if he's a medical intuitionist highcap? Is it possible my condition is graver than I thought? Now I really wish I knew what the guy was. On the websites you can find lists of what abilities the different highcaps have, from the common telekinetics to the rare dream invaders. The one thing they all have in common is that a mutation heightened their brain capacity in some strange way. And that most people pretend not to believe in them but secretly hate and fear them. Except for Cubby, who simply doesn't believe in them.

"Are you okay, Justine? Did you have insomnia again?"

Marnie and Sally stare at me with concern—an unfortunately common occurrence. I need to get out of here.

I point across the floor. "I'm going home to do some paperwork. When I walk in here tomorrow, I want to see that mannequin wearing one of those scarves in a way that makes it look fabulous."

The girls smile. They love mannequin challenges.

Chapter
Three

IT'S NOON when I get back to my sunny neighborhood of apartments, houses, and shops. It's at the edge of the university area, the kind of neighborhood where people have dogs and marriages, but not yet children. I smile as I pass Mr. K., the Greek jeweler, smoking in front of his storefront; then I almost fall over when I see the couple from last night sitting on the stoop of my building. Ringlet girl and the blond guy.

How'd they find where I live? Did Foley send them? I continue my approach like I'm not worried.

The blond fellow stands and smiles. "I bet you didn't expect to see us." He puts out his hand. "I'm Carter." The smattering of freckles across Carter's wide, frank face stretches almost to his ears. He's of medium height and build but wound up, compact. Everything about him says *contents under pressure*.

"Justine," I say, taking his hand.

Ringlets stands and smiles, revealing a chipped front tooth, which gives her a strange, carnivorous beauty. "I'm Shelby." Her outfit—a green flowered shirt and striped velvet pants—is a little crazy.

Carter says, "Our boss wants to talk with you."

So Foley's their boss? "You can tell Foley I don't want anything to do with him. And by the way, Foley *is* his real name."

Shelby curls her pouty lips into a sneer and enunciates his name with breathy, phlegmy disgust. "Foley." She plops down on the stoop, as if her communication is now complete. She is beautiful and grim all at the same time.

"Foley's not our boss," Carter says. "He's one of our targets."

"Please," Shelby says. "Do not speak to Foley again or you will ruin whole thing." Her accent sounds Russian; she's definitely one of the most un-Shelby-like people I have ever met. "Our boss told you he will help you and he will. He has offer you must hear. You will like it."

"Hold on." I begin to feel unaccountably hot. "Are you talking about that guy—" I gesture to my shoulder to indicate the restaurateur's cinnamon curls, just a little too long. "He's . . ." I'm thinking about his pale green eyes, thick rosy lips; his heft, his presence, the sense of excitement I felt around him. "He's . . ." I pause, searching for the words.

"That is him, yes," Shelby says. "Packard. He will prove he can help you."

"Packard saved my life," Carter says. "Packard saved both our lives. Just come to the restaurant and hear his offer."

"How do I know you're not working with Foley?"

Shelby crosses her arms. "Because Foley is buffoon. And we will destroy him."

Sometimes truth really does have a ring. I hear it now. Which makes me wonder if these two are telling the truth about this Packard saving their lives. *Is* it possible he can help me? What's his offer? Maybe it's not so terribly Faustian after all.

Shelby points to a sporty black convertible. "We will drive you there."

It's crazy to take rides from strangers, crazy to hope

some guy in a Mongolian restaurant can do what med-ications and therapy never could. Crazy—unless you're desperate. Packard was right about that.

"If you become frightened, you can throw yourself out of car," she says.

Five minutes later I'm in the back of Carter's convert-ible. I could at least hear this Packard's offer and see his proof. That's my thinking.

I ask about how Packard saved their lives, but they insist I have to wait to talk to him. Maybe he doesn't like them telling people he's a highcap. They say most highcaps try to pass as normal.

I'm surprised when Carter merges onto "the tan-gle"—a nightmarish curlicue of highways that's the fastest, most unpleasant, and most treacherous way to move between neighborhoods. Everybody sane avoids the tangle, which has been blamed for everything from Midcity's industrial decrepitude to, of course, the eight-year crime wave, in articles with titles like "A Dark Snarl at the Heart of Our Fair City."

I hold tight as he weaves around cars and takes curves at high speeds. Who *are* these people?

Finally we're dumped off into East Farley and creep through the industrial neighborhoods north of the river.

"Mongolian Delites is an unusual restaurant," I observe, just to break the silence.

Carter shoots Shelby a glance, then addresses me in the rearview mirror. "Just a request. Don't say anything derogatory about the restaurant to Packard."

"So he owns it?"

Shelby nods. "Yes, but please understand. You must not speak of restaurant."

Carter turns down a narrow, shady street hemmed in by blocky brick buildings. "You especially don't want to comment on the decor."

"Fine. Just tell me this—Packard's a highcap, right?"

They exchange glances.

"Yes," Carter says finally. "Packard sees people's psychological structures."

"That's it?" I say. "He just sees psychology?"

Shelby frowns. "It is powerful highcap gift. Do not disparage it."

I don't know what I was hoping for. Some better power, ideally something curative. I sit back, resigned to a stupidly wasted afternoon.

Mongolian Delites is located in an up-and-coming area not quite near enough to the lake to be hot for condos. It occupies the first floor of a four-story building scooched up to the dirty sidewalk between an ad agency and a refurbished office space. The behemoth Bessler Box Company occupies nearly the entire block across the street, save for a tiny corner deli like a neon-flashing jewel in its flank.

Carter finds a meter right in front and we get out. The name *Mongolian Delites* is painted on the window in fat black brushstroke lettering; gold curtains behind conceal the interior. But the most striking feature of the place is its huge wooden door, which has a massive face carved into it, as if a friendly bearded giant with long, Renaissance-king-type curls is attempting to push his face out through the wood. The face is attractive and oddly comforting.

Carter grips the outer edge of the giant's nose and heaves the door open, splitting the face down the middle.

I follow Shelby and Carter around the perimeter of the main dining room, now populated by lunchtime patrons, past the giant pagoda-shaped mirror that occupies a center spot in the place, and into a wide and deep back corridor I hadn't noticed last night. One side of the corridor is lined with empty booths whose flickering candles add an eerie gleam to the bright Asian paintings along the wall.

We stop at the very end and there he is, restaurateur Packard, sitting sideways in the booth, feet out, head leaned back against the wall. He gazes up at us coolly, a highcap prince in his back-booth throne.

"Justine," he says, like he's trying out my name. "Justine Jones." He clambers out and clasps my hand in both of his. "Impressive."

I mumble my thanks.

"I can't say I've encountered anybody with your level of health anxiety outside of a straitjacket," he continues.

I frown. "You know, maybe I am a bit of a hypochondriac, but when you have legitimate symptoms, it's common sense to worry. Symptoms are the body's way of telling you something. Because even hypochondriacs get terrible diseases—"

Packard laughs. "Oh, that is perfect. You are perfect."

Carter wanders off.

"It's not funny," I say. "Look, I know you can see my psychology, but unless you can give me permanent immunity to vein star and all related diseases so that I never have to worry about them again, I don't see you helping me."

"Oh, I am most certainly going to help you." Packard slides into the booth, and Shelby sits next to him, toying with a swizzle straw. He indicates the seat across from them. "Please—"

I sit near the edge.

"I know what it took to confront Foley last night. You have a strong interest in helping victims, just as many of us do. But your unnatural abundance of fear is ruining your life, and eventually it will drive you insane. Literally. But to us, your fear is a power." I start to protest, but Packard holds up a hand. "Imagine if you could channel all that fear out of yourself. Free yourself of it completely."

I consider this a moment. "That could be helpful."

"You would simply channel your fear into victimizers. You'd weaponize it."

"Weaponize it? Like, attack people with it?"

"Yes." He gazes brightly, like he's a little bit on fire with his mad scheme. "You know how some people hire a hit man to kill an enemy? We're like a squad of hitters, only we don't kill people. We *disillusion* them. We're a psychological hit squad. We've needed somebody in health anxieties for some time."

I choke back a chortle. "I'm sorry; that is just so out of the realm of what I'd ever do."

Carter returns and sets down a bread basket and a steaming plate of kebabs and disappears again.

Packard places a napkin on his lap. "Typically, crime victims or their families hire us. Please, help yourself." He places a tomato wedge on a piece of French bread. "I use my psychological vision to assess the target. Then I put together a team to disillusion the target on emotional, mental, and other levels." He seems like such a maniac at this moment, it's hard to imagine parents ever caring for him, combing his hair, bandaging his knees.

"So somebody hired you to disillusion Foley?"

"Recent victims. And soon they will enjoy a feeling of resolution they simply can't get from seeing Foley dead or in prison. They'll get to see him broken down and repentant, and he'll get to build back better. Disillusionment creates a profound change of heart."

"Like rebooting computer." Shelby inspects a zucchini slice. "Disillusionment crashes and reboots people."

"That seems a bit . . ." I'm at a loss how to finish.

"It's not Foley we need you for, of course," Packard continues. "We need your help for other targets."

"It doesn't even make sense. A hypochondriac attack is unpleasant, but not disillusioning."

Packard seems pleased with my question. "Do you know how they demolish a building?"

"Explosives."

"Right. But they don't toss bombs at it, do they? A demolition expert uses X-rays to find lines of weakness. The weak spots tell him where to put the dynamite. I look at a person as a demolition expert would. I see what they're made of. Their strengths and weaknesses. I see how to bring them crashing down. And health anxiety is a tool I need in my toolbox." He wipes his hands, eyes sparkling. I've never met a man so full of confidence and charisma. "You're right that hypochondria attacks alone won't crash a person, but they will weaken one in preparation for more powerful disillusionists. About ten percent of people have some exploitable anxiety about their health. Did you know that? One out of ten is a hypochondriac. Most manage to hide it." Packard flicks a match and lights the candle on our table. "Of course, not everybody can be disillusioned—"

"Let me stop you right here," I say. "This is all interesting, but getting rid of my fear by dumping it into other human beings . . . I'm not that kind of person. Even if the process could help me—"

"The process won't merely help you; it'll save you. From institutionalization and an early death. Deep down, you must know that's where you're headed."

Our eyes meet. The candlelight adds rosy depth to the mannish angles of his face. "I know no such thing."

"Does it get worse every year?"

I don't answer. Because it does.

He says, "Aren't you curious what it would be like to feel healthy and happy for a while?"

"Healthy and happy?" I repeat his words casually, like it isn't what I most want in the world. "Not if I have to hurt someone."

"Fair enough. But how about a free demonstration? I'll let you zing the fear into me. You'll be free of it for weeks, maybe a month."

"I don't want to hurt you, either."

"You won't. Can you generate a fit of health anxiety right now?"

"Not on command."

"Right." He writes something on a napkin. "Then we'll provoke an attack. Eventually you'll learn how to ramp it up on your own." He turns to Shelby. "Go up to the drugstore and get these."

Shelby reads the napkin. "Oh." She smiles and leaves.

"What is she getting?"

"You'll see," Packard says.

"Yeah, we'll see." I cross my arms. "It's never been things that scare me."

His cheeks harden, like he's suppressing a smile.

I'm a bit nervous now, but I need to see if he can help me. I need to know if what I'm passing up is real. "I'm warning you, when the old ladies pass out the little squares of pizza at the supermarket, I always take one, but I never buy the pizza."

He leans into the booth corner, raises a knee above the plane of the table, and drapes a lazy arm over it. "You'll buy this pizza. It's topped with wealth, health, and perfect happiness." His confidence is captivating.

A waiter brings a bottle of clear liquid and pours us each a fat glass. It smells licoricy. Ouzo. Packard raises his glass, a toast to nothing, drinks it like a shot, and pours himself another.

"I'm no vigilante."

"Naturally." His lips quirk, as if he secretly finds my resistance amusing, and his eyes seem softer now, a soft green gaze under dusky red lashes. I have to look away, like if I stare at his handsomeness for too long, I'll get lost in it. I sip my ouzo even though it's barely afternoon.

He runs a finger around the rim of his glass. "Wealth, health, and happiness. And membership in a glorious and invincible squad."

With this utterance, Packard moves out of the category of *handsome, slightly maniacal highcap* into the realm of *mastermind*.

"You generate such a high volume of fear. It's a rare ability."

"Thanks," I mumble, blushing stupidly. Nobody ever admired me for being screwed up.

"As a disillusionist, you'll zing that fear into criminal targets, and at the same time you'll use your warped hypochondriac's reasoning to draw their attention toward symptoms, diseases, and mortality. In this way, you'll push them into an attack." Packard goes on about how they psychologically attack people as I construct and eat a bread-and-kebab treat. They seem to view their criminal targets almost as computers, and overloading and crashing frees them to reboot without their old hurtful, antisocial behavior.

Then Shelby's back with a brown paper bag. Packard pushes aside the plates and glasses. "Shelby, what do you have in there?"

"I have these." Shelby pulls out a stack of fashion magazines.

I feel cold.

Shelby slaps one down in front of me. "Girl in prime of life gets cancer, page 214." Then another. "Staph infection leads to double amputation for young mother, page 108."

"Oh my God," I whisper.

She puts down the next. "Degenerative corsitis attacks intestines of girl on honeymoon, page 134."

Fashion magazine disease articles. My personal kryptonite.

Gleefully, Shelby slaps down another. "Blood clot in the leg travels to brain. She is only twenty-four. Dies."

I inhale sharply.

Packard shoves it closer to me. "Excellent. Justine is partial to vascular maladies,"

"I can't read that," I whisper hoarsely.

"Vascular? Hmm." Shelby extracts a pink-spined magazine from the bottom of the stack. "Perhaps this—'Hofstader's thrombus strikes down young woman out of blue.'"

I widen my eyes. *Hofstader's.* My second-worst disease. A close cousin of vein star. Some say it's the same syndrome.

Cheerfully Packard says, "We'll start with that one."

"I can't read that. I won't."

Shelby helpfully opens it to the page.

"Thanks, Shelby." Shelby leaves and Packard leans across the table. "You're going to read it. The whole article." He sits back. "That'll do it for you, right?"

I grimace at the image of the woman rock climbing. There's always a before picture where the woman is living her fun life and doesn't know she's sick. "Honestly, I probably shouldn't read this because there really is a possibility I might have a vascular condition, and anxiety could heighten my blood pressure and make it worse."

"Get going," he says. When I protest, he slaps the magazine. "Read."

"I told you—I'm not sure if I want to do this anymore. It's not like I'm going to join."

"You want to leave? Then leave."

There's this silence where I imagine leaving.

He sits back. "You're not joining. Fine, but let's not waste time acting like you don't want a peek behind the curtain. It's human nature."

"Are you always such a know-it-all?"

He fixes me with an intense stare, which I take as a yes.

I stare straight back at him. He *is* right, and I'm not the kind of person to pretend otherwise. "Okay, let's see what you got, mister." And then there's this awkward moment because that sounded sort of sexual.

Coolly I focus on the page. First-person disease articles start in the hospital and flash back to the diagnosis, or else they start with the happy life, like this one, and narrate the course of the disease. This woman made up excuses for the scalp tingles and pinpoint pain. Bad idea. A few weeks later, she cancels a doctor appointment. Precious time is lost. Very common.

Packard sighs impatiently. "How long is this going to take?"

"I don't know." I read another paragraph. Hospital elevator. Heading up to surgery. "Can you please not watch?"

Packard pours himself another drink.

The article talks about the woman's career as an aerobics instructor before the disease struck, something I hate to see. It's always better if they sat on their couch eating junk food all day. I read and read. Nothing's happening. I've never tried to force an attack before.

"What's the problem?" he demands.

"I don't know. I guess it has to come up naturally."

"That's why I got you these magazines to look at."

"It's a lot of pressure, okay?"

He sighs and tops off my glass. "Maybe this'll relax you."

"It'll just dull things. Maybe you could give me a little privacy?"

"How will I know when you're ready?"

"I don't know, but I can't concentrate with you hawking over me."

"I'm hardly hawking."

I snort and get back to the article, but my concentration's shot.

"Idea. How about reading *with* comprehension?"

I frown at him like he's being a jerk, which he sort of is, but I'm feeling far more hopeless than angry. I wanted to know something in the world could help me, even if I wasn't planning on choosing it. I turn away from him and the magazine, hating everything, and I just sort of glare at the horse painting on the wall above our booth. Underneath the horse is Korean writing; you can tell from all the circles. So what's it doing in a Mongolian restaurant? And the elephant salt-and-pepper set is from India. Everything about Mongolian Delites is wrong.

"You're not even reading," he says.

I give him a level look. "What's up with the decor here? All the random ethnic bric-a-brac."

He narrows his eyes, cheeks gone rosy with heat. Slowly he rises up out of the booth and comes around to my side. He plunks his boot on the seat next to my thigh and slaps the magazine. I jump. "I'm coming back in five minutes," he growls. "If you're not good to go, we're not doing it."

"Yikes!" I say as he storms off. But the jolt got my heart pounding like crazy. Fear. This is what I needed. I glue my gaze to the magazine. The picture of the happy girl. "I thought I'd leave the clinic that day with a prescription and some free time to shop. Instead I spent the afternoon getting my head shaved for surgery." And then I come to this sentence: "Emerging research suggests heredity may play a small part in vascular conditions. . . ."

Heredity?

I can feel myself actually breaking into a sweat. I check the cover—last month, May. So they've discovered that vein star syndrome and Hofstader's are *hereditary*? The word swims before my eyes, and I touch my scalp. Were those tingles? This extreme level of anxiety alone could bring on a vein star expansion and leakage. This is bad.

I hardly notice or care when Packard returns and sits across from me. I can literally feel a vein expanding inside my cranium, bulging out in the telltale star shape that distinguishes the disease. Learning this news in an already-tense situation was a dangerous combination. And what if I collapse? What do I really know about these people?

"Ready?"

I look at him like he's crazy. "I don't know what I was thinking. This isn't a fear thing; it's a medical thing."

"You just believe that because you're inside it now."

"I wish." I'm thinking ER, but they have to catch it preleak to do any good.

"Hey," he says. "Look at me."

I don't bother; I have to concentrate on not panicking. Because if it's hereditary, I probably really do have it.

"Trust me. Just for a moment." He takes my hand, and I nearly go into arrest. But when I look up at him, that confident fire of his warms me a little. Wildly, I think, *Why not?* Why not try this?

I take a breath. "A moment." I can't believe I'm consenting to this.

Gently, he arranges my hand to splay flat against the table, palm down. "I want you to feel where the skin on your hand ends. Right where the surface of your skin meets air."

I take another breath. "Okay."

"Now, feel up off the surface of your skin—half an inch or so." He says it so simply that I find myself doing it. It's easy, and I have the funny sense that I've always felt this space.

"That's your energy dimension. It's inside you, and it also surrounds you. It's where your emotions live. When you push out with your awareness, you can feel it and control it."

I stare at my hand against the brown wood grain of the table, pulse loud in my ears, praying that this isn't a long process.

"Can you locate your fear? Where is it?"

"I don't know. In my energy dimension?"

"*Where* in your energy dimension?"

"Can we get to the part where I'm feeling better?" My voice sounds unnaturally high.

"You have so much fear and you're so obsessed with it, yet you don't know where in your energy dimension it lives?"

The answer comes instantly when I focus. "My stomach. A little bit in my throat."

"Right. Keep your awareness pushed out all around you, and around your hand." He slides his hand across the table toward mine, and stops when there's just a small space between our pointer fingers. "You feel that?"

"Yes," I whisper. It's a kind of aliveness around my fingertip. It's the strangest thing.

"You're touching my energy dimension with yours. Actually, I'm doing it for you, but with practice you can learn to feel other people's energy dimensions as clearly as you'd feel an animal's fur." He slides closer, takes my hand, and I stifle a gasp. Sensation overload. He says, "Do you know what would happen if I made a little hole between our two energy dimensions?"

My mouth goes dry. It sounds scary and erotic at the same time. Is this his plan for pulling me out of an attack? "Can you see people's emotions?" I ask.

"No, not in real time. What I see is structural. Don't worry about me—keep your awareness pushed out." He holds my fingers lightly with his, eyes burning into mine. "You've stoked up so much fear, your energy dimension is overloaded with emotion, especially compared to mine. Compared to anybody's. If I made a hole between us, all your fear and other negative emotions would rush into me. Dark emotions rush from the high-emotion body to the low-emotion body. A law of physics, just like siphoning gas. Once the flow starts, they all rush out."

"*All* the negative emotions?"

"Yes."

"What about the positive ones?"

"Negative only. Positive behaves differently." He seems to be waiting for my permission.

"I don't much fancy having a hole in my energy dimension."

"Don't worry; it knits right back up," he says. "Ready?"

"What if it knits back wrong?"

"It won't."

"Wait—will it hurt?"

Packard watches my eyes, and I have this sense of something shifting and lifting in me.

"Wait." I try to pull my hand away.

He holds tight. "You're fine."

"No, something's wrong. And my hand's hot. Why's my hand hot?" I look from my hand to Packard and back to my hand. It's like something hot's rushing out through my hand, and it's making my whole body feel different, like I'm losing ballast, lightening. "What's happening?" He doesn't answer. "My hand . . ." I never finish the sentence, because in a flash, my hand goes from hot to cool, like there's wind in my fingers, and I'm all loose and light. I sit up. "Whoa. What the hell?"

Packard releases my hand. "You'll have to learn to act less surprised when you actually zing your fear into a target."

I move my shoulders, shake my head. I've never felt so breezy and light.

Packard looks on with a kind of arrogant pleasure. "Better?" He resumes his sideways position without waiting for an answer.

"I don't understand."

"What's there to not understand? How do you feel?"

I feel nothing, but it's a wonderful nothing. Nothing's wrong with me. Nothing to be terrified about, or worried about. Or even mildly concerned about. "It's . . . it's . . ."

"It's called peace."

I laugh. I've never felt so light. It's exhilarating. "Wow." I blink a few times.

"Peace and serenity isn't about adding something," he says. "It's about getting rid of something. You just zinged out all your negative emotions, most notably an enormous amount of fear. You'll still think about diseases, but they'll matter as much as who plants their flag on Mars. Few people get to feel this way."

Everything seems different. Richer. More vivid. Just breathing in the spicy smells of the restaurant is a sensual experience, and as I breathe, my silk top whispers against my shoulders. "It's wonderful."

"Nothing's different. You were just so focused on your emotions and yourself that you never fully experienced anything. Very common."

The price suddenly strikes me. "I shot my darkness into you. Are you okay?"

Eyes fixed on the wall in front of him, he says, "I alone can handle it."

I smile at his dark lord talk and don't look away from his handsomeness anymore. I just enjoy him: the wonderful meatiness of his nose, the stray curl that kisses his cheekbone, the rough puff of his lips. My stomach tightens as I imagine running a finger over those lips, and maybe even kissing them. Possibly tracing that finger down his neck, unbuttoning one button. Maybe the next. I swallow, overwhelmed by the sudden desire to feel and taste him.

Ever so slyly, he looks over. "Your experience of life will be unfiltered for about an hour. *Glory hour,* we call it. You're smarter and more perceptive now in every way, and all your senses are ratcheted up. As long as you don't give into your baser appetites, it can be a powerful advantage. Don't worry—you get used to it, and it only lasts an hour. But your immunity to health fears could last for weeks. After that, you'll want to zing somebody again."

I tear my attention away from Packard and sip my ouzo, savoring its tartness, schooling my features, like I do when I'm in an attack. "This has got to go against some natural law. Could this be dangerous? Physically?" Oddly, I find I can say this without fear, as though it's all just theoretical.

Packard laughs, rich and deep.

"Seriously."

He regards me with that look of awe again, like a jungle explorer beholding the mythical winged monkey. "Oh, we have been waiting for you. We should start training tomorrow."

I watch him coolly, but inside, I'm awash with clean, sweet energy. And desire. "It's wrong to go around attacking people."

"Is it? We effect changes in the hearts of criminals— changes they wouldn't come to for years, eons, maybe lifetimes, who knows? And we give victims a sense of resolution."

"That still doesn't make it right."

Packard smiles, like I've made quite the joke. "You're gloring right now, but you're not showing it. An excellent poker face comes in handy for a disillusionist."

"I'm serious. I said I couldn't join." Though all I want to do is stay. And suddenly one thing becomes very clear: if I don't get away now, I might never leave. "The demo's over, right?"

Packard stops smiling.

Fighting my every instinct, I stand and sling my purse over my shoulder.

"This won't last. You'll go back to the way you were."

"I know." I put my sunglasses on top of my head, like a headband. "Thank you, Packard, for all this. But I told you, I can't be in your squad. It's not right to psychologically attack people."

My heart pounds as Packard rises, tall and lean and cool. He is way too alluring—another reason to get out. "Justine, you have a mental illness that will end in institutionalization and death."

He doesn't like that I mean to leave. Probably no one ever has.

It's not easy, but I do it—I thank him again and get out of there. I feel stronger once I'm outside, heading happily down the shady sidewalk. Cars zoom brightly by, a soft breeze kisses my arms and neck, and up above, the sun warms the brick building faces. Best of all, I feel no fear. No fear of fear, even. I can think about vein star syndrome without any sense of doom whatsoever. Flying bricks? No worry there, either. Everything's perfect. Even a crumpled Twix wrapper on the sidewalk seems perfect.

This is the state of mind people search for all their lives, I realize. Hermits in little caves, monks in their moldering monasteries. It's all anybody could ever want.

"Justine! Hey!" A black convertible rolls up beside me. Carter. "I told you I'd give you a ride home."

"I know. That's okay."

"You sure?"

I reconsider. If I went home, I could enjoy a luxurious bath, a delicious meal, rollerblading at top speed along the river. I swing in and sink into the cushiony red seat.

We peel out. Carter shifts again and again, hands clad in racecar-driver gloves, bright hair blowing over freckled cheeks. I think it would be fun to swim, too. Or run. And then it hits me: it would be funnest of all to have sex. I imagine the weight of Cubby's hands on my thighs, the feel of his exultingly hard erection in my hand, skin soft as a rose petal.

"Can you drop me off at my boyfriend's place?" I give him Cubby's address.

Carter smiles.

"Something funny?"

"Glory hour," he says, like he knows exactly what I'm thinking. My face goes hot. "So I hear you're not joining."

"It's not my cup of tea."

Silence. I run my finger along the cool metal door.

He says, "The way I was before I became a disillusionist, sheesh. I was actually one of those guys who would beat you up for looking at him the wrong way. I'd get in fights with whole mobs of guys—the more the better. When I was fighting, it blotted out the feelings, you know? I was a line cook at the time. If I hadn't met Packard, I'd be dead." He jerks into another lane, then another. "Do you know that thing where people look at you with pity and fascination, and you know they're thinking, *You pathetic loser, what is ever gonna become of you?* You know that look?"

"Oh my God." I turn to him. "I can't believe you know the look!"

"All us disillusionists know the look. Used to, at least. You should reconsider," Carter says. "You belong with us."

It feels wonderful that somebody would say that to me. "I would love to join, but I believe in things like right and wrong. And fair trials—what about that?"

"What about the unfair ones?"

And then we're on the tangle. Around and around we go, past dirty buildings, then fat, shadowy pillars supporting industrial-strength bridges, then blue sky. At the very top you can see the glinting cluster of glass buildings downtown, with the sparkling lake beyond. It's heartbreakingly beautiful. And then we're back under a bridge, and that's beautiful, too.

I slide my gaze over to Carter, keenly aware of his pleasure at the wheel and the rage under his surface, cool and inert, like a gun. And I slice my hand into the velvety air.

Chapter Four

CUBBY AND I spend an enchanted afternoon together, lips pressed to naked skin, fingers in mouths, everything everywhere. I'm transfixed by his lusciousness, and he's transfixed by my newfound happiness.

The utter delight of glory hour wears off soon enough, but my freedom from abnormal fear remains, just like Packard said it would. Those next few weeks are the best of my life. They're the best weeks ever for Cubby and me, too. This is what normal people have, I think—the freedom to be happy without worrying that veins in your head might burst or leak. Sometimes when I'm doing things like showering or washing dishes, I smile for no reason.

On day twenty, I notice some scalp tingling, but I force my attention away. Day twenty-two is when the intermittent pinprick sensations start. Day twenty-four: a horrible new theory—what if my false well-being masked significant symptoms? What if I've lost precious time?

Suddenly I'm back to the all-night Internet binges and I'm a zombie at work, standing behind the counter, face frozen in a rictus of glee while I secretly panic.

What if the zing degraded my vascular integrity? After all, I do have a genetic weakness for vein star syndrome. The girls at the shop start giving me the look again, wondering what will become of me. The moments where I know I'm being crazy come less often.

I also find myself cravenly revisiting Packard's arguments. What if disillusionment does reboot criminals and help victims feel resolved? Surely it's superior to locking somebody up or executing them.

Still, it doesn't feel right. What about trials and all that?

Day twenty-seven: Rainy afternoon. Cubby's on his couch, frowning. We've had to stop the movie. "Bodies have pains, Justine."

"People who die unexpectedly have pains, too." I'm using my fingertips to move my scalp around, hoping to alter the location of sensation and thereby prove to myself that it's the musculature surrounding the skull and not a vein star underneath.

"You're fine."

I stand. "How do you know? You're not a doctor. If you're not going to drive me to the ER, I'm calling a cab."

"What happened? You haven't had your vein thing for weeks." He presses his palms to his eyes. "I thought you were over this. You need to decide to get over this."

"*Decide* to get over it?"

"That's right."

"I'm calling a cab."

He holds out a hand. "Don't go."

"Cubby, this is both tingling *and* pinpoint pain, and sometimes it feels like someone's pushing on it. That's new!" I pull out my phone. "If they catch it early enough . . ."

He stands and wraps his arms around me. "Trust me, you're okay."

I pull away. "I'm not!"

"Yes, you are." He watches me put on my shoes and

grab my purse. He says, "I'm not going, because I know it's not real."

"I know it *is*!"

He's silent for a long time. Then, "I don't know if I can do this anymore. If you go."

My heart sinks. "I have to go," I whisper, eyes hot and misty. And like the prisoner I am, I march myself out.

The ER waiting room is a scene of unruly children, germy magazines, and people in the grip of both terror and boredom. One of the nurses recognizes me and scowls. It's two hours before I'm seen, two more hours before I'm lying still in the CAT scan tube while my panic tornadoes.

When I come out, I detect a flash of alarm in the elderly tech's eyes. What did she see?

After some tense waiting in yet another room, a doctor I've never seen before breezes in. "All clear," she says. Nothing else. Just *All clear*.

I feel hazy. "All clear?"

"We didn't find any vascular irregularities. What you have here is anxiety."

After she repeats herself several times, I thank her profusely, bounce out of the hospital, and just walk. No vascular irregularities! All clear! I stroll past gray parking ramps and stone office buildings. I wince understandingly at a woman wearing a pink hardhat. I linger pleasantly at the windows of old-time department stores, where pointy-boobed mannequins in newscaster fashions dangle purses from grasping hands.

It's all quite the bowl of cherries until I consider how suspicious it was that the doctor diagnosed me so fast. I often suspect doctors write notes to one another on my record. *Take with grain of salt*. I don't recall her studying the scan too diligently. Did she study it at all? And what about the alarm in the elderly tech's eyes?

Suspicious sensations return. Were they ever really gone? Clearly the tech saw something; it's this thought above all that spurs me onward to a degrading odyssey of more cabs, more ER waiting rooms, and increasingly stern medical personnel, hating myself every step of the way. The fear hounds me harder than ever—grinding, sickening fear that's all the more oppressive because I remember how great life was without it. I wander down side streets, no longer sure which direction the lake is in, or if I'm crazy or sane, or even whether I'm hot or cold. And I'm rationalizing a return to Mongolian Delites. It was almost like a cure, I tell myself. Sure, maybe they're vigilantes, but they do help people. And anyway, it's not like I'd join forever. Just for now.

Eventually, I manage to reach the restaurant. It's midnight, an hour after closing. I rap firmly on the facedoor, praying Packard's still around. The gold curtains jerk apart and there's Shelby, smiling her chipped-tooth smile. She disappears and the door swings open.

"About time." She wears a silky Japanese dress, and an oversized watch slides around on her slim wrist. She takes my hand and leads me through the sea of empty tables toward Packard, who sits between two men at the bar. The flickering candles make his penny-colored curls shine darkly; his smile is beautiful and slightly evil.

"You've changed your mind," he says.

"Yes."

He regards me carefully, green eyes the color of old moss in sunlight. "You want to join now? You're sure about it?"

"Yes, quite." I say this nonchalantly, as if I'm accepting a mint bonbon from a butler instead of a new vigilante lifestyle from a slightly maniacal mutant.

He introduces the large, agitated, bearded man next to him as Helmut. The anti–Santa Claus, I think as I shake Helmut's hand, wishing Packard would get on with it.

The short brawny man on the other side of Packard jumps off his stool. He has the thickest neck I've ever seen, and he peers at Packard through big round glasses, reminding me, oddly, of a bespectacled caterpillar. "The hypochondriac?" he barks. He seems angry.

"That's right," Packard says to him.

There's this awkward silence where Packard and the brawny fellow are in this stare-off that seems to contain a mountain of significance. I glance at Shelby. She doesn't look surprised. Maybe this is just how disillusionists act. The brawny man shakes his head angrily, then turns and walks out, hands raised in the universal *I wash my hands of you* gesture.

"Everything okay?" I ask.

"More than okay." Packard sends Helmut and Shelby to the kitchen to make kebabs, and I wonder briefly if "kebabs" is a code for something. Once they're gone, Packard slides down off his stool and stands in front of me, all masculine heat and coffee breath.

"I'm ready," I say. "I'm in." I don't tell him I'm only in until I think of something better. I hold out my hand. "Go ahead and make the hole. My fear is all stoked up."

"I'm sure it is." Packard practically shimmers with excitement as he takes my hand. "Push out with your awareness."

"I'm doing it."

"Good." He keeps his eyes on my hand and it starts: the lifting and shifting, the hot hand, the dizzying release of pressure. And the windy feeling in my fingers. Followed by peace pervading my entire being. Pure peace.

I inhale, savoring the bright, vast weightlessness of the world, and lower myself into a chair at a nearby table. Candlelight reflects off the pagoda mirror like ghostly diamonds. Why exactly did I wait so long to return to Mongolian Delites?

Packard brings me a glass of water. It's a small gesture, but perfect, like everything. "Thanks," I say. I take a sip and relish the way its coolness drenches my heart. The moment is perfect. The candles are perfect. Packard is perfect. I close my eyes and savor the freedom.

"Hey!" Packard grabs my ponytail. "Don't do that."

I laugh. "What? Don't enjoy it?"

"Precisely." He lets go of my hair, grabs silverware and napkins, and sets the table around me. "Enjoying it is like driving a car at top speed with your attention fixed on a bug squashed on your windshield. Down that road lies devastation." Fork, fork, spoon, knife. "Our targets are dangerous and diabolical people. You must not get into the habit of devolving into a sensual hedonist every time you zing."

I try not to smile, but I do so enjoy his extravagant talk.

Packard sets out wineglasses, and soon Shelby and Helmut arrive bearing plates piled with skewers of colorful vegetables and fat scallops.

Packard opens a bottle. "Ouzo okay?" He seems to be addressing me.

"For what?"

Packard gives me a stern look. "We're celebrating."

Shelby scoots a chair up next to mine. "Do you have somewhere better to be?"

"No," I say, marveling at how beautiful her thick, dark curls look against the deep red of her dress.

Packard lights more candles. Helmut and Packard settle in, and Shelby raises her glass. "I will toast to you, Justine," she says. "May the targets never see you coming." We laugh and clink and make more toasts. I've never belonged to a squad or a club, especially not a secret one like this. We dig into our food.

"We were all quite surprised when you left last month—nobody has ever declined," Helmut says.

"I was crazy then," I say. The four of us have a good laugh about that. I push an onion off my skewer. You can tell from the sear marks that everything was grilled flat, and later placed on skewers. "You guys are really into kebabs," I observe.

Shelby and Helmut glance warily at Packard.

"Nothing wrong with it, of course." I'd forgotten you weren't supposed to talk about the restaurant.

"There's plenty wrong with it," Packard says darkly.

Quickly I change the subject. "That is such a beautiful dress, Shelby."

Shelby smiles at me. If she were American, she would've had that chipped tooth fixed, and she wouldn't be so beautiful. "I bought dress at Asia emporium. Justine, will you shop there with me tomorrow?" This in a solemn tone, like she's asking for my hand in marriage. "May I bring you to Asia emporium?"

"I'd love to, but I have to work tomorrow."

"But you are disillusionist now," she says.

"I can't just quit my job."

There's this silence where Helmut and Shelby look at Packard.

"Details, logistics," Packard says. "I don't see the rush to shop."

Shelby puts down her fork. "For six years I am only girl disillusionist. Except for Jordan." Apparently Jordan doesn't count. "Male disillusionists are all friends with much male bonding, but I am alone. Regular girls do not want to be my friend, and even if they want to be friend, I must make up pretend life." Shelby's as girlfriend-starved as I am.

"I'll go," I say.

Packard wants us to wait until my training is under way. Apparently I'm already assigned to two targets—the Silver Widow and the Alchemist.

Helmut looks surprised. "Where did they come from?"

"They're new," Packard says.

Helmut makes a face, like something strange is going on. I'm a lot more surprised by the names. "The Silver Widow and the Alchemist?"

Shelby says, "All targets have code names."

"Are they highcaps?" I ask.

"No," Packard says. "We sometimes disillusion highcaps, but the Silver Widow and the Alchemist are human." He turns to Shelby. "Why don't you give Justine an update on the criminal she knows as Foley?"

"Yes, your Foley. One of the illusions that comfort people is, if I have this thing, *then*"—she flows her hand in a graceful movement, a sort of ballet of the fingers—"I will be so happy. Is important illusion for people—around corner is happiness. Can you guess what your Foley wants most in life?"

"Money?"

"To be adored." She spears a beet slice. "So pathetic."

"Yet so common," Packard says.

"To be adored?" I'd feel sad for Foley if I didn't loathe him. I sink my fork into the center of a succulent grilled scallop the size of a baby's fist.

Shelby stares at her plate as she chews. "I infuse target with grim clarity about impossibility of happiness."

"That's your disillusionist specialty?"

She nods.

"She sucks the sparkle out of desire," Helmut adds.

"I do not suck, I give. I give knowledge." She points around the room. "Whatever it is you want, it will not make you happy." She sniffs. "Your Foley, he sees this now. Is despondent. All day he wears pajamas. I take his watch and leave." So the man's watch is Foley's.

Packard glowers. "You know I don't condone robbery that isn't part of disillusionment."

"He would lose watch anyway."

"*Nevertheless.*" Packard turns to me. "Though she's
right—he'll lose everything. It is often necessary to part
targets from their worldly possessions. Steal, bilk, make
them gamble it all away. Right now, our predatory
financial advisor is fleecing Foley. Money helps protect
Foley from the harsh truths of life and what he's done
to people. That's the case with most criminals."

"In this part of the world," Helmut counters. "Once
the resource wars start up, that will change." He goes
on to paint alarming scenarios of overpopulation, mon-
etary collapse, and nuclear exchanges. I can't believe
how many statistics he knows.

Shelby touches my arm. "Helmut's disillusionist specialty is dread about big picture—about world situation."

"It's not *dread* about the world situation," he says.
"It's *clarity* about the world situation. I help people see
that they live in dangerous and threatening times."

Shelby sniffs. "Nothing to be done."

Helmut glares at Shelby; I can feel the ruthless power
of his anguish sure as I can feel the cloth napkin
between my fingers. "It's reality," he adds. "The water
wars will be what kills us."

"Unless a horrible disease gets you first," I say. "Your
own body's working overtime right now finding ways to
self-destruct." It's wonderfully liberating to be able to
talk like this without upsetting myself.

"Who cares?" Shelby says. "We have no chance for
happiness anyway."

Silently we sit, siblings in torment. The moment
stretches on and I have this crazy sensation that I'm

finally home. I smile at the thought. And then I chuckle. And then we all just burst out laughing.

It's exhilarating, just laughing around the table. I have this brief sense of us as supervillains from a B-rate thriller. Except we're more like crime fighters—if there were crime fighters who got their superpowers from being really neurotic, and used them as part of a bizarre and marginally ethical program of criminal rehabilitation.

I gaze across the table and catch Packard staring at me, eyes sparkling in the candlelight.

Later, Helmut gives me a lift home. It's 2:30 a.m. when I get to Cubby's. I let myself in and creep across the living room and down the hall to find him asleep in the snuggly softness of his bed. He's surprised I've come.

I slip in next to him. "I'm done," I whisper, smoothing my hands over the supersoft blue blanket.

He squints. "What do you mean?"

"I mean you were right. I decided to be over the medical stuff."

He opens one eye. "What happened?"

"I can't really explain."

My new disillusionist friends warned me passionately against telling Cubby—for his own good. That's fine with me. Being recruited for a psychological hit squad due to my extreme neurotic tendencies does little to bolster the whole normal-girl image I'm going for. And anyway, it's all just temporary.

"Like a breakthrough?"

"Sort of."

He squints and turns over.

With shock, I realize that he was actually going to dump me. I can't let him. Cubby is everything I ever wanted, everything I always aspired to, and now I have a chance with him. I place a hand on his shoulder. "You were right," I say. "I took your advice. Okay?"

I wait. If he says *okay,* I know I have a reprieve.

"Okay," he mumbles.

I settle down next to him and lay my head on my pillow with a silent sigh.

Chapter Five

TRAINING IS TO START at ten, two hours before Mongolian Delites opens for lunch. I dress in a sleeveless white top, knit maroon skirt, and brown boots, and I put a sparkly barrette in the heavy side of my blonde hair. Wearing a bright and pretty outfit always helps me feel more awake.

Not that I need it. The moment Packard pulls open the Mongolian Delites door and our eyes meet, I feel exuberantly awake.

"Morning." He turns and trudges toward the bar.

"Morning." I follow, drinking in his hotness. What am I doing? I just got my reprieve from Cubby!

"Five minutes," he says, taking a stool in front of a plate of kebabs, of all things. His blue flannel shirt, just a shade darker than his faded jeans, is untucked, and his curls are tousled; he looks like he just got out of bed.

I settle onto a nearby stool with the big strong coffee I got from the corner deli and focus on the *Midcity Eagle*. Another pedestrian has been killed by a brick hurtling from nowhere—this one just west of downtown. That's ten victims this year. The photo shows dashing Chief Sanchez at the scene, dark hair flowing from beneath his signature black beret. He holds up a brick, looking right out at you with his big brown puppyish eyes. The warm feeling wells up in me. There's something downright noble about him and his quest against crime. Like the knights in the books I used to love. I can't wait for him to get the Brick Slinger.

Packard glances over at my newspaper. "Police Chief *Otto Sanchez*. Somebody needs to stop him from wearing those ridiculous outfits."

"I'm impressed with his work so far. The force has doubled their case clearance since he's been in charge."

Packard snorts and eyes my coffee. "Is that regular?"

"Maybe."

"No more for you. Too high-octane. Meet me at the booth." He points at the coffee. "And bring that."

I head back, not exactly thrilled with Packard's bossy attitude. Or the way he insulted Chief Sanchez. A lot of men ridicule Sanchez's elegant suits and berets and his unconventional hair, his dazzling rise from detective to police chief to Midcity's biggest celebrity.

Packard appears with the stack of magazines and a large mug.

"What if I'm a person who likes to drink lots of coffee?" I ask.

"I don't care. All that caffeine energy comes through the zing. I can vent emotions but not caffeine or any other drugs of any kind, so steer clear of them. You'll need your wits about you as a disillusionist." Packard pours most of my coffee into his mug. "You get that much."

I stare into my nearly empty cup, thinking it's never a good sign when somebody informs you that you need to keep your wits about you.

The first order of business is how I'll explain my irregular hours to Cubby. Packard's suggestion: I've landed a job as an assistant in a security consulting firm. Packard has business cards and a phone number and everything; apparently I'm not the only disillusionist who's needed a cover. Packard expects me to quit Le Toile, of course.

When I protest, he slides out of the booth and walks off. I hear a ding from the dining area. He comes back and counts out twenty hundreds. Two thousand bucks—far more than I make in a month at Le Toile.

"First week's paid training. Give a month's notice if you want. That's how long training will take."

"Wow, thanks," I say. "But wouldn't it be okay if I kept a few hours at the shop?" I'm thinking I'll need something to fall back on after I quit the disillusionists.

"This is an on-call lifestyle. Plus, you'll be pretending to be in a different profession. I wonder if you can guess what that might be." He has that glow again. Clearly, this is something I'm going to like.

"I don't know."

He gives me a sly look. It's intoxicating. "You'll tell them that you're a nurse."

I can barely breathe. "I'm going to go around pretending to be a *nurse*?" I've always wanted to be a nurse, but of course, it's impossible for somebody like me.

"Surely you grasp my reasoning."

"Oh, yes," I whisper. Shiver. "People would listen to what I said about health if I was a nurse." I gaze into his pale green eyes. "You've thought of everything."

"I have," he says, like it's a matter of life and death. There's this hush between us where we understand each other on a new level. I feel like he gets the depth of my impossible dream of becoming a nurse, and I suddenly get how important the success of the disillusionists is to him.

I say, "It's all very deliciously diabolical, my friend."

He smiles, and I smile. We're both pretty pleased with the plan. And increasingly pleased with each other.

"Right." He taps his pen on the table. "Anyway, targets will trust you because you're a nurse, but they'll also trust you because, after you zing them, they *bind* to you, because it's your fear they feel. They won't know why they feel a mysterious connection to you, but they will. It makes them easy to work with."

"Does that mean you bind to me when . . ."

"Of course not. I'm not affected by a zing." He gestures between us. "There's nothing—" He pauses. There are many words to describe this smoldering thing between us. *Nothing* isn't one of them.

"Right," I say. "That's good."

Packard looks at me without expression. My heart pounds too hard. He pulls out his laptop, and we go online and order some nursing textbooks. I'm to pose as a nursing student for the Silver Widow case. They've brought her up a few times now.

"You know, I won't go after some poor vulnerable old woman. A hypochondriac attack would be devastating to anyone elderly, because the chances of something being wrong are so much higher."

He gives me that look of awe again; he loves when I talk like a hypochondriac. And I love that he loves it.

"The Silver Widow is as far from poor, old, and vulnerable as a woman can get," he says. "She's a killer."

"Obviously they couldn't prove that in a court of law."

"Not for want of trying. Believe me, we check these people out. You haven't officially met Strongarm Francis, but he used to be a detective, and he does a lot of work to make sure our targets deserve to be hit. Most of them are killers."

"That feels like vigilantism."

"Think of it as a mechanism of nature. Karma catches up with people one way or another. We just speed it up."

I don't see what part of that isn't vigilantism, but I keep my mouth shut. I said I'd give them a fair try. If I don't like it, I'll quit.

"You'll get it when you meet her. Now." He rests his hand on the table between us, and I gaze at its knuckled, sculptural beauty. "Let's see your hand."

"Oh." I flatten my hand to the table in front of me.

"You have to practice feeling that space around you, pushing your awareness out through your energy dimension. Once you have that, you'll work on pushing out while you're touching other people. You'll be able to touch their energy dimensions the way you'd reach out and touch a solid object. These are all things you can practice here and on your own. Once you have that, we'll work on burning the hole."

"You *burn* the hole?"

"With your focus," he says. "Like sun through a magnifying glass."

"It didn't feel like burning."

"It's dimensional. You're thinking physical. Two warnings," he says. "Number one, never go deep inside a target's energy dimension. Stay near the surface. If you plunge into somebody, there's no guarantee you can get back out. Very dangerous."

"But wouldn't you stop at their skin?"

"Your skin would stop at their skin, but your energy dimension would keep going," he says. "Again, you're thinking physical. This is dimensional. And here's the other thing—I'm going to tell you, even though you're not able to zing yet, because it's so important—never zing somebody I haven't told you to zing. If you zing somebody who is not compatible, it will fry your brain."

"Yikes!"

"Your fear is like an electrical charge, and if you zing somebody incompatible, the blowback will destroy your mind. It would be like zinging yourself."

"How do I know if somebody is compatible?"

"*I alone* can recognize safe targets," he says.

"So zinging a random person would be out."

"Unless you wanted to become a vegetable." He gets this faraway look. "Which I suppose might be smart if you were about to be brutally tortured." He slides a piece of paper in front of me. "You can leave as soon as you memorize these numbers."

I stare at the three columns of numbers, not really seeing them.

"I'm serious," he says. "Being a disillusionist is a game of concentration and focus."

I watch him walk off. Frankly, I'm still stuck on the concept of *brutally tortured*.

Chapter
Six

MOST MORNINGS Cubby and I talk and sip lattes at our favorite coffee shop. Our relationship has greatly improved since I had my "breakthrough." Or at least Cubby likes me better. This scrubbed version of me, anyway.

I put in my notice at Le Toile and inform Cubby that I'm considering something new, career-wise, possibly something in security. Cubby finds this amusing. "You do get all worked up about people in trouble, though," he says. "And people breaking laws. Maybe you could get a little uniform and badge."

"Maybe I could."

"Maybe you could be a meter maid," he says.

I hit him with a rolled-up newspaper. Really, I hate lying to him.

I usually show up at Mongolian Delites around nine bearing a large coffee from the corner deli. Packard acts annoyed by this and makes me turn it over to him, but I suspect he's secretly grateful for a decent cup of coffee. Why he doesn't just walk down there and buy coffee for himself or—brain flash!—get better-tasting coffee for the restaurant, I don't ask. Questions about the restaurant plunge him into a mysteriously dark mood. Packard is a man with secrets.

The training continues to be intense, and it's a constant mental struggle to keep Packard in the boss category and out of the man category. Usually it's just the two of us there, alone, until the cooks arrive. Ling, the day manager, rolls in at around eleven. No matter what time of day it is, I notice, it always seems like night inside the restaurant—it's because of the orientation of the windows and the height of the neighboring buildings.

On a typical day, I take his hand and push out my energy dimension to make contact with his. I find I can touch his dimension easily. It feels like a powerful presence, warm and mysterious and inviting. It's especially difficult in these moments not to dwell on topics like how good he feels, or what he would look like naked. But my quickly increasing ability to concentrate seems to be helping.

To his credit, Packard stays businesslike. He's a man who will respect my relationship with Cubby as long as I do. Which, ironically, only makes him more attractive. It doesn't matter. I'll never let Cubby go. My dream of a normal, wholesome life with him is closer now than ever.

It turns out that disillusionist training involves numerous memorization and observation exercises. Sometimes I do multiplication in my head. One Monday, Packard instructs me to move a napkin across the table using the power of my mind. We're sitting across from each other in the booth, and he places the napkin on the table between us and goes back to his paperwork. Some sort of condiments order.

"I don't see how I could possibly move a napkin with the power of my mind," I say.

"All will be revealed," he mumbles.

"Did you just say 'All will be revealed'?"

He looks up. "Yes."

"Who says 'All will be revealed'?"

"I do," Packard says. "Just perform the task."

"The task. Ah, please, forgive me for interfering with your diabolical restaurant supply order."

He scowls down at his papers and forms. He really is one of the most teasable men I've ever met.

I try to move the napkin—I do—thinking, like a fool, that maybe I'm now capable of this sort of thing. And when I fail over and over, I feel more upset than I ought to. It's just that I've never been good at anything, and I so want to be a good disillusionist.

After a discouraging three days of trying to move the napkin—yes, *three* days—Packard informs me it was just a random exercise he devised. "I never imagined you'd do it," he says offhandedly. "You're not a telekinetic."

"What, are you making this up as you go along? Why have me try to move things with my mind if you know I can't?"

He steeples his fingers. "Imagine, if you will, that I asked you to roll a two-ton boulder across a field. You wouldn't be able to do it, but it would be an extraordinary workout."

"God, Packard! Do you know how hard I worked at it?" I twist up the napkin and whip it at him.

He deflects it. "There we go; I knew you could do it."

My mouth falls open. "Very funny."

He just laughs.

"I can't believe you!" I get up out of the booth and clamber onto his side, smashing my hands into his upper arm, pushing him playfully toward the wall while he laughs some more. "You're crazy!" Then I stop short, and we regard each other from a kind of still point, and I'm conscious of my fingers on soft flannel, warm muscle underneath, and that I want to kiss him. I hastily back out and go sit down over on my side again.

And for the first time in a long time, I feel alive. Completely and exquisitely alive.

I practice a lot, even at home. I push my awareness out my fingertips like Packard taught me and touch Cubby's energy dimension, which is pleasantly dense and solid. This is something I try to keep very high in my mind, that Cubby is the good solid sort of man that I have always aspired toward, whereas Packard is simply new and exciting. Furthermore, Packard's a highcap, and highcaps tend to bond with other highcaps. Though oddly, I never see him with other highcaps—that I know of. It's not like you can tell.

Soon I can make contact with a person's energy dimension with a brush of my fingertips. The girls at work have distinct energy dimensions; sometimes their energy dimensions relate vaguely to their personalities, but sometimes not. I'm always careful not to sink into them, though, like Packard warned. I would hate to get trapped inside one of my underlings. Nothing against them.

In training, we move on to burning a hole in my energy dimension, which requires pinpoint focus on a spot just beyond my right pointer fingertip. I spend long hours at the booth concentrating on it. Sometimes Packard comes by and touches it and says whether I've burnt one. After a while, I can feel the progress myself. It feels like heat. Packard seems pleased and proud, and this makes me happier than it should.

I also practice stoking up my fear on command. I still need the magazines, which is sort of embarrassing. If I need a juju item, at least it could be an amulet or an orb or something. Packard likes to tease me about this. And I often tease him about his dark lord talk. One time he actually uses the word *brainchild* in reference to the whole concept of zinging, and I get a ton of mileage out of that, applying the word to pretty much everything he thinks of.

Like mature adults, we develop what I come to consider a very nice friendship over our crackling chemistry. I find I can be honest with him about things like how grateful I am to belong to the group, and how badly I want to excel at this one thing. He often talks about the importance of what we're doing; stemming crime in this crazy way apparently means a great deal to him. He still strikes me as a man with secrets, however. Some mornings it seems clear he hasn't slept, but he's not much for discussing that sort of thing.

It's around this time I remeet the burly, caterpillary man I saw the night I joined—the one who had the mysterious stare-off with Packard and then stormed out. The ex-detective, Strongarm Francis.

"The hypochondriac." Strongarm Francis takes the seat next to me at the bar while I'm waiting for Packard to get done with somebody back at his booth. We shake, and then he looks at me hard through those fat, round glasses. "So. Things going good?"

"So far, so good," I say.

"Good." He looks away, nodding, like my answer is packed with meaning.

"What? Should things not be good?"

"No, not at all."

He's hedging, I can tell. "You sure? Is there something I should know?"

He looks at me with the stony expression older guys use to shut up younger guys—or younger gals. And it works. Because really, where was I going with this? What exactly do I think he's lying about? That things are good? No disillusionist thinks things are good. We're all too screwed up.

Francis demands my mobile phone. I hand it over and

he programs in a panic sequence—an activity that seems to cheer him.

I wait, uncomfortably warm in my green skirt suit—part of my new web of lies for Cubby. I told him I'd be interviewing today, which I feel guilty about. On the plus side, I'm zinging so much hypochondria fear into Packard these days, it seems more possible that I'll run out of it, or somehow get over it. I privately hope I can end my secret life as a disillusionist before Cubby knows anything.

Strongarm Francis says, "Hit the panic sequence and all disillusionists in the vicinity will rush to your side. Me, too."

"What's your disillusionist specialty, Francis?"

"I'm no disillusionist, little missy. I'm a regular guy. Boss's right-hand man." He goes into his briefcase and presents me with a slim metal box that's cool in my palm. "Zam! Stun gun. I made it. This'll knock anyone out." He shows me how to work it and gives me a holster, which he also made.

I zap a coffee cup and nothing happens.

Francis taps it with his finger and it shatters.

"Gosh," I say. "You think I need all this?"

"When you need it, you need it."

Day manager Ling bustles out of the back room, all in black with several pens stuck into her bun like chopsticks. "I'm opening the place up, people." She slaps the bar as she passes. "Get rid of this stuff."

Chapter Seven

MY TRAINING for the Silver Widow is finished by the time Shelby and I arrange to meet at Mongolian Delites for our long-awaited girl outing. She's been out of town, something about a target called El Gato.

I find her at the back booth with Packard and a wiry, forty-something black man with a pointy chin and a smattering of gray at his temples.

He stands up and we shake. "Vesuvius. Self-esteem issues," he explains. "Don't be impressed."

"Great to meet you," I say, pushing out to his surface, which feels soft and uneven, like tangled yarn.

"That was a lame joke, I know," he says. "The 'don't be impressed' bit. Being that I'm self-esteem issues."

"No, it was clever."

"It wasn't." He picks up a saxophone case. "Here goes nothing." He stalks off.

My gaze meets Packard's, and he tips his head in the direction Vesuvius went. "Rips their pride to tatters."

"With astonishing speed." Shelby stands. "Fastest of all disillusionists." She takes my hand and I push easily out to her surface, smooth as polished obsidian, knowing she's probably doing the same to me. I wonder what my surface is like.

And then she pulls away and grabs her coat. "We are late."

"Late?" I turn to see a pale, dark-haired man saun-tering up the aisle, dressed all in black.

"Simon," Packard says.

Simon squeezes past us, slides into Shelby's former seat, and flicks a heavy chunk of black hair out of his eyes. His eyelashes are so thick and dark that if he were a girl he wouldn't have to bother with mascara, though he might do well with a bit of blush—his skin is way too pale, and not Packard's healthy, milky pale, either. Simon looks ninety-eight percent unwholesome.

"Justine, this is Simon," Packard says. "Simon's our gambling specialist." Simon goes for the breadbasket like I'm not even there.

"Nice to meet you," I say.

"Simon," Packard says. "Say hello to Justine."

Simon inspects a piece of bread and puts it back in the basket. Then he looks up at me, eyes a beautiful royal blue. "Fear of disease, huh?" So unimpressed.

Shelby nudges me. "We are late."

"That wasn't a hello," Packard says.

"Since when do we need such a specialized function?" Simon asks.

"Since we have cases that require it."

"We already have fear so well covered. What use—"

"Simon, have you suddenly developed highcap pow-ers that grant you infallible psychological insight into our targets?"

"I don't need a highcap power to know when I'm being bullshitted."

Packard gazes pleasantly at Simon. "Disgruntled?"

Shelby pulls at me. "Come on."

"Wait," Packard says, not taking his eyes from Simon. "Simon wants to greet our newest squad member."

More tense silence. I almost empathize. Not too long ago I sat there, wanting to walk off and not being able to. Shelby pulls at me again, and this time I go with her.

"Shit! What was that?" I ask her once we're outside.

She shakes her head, like the answer is too vast to verbalize, and walks faster, shirt and floral scarf clashing in the evening breeze. "Is stupid. They are always in fight." The streetlights are just flickering on, and a bus appears in the distance. "This is us," she says.

"What did Simon mean by being bullshitted?"

"Oh, Simon, you know, he is like teenager, I think. Always somebody is lying, always Daddy is wrong."

We find a seat together in the front. The bus is air-conditioned to arctic extremes; all I have on is a black cashmere tank top with a slim green skirt and strappy sandals. I rub my arms. "So Packard would never bullshit us?"

"I do not say that. I think everybody is liar. However, is not for us to become agitated about it. There is nothing to be done."

I smile at her grim attitude.

"The time for Simon to question Packard is before he joined, that is all," she says. "After you join, pffft. You cannot decide not to be disillusionist as one would decide to change shirt, you know?"

I nod like I would never dream of that and turn my attention out the window. We rumble north past warehouses and machine-parts fabricators. Midcity makes a lot of things that go in other things.

"Simon, he is also jealous, I think. He imagines you and Packard have special relationship. I have heard him say you joke together, and that Packard drinks from your coffee cup."

"Well . . ." I try to remember when we started sharing a cup. "Packard hates the coffee at Mongolian Delites, so sometimes I let him have mine. You know how training is. You talk about stuff, get sort of buddy-buddy. Packard has that dry sense of humor. He likes to joke around, you know?"

She regards me strangely.

"What?" I say.

"Packard does not joke around. Especially when training. Training is arduous."

"Well, of course, yes, it's arduous, too. . . ."

"You joke together?"

My face flashes hot when I realize what she's thinking. "There's nothing romantic going on!"

"This is why. This!" Shelby narrows her eyes. "He has seemed lighter and I did not understand."

"Trust me. Cubby is the only man I want."

She smiles and says nothing. Pointedly.

"Cubby is the only man I want where I will *act* on that want. Okay?"

"You and Packard," she says, like it's a crazy new concept.

"And even if Cubby weren't around, I wouldn't go after the boss. The whole power imbalance issue, it's wrong in every way."

"Yes, that would be very much power imbalance. Very much." She nods. "I never see Packard with girlfriend. But then, what would he do? Take her to Mongolian Delites?"

"He certainly is a workaholic," I observe.

She shoots me a look. "He jokes?"

"Not overly."

Shelby dings the stop signal in a neighborhood of giant used-car lots that are lit up like circuses, and tiny Asian groceries and manicure places. We step out and almost get knocked down by a pack of boys on little bikes, then pass by a pair of young girls in huge motorcycle helmets playing hopscotch.

"Oh, that is so sad," I say.

Shelby links her arm in mine. "I will never wear helmet. You do not wear helmet either."

"I can't wait until Chief Otto Sanchez gets that guy."

"Police will never catch him."

"Sanchez'll catch him."

Shelby says, "He is only a man."

"I know." I shrug. "Still."

"If Brick Slinger is caught, it will not make city safer. Another will emerge to kill." In spite of her words, there's very little charge to Shelby's grimness today; she must've zinged recently, I think. That's what disillusionists say when a fellow disillusionist seems saner than usual.

I say, "If another emerges, Chief Sanchez will get that one, too. And the next and the next. He'll take them all down."

"I think you wish Chief Sanchez would take *you* down."

I laugh.

After the next block we head into a cavernous warehouse that's honeycombed with retail and restaurant stalls, a kind of high-tech bazaar.

We walk around and I quiz her about other disillusionists, like Jordan, the woman she'd mentioned that first night. "Very unpleasant, Jordan the Therapist," Shelby says, inspecting a decorative fan. "Steer clear, you know? Her mania is"—she wrinkles her nose— "aggressive. And then there is the Monk, most dangerous disillusionist. Destroys people's faith. None of us have met him. Sometimes Packard must contact Monk through wilderness guides."

I forgot how fun it was to shop with a girlfriend. We try on dozens of pairs of shoes. I buy a Chinese dress just like hers. Afterward, we go for a late dinner of spicy noodles at a Thai restaurant back in the Delites neighborhood. We talk and laugh and discover we like similar books and music.

Over mango shakes, I learn that Shelby came to Midcity as a mail-order bride at the age of fifteen, left the guy at eighteen, and went to work as a maid at a hotel on the edge of downtown, just below the river. I know it. It's near Cubby's condo.

"I would save my pay to drink and eat alone at Mongolian Delites, and that is how I met Packard," she tells me. "I still love kebabs. Packard and other disillusionists hate them, of course."

"If they hate them so much, why do they always eat them? And if Packard's so damn sensitive about the restaurant, why not change it, or sell it?"

"Nobody has told you?"

"Told me what?"

"About Packard and restaurant."

I look at her blankly.

Shelby parts her pretty lips in surprise and leans close, all dusky intensity, as if this tidbit demands an extra flourish. "Packard is prisoner there. He is prisoner at Mongolian Delites. He has not been outside restaurant for eight years."

"What? Are you talking about some sort of house arrest?"

"No, Justine, he is prisoner of another highcap. I cannot believe nobody told you this. Packard, it is hard for him to speak of it. Nemesis imprisoned him there for life."

I blink at her, dumbfounded.

"Have you seen Packard out of restaurant? No. He can go into kitchen, bathrooms, dining areas and broom closet only. He is thirty-three, I think. So he has been inside since age of twenty-five."

"That's insane. It's impossible!"

"It is not impossible. There are highcaps with such powers."

"So he can never leave? Ever?" And suddenly I see it. I see the caged animal in him. "Oh my God. That is horrible. He has to get free."

Shelby shakes her head. "He cannot. Packard's nemesis is highcap with power of force fields. It is as if he can speak to building, interface with building. He can make force fields, even change shape of walls. Nemesis spoke to Mongolian Delites building. He said, 'You must never let Packard leave.'" She describes how an invisible wall traps Packard, even if the door is open. The sadness of it steals my breath.

"Packard cannot change menu; that is why we must eat same things. He cannot change hours or layout of space to make private place in back. Always he lives in public. Even silly decor, if he smashes knickknack or burns a wall hanging, tomorrow it is back. Force field creates, what do you say? Continuity. You should look on Internet. There is something on Internet of this highcap mutation. You have studied highcaps on Internet, right?"

"Yeah," I say distractedly. I looked up Packard's mutation, of course. Seeing psychological structure. There was hardly anything on his type. "How could I not know this?"

"He loathes to speak of it." The waitress brings the bill, and Shelby snaps her credit card over it. I can tell she's tired—it's after midnight—but I ask her more questions. I need to know everything.

She tells me how Packard purchased the restaurant from the owners after his imprisonment, and about his unsuccessful attempts to escape, to remodel. "We believe Packard sleeps on little bedroll that he lays out next to booth. He is cut off from world. From friends and loved ones," she says.

"They can't come and visit him?"

"All those who knew Packard—or knew of him— think he is dead. Even if they saw him, they would not see him, would not believe it is him. If I saw woman who looks like my dead nana, I would not think it is her.

Strongarm Francis says nemesis worked with powerful highcap revisionist who revised minds and memories of those around Packard. This is part of imprisonment, you see. He is isolated in all ways."

Packard doesn't seem so teasable anymore; his darkness and gravity have new significance. "Who is this nemesis?"

Shelby shakes her head. "Packard will not tell. Nobody knows."

"Have you tried to find out and, like, do something about it?"

"Packard forbids it. He says nemesis is evil and dangerous. Such investigation could alert and anger nemesis. What if nemesis decides to put Packard where we cannot find him? What would happen to him? To us?"

"Why doesn't Packard kill him? Not that I'd condone it, but . . ."

"If nemesis dies, Packard is trapped for good. As long as nemesis lives, there is chance he will change mind."

"We have to help free him."

"He cannot be free, Justine. Even Packard accepts this. And you must, too."

It's well after midnight when I'm banging on Mongolian Delites' window. The restaurant closed over an hour ago. The staff would've just gone home.

He opens the door wearing a black T-shirt and holey jeans. An outfit for lounging at home. Because this is his home.

"When were you going to tell me?" Seeing him now, I feel this immense sorrow for him. "I thought we were friends."

He gets this strange look—eyes bright, and not in a happy way. "I wasn't aware I was beholden to give you every fact of my existence."

"Every fact?" I push past him and walk in. "How

about the single most important, unthinkable, and out-rageous fact of your existence?" I hear the door shut. I turn. "God, Packard!"

He strolls over to a table by the curtained window where a lone candle burns over a magazine and a coffee cup. He flips the magazine closed and turns to me, more composed now, though his green eyes still shine—with pain, I think. "It's hardly the most important fact of my existence," he says. "Unthinkable and outrageous, though—I'll give you that."

"We have to get you out of here."

"Leave it."

"I won't. There's always a way."

"I've been in here eight years. *Eight years.*" It sinks in even deeper when he says it. "I know every detail of the strength and limits of this prison. Every excruciating detail."

"So you just give up? Like a man helpless to change his circumstances?" I don't know whether I'm madder at his nemesis or at him for accepting it.

"Leave it."

"I won't leave it. It's wrong. And surely you haven't tried everything. I'm new, maybe I have new ideas. It's not right that we wouldn't keep working on it. Doesn't every villain have an Achilles' heel? What about disillusioning this guy? Attack him and crash him?"

"If you knew my nemesis, you wouldn't say that so lightly. You might not even say it out loud." His voice sounds gravelly. "You certainly wouldn't consider try-ing to disillusion him." He looks at the door. "I won't discuss it further."

My eyes go to the magazine on the table where he'd been sitting, one of his many travel magazines about tropical beaches. He moves in front of it. "Now that you know this is my prison, maybe you could respect the pathetically small amount of solitude I have?"

And it hits me like a punch in the gut: the magazine he's hiding is *a travel magazine about tropical beaches*. He was fantasizing. He'll never smell that salty air. He'll never wiggle his toes in the warm soft sand. He never even feels the sunshine on his skin! "I'm so sorry."

He snorts. "Oh, please. Don't."

"Don't what? Be sorry you're trapped for life?"

"That would be a start. I'm fine."

"Fine?" I reach around him for the magazine. "This is fine?"

"Don't!" He grabs my wrist and I let go; the magazine slaps onto the floor. The wild way he looks at me—I understand him completely in this moment. He doesn't want me feeling all sad and sorry for him.

"Shit," I say. "I didn't mean to look at you all pitying and—"

He holds my wrist tight between us, searching my face. My blood races; I'm seeing inside him for the first time.

I say, "That's not how I'm looking at you."

The world around us seems to have fallen silent, save for the sounds of tires on wet pavement outside, and my ragged breathing. And his ragged breathing.

He tightens his grip. I turn my hand and press it to his chest, feel his heart thumping through his warm, soft T-shirt.

He says, "It's certainly not how I'm looking at you right now."

This strange calm descends over me as he moves his hand over mine, trapping it to his heart. I'm about to cross some line, and I don't care. Frankly, I'm trembling to cross it. Or maybe I'm just trembling.

He slides his hand off mine, and I close my fist over his T-shirt, grabbing fabric, pulling him toward me as he runs light fingertips over my shoulders, the sides of my neck. He brushes his lips over mine, soft and warm, a feathery kiss at the top of my lips, the bottom, pulling me closer. I relax and mold to him, enjoying the shivery goodness of the way he kisses me.

I sigh, like all the harshness is going out of me and there's just the pure pleasure of Packard. And right there I feel this change come over him, a quickening in his whole body, and he shifts his hands to my back and pulls me to him hard, chest to chest, lips soft and moist.

He pushes my lips open with his, and we sink into each other. It's crazy and wonderful; every part of me is melty with desire. It's all just breath and body between us.

"Oh, God," he says into my lips, cupping the back of my head, kissing me harder. I grab the back of his shirt and pull him closer. I want to eat him up!

"I have been waiting so long," he says. "And waiting. And waiting." His breathy kisses intoxicate me and send waves down between my legs.

"I have, too." I realize it only as I say it, and it's like I can't get enough of him, and I fall deeper into the thrilling hardness of his erection between my legs. I slide up on him, and then down, and the feel of him magically penetrates to the deepest places inside me. Even so, I can't get enough of him.

He curls his hands down around my bottom and pulls me to him firmly; then he slides his hands lower and knits his fingers under me, actually lifts me up. I wrap my legs around him and it's the most natural feel in the world, being mashed together, straining into each other. I grab his curls, lost in the sensation of his cock and the rub of his whiskers on my cheek. The room whirls around and suddenly I'm sitting on the table and he's kissing me—soft, short kisses. He kisses up my neck, lingering tantalizingly over my ear, doing warm breathy things that feel illicit, especially once his tongue gets involved. Then he bites down on my earlobe, hot and sharp, and a swoon moves through me, like unexpected sunshine on my stomach.

Time slows. I touch his chest, relax into this new deli-cious thing, and he trails his fingertips along my shins, my knees, my thighs. I like a man to touch my legs—knowledge Cubby frequently exploits.

A wave of panic. "Shit," I say. "What am I doing?" He feels me freeze and slows. I slide off the table in a daze. "This cannot, will not—oh, man," I say. "What am I doing? I have a boyfriend." Though I showed up at his place in the middle of the night. That is not boyfriend-having behavior.

He watches me warily, skin flushed with passion.

"I'm sorry, this cannot . . ." I turn away, finger a salt shaker on a nearby table. "I shouldn't have come. I shouldn't have let this happen. Cubby means everything to me."

"Right." . . .

I turn around. "What's that tone? Are you being sar-castic?"

Packard waits. Like I'm supposed to figure it out.

"Come on, let's hear it. You don't think Cubby means everything to me?"

"I should let you come to it on your own," he says.

"No, do tell. I bet it'll be amusing."

"Fine." Packard crosses his arms. "The *idea* of Cubby means everything to you, but the man himself means nothing. You barely know him. It's as if you're shopping for the life and the safety he represents. You're mesmer-ized by men who are stable and secure—men admired by society—but that's just you groping for the safety and security you don't feel. Because you've always been a misfit. Fearful. Rejected by others."

The insult of this cuts so deep, I'm speechless.

"And Cubby's one of these high achievers who don't feel deeply," he continues. "Life doesn't touch him, which is why he likes to have you around. You make him feel something. Your chaos. Your instability."

"I can't believe you used your stupid mutant powers to analyze us like that. And got it wrong, by the way."

"I got it right, Justine. Feel into it. Your sense of being a misfit blinds you to what your heart really wants. When you get around solid, upstanding men, you're like a bird with tinfoil. It makes you incoherent on a romantic level."

"My affection is incoherent unless it's for you? That's the line you're giving me here?"

"This is real." He points out the door. "That isn't."

"I think you're the biggest manipulator I've ever met."

"I am." He lowers himself onto the table. "I'm the biggest manipulator you'll ever meet. But not at this moment."

"Yeah, you're just a guy boiling me down to empty psychological tendencies."

"You came here in the middle of the night. You wanted to know."

"Right, I did. It was really poor behavior for somebody in a relationship." I grab my purse. It's time to leave. "But here's the thing—Cubby and I have a great relationship. Which proves that you only see what you want to see. Your beloved mental power isn't infallible."

"Oh, my mental power is infallible," he says. "But I never said I loved it."

Chapter
Eight

OVER THE NEXT FEW DAYS, the kiss haunts me, floating through doors, turning up in quiet corners with a *whoosh* of sensation. I avoid Cubby because I feel like he'll be able to look at me and tell. But I finally catch up with Shelby one hot afternoon. We take iced coffees to a bench on the lakeshore, watching kids play in the sand by the water's edge—all of them wearing helmets. Some even wear protective gear on their chests, like little hockey players. It's enraging that children at the beach would have to dress that way because of some psycho.

Shelby points to a couple stretched out on a picnic blanket next to a basket, a bottle of wine, and a rifle. "They think rifle will ward off Brick Slinger?"

I stir my coffee. "The Slinger needs to be slung." We watch the kids a little more, and finally I muster up the courage to tell her about kissing Packard, begging her not to tell the others. I finally belong, and I don't want to be different or set apart. She understands. If there's one thing disillusionists understand, it's the desperate desire to belong.

"The kiss was a mistake," I say. "A stupid mistake."

She inspects my eyes for signs that it wasn't.

"He's wrong that I'm with Cubby out of being a

misfit." I look away. "I hate keeping all these secrets from him. I have to come clean."

"You cannot! He would want you to quit."

"Yeah."

She looks at me like I'm crazy. "You do not plan to repeat kiss?"

"Definitely not."

"You must not tell Cubby, then."

We walk to the pier for Shelby to feed the seagulls, analyzing Cubby, Packard, and the kiss as only girl-friends can.

"I still can't believe he's trapped and none of you know why, or who this nemesis even is," I say.

"None of us know anything, yes." Shelby pauses with a saucy look. "Except I know one small thing."

"What?"

"I said I would not tell."

"Did you give your word of honor?" The disillusion-ists take their words of honor seriously. Like blood oaths.

"No, I did not give word of honor." She snaps the lid over her coffee. "And it is not telling if I show you."

Fifteen minutes later, we're in a cab bumping north down deserted, garbage-strewn streets, past fortress mul-tihousing. People watch us from darkened doorways.

Shelby directs the driver to a tall concrete apart-ment building that's composed of massive rectangular blocks stacked willy-nilly, like a giant baby made it. Random blocks are painted blue. The rest are concrete gray.

Shelby gets out. "Wait for us, please," she says to the cabbie.

I join her on the sidewalk across the street from the building. The air is stifling this far from the lake, and it smells like rotten eggs and curry.

She turns to me. "Do you give your word you will say nothing of what I show you?"

"I give my word," I say, hoping I won't regret it.

She points upward. "Look at blue square on end of fourth floor. What do you notice?"

"It has more peeling paint than the others?"

"Look better."

And then I see it: large eyes, elegant curve to the nose, the beard with the upturned curl at the end. "Whoa! It's the same face as the Mongolian Delites door."

Shelby smiles.

"Same expression, same . . . everything." Except this face isn't wood; it seems to have been formed by an artist scratching away blue paint to reveal gray.

"Two years ago I saw this and told Packard. He said that I am like woman who sees face of Jesus in two-headed calf. He never wants to speak of this face or that face or any face ever again. He says I must never come here again." Shelby crosses her arms. "I have reflected on it. When Packard keeps secret, it is always about nemesis and his old life. Everything else, he does not care. So when he keeps secrets, I know it is this. I believe bearded face to be logo for highcap nemesis, type of fingerprint, I think. Like face of little girl on box of brownie mix, or skull face on canister of pepper spray."

"Where did you get that idea?"

"Reading on Internet."

"Do you ever think about going up there?"

She's silent for a while. "Packard would forbid it."

"If he knew," I say. "What if there's something to learn here? Something that could help him? He deserves to be free."

"Many people deserve many things. And we cannot anger nemesis. What if he lives there?"

"What if he does? Why should the nemesis be angry

about two women walking around in an apartment building? It's a public place."

Shelby considers this.

"Don't you kind of want to check it out? Just a little bit?"

She smiles her foxy, chipped-tooth smile. "A little bit."

We tell our cabbie to wait some more and head toward the front door. Two raggedy boys run out.

"Children! Come!" Shelby calls after them. "Please, come!"

The children stop and regard Shelby with suspicion. She kneels and digs a package of licorice out of her purse. "I will give you each piece of candy if you will let us in and tell us how to get up to that apartment." She points at the fourth floor. "See? Where it looks like face?"

The boys stare at the licorice.

"Shelby, they can't take candy from strangers." I pull out my wallet. "Five bucks each to get us up there."

The older boy puts his hands on his hips. "Five bucks each and the candy. The whole pack."

"You got it," I say.

We follow them into a grimy lobby. One wall is covered by squares of cracked mirrors; the other side is blue concrete with an elevator in the center. The older boy, who's maybe nine, points at it. "Stay out." He leads us into a stairwell that smells like urine and mint. We step over bags of garbage and a few bundles that turn out to be sleeping people. It makes me wonder what's in the elevator.

"You know who lives in the apartment where we're going?" I ask.

"Not our floor," the boy says.

"Not our floor, not our problem," the younger one adds mysteriously.

Soon we're standing in front of #401, the last door on a moldy-smelling corridor that feels subterranean. The lighting fixtures have little cages around them. The boys are long gone.

Shelby gives me a questioning look that turns to horror when I knock. She whispers, "What if it is, you know—"

The door is opened by a girl, maybe twenty-one, twenty-two years old. Her long, stringy white-blonde hair creates a dramatic contrast with her thick black eyeliner and strappy black tank top. She's frighteningly thin—her torn jeans would fall right off her if they weren't held up by her black belt. She has a wary air of damage, like a hurt stray cat.

"Can I help you?"

"Umm . . ." My thought was to pretend we had the wrong door, but no way is this the nemesis. Packard was sealed up eight years ago; this girl would've barely been out of her Disney movie phase.

I glance nosily into her place, which is normal-looking save for a large hole in one wall, like someone went at it with a sledgehammer. On the endearing side, she has pretty paisley curtains on the windows, and a big, beat-up picture book of horses on the coffee table.

"Excuse us, we have wrong door," Shelby says. "We are looking for somebody else."

The girl seems disappointed. "Maybe I can help find who you're looking for. I know everybody in the building."

"No thanks," Shelby says.

"We were more looking for information about somebody," I say. "You probably don't know him. . . ." I feel Shelby's eyes on me, but there has to be a reason Packard told Shelby to stay away. "A man named Packard? Reddish brown hair, tall, good looking? Very, very intense."

"Highcap? Sees people's tendencies and shit?"

"Yeah."

She nods. "Sterling Packard."

"You know him?"

"Knew him. Guy was shot dead eight years ago." She turns and strolls into her small room. Shelby and I take this moment to exchange glances. "Man got his head blown off. Couple guys in masks. You didn't know?" She flops down on a ratty pink couch. "My name's Rickie. Come on in."

We step over the threshold. "I'm Justine, and my friend here—"

The door slams behind us before I can finish, and the horse book lifts off the table and traces an arc through the air, gaining speed, spinning like a Frisbee right at Shelby, who's still mesmerized by the self-slamming door.

"Shelby!"

Too late—the book clonks Shelby in the head, knocking her to the floor. I kneel over her, squeezing her shoulders. "Shelby!" Unresponsive. "Shit!"

Rickie laughs, and I catch movement out of the corner of my eye—the book, circling back toward me. I flatten over Shelby just in time; it sails over me and smashes into the wall, embedding itself in the hole. Rickie laughs as the book trembles, dislodging.

"Goddammit!" I lunge across the room at Rickie, avoiding the book as I heap onto her, trying to pin her arms and legs and stop her from making stuff fly through the air. A flurry of spoons and cups hit me in the back. Then I see bigger stuff tremble, including a large trophy. Rickie gets hold of my hair and my shirt, keeping me over her, exposed to the next round of stuff. I twist and pull, but she has a real grip on my hair. It hurts. And then I do what I should've done all along— I whip out my stun gun and give her a good jolt in the gut. Her laughter ends with a shriek, and everything airborne falls to the floor as she crumples under me.

I rush back to Shelby, who's unconscious and bleeding from the forehead. I heave her out of there by an arm and a shoulder and sit her in the hall.

Down a ways a door opens and two black guys in warm-up suits saunter out. One of them points at Shelby and laughs. "Rickles getcha?" His wraparound sunglasses are so dark you can't see his eyes.

"Quick, help me get her to safety," I pant.

"Don't you worry, Rickles can't hurt you out here," the guy with sunglasses says. "Rickles can't come out in the hall, and Rickles's voodoo don't work out here, neither."

I look up at him. "Are you saying that girl's trapped in there?"

"Oh, yeah. She's been in there, what . . . ?" He looks to his friend.

"Good three years," the friend says.

Sunglasses nods. "I'm telling you."

I kneel in front of Shelby, who's coming around, groggily insisting she's fine.

"Some kind of electric fence. Whatever she says, don't you go in there." He turns his head and points to a scar on his cheek. The friend shows off scars on his head and leg. They both seem amused.

The friend goes and gets towels, and the three of us fall to cleaning and inspecting Shelby's forehead gash. We're divided on the need for stitches.

"Please, I am fine." Shelby presses a towel to her head to prevent further inspection.

The guys leave.

"Head wounds bleed a lot, but it's nothing to worry about," I assure her. "Let me look at your pupils."

"No. You are not really nurse."

"Do you feel nauseated or sleepy?"

"Stop. I am fine."

I bite my lip. A hard blow to the head can lead to

a vein star–type vascular bulge and rupture. I want to warn her, but on the other hand, the anxiety of knowing this could elevate her blood pressure and exacerbate it even more.

"Stop looking at me like that." She shifts her eyes sideways, toward the door. "Telekinetic."

"Seems so," I say.

A voice: "Hey! What the fuck?"

Rickie's at the door, hands flattened against nothing, like a mime. She's trapped, just like Packard. Are there others?

"What'd you do to me?" Rickie demands.

"What'd you do to *us*? Why would you attack us?"

"Why? Lemme think for a second." She scrunches up her face. "Oh yeah, I remember. Because I can. So what did you wanna know about Sterling Packard?"

"So now we're going back to conversation?" I say.

"You got questions; I got answers."

I stand up, face her across the threshold. "Like we trust you now."

"Come on, try me," she says. "'Cause I got more I can tell about Packard."

"We will hear it," Shelby pipes up from the floor.

"Now we're in business," Rickie says. She disappears into her place. A minute later she returns waving a scrap of paper. "It'll cost you."

I stare at the paper.

"My info's good." She extends the paper through the invisible wall. Closer and closer. I snatch it away. A shopping list.

Two hours later we're back in the hall with a case of tequila, ten bags of French Onion SunChips, a book on pigeons, and an ant farm. We arrange the stuff in the hall just beyond her reach. Lastly the ant farm. I slide the box sideways so she can see the edge of it.

"Slide it out. Let me see the whole front of the box."

I comply and Rickie stares at it for a long time.

"I always wanted one of those," she says quietly.

"And it's Plexiglas. Unbreakable."

She's too engrossed in the box to get my joke. "Does it come with the ants?"

I read the contents list on the back. "Oops."

Rickie looks like she's about to cry. "What good is it without the ants?"

"If you answer our questions today," I tell her, "we will give you all this stuff. If your answers prove true—and believe me, we will check them—I will personally bring you a jar of ants."

"It can't just be the ants. It has to have the queen."

After further negotiation, we decide I'll bring C batteries, more tequila, and a jar of ants to include a queen if her answers are true. As if we have a way to verify them.

She wants a tequila up front. I hand it through. "So you know Packard."

She opens the bottle and throws the cap over her shoulder. "Knew." She takes a swig. "Man was like a fucking rock star, you know? Everybody loved him. Wanted to be in his gang." She pulls a chair to the doorway, settles into it backward, and takes another swig, seeming very much like a girl pirate. "First time I talked to him I was a kid, new out on the streets, living at this abandoned house with a bunch of other highcap runaways. I remember I was hanging in the doorway and I see this shiny blue boat of a car roll up, and people jump out of it. Sterling Packard and his gang. One guy with a long coat and chains and shit, girl in some sort of riding outfit. Couple of muscle guys. They all come up, and Sterling Packard, he wants to know is Stoolie Black around. Stoolie was one of the older kids at the house, a short-term prognosticator. Stoolie'd helped

Sterling and his gang on this one job once—some sort of complicated robbery. So I tell Sterling Packard, you come in, and I'll get that boy."

"A robbery?"

Shelby gives me a look.

"Yeah. A robbery." Rickie wipes her mouth with the back of her hand. "So I come back down with Stoolie. And I'm like, 'Hey, I'm a telekinetic, man. You should take me with.' And Sterling Packard, he grabs this horse book that's there, right?" She points back at the horse book. "That exact one. And he's like, 'Can you embed this motherfucker in that wall over there?' And I just laugh. I say, 'Who can do that?' Telekinetics don't have that level of force. And Sterling Packard, he points right at me and he says, 'If you practice, you can do that. And once you're good enough to embed this book in that wall, come find me and you can join my crew.'" She dangles the bottle from her fingertips, arms stretched long over the back of the chair. "And you saw it, right? I fucking can now. That and more." She sighs. "Sterling Packard, he had a code. He came up on the streets from pretty young—even younger than me, I think."

"What? None of you have families?"

"Highcap kids are trouble for families. Tons wind up on their own. But Packard, he put things together. It was bad, him dying. And I'll tell you this—that horse book is way heavier than the bricks that showoff in the news is throwing around. Bricks are half the weight."

"So who put you in here?" I ask.

"That's what I want to know. I'll tell you this—it involved a revisionist, because everybody thinks I'm dead. You try to call them and they think it's a crank." She drinks some more. Softly she says, "Woke up one day and I was here."

"You ever hear anything about Packard having a nemesis?"

"Of course." She lowers her voice. "Henji."

"What's his deal?" I say, hoping it doesn't cost us another shopping trip. "This Henji?"

She shakes her head. "You don't want to know Henji's deal. Good luck finding anybody alive that even knew Henji. Henji left on a ship when he was eleven. Pretty young age to go travel the world, you know? But it's pretty young to be a mass murderer, too."

"Henji was a mass murderer?"

"He could kill people with a thought. Shit, I was barely born when it all went down, but they say Packard sort of adopted him, the way older kids adopt younger kids outside. A group of them were squatting in this old abandoned school by the river. All I know is one day Packard and Henji had this fight that leveled the school where they lived and Henji took off. And Packard stayed behind. Grew up to run highcap gangs, and then he got shot in the head."

Shelby asks, "Could Packard have had another nemesis?"

Rickie stares at her like she's nuts. "I think you only get one. Isn't there a rule like that somewhere?"

"What was Henji's specific power?"

"To kill. I get the creeps just talking about him." She raises a hand to indicate the end of that line of questioning.

"Could it be force fields?"

She shrugs. "Sure."

I look over at Shelby. Is she thinking what I'm thinking? Could force fields level a building? Could force fields kill? Is the face the mark of Henji? I turn back to Rickie. "Can you think of any reason why Henji would put you in here?"

Rickie narrows her eyes. "Henji's gone."

"But what if he wasn't?"

"What are you saying?"

"Is there anything you could've done to make Henji mad?"

She regards me with horror, as though she's spotted a scorpion on my nose. "Henji?"

"I'm not saying—"

"Henji's back?" She stands unsteadily. "Wait, you think Henji's the one . . . Why would Henji put me in here? Look, I never did anything to Henji, I swear. If I hurt somebody he knows, I swear—" She straightens up. "Did Henji send you?"

"No."

"There's something you're not saying. I could tell that this whole time."

"It's nothing like that—"

"Then why'd you ask that out of the blue? I would never do anything against Henji. I don't even know him. He was before my time!" Rickie backs up to the couch. "I don't like this. You guys have to just get out of here. And I will never talk about Henji again—you tell him that. And if he wants to know, I would be the most loyal person, and I will never say his name again." She hugs her bottle. "God! Just get away. Don't come back here."

As soon as we push the stuff in, the door slams. We rush down the stairwell, spooked.

"Henji. Henji imprisoned both," Shelby whispers. "It has to be."

"Right, but why?" I lower my voice. "Henji leaves at age eleven, after the fight with Packard, but then he comes back years later and imprisons Packard for eternity. What's that about?"

"I do not want to investigate this further," she whispers. "I do not like this."

"And here's another thing: I don't see Packard as a criminal. No way." We cross the lobby and push outside. The air is like a blast from a furnace.

"Packard is prisoner now," Shelby says. "We are his gang now."

"Shit." I stop, pulling Shelby to a stop. "We know Henji's been back at least eight years, right? Because that's how long Packard's been trapped."

She stares longingly at our cab across the street. "Yes."

"Okay, what started eight years ago?"

"I was still maid then."

"Eight years ago was that notorious first summer of crime, remember? The holdup gangs that could read minds? And then the pickpockets, the open-window robberies? Remember? It all started *eight years ago*."

Her eyes widen.

"Henji's behind the crime wave. He comes back, puts his rival Packard away—I mean, isn't that the first thing a nemesis would do? And then he starts destroying lives." I feel this surge of anger toward Henji. "This guy has to be stopped."

She clutches both my arms. "He can kill with thought! He could be somebody we already know. He could be listening now. And what if you alert him and make things worse for Packard?"

"How do you know we won't make things better? Frankly, I'd like to hunt this jackass down on my own behalf as a pissed-off citizen of Midcity who's sick of people being terrorized."

"No, Justine—"

"We could at least *locate* Henji. A little knowledge never hurt anybody."

That night I hop on a computer—at a coffee shop, just to be safe. There are no mentions of Henji anywhere, which I find ominous. I learn more about the force field ability among highcaps, however.

Power over force fields—or "structural interface," as

most sites call it—is rare. The theory goes that force fields people can actually interface with the atoms of a building. They can also modify architectural details and get impressions of important events that transpired inside—not like a movie camera but flashes, images, according to the sites. Like a "dimly remembered dream," one says.

Chapter Nine

I LEAN AGAINST THE STONE WALL outside Delites; today's the day I'm to pick up my uniform and instructions for the Silver Widow job.

I haven't faced Packard in the week since the kiss. Part of me is eager to see him, and part of me feels like everything's spinning out of control and seeing him will make it spin harder. So I lean on the sun-warmed wall and watch the employees of the Glorybell Ad Agency wander into the door down the way. A lot of them wear helmets with their business casual clothes. There's talk that the Brick Slinger is due for another strike.

Is Henji responsible for the eight-year crime wave? It makes sense. And then there's Chief Sanchez. He's the first one to make any progress against it. What if Henji goes after Sanchez? How does Sanchez fight an enemy who can kill with a thought? Chief Sanchez has his own motto—the papers have been making much ado of it lately—something like, "Guarding citizens from evildoers of all kinds." But not Henji's kind, I think wistfully.

But Chief Sanchez will keep fighting no matter what—that's how he is. Does he know about Henji? Would that information be valuable to him?

It occurs to me here that Packard and Chief Sanchez are natural allies, which makes me a natural ally of Chief Sanchez. I get a real charge out of this thought. By crashing and rebooting criminals, Packard and the disillusionists and I are helping Sanchez in his mission. I turn my face to the sun, resolved not to let any doubts cloud my mind today—doubts around the vigilante bit and all the secrets and shadows lurking just beyond the light.

Carter squeals up in front of the restaurant and jumps out of his convertible, all ruddy face and windblown hair. "It's an asshole driving convention up on the tangle." He slams the car door. I can feel the rage wound up tight inside him; even his body looks more compact.

"You need a zing."

"Damn straight." He plugs the meter. "Goddammit!" He starts smacking it. "Come on, motherfucker!"

I turn and trace the wooden plane of the giant's cheek, admiring his dashing Renaissance look. He would be perfect with a sword and a ruffled collar, like a knight. Why would Henji use such a pleasing symbol? Or doesn't he have control over it? If it's really like a fingerprint, he wouldn't have control. He probably wishes it was a viper head or something.

"You going to open that door or hump it?"

"Yeah, yeah." I open the door.

Carter heads back, but I stop to say hi to Helmut and Simon at the bar. Helmut greets me like a civil person. Moppy-haired Simon is silent.

"Hi, Simon," I say.

Simon hops off his stool, brushing my arm—did he just touch my energy dimension? "You're not a disillusionist. You're a decoration."

"Excuse me?"

"You imagine you have diseases you don't have," he says. "It's a preening, pathetic specialty. You've got nothing."

"Are you saying I'm not screwed up enough?"

"That's what I'm saying," Simon says. "I don't know why Packard even has you here."

Helmut frowns. "Take it down a notch, Simon. Only a fool criticizes somebody he hasn't seen in action."

"That's okay," I say. "Simon's entitled to his opinion." I turn to Simon, hoping he can't tell how he's hurt my feelings. "Let's see, your area is gambling. Winning and losing money. My area is the fact that you depend on a flawed and decaying piece of meat for survival. My area is mortal terror." I stare into Simon's deep blue eyes. "My area is the loss of everything."

"You deal in imaginary loss," he says. "I give them genuine loss."

"Both of you—" Helmut barks. "Tone it down. There's enough strife on this planet."

Simon smiles and walks off.

Helmut turns to me, full of despairing gravity. "Don't listen to him. Simon is one of our best, but he's an artist—a very dark one. He'll warm up to you."

"I don't know if I want him to warm up to me."

Helmut updates me on the impending nuclear exchange between India and Pakistan. This does not make me feel better.

Finally I go back. Carter's sitting with Packard, who glances up and smiles. My goose bumps go full flare. "Justine," he says.

"Packard." I take the seat next to Carter, who's firing up a laptop.

Packard launches into the meeting. "Skin conditions will be the Silver Widow's Achilles' heel," he informs me. He's identified the perfect disease: Osiris virus, a skin syndrome that's so amorphous, its very existence is hotly debated. Amorphous syndromes are ideal for the hypochondriac. You can't rule them in and you can't rule them out.

"I've never related to skin diseases," I say dismissively.

"They're so nonvital. I mean, with internal organs, you can't see them, so you don't know what's going on. But skin?"

"Oh, you'll see that skin hypochondria can be quite profound," Packard says. "Imagine what would happen if you could touch and inspect and irritate the vascular walls of your brain?"

I concentrate on folding my napkin into an insanely meticulous square. "I guess it would be more participatory."

"Among other things." Humorously, he adds, "You shouldn't automatically write off one thing because you're better acquainted with another."

"Yeah, yeah," I say, seemingly bored, like I didn't catch that double meaning. Like my pulse isn't racing.

Carter works on emailing me articles on the Silver Widow's trial. He tells me they couldn't get a conviction due to circumstantial evidence.

Packard points at the screen. "Send her this one, too," he says. "And this." His eyelashes are long and thick—the sort of detail a mother would enjoy in a baby. I have to get away from him.

He looks up and catches me staring, and smiles. "Just because it's an unknown quantity," he says, "doesn't mean it might not be superior in every conceivable way." He's playing. It's actually kind of funny.

I raise my eyebrows. "I know what works for me."

"You know what's *familiar* to you."

"It's familiar because it works, and because I'm committed to it," I say.

"But what if your commitment only holds you back? What if what's familiar has no ability to recognize and appreciate the full truth of you? Don't tell me you haven't imagined how it would feel to fully indulge the unknown quantity—"

"You think I've imagined it?"

Carter looks up. "What the hell are you guys talking about?"

"Skin diseases," I say.

Carter returns his attention to the screen.

Simon appears and slides in next to Packard. "I feel so left out," he says. "Justine has touched everybody's energy dimension except mine."

"How would you know? Maybe she has." Packard glances at me and I give him a look that says no. Packard instructed me to practice on everybody, but I never did Simon.

Packard raises his eyebrows scoldingly.

I twist my lips in an oops face.

"My, what robust nonverbal communication. Aren't you two cozy." Simon puts his hand on the table, grinning. "Try me, Justine." Like he thinks I can't do it.

"I don't see what the big deal is." I touch his hand and push out with my awareness, but as I near his energy dimension, I have this sense I'm closing in on something disturbing; I feel shaky and clammy. I try to press on, but I can't force myself to push out all the way to him any more than I could force myself to chew and eat my own tongue.

Simon's blue eyes are aggressively innocent. "Something wrong?"

"No." I keep trying. My repulsion grows stronger; sweat blooms down my back.

"Enough!" Packard pulls our hands apart.

Carter snorts. "Christ, Simon."

I breathe hard. "What's going on?"

"Some disillusionists have reactions to certain energy dimensions," Packard says. "It happens to the best of them."

"Never happens to me," Simon says.

Packard glowers at him. "It's okay, Justine."

But it's not. It feels like the residue of Simon's energetic dimension clogs my throat. Am I actually going to throw up? I need air.

Packard says something I don't register; I get up and beeline out through the dining room and straight to the bathroom.

I push open the door to find a woman washing her hands at the last sink. Smarty glasses and a neat gray ponytail, like an upscale librarian. I sit in the wicker chair near the stalls, head between my knees, willing her to leave. What if this happens when I'm with a vile and dangerous target? Will I be a failure as a disillusionist now, too? Maybe Simon's right. Maybe I don't belong here.

Clicks across the floor. Sensible black heels stop in front of me. "It's a miracle everybody's not throwing up all the time," the woman says.

I raise my head. "Excuse me?"

"All of it. Packard, this restaurant, this world. The outrageousness of the human condition. The best you can hope for is to comprehend the full horror of it. Because things will never get better. I guarantee it."

I squint at her.

"I'm sorry, I should've introduced myself. I'm Jordan. The therapist. I understand you're our new health anxieties specialist."

"You're a therapist?"

Jordan frowns at my incredulous tone. "I deliver the truth that other therapists spend their lives trying to minimize. Deep down, my friend, we're all crazy and twisted." Her eyes dance as she speaks. "Nobody and nothing gets better."

"Well, we're crashing and rebooting criminals. That's something better."

She rolls her eyes. "Oh, maybe we're *rebooting* them. Doesn't mean it's not crazy and twisted."

"What do you mean?"

"Why are we rebooting them?" she asks.

"Because they need a change of heart."

She smiles down at me like I'm an idiot. "Why?"

"Who cares why?" I say.

"Why *always* matters."

"We're helping them turn good."

She adjusts her glasses and peers at me intently. "I have a riddle for you—when is good not good?"

"Is this one of those mind twisters? Or like a definition thing? It doesn't make sense."

Jordan snorts. "You people."

"I give up. When is good not good?"

"I'm the therapist. I ask the questions."

The door swings open. Packard. "Are you okay?"

Jordan folds her hands. "We were just having a nice chat."

"Can you excuse us, Jordan?" Packard says.

Jordan smiles wide and pushes out the door.

"Watch out for her," he says as soon as she's gone. "She's the most dangerous disillusionist that you're going to meet."

"I thought the Monk was the most dangerous."

"You'll never meet the Monk." Packard kneels in front of me. "You're sure you're okay?"

"No," I whisper, because I have this overwhelming urge to touch him.

"Don't let Simon undermine you. Some disillusionists have aversions to some energetic dimensions, that's all. Simon guessed you'd have an aversion to his. He set you up."

"What if I get an aversion when I'm with a dangerous target?"

"You'll handle it or we'll move you to another case."

"What if I fail with all of them?"

"You won't."

"How do you know? You can't see the future."

"No, I can't," he says. "But I can see you."

My stomach feels funny. I don't know what to say.

"Trust me." Packard stands. "Simon's jealous. He sees me fast-tracking you with all this training—"

"You're fast-tracking my training?"

"That's not important. You have the Silver Widow next week and you'll do brilliantly. You're more than ready."

"Great." I go to the sink and splash water onto my face. "A cheater on Cubby. Brilliant at attacking vulnerable old ladies." I turn to Packard, blotting the drips on my face and neck, thankful he can't hear my pounding heart.

"The Silver Widow brutally murdered her husband," he says.

"So you say, but maybe she killed him in self-defense."

"It was a torture kill."

"How do you know?"

"I was going to go through all this out there. . . ." Packard looks at my eyes, one and then another, the way a man will when he's near. "According to the chronology the coroner established, the Silver Widow drugged her husband into unconsciousness, gagged him, and dragged him to a secluded part of their backyard. Near an anthill. She somehow managed to dig a vertical hole, burying him up to his neck so that he was completely immobilized."

My pulse jumps as Packard touches my cheek where a droplet of water was tickling.

"The Silver Widow then proceeded to fill his ears with honey, and the ants swarmed out of the anthill and crawled up into his ears to eat it. When they'd consumed all the honey, they continued on, as ants will do, to consume his brain. Ants were crawling through his nearly empty cranial cavity by the time his body was found."

It takes me a while to comprehend the many dimensions of horror here. "Oh my God."

"Once she had him drugged, it would've been far less trouble to drown him in the pool, or even bury him alive. The ants were a great deal of extra effort. She's crazy and dangerous, but we'll turn her around. In disillusionment begins reform."

"So did he wake up? Was he conscious when . . . uh!"

"He was probably conscious for part of it," Packard says. "He seems to have struggled. As much as a man buried to his neck can struggle."

I slap my hands over my ears.

He draws nearer, wraps his hands around my fingers, pulls them gently from my ears. "You're okay." He presses my palms together inside his. "The trick is to not let yourself picture it."

I breathe in his spicy curry scent. "Ants ate his *brain*, Packard."

"I know they did."

"How long was he conscious? How much of his brain would they have eaten before—"

"Hey, look at me."

I look up into his pale green eyes, acutely aware of his hands enclosing mine, and of our physical nearness in this private space, and the heavy rise and fall of his chest. The charge between us thickens.

"There is no end to the darkness of the human heart," he says. "But Justine, you are part of a powerful squad that's changing things in a real way. You'll destabilize her, and other disillusionists will strip her of her illusions, and she'll crash into the horror of who she is, and she will come out the other side. That is what we do."

"It's all just overwhelming," I say. Though it's not the Silver Widow that's overwhelming now. It's the warmth of Packard's hands. It's the urge to pull him to me, breathe him in, press my lips to his neck, press my body to his.

He tightens his hands around mine. "You'll be brilliant, Justine, I know it. You are perfect for this. You'll take your time, and when you're finally there . . ." He pauses, and the heat between us grows fierce and luxurious. "God, it'll be glorious," he whispers.

Shivers sparkle through me—good shivers—and nothing seems real anymore. And God help me, I push out with my awareness to touch his energy dimension.

A sharp intake of breath; Packard looks at me intently.

My heart pounds, and I'm teetering on the edge, drawn to him. Our lips meet.

A click. A creak. We pull away from each other and I turn to see a big freckled face in the door—Lana, the day cook.

"Oh," I say.

She mumbles and backs out, pulling the door shut.

"Oh." Packard steps back. "I didn't come in here for this."

"I didn't either."

There's this silence where it seems like one of us ought to utter a sentence that begins with the word *yet*.

Chapter Ten

I STEP OUT onto the stoop of my building and nod to Mr. K., who's looking squarish and sweaty in his shirt-sleeves, having one last smoke before his shop opens. He nods back. For the first time ever, he's wearing a bike helmet.

I find myself wishing we could go after the Brick Slinger and Henji and the rest of his criminal highcap buddies, even though I'm frightened out of my wits just going after this one human woman.

I wind my hair into a ponytail. My red shirt has a chest patch that says KENNEDY POOL CLEANING; I wear it over shorts, my black one-piece bathing suit, and my shoulder holster, which holds my stun gun. My fashion magazine—we finally found an old one that has a vein star syndrome article—is rolled up in my fanny pack.

Carter pulls up to the curb in a silver van, and I swing into the passenger seat.

"Hey hey hey." He's grinning. "Gonna be a hot one."

"You had a zing?"

"Yesterday." He speeds off. "So what's new?"

"What's new? Well, I'm fairly nervous, because this Silver Widow is my first live target, and she sounds like, oh"—I whisper dramatically—"*a bit of a maniac.*"

He laughs. "It'll be fine."

Of course there's a lot more new than that. Like, I

kissed Packard and I wanted to again. It's not fair to Cubby. I've avoided him for over ten days now.

We review pool-cleaning techniques and our family backstory, which involves us growing up in a desert town, which I find to be an odd touch. "Did the fact that we grew up in a desert town contribute to our great love of water and pool cleanliness?"

"Why not?" he says. I'm to pose as the pool boy's sister who sometimes helps out, and I'm to befriend Aggie—that's the Silver Widow's real name. He takes the tangle and spins off southbound, toward the horsey suburbs.

Carter feels it will be easy for me to make friends with her for two reasons. One, the disillusionists who had her first effectively isolated her, so her social life mostly consists of workers and servants now. Two, she really wants to have sex with him, and he's somehow implied that he does nothing without his sister's approval.

"You wouldn't, though, right? Have sex with a target?"

"It won't come to that," he says.

"But you wouldn't, right?"

"Packard saved my life. I would do anything for that man. But it won't come to that here, thank God. Aggie is the single most frightening female I've ever met. Everybody's a plaything to her. She's like a mean little girl with dolls, and you're the new doll."

Instinctively I run my hand through my long blonde hair. It took two and a half years to grow it this long.

"Say, are you wearing your stun gun?"

"Yup." I flip up my shirt.

"Stow it. I don't like those things around when we're working in a pool."

Carter and I pull buckets and implements out of the van and haul them around to the back of the Silver Widow's white stucco mansion to her pool, which is the shape of a peanut. Lushly landscaped acres unfold beyond it, complete with gazebo, babbling brook, and clusters of flowered trees. It would be beautiful if I didn't know that ants ate a man's brain out there.

"Howdy, ma'am." Carter tips his pool-boy cap to a forty-something woman in a wavy blonde movie star bob. She clicks slowly across the veranda, lovely and leggy in a silvery swim cover-up. Aggie, a.k.a. the Silver Widow.

Aggie is one of those women who never lost their baby cheeks. Hers are covered with a thick application of shimmer powder. It's the kind of makeup choice that would cast her entire mental landscape into question if the business with the ants hadn't already accomplished this. Her fingernails and toenails are polished silver, and her platinum earrings and bracelets jangle brightly.

I hold my breath, praying I'll be able to touch her energy dimension and not screw up like I did with Simon. Unfortunately, she doesn't offer her hand when Carter introduces us.

"Perhaps you'll both join me for snacks in the conservatory after you're finished up."

"That would be lovely," I say.

Carter grunts, and then we head to the far end of the pool with our equipment. Aggie positions herself on a lounge chair under a cabana near the house.

"What's up with the gruff act?" I whisper.

"It's my act for this job, that's what's up."

"It suits you," I say. The pool-boy shirt and shorts suit him, too. He hands me the parts of a long-handled net and I fit them together.

"I'll have you work a little; then you'll go to the conservatory first, without me. This may just be the ground-laying day. Don't introduce a skin disease if it's not natural."

"Don't worry."

Aggie's phone rings shrilly across the pool. She answers, placing the back of her hand over her forehead—a tragic pose.

"I don't know if this is helpful," Carter says, "but the last two times I was here, I saw her inspecting her arm, some pimple or something." He taps the back of his arm to show where it is.

"That could be very helpful," I say.

Carter moves some plants; then he opens a door and attaches a hose to a nozzle. "This is a vacuum cleaner," he explains, "except it sucks water instead of air. I'll vacuum while you net out the leaves."

I wipe the sweat out of my eyes. "I wish we could just jump in."

"If you make it look like part of the job, you can."

"Nah, I don't want to be wet."

Netting out the leaves is not as easy as it looks, and it doesn't help that I'm feeling so nervous about touching Aggie's energy dimension. I start a measly pile at the corner, watching Aggie from time to time. I'm working on getting a pesky leaf when Carter comes over.

"I find this job sort of calming," he says. The sound of a door. Aggie's gone. "Act natural. She watches from that big circle window upstairs."

I look up, wondering if she watched her husband from that window. Did he jerk his head around, trying to shake off the ants as they gnawed away at his brain?

"Is that who hired us to disillusion her? The husband's family?"

"Packard wouldn't tell me." Carter gazes out at the lawn. "It's sort of strange, because usually he tells us the client. In fact, he always tells us."

"Did he say why he couldn't?"

"Nah," Carter says. "Maybe the client wants to be confidential. Anyway, you don't have to rush with

Aggie. Simon's scheduled for her after you, and he's pretty busy right now."

"Simon's after us?"

"Yeah. Eventually you'll have to think of a way to work him in."

An hour later I'm sitting in a white loveseat in Aggie's glass-walled conservatory, a sort of terrarium for the wealthy, listening to Aggie talk about the revoltingness of infrequently cleaned pools.

I've never hunted, but I wonder if this is how the hunter feels—the anticipation, the uneasy thrill. The power of the weapon. Flashes of fear, flashes of pity.

She tells me how once at a five-star hotel she'd felt slime on a pool tile. "What was that? What was I touching?"

I sip my champagne and consider the question. "I'd say it was a thin skin of algae."

She shudders. "Disgusting. The whole place was slimy. Even the people who worked there. No offense."

"None taken," I say. Though being that she said 'No offense,' I'm pretty sure some was in there.

Aggie stretches her arm across the seat back in a pose of dissolute glamour I rather like. The conservatory doors are wide open, providing an unobstructed view of the expanse of the grounds, the expanse of the pool, and the expanse of Carter's muscular shoulders.

Aggie stares at him as she gives her opinions on the revolting rubberiness of mushrooms, the revolting sliminess of dogs' noses, and the disturbing three-fingered hands of Disney characters. After each anecdote, she raises her shoulders practically to her ears: "Guh!"

I titter along. I dealt with women like her at the dress shop enough to know that the point of these anecdotes isn't that mushrooms, dogs' noses, and cartoon hands are revolting. Rather, she's just showcasing her dramatic distress, as if it adds to her personality. Her expired husband loved mushrooms, she explains. I tell her I'm sorry.

"I'm not," she says.

She holds forth on other subjects, playing with the silver zipper on her shimmery silver cover-up as she speaks. The cover-up is a kind of sparkly minidress, bejeweled where the hood meets the collar. When the light hits it just right you can see the outlines of a silver bikini underneath. She's paired it with silver kitten-heeled sandals for what I have to admit is a highly god-damn impressive outfit. A kind of space-age glamour look.

Aggie refills her glass, then leans across the corner of the glass table and tops mine off. "This is very exquisite and expensive champagne. Don't you like it?"

"I like it very much," I say.

"Yet you've hardly drunk any."

"Yes, I have. It's wonderful."

"Don't tell me," she says sweetly, "that you *are* doing something when you *aren't*." She watches my eyes for an uncomfortably long time. "Worse than that," she continues, "is if you tell me that you *aren't* doing something when you *are*."

"Who wouldn't hate that?" I say, wondering if she suspects.

She narrows her eyes. "I don't like deception."

I stare at her dumbly. My nervousness has gone right to my stomach, which is feeling unpleasantly floaty, like helium got in there.

"What was your name again?"

"Justine."

"Carter tells me you're in nursing school. What sort of nurse will you be?"

"RN. Concentrations on medical/surgical, burn unit, dermatology."

"Oh, Justine!" She throws her head back in a weird silent laugh. "That is so funny, because I'm such a hypochondriac. You can't even imagine."

Actually, I can. Specifically, she's just revealed to me that she is a social hypochondriac. The social hypochondriac makes her fears public, even if they're under control. She gets a thrill out of discussing symptoms and diseases the way kids enjoy scary stories around a campfire. My approach to her spreads out in front of me like a mandala—intricate plays informed by a body of understanding I've been building all my life. Though certainly not for this purpose.

"There was a time when I would just flip out—just fulllllliiiip out." Platinum bracelets jingle as Aggie waves her free hand around. She always has to be the most dramatic one in the room. Soon, hopefully, she will be.

A splash from the pool. Carter's in the water again.

"Aggie—" I look hard into her gray eyes. "Did you used to watch *The Brady Bunch*?" She nods. Of course she did. "Do you remember," I whisper, "when Peter thought he had that tropical fever?"

She claps a hand over her mouth. This was a memorable episode for all child hypochondriacs. "Oh my God!" She sits next to me. "'Look at my rash, Marcia!'"

We laugh and turn our attention to Carter, who's splashing loudly in the pool, hoisting tubes over the side, and then he gets out, skin shining wet. I'm feeling proud of how I'm bonding with her, girl to girl.

"Mmm," Aggie says. "God, he's so pluscious. So pluscious and sexy."

"Very sexy," I say. "Especially when wet."

Aggie turns to me slowly. Eerie smile.

I freeze. I forgot I was supposed to be his sister. "Speaking objectively," I add. "Girls have always said—"

"That didn't sound very objective to me, Justine. I don't think you're objective about your brother at all."

"I'm just proud of him."

"You're more than proud." She smiles saucily. "Do tell."

"There's nothing to tell."

She clutches my forearm. "I can smell when people are keeping secrets. I smelled it on you the minute I met you. Do you remember what I said about deception?"

I feel cold. Better the secret she suspects than the real one, I decide. So I go forward. "Some secrets are best kept."

"You don't have to be ashamed. You can say or do anything in front of me." She presses her fingers harder into my arm. "People are so puritanical about sex in this culture. It's just somebody putting a body part somewhere and moving it around a bunch, you know? It shouldn't matter who those two or three people are."

I nod. "There *is* a lot of emphasis on who the people are." I should be using this opportunity to contact her energy dimension, just to make sure I can do it, but I can't seem to pull myself together.

"We'll get along just fine." She releases my arm and together we gaze out at Carter. It's here that I spy the pimply thing Carter mentioned. An irritated skin bump. Perfect.

She grabs the champagne bottle. "Come on."

I snatch my fanny pack and follow her through arched French doors into a huge room with a blinding white and silver color scheme. A silver fireplace chimney soars up a full three stories above thick white carpeting that's unbelievably soft on my bare feet.

"Incredible," I say.

"I redecorated last spring." She leads me through several more white and silver rooms, up a white carpeted staircase and into her bedroom, a menagerie of white silks and crystals. I wonder if Carter's seen it. I don't know him very well, but I think all this white would freak him out. All that white would freak any man out.

Aggie smiles. "This is gonna be great." She pours herself more champagne while I eye her blemish.

"What?" she says.

"Oh, nothing. Sorry." I'm laying groundwork. I know exactly how to work with her. It's like I was born for this. As long as I can contact her energy dimension.

"Right. Nursing school. But it's just an arm bump." She doesn't touch it or even look at it. She knows damn well it's there.

"Good," I say. "You've had it checked out."

"No. But believe me, I'd know if it was skin cancer."

"How long has it been there?"

"Too long for a piphis infection. It's nothing. I know it."

"I agree it's not piphis," I say.

"Justine—" She widens her eyes. "Have you ever seen a flesh-eater piphis?"

"In my volunteer work at county, yeah. I worked with a young guy, maybe eighteen, who lost his leg from it. It was all over his face and scalp, too."

She settles into a chair, bottle in hand, repulsion and fascination playing across her plump features. "What was it like? What did it look like?"

"Like acid ate his skin away. And entire chunks of his leg. He had to be in a special chamber."

She parts her lips. Her face glows. She wants more.

As I go through the more graphic details I have this flash of intuition: she watched her husband struggle and die. She watched with this same shudder, this same glow.

"Enough!" She raises a hand, bracelets jingling. She crosses the room and flings open a door while I dump my champagne into a crystal vase of white roses.

"Come here, Justine. We're going to surprise Carter."

I follow her into a huge walk-in closet lined with hanging clothes, shoeboxes, and suitcases frilly with airline tags. A white marble table stands in the middle, piled high with scarves and jewelry and shoes. Most everything is in whites and silvers.

"So I guess it's safe to say you've decided you're a winter."

"I like everything fresh. You know . . ." She wipes her hand across the space in front of her face, as if to wipe her personal windshield. "Pure." She turns her attention to a corner rack, explaining how she buys three of everything. "You can lose one, shrink one, and you still have one. But sometimes maybe . . ." She gives me a playful look, then pulls a garment from a rack—a swimsuit cover-up identical to the one she's wearing. She holds it out to me. "A present for you, Justine."

"Oh, I couldn't!"

"Try it on, go ahead.

"Really, thanks, but I couldn't."

She frowns. "You don't like it?"

"No, it's gorgeous." I touch the fabric.

She throws it on the table and points at my shirt and my shorts. "Off and off."

I strip down to my matronly black one-piece bathing suit and pick up the shimmery cover-up, but then she snatches it away. "Hold the presses. You have got to be kidding."

"What?"

"That suit." She rummages through an enameled chest of drawers and pulls out a silvery bikini just like hers.

"Oh, this is way too generous," I say.

She pushes the wad of silvery fabric into my hands. "Put it on."

I look around. "Do you have a—"

"You don't have anything I haven't seen before." She snatches it back. "Out of that suit."

She waits, and I wait, feeling awkward. She's pushing me. Why?

I peel off my suit like I don't care. Aggie stares at my naked body, which makes me feel vulnerable. This is a woman who immobilized her husband and let ants eat his brain, after all.

"You're very fit. Do you work out?"

Maybe I'm a little slow, because I'm only now getting the idea that she aims to have sex with Carter and me, at the same time. "I rollerblade and stuff." I hold out my hand for the suit; she playfully raises it above her head, out of my reach. I grab for it, briefly touching her arm, and right there I contact her energy dimension. She feels dense, oddly like metal. "Come on," I say sternly.

She drops the fabric into my hands. "Somebody needs more champagne."

I feel better once I'm zipping the shimmery cover-up over my new suit.

"Um, no." She comes up to me and, looking into my eyes, lowers the zipper ever so slowly. "I think he'd like it better like this, don't you?" She hovers close, like she might kiss me. I'm thinking I'd better zing her fast, while there's still the promise of sex in the air. Once the promise is gone, she'll turn.

"Now. Shoes. Can you take an eight?"

"Oh, Aggie . . ."

"Look, you and me and Carter, we are having a champagne luncheon together"—she tilts her head in a way that indicates a lurid world of meaning behind *champagne luncheon*—"and you must wear a champagne outfit." She yanks a shoebox from the bottom of the stack. "These ones have some crystals missing. I was going to toss them."

I slip them on. They look awesome. She takes my hand and leads me out into the bedroom and we stand together in front of the full-length mirror, looking like a mentally unbalanced supergirl team. She's the hot sexy one and I'm the sassy jock who cleans up moderately well. I'm actually thinking here that I really want to show this outfit to Shelby and maybe wear it some other places. There are no pools in my life, but that could change.

The Silver Widow's next operation involves me undoing my ponytail and her sitting on the corner of the bed and brushing my hair with long, deep, firm strokes. If I wasn't so tense I'd enjoy this; when you're a medium-pretty woman, it feels wonderful to have a very pretty woman fawn over you. "The color of golden honey." She puts down the brush and smoothes my hair.

"Sort of a boring color," I say.

"No," she says, lips to the upper edge of my ear. "It's not boring at all."

"Oh, it is," I say.

It's time.

"I'm thinking of changing it, actually," I continue. "I have a magazine photo to show my hairdresser. I would love to get your opinion on it, actually."

"Let's see it, sister." She flops back onto the bed and lies there, hands folded behind her head.

My fanny pack is by the door. I walk over, pull out the magazine, flip to the article, and skim frantically, stoking my fear. Misdiagnosed headaches, the vein star a ticking time bomb.

"Let's see!"

"Hold on," I say.

"He's very diligent, isn't he?"

I'm almost there. I scan further: "Three weeks ago I was swimming in the sparkling ocean. Now I'm hooked up to four different machines. I've placed a seashell I found on the beach next to the blue plastic sputum tray on my bedside table. That is the closest I'll ever get to that beach again." My heart beats like crazy.

"I asked you a question," Aggie said. "Is he diligent? Is your brother *diligent*?"

I stalk toward her, vibrating with fear. She's stretched out on the bed, dangerous, yet vulnerable to my power. This crazy dark excitement washes over me. "Very diligent," I say, sliding onto the edge.

She sits up and grabs the magazine.

I look over her shoulder. "No, this page." I turn the pages until I find a hair color that strikes me as pretty. "Here." My natural brown, before I went blonde.

"Nah. I like you as a blonde."

"Just a thought," I say, staring breathlessly at the blemish on her arm.

"What the hell kind of outfit is this woman wearing?" Aggie flips the magazine over to see the cover. "This issue's from 1998. Why are you reading a magazine from 1998?" She catches me staring at her arm. "Don't look at it," she says.

I give her my impression of a nurse trying not to look concerned. My fear is stoked so high, I'm trembling. I touch her arm. "You need to get it checked out."

"No!" She pulls away.

I nod gravely, picturing the airline tags on the suitcases in her closet. "You wouldn't have spent any time in Atlanta recently. . . ."

Her eyes widen. I'm hoping Carter doesn't interrupt us now. "Just the airport."

"When?"

"Last month."

I look down.

"What?"

"Atlanta is a major Osiris virus cluster."

"A what? I never even heard of that."

"Do you ever have any sensation around your upper arm? Skin sensation?"

She tightens her lips, shakes her head. "Never," she says. "Never." She claps her hand over the pimple.

I happen to know she's lying. Skin is always flooded with sensation; you only have to draw your attention to it. It's one of those things the human brain filters out.

"It's just a pimple."

I move closer, place my hand over hers. "Let me look at it. I'm sure it's just a pimple."

"No."

I gaze into her eyes. "Let me rule it out." I slide my hand down to her forearm and push my awareness onto the surface of her cool, hard energy dimension. I can't believe I'm doing it. She tries to pull away, but I tighten my grip and burn the hole.

I struggle to keep my expression neutral as the fear surges out my hand, finding and animating her fear, filling her. It flows and flows, and just as I'm thinking it might never end, it does, and there's wind in my fingers, and peace in my heart.

"God, do you think it's something serious?" She bolts up off the bed. "I knew it was serious!"

I sit there replaying the surge in my mind, the madly satisfying rush of my fear into a perfectly analogous vessel. The cool calm it left behind. It's like nothing I've ever experienced, even with Packard.

She scratches her leg. "Well? What do you think?"

"I can't say," I whisper.

Aggie rips off her cover-up and inspects her skin in the mirror. "I'm totally freaked out now! I knew I shouldn't've gone to stupid Atlanta! Is it contagious?"

"Infectious," I say, thoroughly exhilarated and even a bit debauched. I have to concentrate. I have to get her rolling.

"Shit! I touched things in that airport. On the plane.

Interacted with the workers. No offense. What if I have it? Look at it—use your nursing skills."

"Come here."

She obeys. Now that my fear is in her, I have this crazy sense that she's mine. I take her arm and pretend to inspect it more, dizzy with pleasure. Her skin is as soft as it looks. I take a centering breath and do a Packard number exercise: $11 \times 39 = 429$. "If you're lucky, it'll stay dormant," I say. "Stress aggravates it. You don't want that."

"What? What are you seeing?"

"There are sometimes tiny filaments involved around the lesions. And that's what I'm looking for, but I don't have any equipment."

"Shit."

I stand, keenly attuned to my surroundings, to Aggie. The skin fixation, the method of killing she used—it all links up in my mind. He had an affair, and the death was cleansing: a brain picked clean. Her white decor is cleansing, purifying for her.

"The truth is, they barely know anything about Osiris virus. Most doctors are reluctant to diagnose it. A lot of them will say it's a pimple, or psychosomatic."

"You really think I have it?"

"I'm sorry; I'm just not qualified to make a diagnosis." To a hypochondriac, this answer is worse than a yes. It's like saying, *Yes, but it's so horrible that I'm hedging.* "Do you have a computer?"

Aggie gets this haunted look in her eyes. She does not want to go online. She knows what will happen there. She swallows, and I have this strange urge to touch her throat, trace the path of her swallow to the nook of her neck, like I'll touch my own fear there.

I say, "We could get the latest research and see the photos for better comparison."

She is still. She does not want to go. But she will.

Soon we're sitting together in her office, embarking on the most dangerous voyage a hypochondriac can take: the online odyssey to rule out a condition, which is like trying to rule out the probability of getting sucked into quicksand by standing in it. She scratches her arm now and then. Osiris virus patients often become so focused on the sensations of their skin that they create their own lesions. Most get diagnosed with delusional parisitosis. I watch and wait, breathing in her floral perfume.

A voice from downstairs. "Hello?"

"I can't deal with Carter now," Aggie says, fixated on a pimple photo. "Tell him to reclean the pool. I'll pay him double or whatever. You have to stay and help me with this." This is the binding that Packard talked about, I think. She feels attached to me, thanks to the zing.

I rush down the stairs and through the carpeted world of white and find Carter in the conservatory. He raises his eyebrows, as though he's surprised to see me.

"Champagne brunch is cancelled, Carter. We need more time."

He draws near with a crooked smile. "What's going on up there?"

"I zinged her. And we're kind of in the thick of it." Carter smells like newly mown grass and sweat. I have this weird urge to taste his skin. Glory hour.

"Why'd you take her clothes?"

I snort. "Please, these are duplicates. Look, Aggie wants you to clean the pool again. She won't be watching."

"Nice going."

Aggie and I spend the next half hour examining images of seminal urticarias, which resemble pimples. Then we arrange to meet the day after tomorrow, and we exchange numbers like it's the most natural thing in the world. I leave her at an Osiris virus site full of first-person accounts. She'll be there for hours. Tomorrow she'll see a doctor, but no matter the diagnosis, she'll think she has Osiris virus. That's how it works. I grab my fanny pack and leave.

Soon I'm outside on the sunny veranda, breathing in the fragrance of the flowering trees; Carter is nowhere to be seen. A breeze blows cool, soft kisses on my bare arms and legs as I stroll to the edge of sparkly sapphire water, consumed with the desire to swim. I throw down my fanny pack, pull off my cover-up, and slip in. I dive deep under and skim along the bottom, water like cold silk on my skin. Then I come up and float on my back, eyes shut tight to the sun. A cardinal chirps, and a lawn-mower hums in the distance. I no longer know which direction the house is in, or which direction Midcity is in. I just float, sunshine shapes swirling on the insides of my eyelids. I float like a compass needle with no poles to point to.

A soft splash. I open my eyes and there's Carter in the pool.

"Hey!"

"Shh!" Carter swims on his side, hair like bright metal. "You sure she's *ocupado*?"

"Definitely," I say, watching the bright water stream off his smooth shoulders.

"What a nice, clean pool," he says. "We did a fine job on it."

We splash and swim around and it's all wholesome fun until I start thinking about sliding my hands around the wet contours of his glistening muscles and maybe wrapping my legs around his waist. "We should get out of here," I say.

He smiles. "Beware the glory hour."

"Oh, you think you're a bug on my windshield now?"

"I think I might be."

"Right." We hoist ourselves out, and Carter throws me a towel. I dry off, watching the small, bright ripples on the surface of the pool bounce from side to side, distorting the pattern of tiles deep below.

Chapter
Eleven

WE SPEED DOWN the Falconbridge highway, pastures and cornfields behind us, strip malls and developments increasing in density. I'm sitting on my towel, still in my wet suit because I forgot to grab my old clothes from Aggie's master closet. No way was I going back in that house.

"That was fun," Carter says, "but don't tell Packard we swam like that. He'd be angry that we risked our credibility."

"I'll never tell," I say, happy to be a trusted member of the squad. Doing work that means something.

We pass a sprawling suburban hospital. You can see a few people in the windows, and I even spot an IV bag on a pole—a sight that once filled me with dread. Not anymore. I sigh a happy sigh and tell Carter about Aggie and me in her closet.

"She is so smart," Carter says. "You used to manage a dress shop, right?"

"Yeah."

"She was seducing you with clothes. She sensed that was a way to get to you. God, she is so dangerous. But you did great. It's great you joined us."

I smile. My squad depended on me and I came through.

"It'll be easier from here on in," he adds. "Eventually

she'll roll on her own, without your help, maybe after a few more visits."

I go back to the zing, replaying it in my mind: touching her, making the hole, the glorious surge.

Later, we discuss Packard's imprisonment. "I didn't even know he was trapped until last week. It's unthinkable. It just shouldn't be."

Carter is silent for a long while. If it weren't for the hit of rage I get off him, I'd think he didn't hear the question. "If I knew who that nemesis was," he finally says, "well, I would want to kill him, but that would just cement Packard's imprisonment. Or else maybe I would just destroy his face and break his fingers and . . ." He's looking pale and somewhat overcome. "It's probably good I don't know who or where he is, because I would definitely kill him."

"So the nemesis is male?"

"I don't know. Seems likely."

"That anyone would trap Packard like that . . . it's all so farfetched."

"You're not a highcap, Justine, but this afternoon you drew energy off your dark side and attacked a woman with it. A lot of people would consider that farfetched. And you can touch energy dimensions. You're living in a world now where that sort of stuff happens."

"I don't know about *living* in it. I consider myself more of a visitor. Between you and me, Carter, this whole thing is just a temporary gig."

He turns his wide freckled face to me, incredulous. "Temporary?"

"I love being part of a gang—don't get me wrong, I really do. Everybody's been great, and my whole health anxiety problem is under control for the first time in . . . well, ever. But I'm not completely sure how I feel about what we're doing, and this whole double life and keeping secrets from my boyfriend? Ultimately, I plan to figure something else out. Possibly sooner than later."

He stares. "You're planning on leaving."

"Not right away. And it's not that I don't like everybody so much—"

"Does Packard know—" He pauses here, rephrases with care, it seems. "Does he know you see this as temporary?"

"He never asked me for a specific commitment and I never gave one."

Silence.

"What?"

"You two never discussed the whole long-term aspect. . . ."

Carter's nervousness scares me. I finger the gem on my cover-up zipper. "What about it?"

The van wheels hum as we cross over a bridge, metal angles and rivets whipping by. "Justine, this should be a happy time for you. Sheesh, you've successfully zinged your first target. Why would you ever want to leave?"

"What are you getting at, Carter?"

"Just tell me, what could possibly be better?"

I don't answer. I'm waiting.

"Shit," he says. "You should talk to Packard about this, not me."

"Carter, are you suggesting I won't or can't leave?"

He looks at me warily.

"Are you?" My glory-hour feelings are definitely starting to fade.

"I can't believe Packard didn't . . ."

"What?" I demand.

Carter purses his lips, as if this will keep him from telling me. And then he says, "You can't leave. Basically."

"What do you mean? Maybe Packard just plans on letting me be a temporary person."

"That's not how it works. You've been zinging for what? Maybe a month or two? Do you have any idea what would happen to you if you stopped at this point?"

"I'd go back to the way I was. Right? I mean . . ."

His silence scares me.

"Right?"

"No," he says eventually. "You can never go back. Zinging rearranges things inside your brain. If you stopped now, you'd be worse than you can imagine. At this point, if you go four, five weeks without a zing you'd be looking at irreversible brain damage. Basically."

I feel ill. "No."

"You can never go back. You can never stop."

"No, that can't be. After that first zing, I know I came back a month later, but I think I would've gotten through it."

"After one zing, sure, maybe. But if you stopped now, you'd be a million times worse."

Panic clenches my gut. Even the van's hum sounds different now. More strident.

"You've zinged Packard probably dozens of times," Carter continues. "And now you've zinged a target. I don't need to tell you how powerful that is. You can't stop now. The neural pathways are in place and you're addicted to zinging. You can't live without it. If you stop, you'd be a vegetable. Christ, I just assumed you knew going in." He turns to me, gaze full of concern. "You're in a permanent relationship now. You are a minion of Packard, Justine."

I stare back, openmouthed, sensing the truth of his words.

"Maybe I shouldn't've said 'minion.' It's like a symbiotic relationship. He scratches your back and you scratch his." Carter winces. "It's not that bad. You need him to identify safe people to zing, and he needs you to zing them."

"You call that symbiotic? When he has power over whether we're vegetables, and we can never be without him? That's not symbiotic. That's complete dependence." I feel hollow. "Screw that. I quit. Right now."

He eyes me nervously.

"If it gets bad, maybe I'll find my own people to zing."

"And risk the blowback? That's even worse. You may as well shove an ice pick through your eye."

"I don't care. I'm not a goddamn minion. I won't live in servile dependence. If I'd known that . . ."

"You would've never joined," he observes. "And you would've died."

"Says Packard."

"Don't leave, Justine. We're doing important work that transforms bad people. You would've probably ended up staying anyhow, but now that you know you can't leave, that's the only reason you want to."

"It's as good a reason as any."

Mysteriously, Carter chooses this moment to pull out his phone and make a call. "He up for visitors?" Apparently, the answer is yes, because the next thing I know, he's doing a U-turn. "Packard's going to kill me for this."

"Where are we going?"

"To visit Jarvis."

"Who's Jarvis?"

"You'll see."

A half hour later, Carter's rapping on the bright green door of a tiny townhouse that's crunched shoulder to shoulder in an endless row of tiny townhouses out near the airport. I wait nervously, cold in my silver cover-up, cradling the pineapple we purchased on the way over. I'm definitely not glorying now.

The door is opened by a black woman in nurse's scrubs.

"Mel," Carter says. "We came to say hi to Jarv. And give him this . . ."

I hold up the pineapple.

She smiles. "Come on in. We're just watching the news."

Carter introduces her as Melanctha, Jarvis's private nurse. We follow her to a living room. "Jarvis," Melanctha says, "Carter and a friend to see you."

Jarvis, an obese black man in a recliner chair, stares blankly at a giant TV. His hair is pure white, though he can't be older than forty-five. Carter takes the pineapple from me and sets it gently in Jarvis's lap, like it's a baby. Jarvis lowers his gaze to it as Carter kneels next to him. "Jarv." Carter grips Jarvis's forearm, and Jarvis moves his eyes off the pineapple and locks onto Carter's face.

Melanctha claps. "He recognizes you!"

"Hey, buddy!" Carter says. "Good to see you." Jarvis continues to stare at Carter, though it looks more like a space-out than any kind of recognition. Carter shakes Jarvis's arm. "Hey, Jarvis!"

A commercial with people singing about pickles comes on the TV. The song takes over the room.

"I've been steaming veggies for him this week, and boy, has it been helping with the blood pressure," Melanctha says.

"I'm glad," Carter says. "Hey, buddy, this is my friend, Justine." Carter takes my hand and puts it on Jarvis's fat, warm shoulder. "Jarvis can feel you, but it's like he's trapped in there. Go ahead, touch his energy dimension. It comforts him."

I look over at Melanctha, who shrugs.

"It reminds him he's not alone," Carter adds.

I push out and stifle a gasp. His energy dimension is blank. Terrifyingly blank—like blank eyeballs. It's horrible. "Good to meet you, Jarvis," I say.

Carter and Melanctha watch Jarvis for a reaction, but he just stares at Carter. I wait nervously; I'm getting that Jarvis was a disillusionist. Slowly, I pull my awareness back, but I keep my hand on his shoulder out of politeness. There's this awkward moment where none of us say anything.

The TV drones on. The news is back. Another brick attack. Victim in a coma. My heart calms when Chief Sanchez comes on and explains that the hoodlums have developed high-velocity catapults that can put spin on the bricks, his voice like a deep, plush blanket. "We're making splendid progress in this case," he says. Obviously he has to act like it's not highcaps, but I'm sure he knows it is. I wonder again if he knows about Henji.

I squeeze Jarvis's shoulder. "I'm really glad to meet you."

Carter stands. "We can't stay," he tells Mel.

"Vesuvius and Shelby and a few of the others sat with him yesterday morning."

"Good."

I'm relieved when we get back on the road.

"Jarvis was angst," Carter says. "He was a powerful disillusionist. Great guy. Funny as hell."

"And he quit?"

"He couldn't handle being the minion of a white man after a few months. Suddenly it just started getting to him. It's not easy for anybody—we all get around minionhood in our own ways, but being black, it got to Jarvis a whole lot worse. Vesuvius struggles with it, too, but not like Jarvis. It was so maddening to see him go down and not be able to stop him. Did you feel his nothingness? That's what'll happen if you quit—or if you zing the wrong person and get blowback. It fries you blank. So . . ." There's this silence when he looks at me tenderly. "Please."

I slide my fingers along the smooth grain of my seat-belt, up and down, quietly mortified. Carter keeps looking over at me, and I know that he'd feel a whole lot better if I assured him I won't be quitting or zinging random people, but I'm not in a generous mood. And honestly, I don't know what I'm going to do. Well, that's not entirely true.

"You think you could drop me off at the restaurant?" I ask.

He nods energetically. "No problem."

Chapter Twelve

I STORM UP to the wooden face, grab a nostril, and fling the door open. Early dinner. A few tables occupied. Staff and diners stare as I stomp through. Outside of a glamorous poolside context, my Silver Widow outfit is bizarre.

I head back and find Packard's booth empty. I retrace my steps through the dining room and into the kitchen, almost crashing into Morgan the cook, who's busy with a knife and a pile of peppers. On the far end of the kitchen, I spy Packard, spoon in hand, lingering in front of a large pot. He smiles when he sees me, all innocence and tousled hair. "My goodness, Justine. You look ravishing."

I grab an iron skillet off a nearby rack and fling it across the room at him, hitting a stack of bowls on the dishwasher. They crash onto the stainless-steel counter and down to the floor.

"Shit!" Morgan says.

Packard fits a lid over the pot. "Morgan, can you give us a moment?"

"I'm in the middle of two operations," Morgan says. "Take them elsewhere."

Morgan picks up his chopping board and a bowl of peppers. "Don't let the kebabs burn." He storms out.

Packard turns to me. "You zinged her—"

"You craven parasite!" I grab another pan and stalk toward him. I'm not the hitting type, but I might be now. "How could you not warn me?" I lift the pan up and smash a tray of wineglasses fresh from the washer; glass flies everywhere. I want to take down the whole damn restaurant.

"You wouldn't have joined."

"Damn right I wouldn't have joined!"

"You were on your way to institutionalization and death. I saved your life!"

"You didn't save my life. You stole it!" I throw the skillet into the curry corner, shattering jars in an explosion of orange powder. "This was supposed to be temporary, and now I'm your minion, totally enslaved to you? That's not what I would've chosen under any circumstance."

"I know," he says softly. "You wouldn't have taken the save. Until it was too late."

"That should've been my choice." I grab the front of his white shirt. "All I ever wanted was to be cured. I thought, meeting you, that I had a chance. I thought I was closer, goddammit, but I've never been farther away." I close my fingers around the fabric, twisting, half wishing it was his neck. "I thought we were together in all this. I thought we were allies and friends, and that there was honesty between us."

"I never lied to you. And I saved you."

"Stop acting like it's a favor. You did it because you wanted to. Is this what you meant by allegiance? Your allegiance to whatever is so important that you had to steal my independence?"

This flush of heat comes over Packard's face—a swell of emotion that seems to rise from a dangerous place inside him. "Yes," he says with brutal resolve. "Yes."

I tighten my grip. "So basically, you did the same thing to me that your nemesis did to you."

"It's not the same."

"It's exactly the same!"

"I create. My nemesis destroys." His angry passion makes a radiant heat I can feel in my fists, my belly. "He destroys."

I don't know if I want to kill him or fuck him right there on the counter. I push him away. "I will never forgive you, Packard, and I promise I will get free of you. But not like Jarvis."

He fixes a gemlike gaze on me.

I harden my resolve. "I'm telling you, I will never forgive you. I'll continue on for now because Carter and Shelby and everyone else is counting on me, and obviously I have to anyway. But I am going to get free of you."

He says nothing. Smoke leaks from the roaster oven.

I brush a plate off the counter as I leave. The crash is unsatisfying.

Chapter
Thirteen

SHELBY DECORATES the way she dresses. Her apartment is a mad cornucopia of paisleys, florals, Oriental rugs, and optical-illusion art that hurts your eyes.

She sits in a red-and-white zigzagged chair, teacup in hand, listening to me rant about how Packard fooled me and how I'll never forgive him. Like Carter, she's stunned Packard didn't warn me that being a disillusionist was a permanent situation. She clearly had no idea that I didn't know.

"When I joined, Justine, he was so very clear. He sat me down, he said, 'Once you are in, you cannot leave, you cannot unjoin.' He said this to all of us."

"Not to me."

She shakes her head, staring into the blackness of her tea. "When he does not have right mix of disillusionists, he simply does not take case. I have never heard of him, what do you say, hoodwinking some person as he has hoodwinked you."

"I might go stronger than hoodwinked."

"He tricked you."

"But of course he says he saved my life."

"If he says he did, perhaps he did."

"Or perhaps he really really needed a hypochondriac to join up for the Silver Widow. What's so important about rebooting the Silver Widow that he'd trick me?"

"Who is client on Silver Widow?"

"Packard won't tell."

"But we always know client."

"This one's secret."

"I have never heard of that. Always we know client."

"Something's going on. Some larger evil. That's what Jordan the therapist implied, and I kind of agree."

"Oh, Jordan, no. Do not listen to Jordan."

"Maybe this goes back to Henji. Either way, I'm getting out." I wander over to the window. I can see my new used car, a Jetta, from here. I was pretty proud to be able to buy myself a car—until I learned what it really cost me. Beyond is a stunning view of the belly of the tangle—dozens of fat pillar legs rising up from a bed of tires and forgotten shopping carts under massive concrete curves. "You need curtains."

"Why should I cover it?"

I sense a Shelby moment coming.

She joins me at the window. "People want view of beauty. Pfft. I say, do not give me lies. Always they try to fix it, but nothing will make it better. Same as life. You wish to be free, but there is no such thing as freedom. You can redecorate dungeon to give illusion of freedom, but you are still in dungeon."

"I should've had the choice."

"Choice is illusion, same as happiness and freedom. Yes, it is unthinkable indeed that he did not warn you," she assures me. "But he is not wicked, Justine."

"I'd say trapping me in a life of dependence is pretty wicked."

"You are trapped in dependence upon oxygen and water. Is that wicked?"

"It's not the same thing. But in a way, it serves me right. I rationalized being a vigilante when I knew it was wrong, and I wasn't forthright about my plans to leave. Now I'm the minion of a mutant." I glare out at the tangle.

When I'm honest with myself, I'm angry about more than my loss of freedom. Crazy as it sounds, I'm angry about the loss of us—me and Packard. He's like nobody I ever met. He made me feel alive in a way no other man ever has. I wanted him, and in my heart, I was moving toward him. We were moving toward each other—I felt it. But he tricked me and stole my freedom. Taking a person's freedom breaks some universal law of relationships; that's all there is to it. It rules a man out utterly and completely. This is something that makes me angry, and very, very sad. Most of all, it hurts like hell.

"I have idea for you to feel better. You will like it."

"What is it?"

"Something to help you see from better perspective. Later, not now. You will see." She gazes out at the tangle's underbelly with a pretty little Shelby smile.

Chapter
Fourteen

THE DAY AFTER the next, I arrive at Aggie's place wearing a dowdy T-shirt and khaki pants, hair in a ponytail. That was Shelby's advice: *Dowdy and weaker friend is powerful disillusionist position.*

"Oh, Justine, thank heavens you're here!" Aggie grabs my arm and pulls me in the door. She's wearing a layered beige outfit, sort of a sexy desert traveler look. She introduces me to a pair of women sitting in the living room, both wearing white medical jackets. Sasha and Elaine. "We'll be a few minutes." With that, she rushes me upstairs.

The white medical jackets have me worried.

She slams the office door and strips off her outer layer, a loose linen shirt. My stomach jumps when I see the gauze patch taped onto her upper arm.

"Are those two women nurses?"

"No, you're the nurse," she says. "They're the beauticians. They used to work in LA, too, so they know what they're doing. I've had it with Midwestern corn-fed hairstyles. You know? *Uh!*" She rubs her arms. "I slept horribly last night, because whatever skin wasn't pressing on the sheet—" She gyrates her shoulders. "*Uh!*"

I'm shocked at how fast and hard she's fallen. That's the goal, though—to get the target rolling, as they say.

Nevertheless, I feel this burst of compassion. I force myself to remember her husband—buried, helpless, ants streaming in and out of his ears.

She grabs a Tupperware off the desk and hands it to me. "A cellulose filament I picked out of my arm is in there."

A tiny white filament rests on the bottom. Supposedly the filaments are the excrement of the Osiris parasite, though this one looks suspiciously similar to the carpet.

"I need you to examine it." She leads me over to the corner, where she has a microscope set up. "You have to check it for me."

I stare at the microscope. I've never used one in my life.

"What's wrong?" she demands.

"Nothing. I'm just thinking."

"Something's going on."

I straighten up. "I need tweezers. And latex gloves."

"'Cause you don't want to contaminate *yourself*?"

"It's procedure."

Aggie's eyes are small and shiny; even her face looks smaller. "I'll ask the girls. Next time, bring your own shit." She pulls on her outer layer and leaves.

The microscope bristles with knobs and trays and slots. I can't even turn the thing on. I collapse in the chair in front of it, feeling deeply weary. Why is crashing this woman so goddamn important that Packard would entrap me as he did? Is there a larger purpose? Something with Henji? And how do I get free? Because there has to be a way. There's always a way. As I twist knobs and push buttons, I find myself desperately missing Cubby. With all this craziness, I just want to be with him.

"Everything okay?" Aggie's standing there, holding gloves and tweezers. How long was she watching me?

"No," I say. "This microscope isn't powerful enough."

"It's the most powerful one a person can buy."

"But not the most powerful one a medical professional can get. And it doesn't have the ultraviolet settings I need. Let me take the filament to the lab at school where I can perform the tests."

"Can we go there now?"

"Students only. I'll go tomorrow morning. I'm sorry, Aggie, that you had to spend all that money on a microscope."

"What do I care about money? Hell, I'm flying first class to Florence, *Italy*, next month to see this one doctor who treats it. Charges up the wazoo."

"Wow." Visit to foreign specialists. Aggie enjoys a level of hypochondriac opportunity I'd barely dreamed of. We discuss more medical stuff. If anybody was listening in, they'd think we were two doctors, except for the fact that Aggie frequently repeats herself, then screws up her face and says, "Did I already say that?"

My fashion magazine, rolled up in my purse, calls to me like an evil beacon. Here she is, obsessed with an imaginary disease all from one zing, and I'm yearning to do it again.

"You want a drink?"

"I'd love one," I say. "But are you sure you should mix alcohol with your prescriptions?"

"It's fine if I balance it with something speedy." She grabs my arm. "Don't tell Elaine and Sasha about the virus. I don't want them to not work on us out of fear for infection." Philosophically, she adds, "Infection is a risk they always take, so they're used to it. It's their fault if I infect them."

I assure her that I won't tell, and soon we're downstairs, sipping champagne in her spa-like bathroom as Elaine and Sasha set up their mobile beauty parlor. There's a plasma-screen TV embedded right into the sparkly wall. The sound is off, but the picture's on. A local celebrity newscaster shows off his shower, which is constructed as a waterfall.

"Ugly," Aggie says.

Sasha, who has purple glasses and unnaturally red hair, shows me a book that has brown hair color swatches pasted to its pages. I compliment the collection, unsure why she's showing it to me.

"You didn't change your mind, did you?" Aggie says.

"About what?"

"Your new hair color. I shoulda told you to bring the magazine."

"Oh. I did bring it."

"What, you carry it around?"

"Yeah, actually." I get out the magazine and turn to the photo, a dozen pages or so after the article.

I feel Aggie's eyes on me. She finds it suspicious that I carry it around with me.

"Chestnut," Sasha says.

Suddenly I really like the idea of getting my old hair back.

Aggie holds a swatch to my cheek. "Finally the drapes will match the carpeting."

"Too dark," says Elaine, who has a boy's haircut and dangly silver earrings. She seems to be the boss.

After some debate, followed by harsh mockery of the model's chunky 1990s' boots, it's decided Sasha will cover my head in foils, alternating shades of brown for *dark dimensionality*. That's the term they use. We go to. Elaine soaks and scrapes Aggie's nails—without wearing gloves—and Sasha puts foil strips into my hair, and they're both half watching their show.

"Oooh, Chief Otto Sanchez," Sasha says to the TV screen at one point, "you can detect and inspect me any day of the week."

I look up to see Sanchez gazing down at me. He shows a brick to the camera, grave expression in his big brown eyes. It's the same footage from two days ago at Jarvis's.

"I bet he's bald under that beret," Aggie says. "That's why he wears it all the time. And the hair's a wig."

"I just wish he'd catch that bricker," Elaine says sternly. "One of the victims was my neighbor. She was so nice, and she had this little poodle—God, they can't catch him fast enough."

"Sanchez'll get him," I say.

Sasha says, "I got this little chain thing where you clip your wallet to your purse so the highcaps can't suck it out with their freak powers. Like the cowards they are."

Elaine shakes a nail polish bottle angrily. "Sanchez needs to get cracking."

"He doubled case clearances over the last year," I say.

"Too bad crime tripled," Sasha snaps. "Sanchez doesn't need more cops. What he needs is to round up all the highcaps and just shoot 'em. He should find a way to identify them, like genetics or something, and just take 'em out."

I feel cold. "That wouldn't be right, and he would never do that."

"He *should*," Sasha says.

"I don't like talk like that," I say. "That's a horrible thought on every level."

"I agree," Elaine says.

"Regular humans are responsible for crimes, too," I add. "Should Sanchez shoot all of us?"

Sasha frowns. I'm thinking it would've been smarter to have this discussion after she was finished coloring my hair.

Aggie pipes up. "All I can say is why would Sanchez wear that beret and that wig if he wasn't bald as a baby? And that's final."

Eventually Sasha has my whole head covered in foils, which gives me the look of a space-age lion.

"So," Aggie says. "How do you think your new hair will go over with you-know-who?"

I flash on Packard. I want to punch myself in the face. "You don't think Carter'll like it?"

"Oh," I shrug. "I wasn't even thinking of him."

Aggie raises her perfectly shaped eyebrows. "Who were you thinking of?"

I sigh, hating myself on about five different levels. "Somebody I don't want to be thinking of."

"Ooooh! Another man!" Aggie exclaims.

Elaine has moved to bathing Aggie's toes. Aggie sees me staring and gives me a warning look. If she really had the parasite, Elaine would be infected. I shudder inwardly.

"Compare and contrast," Aggie demands.

"There's no comparison," I tell Aggie via the mirror. "I just have to get hold of myself."

Aggie makes her goofy face again. "That's no fun."

I slam the rest of my champagne, and Sasha refills my glass.

Aggie shakes her blonde curls, a marvel of generosity and cruelty. "Details, sister."

I study the tile pattern around the mirror. The whole world seems to slow and hush whenever I think about that kiss; then I think about how Packard betrayed me, and I go seasick with anger. "It's just some guy who I should never have gotten involved with, and he screwed up my whole life."

"Mmm!" Aggie says brightly.

"It's like he's consuming my mind. I kissed him once— twice if you count one where we were interrupted right away. But it'll never happen again. Because he is a destructive and dangerous person." Sasha turns my chair and checks under some foils. "But I can't stop thinking about kissing him. It just keeps replaying in my mind, over and over. And since I've met this guy, I've done things I would've never imagined doing a few months ago."

"Really!" Aggie rubs her hands. "Gimme the details of the kiss. Set the stage."

"Oh, I was upset about something I'd heard." I can't believe I'm telling her, and I can't stop; it feels too good. "We were at this place where we hang around. It was one of those kisses that lights up every molecule in your body, you know?" Suddenly I'm trotting out every little tidbit—the position of his fingers, the way he tasted.

"Does Carter know?"

"It's not Carter I'm worried about. I have a regular boyfriend who's the one for me, and I betrayed him. I have a great life with him, and he makes me a better person."

"Hold the presses. So you have three boyfriends." She counts off on her fingers. "One, this regular boyfriend. Two, the destructive one. Three, your brother. Right?"

"Yeah."

Sasha smirks.

Aggie scratches discreetly at her arm. "I say go with the hot destructive one."

"No way. I need to get free of him."

"Since you don't want him, I want to meet him."

"I don't think that would work."

Aggie frowns. "You want to get free of him, but I can't have him?"

"It's complicated."

"If he likes *you*, I'm sure he'd like me. That came out wrong, but you know what I mean." She scratches her arm vigorously. "Bring him over."

"It's impossible." I hate the focus I've put on Packard. Thankfully, Sasha wants to put me under a dryer, then wash my hair.

Twenty minutes later I'm a brunette, all dark

dimensionality with a deep side part and waves down past my shoulders.

Aggie closes one eye and then another, like she's having focus trouble. "You like?"

"I love it." We discuss my hair—everybody agrees my new color is prettier—and I wonder now what Cubby will think. Tomorrow's Friday, our standing date night. I cancelled the last two with excuses involving my new job, but if I'm honest with myself, I didn't want to face him after the kiss. Now I'll come in with this new hair. Will he feel like I'm pulling away? Am I?

Aggie grabs the magazine and finds the page with the brunette model for comparison. Suddenly the napkin marking the vein star page floats down to the floor. Aggie picks it up. "Mongolian Delites. That's the restaurant with that big face on the door, right?"

"Uh . . ." Somebody would've brought her so Packard could see her psychological structure. He can do his thing through photos, but he prefers to see the targets in person.

"Yeah," Aggie says. "It is."

I extend my hand for the napkin. It makes me nervous that she has it.

"Testy."

"I need it to mark a page."

She holds it away from me. "Mongolian Delites," she says.

I freeze.

She makes a big show of inspecting the napkin. "Mongolian Delites." She lets her syllables flow musically. *"Mongolian Deelites."* Full of medications, destabilized by me, and still she zeroes in on my anxiety about the napkin, like a shark smelling blood. "What's wrong, Nurse Jones? You don't want me to know you go to *Mongolian Deelites*? I think something's up with *Mongolian Deelites*."

"Nothing's up with it."

"Oh, I know when something's up. Maybe this is where you and your destructive boyfriend hang around. I should check it out."

I practically fall out of my chair. She could wreck the whole operation! I grab the napkin out of her hand. "The problem, Aggie, is that the napkin was marking this article." I open it up to the vein star syndrome page. "But it's such a disturbing article, I didn't want you to see it."

"Oh yeah?" She takes the magazine and reads as Sasha and Elaine pack up their beauty tools.

"I'm writing a paper on it for nursing school." I read along, stoking my fear; then I rest my hand on Aggie's shoulder and push out to the surface of her energy dimension.

"When you're in nursing school, you see the full horror of what can go wrong with the body, and how medicine hasn't changed from the dark ages. You know what today's most important surgical instrument is? The saw. Sometimes it's tiny, like a scalpel, and sometimes it's giant, like for a knee operation. And then after that you have scrapers and needle and thread." I'm starting to burn the hole. I look at us in the mirror, my dark dimensionality hovering over Aggie's brightness. "Throw in some drugs, which are just mashed-up plants . . . God, the battle against disease is so hopeless."

Aggie's face changes completely as my fear surges into her—she gets this exaggerated expression, like a Greek tragedy mask. "That's one of the most disturbing things I ever heard!"

I close my eyes. "I know." When I open them, the world seems to have dialed up a degree in hue, brightness, and saturation. I feel beatific.

Aggie jumps up from her chair and scratches her thigh

through her white pants. "Uh! I thought getting my nails done would make this better." She scratches her skin rhythmically, frenetically, seeming more animal than human. Then she dashes from the room.

Sasha and Elaine click their beauty boxes shut.

"I better go find her," I say.

I find her upstairs, embarking on an ambitious multimedia skin-mapping project. It involves life-sized diagrams of the human form on the wall, a complicated system of eighty-four "zones," digital images of anomalies, and lots of string.

Two hours into the project, I make up an excuse to go. She acts funny about my leaving, and I get the idea she's thinking about forcing me to stay. For the first time it occurs to me that her criminal creativity could be turned against me.

Chapter Fifteen

I SHOW UP at Cubby's the following evening at six. My new hair color shocks him, though he claims to like it. But all I can think about is the kiss. Cubby keeps looking at me strangely, and I know it's because of the hair, but part of me feels like he sees the kiss all over my face.

"I'm so sorry I've been AWOL," I say, wrapping my arms around him. "I missed you."

"You were busy with all that training. It's cool." He pulls back and looks at me. "It's so different."

If he only knew how much is different. "Well, the one thing that's not different—" I kiss him long and hard.

"Wow." He looks at me quizzically. "Is something up?"

"No!" I grab two plates and a jar of red hot chili pepper flakes and bring them out to the coffee table in front of the TV.

He settles onto the couch. There's a double-cheese pizza on its way, and an action adventure movie ready to roll.

"I'm not really used to the hair yet myself," I admit. "It was an impulsive decision." I flop sideways onto the couch and swing my feet onto his lap.

He rubs my toes just how I like, reinvigorating my guilt about the kiss.

"I know I'm making all these giant changes all at

once, and I'm sorry because I know it's not fair. . . ." My chest contracts; I feel like Packard is sucking the air out of me.

"Hey, I'm proud of all your changes, Justine. Suddenly you're coming into your own as this woman of action, and you have control of your health situation. That alone is impressive. I mean, how long has it been since you went to the ER, or even had one of your head tingle things? Two months? Not only that, but you've gotten yourself this new job that pays well, and no, I don't like that it's this secret security thing, but I can deal. Okay, maybe the hair . . ."

I kick him. "I knew it!"

"But I'll get used to it. The point is, you hardly ever used to do things like that."

"I just want you to know, I'll never lose sight of the larger picture. The things that mean the most."

He squeezes my foot. This is the real and true thing, I think. Right here. Cubby rubs my foot with one hand and works the remote with the other. We can't start the movie until the pizza comes; that's one of his personal rules.

The doorbell rings a hundred channels later. "That was fast." Cubby hauls himself up. Moments later he's calling me to the door. "Somebody for you."

My heart jumps. Disillusionists would call first. I flash on the Silver Widow. Could she have followed me? It's just like something she'd do. I rush across the condo and round the corner to find Strongarm Francis at the door, looking caterpillary as ever with his giant round glasses and thick, tendony neck. Packard's right-hand man.

I make my introductions. "Francis and I work together," I tell Cubby.

Francis says, "Sorry to barge in, but we need Justine for a quick trip in the field. Unexpected eventuality."

I feel faint. Am I in trouble? What if the Silver Widow burst into Mongolian Delites? What if Henji discovered we were asking about him?

"It's six o'clock on a Friday night," Cubby says. "We just ordered a pizza."

I place a hand on Cubby's chest. "Cubby, every once in a while I'll have a trip like this. Not often." I glance at Francis, who nods. "If it wasn't important he wouldn't be asking. Francis, how long will this take?"

"Hour tops."

"But we just ordered pizza," Cubby says.

"How's about this," Francis says. "I bring her back with two pizzas, on the company. Piping hot."

"What's up?" I ask Francis once we're in the elevator.

"Your hair is brown," he says.

"I colored it. That's not against the rules, is it?"

"No, but I brought a brown wig for you to wear for a disguise, and now it's outmoded. Got your weapon?"

"No."

"Did I or did I not instruct you to have it at all times?"

"I was having pizza with my boyfriend."

"You need to wear it or carry it at all times. When you need it, you need it."

"Did something happen?"

"Not yet," he says.

His car is a boxy black Buick—just the kind of car I'd imagine for him. We get in and he reaches under the driver's seat and pulls out a revolver, empties out the bullets and hands it to me. I never liked holding guns when we went to the range as kids, and I don't like it now. And this one is much bigger and heavier than the lady revolver I had. "Look here, every chamber is empty, okay? Have it on you, in your belt strap or something, like you're hiding it, but make sure they see it."

"Make sure who sees it?"

"Our clients, the Mandlers. Six months ago the Man-dlers hired us to crash the man we refer to as the Bon Vivant. This is the final meeting."

"There's danger at a client meeting?"

"We need to confirm their expectations, that's all." He hands me sunglasses and a baseball cap. "For the duration of this meeting, you're acting invisible. Know how to do that?"

"Yup." I put the gun in my pocket. Francis starts up the car and pulls out. "So that's it? Nothing's wrong or anything?"

"Should there be?"

"No."

He gives me a look. Then, "No commentary, no mat-ter what happens. Especially once we're with the target. Can I have your word of honor on that?"

"Why would I say anything?"

Francis waits.

"You have my word of honor."

This seems to satisfy him. I love how much stock the disillusionists put in one's word. It's nice that they would value something like that.

"The Bon Vivant is indirectly responsible for the death of the Mandlers' son. He ruined the boy, who then drunkenly crashed his motorcycle, wound up in a wheelchair, and shot himself two months later."

"So they hired us."

Francis nods.

"So who's the client for the Silver Widow? Is it the dead husband's parents?"

Francis stares ahead. I'm almost thinking he didn't hear me, but then he says simply, "That's confi-dential."

"I thought we always knew who the client was."

"You don't with this one," he says curtly.

"But with others we do, right? It's weird that we wouldn't know, right?"

He gives me a stern look through his thick glasses. Have my questions made him uncomfortable? "Focus," he says. "Try that stuff on."

I try on the sunglasses. "Why the disguise?"

"Insulation. I am the only face of the disillusionists. If I bring one of you for an assist, you're disguised."

"So that's what this is? An assist?"

"What did you think it was?"

"Clients think you single-handedly do the disillusioning?"

"Ideally."

Friday evening traffic is sluggish along the Midcity River. I scan the old brick buildings, looking for more faces. I'm always on the lookout now. "Maybe they think you're some kind of a highcap."

"They might."

"So why doesn't Packard hire highcaps to disillusion people?"

"Highcaps can't do what you do," Francis says.

"Plus, all the highcaps who knew Packard think he's dead, huh?"

"Seems so."

"What would make the nemesis do that to Packard?"

"I'd like to see you cut down on the questions and concentrate on this."

"Fine." I put on my hat and look in the visor mirror. The giant sunglasses make me look like I'm trying to cover a black eye. "Just let me ask you this last thing, Francis. If I suddenly wasn't a hypochondriac anymore, maybe got miraculously cured, then I wouldn't need to zing anyone, would I?"

"Yeah. Heard what you did to the kitchen."

"If I got cured, I'd be able to leave though, right? I'd be free."

He scowls at the road, and I recall that first time I met Francis. Or rather, didn't meet him—the night I'd ended up at Mongolian Delites desperate for a zing. Francis had walked out mad. And then later, had urgently inquired if things were okay.

Oh my God. "You knew," I say. "That night I came back, you knew Packard was going to let me join without warning me what I was in for."

"I thought it seemed likely."

"How could you have let him?"

Francis grunts. "You don't *let* or *not let* a man like Packard do anything."

"You could've warned me."

"At that point? Would it have stopped you?"

We drive in silence.

"Why did he need a hypochondriac so badly? Is this all about the Silver Widow?"

He shakes his head. "No, and don't ask me any more questions. My advice is to be an excellent disillusionist."

"As a way out?"

"My advice is to be an excellent disillusionist," he repeats.

"Are you saying the way out of this is through?"

"That was a question."

After a few more nonanswered questions and then stony silence, we get to a deserted Burger Qwik and park nose-to-nose with a blue BMW. I get out and hang back, leaning on our passenger door in the drizzle while Francis confers with the Mandlers—a well-dressed couple in their sixties who have matching short silver haircuts. They look like they came from a pharmaceutical ad. Mrs. Mandler hovers an umbrella over the three of them. Mr. Mandler balances a briefcase on the hood and nods toward the restaurant. "He in there?"

"Nearby. Now here's what happens," Francis says. "You give me a gander at the money so that I know we're in business. Then I take you to see him. Once I satisfy the terms of our agreement by showing you the man disillusioned, you will hand that case over and our transaction is complete."

"I can live with that." Mr. Mandler opens the case, and Francis checks the money. When I'm quite certain the woman is watching me, I pull my jacket aside to display my gun, like they do in the movies. I'm guessing Francis wants them to understand that we will be able to protect them from their newly disillusioned enemy.

Francis leads us across the Burger Qwik parking lot and into the adjoining parking lot, heading toward a coffee emporium—a bright, cozy island in the rainy darkness. We probably look like a double date—the sophisticated pharmaceutical couple with their domestic dispute friends.

"He's been spending most of his time this week in coffee shops," Francis tells the Mandlers.

"Not looking for new victims, I hope," Mr. Mandler says sternly. "That was the whole point of this exercise."

"Mr. James Hermann is not looking for new victims, folks. Ready?"

"We've been ready for three years," Mrs. Mandler says levelly.

Francis pulls open the door, and we follow him into the bitter warmth of the coffee shop. He leads us past tables of students with their backpacks and laptops and around a condiment station. I spot a lone man hunched over a cup at a far corner table. The brim of his baseball cap shields his face, and his dark overcoat is buttoned all the way up. It's a look that says flasher or derelict. He curls his hands around a paper cup, as if to warm them on a hot beverage, but when you get up close you can see the cup is empty. "Almost finished," the man mumbles, not looking up.

The Mandlers exchange careful glances.

"We're just here to talk to you," Francis says.

He still won't look up.

"We know you as James Hermann," Francis continues.

Hermann pulls tight into himself—a movement that reminds me of a turtle.

Mr. Mandler pushes past Francis and looms over Hermann. "Don't act like you don't know what's what, Hermann," he barks. "You knew the lay of the land well enough when you were destroying our boy—Hey!" He bangs his fist on the table and Hermann cringes deeper. Then Hermann peers up from under his cap, and I get a look at his small nose, big forehead, and the way he peers out at the world, as if from a distant location inside himself.

I gasp. Shady Ben Foley. He looks a decade older, and he's lost all kinds of weight.

Francis shoots me a warning look.

I can't believe it. Shady Ben Foley, disillusioned. I feel this crazy sense of triumph and relief, like something's over.

"You killed him," Mrs. Mandler says with rumbly conviction. "You took our healthy, happy son and you broke him in two." She outlines Shady Ben's crimes in a memorized-sounding speech. Mr. Mandler seems to glow; maybe he feels the relief and triumph, too. Or maybe he's burning through the last of his hate. I find myself wishing Dad could see Shady Ben like this.

Strangely, though, the more I study his dull eyes, the harder it is to stay mad. Foley is just so unlike his old self. At one point I have to remind myself of what he did to us back then, and his words at Mongolian Delites that night—*Forgot what a perfect mark your pop was*—in order to stop feeling sorry for him. Now I'm glad for my disguise.

Suddenly Foley speaks. "I know what I did to your son." He pauses, as if to meditate on it, then whispers urgently, "I know better than you what I did to your son." I have this sense that he's being sincere, that I'm seeing the sincere Ben Foley for the first time ever. His words have that ring. More than that: it's like the truth of it is alive in him, ripping holes in his soul.

"You think you can squirm out of it?" Mr. Mandler demands, though it's pretty clear to me that Foley's not trying to squirm out of anything.

"You have no reason to accept an apology," Foley says. "Just know that . . . what I did . . . I know." He continues to peer out at the space in front of his small nose with this expression like he's smelling something terrible, even though there's no smell. After a long silence he begins a new thought. "Nothing . . . nothing . . ."

We wait. Again, I think back to the Foley I saw at Mongolian Delites, the way he insulted Dad, so close and threatening with his onion breath. I can't believe it's the same man.

Foley stares at the Mandlers, face open and soft. "I don't know what you want. I don't know. . . ."

The Mandlers look baffled. They don't know either, now that he's disillusioned. I sure don't know what I want from him; it's like something inside me has evaporated. Instead of being an enemy, Foley just makes me uncomfortable clear to the bone. I pull down my cap.

A voice behind us. "Everything all right here?" Foley shrinks and I turn to see a young coffee shop employee. His name tag says TED, ASSISTANT MANAGER, and he points at Foley. "Hey! You know the rule."

Strongarm Francis presses a twenty-dollar bill into Ted's hand. "Want to give us a minute?" Ted walks off. Francis turns to the Mandlers. "My assistant and I will wait out at the car." The Mandlers look bewildered. They don't want to be left alone with Foley.

I follow Francis out. "I never thought I'd feel bad for Foley. . . ."

"That's natural."

"But why would we need guns?"

"Look and learn, little missy." He leads me back out into the drizzly night and around the side of the building, coming to a stop just a few yards away from the window next to Foley's table. The Mandlers are still talking with Foley. It seems like they should see us, but of course they're in a bright place and we're out in the dark.

I cross my arms over my chest. "It seems wrong."

"It's far from wrong. Disillusionment is a state of truth. We stripped away his illusions, his rationalizations, and his creature comforts. Now he sees things clearly."

"That was clarity?"

"Part of what you're witnessing is the excellent finishing work of the Monk. He's got some spiel about the need to destroy hope because hope destroys the present moment, something like—hey!" Francis points to the window. "In there. Look look look."

Mrs. Mandler is walking away from the table.

"Is she coming out to find us?"

Francis says nothing as she goes up to the counter. "There it is," Francis says. "There it is."

"What? That she's getting a cup of coffee?"

He nods. "We're almost through."

After a few minutes, Mrs. Mandler leaves the front counter with a tray of food—sandwiches, chips, maybe a cookie or two from what I can tell.

"No way. They're feeding him?"

"The client is free to help the target out. We don't take a position on that."

"But they paid to have him disillusioned."

"Buyer's remorse. Very common. The clients are good people who went down the road of vengeance. They now recognize the target's humanity. Nobody thinks they'll recognize the humanity in an enemy until the moment they do, and it most always changes everything."

He goes right up to the window and knocks. The Mandlers look angry when they discern Francis. Francis points to his wrist.

"The Monk couldn't do that kind of excellent work without the target being thoroughly destabilized first. Like the fine work you do to remove a target's security of health and mental well-being." He flips out his phone as we walk back to the cars. "What kind of pizzas you want?"

"What?"

"You and the boyfriend. Pizzas."

"I don't know." I can't imagine eating at this point. Francis orders one pizza with cheese and one pizza with everything.

Eventually the Mandlers emerge from the coffee shop, walking briskly toward us, sans umbrella, even though it's still drizzling. "This is not what we signed on for," Mr. Mandler says when they reach us. "This is not disillusionment. This is financial and personal ruin of a man. I don't know what you did, but this is not what we signed on for."

"*Au contraire, mon frère,*" Francis says. "That's disillusionment as I presented it at all meetings. A lack of illusion. Your Mr. Hermann now lacks illusion."

"He lacks everything. He doesn't have a home."

"Shelter frequently plays a central role in the maintenance of illusions, and I saw fit to cause him to lose it."

"I suppose it went to you."

"Firstly, you were told up front that financial ruin might be part of the process, and you and Mrs. Mandler couldn't have been more pleased. You were informed of this, incidentally, during a recorded transaction. Secondly, Mr. Hermann's own choices led to this. And lastly, let's be honest, Mr. Mandler—you're not

uncomfortable with the financial ruin. You're uncomfortable with the results of the disillusionment you
ordered. And that was something you were warned
about. Naturally, you are free to assist Mr. Hermann—"

"Damn right I will."

"But you will pay my fee."

"Why don't you sue me for it?"

In one angry, fluid move, Francis grabs the man's collar and throws him up against the side of his vehicle;
then he pulls out his gun and presses it to the man's
cheek.

"Stop!" the woman cries.

"Don't doubt my power or my scope, Mr. Mandler,"
Francis says. "Have your wife hand my assistant the
cash, or there'll be trouble. Break any one of our agree-
ments and there'll be trouble."

Mr. Mandler stares at Francis through his nonsquished
eye as Mrs. Mandler takes the case out of their trunk
and hands it to me. Francis tells me to check it and I
comply. Lots of large bills in packs.

"Okay," I say.

Francis lets Mr. Mandler go.

Like two statues, Mr. and Mrs. Mandler watch us
drive off.

"My God," I say.

"We don't tend to have happy clients. We destroyed
some important illusions for these two. They thought
they'd heal seeing the Bon Vivant suffer. That was an
illusion. But Foley will bounce back good now."

"It all seems a bit much."

"Incarceration and execution are a bit much, too. It's
all a bit much."

"Will we take the Silver Widow's stuff?"

"Simon's on that one. She'll gamble it all away.
Preferable for the target to lose their assets on their own
steam."

We ride in silence. I stay in the car while Francis goes in to get the pizzas. They fill the car with a warming, comforting scent.

"Looks like you'll be a little late," Francis says. "I tried. Yell at Shelby if there's fallout with the boyfriend."

"What do you mean?"

"She's the one who insisted I take you on this close."

Cubby lets me in, clearly unhappy. I'm a half hour late. "How was the unexpected eventuality?"

"I would've so much rather been here with you." I head into the kitchen with the two pizzas, wishing I could wipe everything away and have this evening be normal. The first pizza we ordered is there, open and cold. "You only ate one piece. You must be starving!"

"I don't want us to sit down to a fresh, piping-hot pizza when I'm not hungry and you are. It's only fun if we're in on it together."

"Thank you," I whisper, touching his shirt. "Thank you."

We start up the movie—a big action-adventure spy thriller—and dig in. Cubby's mood lifts once the pizza hits his stomach. He declares Francis's pizzeria to be better than our usual one, and he even copies down the number off the box. He's also excited about the movie because it has time travel in it, and he loves time-travel stuff. I try to taste the pizza, try to follow the movie, try to enjoy Cubby's safe and good world, but there's something weirdly insubstantial about it. Like it doesn't matter.

Halfway through, Cubby pauses the movie and comes back with cookie dough ice cream and spoons. "Surprise!"

I try to feel excited. "Yum!"

He sits and hands me a spoon. "What's wrong?"

"It's nothing."

"Your secret mission got you down?"

"You've been really nice to not ask," I say.

"Is that it?"

"Yeah. That and more. Just life, I guess."

He smiles. "Life? What's wrong with life?"

"I don't know . . ." I stare at the floor. "How does a person tell if they're doing the right thing?"

Cubby barks out a laugh. "What? With your security job?"

"Yeah."

"Are you protecting people?"

"I don't know. You could look at it in so many different ways."

"Oh, Justine! You think too much." He works his spoon into the container and pulls up a spoonful that's half doughy nugget. "You always care about making things better and helping other people. You'll know in the end." He makes an airplane noise as he moves the spoon toward my mouth.

"Stop it, Cubby!"

He keeps it inching to my lips. I open up and chew on the yummy doughy chunk and push everything out of my mind.

I grab the remote and flick the movie back on. Clues add up. Another car chase. The handsome good guy kicks ass. I lean into Cubby's chest, sort of burrow in, appreciating him more than ever.

"Hey, you trying to dig to China?"

"No, I'm trying to dig into you," I say.

"Stop. It tickles."

"I can't stop."

So he turns his attention to me and starts tickling my stomach. I retract into a little ball, like a spider, but he's on me, tickling, and I tickle him back, and then he has my wrists in one hand.

He puts his lips to my ear, my cheek, and I loosen

away from myself and wind around him there on the couch. We burrow into each other, and it's wonderful.

That night I lie awake as Cubby sleeps. I used to be upset when I couldn't fall asleep, but tonight I get something out of watching him there—just watching him sleep, peaceful as a lily pad in a hidden pond.

Chapter
Sixteen

THE GOOD FEELING dissipates the next morning. I'm with the Silver Widow, who is more obsessed than ever with her multimedia skin-charting project. We also spend time discussing the cocktail party she's planning. She's been trying to get me to promise to bring my dangerous boyfriend, a promise I obviously can't make. As usual, I have this sense she wants me to stay at her house indefinitely, like I'm her big doll. I have my stun gun on me, and when she offers me a drink, I refuse. This upsets her greatly, which makes me very suspicious and worried. I zing her and get the hell out of there.

I ride off glory hour by rollerblading twenty miles with my iPod cranked, but I can't stop thinking about Foley, broken and alone. Will he really bounce back good now like everyone says? And will Aggie? Who hired us to disillusion her? And why is this client such a secret?

I spend the latter part of the day buying pretty things with my new money: dark velvety curtains, bright pillows, a green rug, and an old Japanese painting of a bird on a branch—all things too big to be teleported out the window. No way am I keeping my windows closed in this heat. I hate that people would have to do that. And like other kooks who believe in highcaps, I've taken to keeping my purse and laptop and other valuables in closets and drawers so the telekinetics can't access them.

I run into Shelby a week later. I'm on my way into Mongolian Delites for a meeting about our next target, the Alchemist, and she's on her way out. She grabs my hands there in front of the carved door face. "Your hair is color of chocolate. Very beautiful for you, I think."

I mumble my thanks. I'd forgotten about the hair.

"You do not return my calls. Did you not see him? Foley?"

"You should've warned me, Shelby. I would've liked to prepare." I don't know why I say this; it's not why I'm mad. The truth is, I don't know why I'm mad.

"I thought you'd like it."

"I didn't. It was terrible!"

"Pfft. If you believe life is only for happiness and butterflies, then yes, disillusionment is terrible. Francis told me that the Mandlers fed your Foley. Did that not cheer you? Is transformative action. The Mandlers pitied him, and their hatred was transformed. They will not go through rest of life bitter and angry. It was happy ending, and I thought you liked happy endings."

"That was a happy ending?"

"You did not think it so?"

"No." I sigh and touch the giant's carved cheek. It's such a nice face. You just want to touch it.

She gazes down at her electric-blue boots. "I am sorry."

"No, I'm sorry." I pull my hand off the face. Am I touching it too much? "I know you were trying to make me feel better."

Helmut comes up. "New hair. Don't be late for the meeting." He goes in.

"Men," Shelby says. "It is enchanting and lovely."

"My meeting's starting." I kiss Shelby on the cheek, her preferred hello and good-bye, and go in.

Packard's back in the booth with a group of guys. He very nearly twinkles as I walk up, which makes me think he likes my chocolaty new hair color, and this pleases me until I remind myself of his crimes against me.

"Hey, guys." There's nowhere for me to sit. Helmut offers me his place next to Packard. Instead, I grab a chair from the front.

Packard introduces me to Enrique, a young Latino with a whisper of a fuzz mustache and gold hoop earrings. "Ennui," Enrique says with a sigh.

"Ennui," I say. "Wow."

Wearily, he waves me off. The other man, a blocky football-player type, is named Jay. His light brown hair is peppered with gray, and he has happy, crinkly eyes and dimples and a big jaw.

"Jay is our alcoholic," Packard says.

Jay smiles, unruffled. He's the likeable sort who's friends with everybody. I don't say hello to Packard himself, and Packard doesn't say hello to me. Nobody notices because the introductions felt hello-like. Packard and I are so far beyond hello.

The purpose of this meeting is to fill Helmut and me in on the Alchemist, whose real name is Connor, and to teach us sheepshead, Connor's favorite card game. Jay and Enrique have already infiltrated the Alchemist's Thursday sheepshead club, and two more spots in the club will open up soon. Helmut and I will fill these spots.

"You ever play bridge?" Jay asks, dealing out cards two and three at a time. I haven't, but Helmut has. "Bridge helps a little."

I immerse myself in the conversation, avoiding looking at Packard, but I can feel him all the same; being near him makes me feel intensely alive, as usual. I remind myself that feeling alive is not always a good thing. People feel intensely alive during hurricanes and wars.

Packard gathers his cards. "Your work on the Alchemist

must take place entirely within the context of these Thursday-night sheepshead games."

Our eyes meet, and my pulse pounds through every nook of me.

"Same as Jay and Enrique," he adds. "No outside contact. No solo contact."

The way Jay and Enrique trade glances suggests this has been the source of some discussion.

"There's no reason why this shouldn't be a routine disillusionment," Packard adds, a statement that implies quite the opposite. I catch Helmut's eye. He senses something odd, too.

Enrique slides down in the booth. "The Alchemist is a chemist, right? He creates and ingests his own drug mixtures, and that's been slowing us down. Every Thursday I zing him with the highest-octane ennui this side of the Atlantic, and it slumps him for a while, but then he's back up. I can't get him rolling."

Jay nods. "He's not the greatest chemist in the world. The drugs he mixes for himself . . . let's just say some of his mixtures are more successful than others, but it's been enough to foil us."

"The key to destabilizing the Alchemist is to get him to start drinking again," Packard adds. "That's all we need, and that's why you're on this, Justine."

Enrique tugs on his leather jacket sleeve. The jacket looks like it's been through three lifetimes of hard use, just like Enrique, even though he couldn't be older than twenty-one. "Guy's got a day job as a chemist for a shampoo company," he says.

Packard turns to me. "I'm convinced the Alchemist will resort to drink if his health anxieties get reactivated and he thinks he's dying. Helmut will be your ride to and from all functions, and he'll pose as your romantic companion. He'll always accompany you."

"Okay." Awkward pause. "Is there something I should know about this Alchemist?"

Nobody says anything. They all just look at Packard.

"What?" I ask. "Is he some kind of a rape, torture, murder, chop-'em-up guy?"

More weird silence. Finally Packard speaks. "He doesn't chop them up."

"Oh."

"And it's always drug-assisted. His own concoctions, of course."

"You're sure about this?" I say.

Packard nods. "I'll give you the file. And you can talk to Francis."

They all watch me to see what I do.

I just laugh; I don't know why. "Well. Sounds like a good candidate."

Jay smiles, and Helmut and Enrique look relieved. Packard stares at his little stack of cards.

"I'm sure you'll be fine, Justine," Jay says. "He goes after women at dance clubs. He wouldn't get his victims from his weekly card game."

I'm pleased to have such an evil target, though I'll definitely want to confirm it. My new rationalization is that I'm only a vigilante on a case-by-case basis.

Enrique leans toward me: sharp, dark stare. "One thing, though. The man gets a little clingy after you zing him. Whenever I charge up his ennui, he just wants to complain to me. Fucking tiresome. The man's complaints are so trivial."

"Not for long," I say.

Jay claps once. "Excellent." He gives Helmut and me cheat sheets with card rankings and explains the play. It's a game of tricks and trumps and bluffs where queens and jacks beat most kings and aces. "You guys don't have to be pros at this," Jay says. "Some players still use cheat sheets. Sheepshead is pretty much only known by elderly farmers. They were shocked when I told them I had a couple players I could bring in. Shocked."

Enrique snickers.

I learn the game fast. I love cards, and I love hanging around with my gang, even with Packard there. An hour into it, Helmut and I are good enough that we can play for money.

Helmut's playing style is methodical: his lips move a lot—counting trumps, I realize. Jay is more interested in socializing than winning hands; he doesn't make a big move unless he's sure of himself. Enrique is an astonishingly good bluffer. And the only word to describe Packard's style is swashbuckling. His throws are sometimes reckless and sometimes brilliant—usually both. He controls the hands no matter what he holds. People eye him when they make a play, and they monitor his reactions when somebody else throws down. This was what he was in life, I realize: a man who did brazen things and galvanized people. And now he's the prisoner of Henji, the highcap who can murder with a mere thought.

A few hours later, Helmut's standing and stretching. I can see just a few civilians left out in the dining room. Jay has to go, too.

"Guys," I say, "I'm on a winning streak here."

Enrique throws down his cards. "Can't play with three."

"Stick around, Justine," Packard says. "We need to talk diseases for the Alchemist."

"Can't you just email me the stuff?"

"No."

The guys leave and I slide into the booth across from Packard.

He adjusts to his usual sideways sitting position, not looking at me for a long time.

I wait, heart beating a million miles an hour.

Finally he looks up. "It's fine with me if you don't want to work on the Alchemist case. You can say no and I'll say I changed my mind. You're the only one who's not here by choice."

"Is that an apology?"

"No, it's an option."

"Don't treat me different than the others."

"I'd think twice about sending Helmut after a serial killer who targets men who look like opera singers," Packard says. "I'd think twice about sending Enrique against, say, a serial killer who targets young, jaded Latinos."

"You'd think twice, but you don't let them pick and choose cases. From day one, I was slated for two cases—the Silver Widow and the Alchemist. Have you decided I can't handle this one?"

"No, certainly not."

"Then what?" Is he frightened for me? And then it occurs to me that maybe there's something he doesn't want me to figure out.

"Listen," I say, "I'm going to find a way to get free of you. But until then, I plan to be the best goddamn ally I can be to my fellow disillusionists. Those guys need me and I'm going."

"The more I think about it . . . it might be a mistake," Packard says. "Maybe I'm rushing this phase."

"Wait. You have a plan with *phases*?"

"I meant this phase of the Alchemist's disillusionment."

I don't buy it. Something strange is afoot. "Tell me this: who's the client on this one?"

"The identity of the client is confidential and not germane to our conversation. This is about you and the Alchemist and his victim profile."

"What? I fit a profile? The Alchemist has a specific victim profile that would put me in danger?"

"Yes."

"What?"

"The victims are all very beautiful."

I roll my eyes. "Get off it." But honestly, I can barely breathe. Or think.

"It's true, and you need to know." He shifts to sit up properly. "And yes, Jay and Enrique have met the Alchemist, but I alone have gazed into his heart. I alone see him for the monster he is. Far more dangerous than the Bon Vivant or the Silver Widow."

I feel cold. The way he says it, I don't doubt him.

"You can refuse. I'll tell the group I changed my mind on tactics. This is only your second target, and I wouldn't blame you."

I've never seen him like this. Is he feeling guilty? "I'm going. What's the disease?"

A pause. Then, "Are you familiar with Farthing-Dollop syndrome? Or aplastic spindler neuroma?"

"Neuro stuff. Sure."

"I see the Alchemist toggling between those conditions. He controls his hypochondria by controlling his thoughts, so he may not have fallen into an attack for years, but the fear is very close to the surface. And here's something else—he probably hasn't been to a doctor since childhood, so you'll be the only medical professional he's spoken with for eons." He takes a deep breath. "It's a loaded situation. Maybe too loaded."

"It sounds like it's loaded in exactly the right way."

He sits up. "You know what? It's off. I'm not sending you on this one."

"What?"

"I don't like it." He stabs his finger into the table a couple times. "I have made my decision."

"You can't pull me off! They're going to think I chickened out."

"It's my decision," he says.

"I'm going."

"I'll instruct them not to bring you."

I let my mouth fall open. "I can't believe you're taking even more choices away from me."

No answer.

Heat rises in my face. I want to help the victims. And I want to know his secrets. "Okay, you know what I'm going to do? I'm going to do a little online research and I'm going to find out Connor the Alchemist's last name and where he lives—I bet he's been in the news, and I bet it takes me all of one minute. And then I'm going to hunt him down. And then I'm going to zing him."

Packard's cheekbones are pink. "Don't."

"What, are you going to stop me? Are you going to come after me?" This is a little mean, I know.

A bemused light dances in his eyes. "You're not the kind of woman to do something so foolish out of defiance."

He's absolutely right, of course. Which enrages me. It makes me want to . . .

I sit back and smile, mirroring him exactly. "You're right. I'm not the kind of woman to do something foolish out of defiance. I am, however, the kind of woman who would do something foolish just to prove that you can't tell me what kind of woman I am." And this actually *is* the sort of thing I'd do.

"You wouldn't!"

"I've made my decision."

He gazes down at the deck of cards, eyelashes a deep fringe of cinnamon brown.

I grab my purse and stand. "Try and stop me."

"Wait, wait." He glowers up at me and I glower back, twisting my purse strap around my wrist, which echoes the twistiness in my stomach. "Give me your word that you won't contact him outside the card game."

"Then let me go to the game as planned."

He relents. I give my word and sit back down.

"Take heed, Justine. The Alchemist is vulnerable to you, but don't underestimate him. Walk away if something doesn't feel right."

"If something doesn't feel right? I'm going around as a fake nurse getting people to have hypochondria attacks."

We both would've thought that was pretty funny back when we drank coffee out of the same cup and shared private jokes. When our affections were sunny and uncomplicated. It was just a few months ago, but it seems like another world.

Chapter
Seventeen

I PULL OPEN the gold-handled glass doors of Le Toile and sashay across the marble floor with an exaggerated frown and crazy swaying hips in one of my famous "Ms. Fancy Customer" imitations I used to do for the girls.

Marnie and Sally just smile and nod and go back to their work behind the counter.

I'm shocked they think I'm a real customer. But then again, I have brown hair now, and it's been nearly three months since either of them have seen me. I try an inside joke: "Do you have any other Dondi Viva dresses besides these?"

They regard me glumly.

"Couldn't you just go back and check for me?"

This does the trick. They both scream and come out to hug me. We catch up on store gossip, and I give them vague details of the secret job that covers my secret job, and then I buy three pretty dresses I never could've afforded in the old days. I probably seem like Cinderella to them.

The truth is probably closer to Little Red Riding Hood. Possibly even the wolf.

I'm wearing one of those dresses two weeks later when Helmut picks me up for the card game. It's a green

long-sleeved number with a black embroidered V-neck;
I've paired it with black boots. Greens, browns, and
blacks look best with my new dark hair. The whites,
pinks, and blues I used to wear are out. Baby colors.

We head toward Elmvale where our hosts Leann and
Leroy live. Helmut's suit and shirt and tie are all the
same shade of brown—a sort of exotic look when you
add in his black villain's beard. He does sort of look like
an opera singer.

"Helmut, don't you ever feel uncomfortable about
how much power Packard has over you? You're totally
dependent on him."

"I know. But I couldn't have gone on as I was."

"What if he died?"

"I think he would send us to another highcap with a
power like his."

"You sure there are others like him?"

"There would have to be." He turns down the radio.
"Do you understand how the highcap mutation works?
How different highcaps get different powers?"

"No."

"The mutation involves a kind of wildcard DNA
that's blank until you tell it what to do, like stem cells.
That's why it's impossible to test for. The highcap baby
who first wants a toy from across the room, that highcap baby becomes a telekinetic. It has told its gene, I
want to cause objects to fly through the air. Which
explains why most highcaps are telekinetics. A different
highcap child might try to divine its mother's thoughts,
so its mutation would take the form of telepathy.
Another might strive to interact with its napping father.
That one turns into a dream invader. The impulse to
hide the truth creates a revisionist."

"So as a child, before trying to get toys or communicate, Packard tried to . . . understand?"

"Exactly. Which forever determined his power. If one

child went that route, others must have." Helmut looks over. "Of course, this isn't helpful to you. You want to know how to leave us."

"Yes."

"I'm sorry. If I knew, I'd tell you."

I nod; I believe him on that.

"For the record, you should've had a choice," he adds.

We enter Elmvale, an old first-ring suburb that kept its 1950s features—like Big Boy restaurants and tilt-roof drycleaners—intact.

I watch his face, wondering how much he knows. "So what's the deal with Packard's overall plan? The whole business about phases?"

Helmut shoots me a look. "What do you mean by phases?"

"As in, this phase of Packard's plan."

He pulls up in front of a wood-and-limestone bunga-low, shuts off the engine, and turns squarely to me. "Do you know something about Packard's plan?"

"Do you?"

Helmut pulls the keys from the ignition, evaluating, I'm guessing, whether to tell me what he knows. "I have thoughts."

"I do, too."

"Why do you say there are phases?"

"It's just something he said last week after our card game, when I stayed behind. He was worrying about me up against the Alchemist and he goes, 'Maybe I'm rush-ing this phase.'"

"He specifically used that word?"

"Yeah. Like the Alchemist is a phase. And when I gave him shit, he acted like that's not what he meant."

"This *phase*." Helmut stares at the steering wheel.

"And Jordan the Therapist implied he has a larger purpose."

"You can't listen to Jordan," Helmut says.

"Why? Is she a liar?"

"No," he says simply, "she's not." He turns to me. "It's interesting she implied he has a larger purpose. I agree, and I feel it directly involves you."

"Because of the way he tricked me into joining?"

"That, and because the Silver Widow and the Alchemist both materialized out of nowhere the instant you came on board. I know they're not ordinary cases, yet I haven't been able to discern anything particularly extraordinary about them."

"Except the client is secret on both."

"The Silver Widow client is secret, too?"

I nod.

Helmut looks thoughtful. "The obvious idea is that these projects relate to his freedom or his nemesis, but I don't see how. They don't relate to each other, either. You know, I've long wondered why Packard would devote his considerable powers of insight to assessing and rebooting criminals. I can assure you, justice is *not* a topic he feels passionate about. As a psychological hit squad, we do indeed make a great deal of money, but there are ways he could use his gift to make far more. And why does a man trapped in a restaurant need money anyway? Now these cases."

"Here's a theory: Packard has been in there for eight years, right? So we know the nemesis became active eight years ago. And that's when the crime wave started."

Helmut draws back. "Interesting."

"It is, right? What if the nemesis started the crime wave? And Packard fights him indirectly by fighting the crime wave?"

"Packard himself as the client? Fighting crime just to stick it to his nemesis?" Helmut chuckles.

"Why not?"

"Seems a tad oblique. And how does that involve you?"

"Maybe health anxieties completes his set."

"Then why hasn't he bothered to replace angst? Jarvis went off the deep end years ago—he was one of the first disillusionists. Come." We get out of the car. Helmut links his arm in mine as we proceed up the walk. I wish I could tell about Henji, but I gave my word to Shelby. We stop on the stoop under a wooden plaque with the names LEANN & LEROY burnt into it, and Helmut presses the doorbell. Cheerful chimes sound. "If you notice anything else . . . if he says anything . . ."

I nod.

"You disarm him, you know."

"Apparently not quite enough to get free."

The door opens, and Leann—a handsome, redheaded woman in her forties—ushers us into a living room that's stocked with frail Victorian furniture and glass figurines. This highly breakable environment increases my nervousness. Leann introduces us to Leroy, and then to Enrique, whom we pretend not to know. Jay we supposedly do know. After that we meet August, a small, gray-haired fellow in a hand-knit sweater who might actually *be* an old-time farmer. And then there's Connor, a.k.a. the Alchemist. As we shake hands, I try to touch the surface of his energy dimension. To my total horror, I find it every bit as repellent as Simon's.

I reclaim my hand as quickly and as naturally as possible. Whereas Simon's energy dimension was offensive, Conner's is scary. This is a problem. I lock arms with Helmut as the four of us get acquainted.

Connor's around my age, maybe thirty—a shortish, stocky fellow with fuzzy light brown hair and eyebrows and a square of whiskers on his chin. A soul patch, it's called, though every time I look at it I think of pubic hair. He stands proud, eyes bright—a demeanor that seems more cop or soldier than shampoo chemist. Or psycho—though Francis and his file convinced me otherwise on that point. Connor wears a suede vest over a Nehru collar shirt, and tells us he grew up on a base in Germany; that's where he learned sheepshead. When I reveal I'm a nurse, he falls silent and bends slightly backward. Then Leann's there with drinks.

"What kind of nurse?" Connor asks in a gravelly tone.

"RN, neuro, ortho, medical/surgical."

Connor does a fake shudder and walks off. I see now how to work him; I just have to get over the repellence. I have to.

I turn to my fellow disillusionists, lowering my voice. "I need to sit next to Connor, and I need you and Enrique to pitch me medical questions. But wait until after I visit the bathroom. Enrique, did you have any trouble with this guy's energy dimension?"

"Nah."

We head toward the table as a team. Jay settles in and spreads out, looking every inch the decadent man of leisure. Helmut maneuvers it so he's next to me and I'm next to Connor. Leroy's the first to rotate out.

We throw our fives to the pot and Jay deals. August picks up the blind, which means he plays against the table with or without a partner. Leroy comes in with Bugles, warning us new players about August's prowess, and in fact August does win the hand, using Jay as partner.

I visit the bathroom with my purse during the next deal and stoke up a hot, prickly mass of fear that mingles unpleasantly with my nervousness. I have got to zing this guy!

It's during the fourth hand that Enrique asks me about my job. Do I work in an emergency room like in the movies?

"Oh, the ER is sometimes like the movies," I say. "But to me, the real drama is the chronic degenerative condition. We had a young poet in with aplastic spindler neuroma last month. It started in his foot!" I look around. "I mean, who of us hasn't had foot pain?" Connor stares at the delicate crystal pretzel bowl. "Before he knows it, he can't get around without a walker because his muscles are that atrophied, and then he's in a wheelchair . . ." I have hold of my fear now. I just need to touch the Alchemist's energy dimension and burn the hole. "He could feel himself weakening little by little, but he couldn't do anything about it."

I turn and rest my hand on the Alchemist's bare arm. "Could you pass the pretzels, please?" I feel sick when I push near his energy dimension.

He passes the bowl, casting a cold look at my hand on his arm. Quickly I let go. I stuff a few pretzels into my mouth. "There's nothing worse than witnessing your own horrible degeneration."

August and Leroy are rapt. Connor keeps his eyes down.

I eat another pretzel; then I hand the bowl back to him, placing my hand on his arm again, my heart pounding like crazy. "Sorry, I can't have these in front of me anymore." Again I fail to connect.

Connor slams the pretzels down in front of August and turns back to me, glaring at my hand and I have to let go. Then he excuses himself to go to the rest room.

I shake my head at Helmut as the guys argue: *I didn't get it.* Enrique sees. I twirl my finger: *I need another go.*

Leann pulls up a chair next to August and turns the conversation toward the brick attacks. Elmvale's been spared, but she worries all the time that maybe they're due. She ought to weed her garden, but she's scared.

Leann's been so sweet, so welcoming, it steams me to

think of her being frightened to go out into her own yard. She shouldn't have to live in fear like that. Nobody should.

Farmer August informs us that he doesn't believe the highcap hogwash, but he's hard-pressed to imagine a catapult shooting a curveball.

During the next hour of play, Connor makes himself big. He invades my space with his elbow, splays out his knee so I have to move mine, and sometimes he looks at me with disturbing directness. It will be weird to touch him again, and it's getting uncomfortable to hold all the fear.

Jay brings up the subject of the hospital an hour later. Again I touch Connor's arm, pretending to be extra animated in my description of a painful exploratory procedure. No go. He looks at me, at his arm, then back at me. We've entered a creepy silent conversation.

Two deals later, Connor picks up the blind. You only pick up the blind when you feel you have the strongest hand, or when you're bluffing, which I know he is, because I have all the good cards for once and the blind should've been mine. I'm in a position to crush Connor, but I don't want to be aggressive toward him. So when the play starts up, I squander my trumps on junk for two hands in a row.

"Hold on, hold on," Connor says when I lay my last card on the last trick. "What are you doing?"

I freeze. "What?"

"Did you just let me win?"

I paste on a face of confusion. "No. I thought . . . I was . . ."

"You forgot queens are top trump? No." He shoves the money back to the center of the table. "I'm not taking the pot. Hold it over."

"It's your pot," Leroy says.

The Alchemist bores right into my eyes. "You didn't play that natural, lady."

"It was a mix-up," I insist, shaky from holding so much stoked fear. My blood pressure has to be spiking.

"Connor," Helmut says, "she hasn't been playing all her life like we have."

"She wastes a red queen when she has a ten?"

"I was thinking diamonds were trump," I say.

Connor shakes his head. "No you weren't."

"Why would I let you win?"

"Because you wanted me to think you can control the game."

Helmut puts his arm around my shoulder and leans forward, addressing the Alchemist across me. "Take it from me, friend, she's not that good a player."

I make a jokey surprised face. "Helmut!"

August gathers up the cards for the next deal. "Don't quibble, kids. I'll have all your money by midnight."

Jay makes a toast to that, and challenges everyone to sweeten the pot by five bucks each for the next round. A sullen Connor throws in. Will I ever be able to zing him? My cohorts don't ask any more nursing questions. Simon's words echo through my mind: *You're not a disillusionist; you're a decoration.*

"Maybe you should ask your boyfriend Helmut to teach you a little better," Connor says at one point, endowing *teach* with creepy significance.

"Yeah well . . ." I look away, wondering what Packard saw inside him.

Later on, Leroy appears wearing a train conductor's hat. He wants the group of us to go down to the basement to see his model train set. I duck into the bathroom instead. I need to be away from everyone for a minute.

I nearly run into Connor on my way out. "Oh!"

He puts up his hands, as if to enforce his personal space.

"How's the train set?" I ask.

Connor stands up straight; he's a hair taller than me. "You talk about nursing too much," he says. "Your mind is in the medical gutter and you need to pull it out."

"It's my profession," I say, underarms and spine drenched with sweat. Something tells me not to touch him now.

He says, "I've noticed nurses on TV don't wear those white nurse dresses and nurse hats anymore." His tone of voice is oddly elevated, like his throat is constricted. "The little white hats? The stockings? You don't like being put in that outfit?"

Shivers rain over me. Casually, I say, "Nurses haven't worn that outfit since the eighties."

"Why? Is it because you don't like being put in that outfit?"

"It's just not very practical."

He bores into my eyes. "Whether that outfit is practical should be in the eye of the beholder, wouldn't you agree?"

"Not exactly."

"They don't like being put in the hat, huh?"

Connor's starting to frighten me on a primal level. "No," I say, "they don't like *being put in the hat.*"

Footsteps tromping up the basement stairs. I'm relieved to catch sight of Helmut at the other end of the hallway. "How were the trains, Helmut?" I chirp.

"Comprehensive."

Connor enters the bathroom and I head toward Helmut, who lowers his voice. "Everything okay?"

"Just a strange discussion."

Helmut and I rehash our Packard theories on the way home. Nothing new. He also tries to cheer me up about my big failure, but I feel terrible, not to mention the fact that I've stoked my fear twice and I really need a zing.

I could go zing Packard, but I don't want to. It'll dissipate a little, and anyway I'll see the Silver Widow tomorrow at her cocktail party. I'll wait until then.

Chapter Eighteen

BESIDES DRIVING like a maniac, Carter reveals his anger by arriving late to everything. The worse he needs to zing somebody, the later he runs. So I'm surprised when I hear my buzzer fifteen minutes early on the night of the Silver Widow's cocktail party. This is the night I'll be passing Aggie off to Simon.

I press the intercom. "Hold on. I'm not ready yet."

Cubby's voice: "That's okay, take your time."

Cubby! My heart sinks. I forgot to cancel our standing Friday-night date. I grab my shoes and my handbag and carry them down the three flights of stairs, barefoot. The shoes and handbag are velvet, and they go with the brown velvet gown I'm wearing, which is easily the most beautiful piece of clothing I have ever owned. It's the same shade of brown as my hair, with silver sparkles around the neck and the waist. I fling open the downstairs door.

"Wow!" Cubby's smile quickly fades. "Uh-oh."

"Cubby. God, I . . ."

"Right. Work. Right?"

There's this horrible silence where my heart sinks some more. "I'm so sorry."

"I didn't think you'd dress like that for a movie and pizza. It's all about work now."

"No, it's about me trying to be a better person, and I swear—"

"I hardly need you to be a better person. What I needed was a simple call. Some consideration."

"It won't happen again, I promise."

Cubby looks at his shoes.

"I am so sorry."

The silence thickens.

I say, "We're still on for having the new neighbor over Wednesday, right? I swear I'll make the best dinner. I picked out these great recipes."

He shakes his head. "I can't believe you forgot. We just talked about it the other day."

"Please don't be mad, Cubby." A car idles nearby. Loud, rumbly. "I'm so sorry—"

Cubby's expression hardens. I look around to see Carter in his convertible. For the first time I notice Carter and Cubby have the same wholesome blond good looks. Except Carter's wearing a tux and picking me up in a fancy convertible with the top down, and I'm in the prettiest dress I've ever worn.

"This is grand," Cubby says. "So grand." I start to say something and he puts up a hand. "Just go."

There's no talking to Cubby when he's like this. "Wednesday." I kiss him and go.

Carter, to his credit, does not get out to open my door. He stares straight ahead as I get in and pulls out slowly instead of peeling out.

"Men, huh?" he offers a few blocks later.

"It was my screw-up." We ride in silence, with me feeling really guilty, and there are also tingling sensations in my left temple, and I'm trying hard as hell to assure myself it's nothing.

Carter honks in front of Shelby's apartment, and she emerges in a bloodred ruffle gown. Very flamenco. We make a fuss over how beautiful the other looks as she squeezes into the front seat with me.

Shelby is Carter's date for the evening, and Simon is to be mine. It was my big idea to pass Simon off as the destructive, intense, good-kissing, mind-overtaking boyfriend I'd described to Aggie during our beauty afternoon; she's been pestering me to let her meet him ever since, so I promised I'd bring him to the party. I was describing Packard, of course, but Aggie doesn't have to know that. I'm confident she'll try to take Simon away from me. I'm confident she'll succeed.

The party starts at ten. The four of us are dining at Mongolian Delites beforehand with Packard.

Maybe half the tables are occupied, lights low, candles flickering. I spy Packard leaning over a table of four, playing the dashing host in a smart black dinner jacket. He glances at us briefly.

"This night would be perfect if *he* was not going." Shelby's nodding toward Simon, who's sitting with Carter and Enrique at the bar.

We stroll over. Simon swivels around to face us. He's wearing an iridescent green suit coat with a net shirt underneath, and black pants and boots. We both just stare at the net shirt. You can see his tattoos through it.

I give him a smirk. "That's an attractive outfit."

"You told me I was going in as the destructive boyfriend," he says. "I ask you, what kind of mother-fucker would wear something like this?"

"I said destructive, not deranged."

Simon says, "A little deranged will be just about right from what Carter tells me."

Enrique sighs. "Sexual politics are so predictable." His diamond earrings sparkle in the candlelight.

Shelby sits down next to him. "You need a zing."

I take a stool at the end next to Shelby and the bartender brings us ouzos. What I really need is a zing.

Packard comes by. "When does her party start?"

"Ten," Shelby says.

Packard looks dashing tonight. I hold my breath, as if that will lessen it. He says, "As soon as some orders clear out, I'll have them start our dinners. You staying, Enrique?"

Enrique sighs. "I suppose."

Packard and Shelby discuss what kebabs to make. I try to focus my attention on picking candy pecans out of the nut bowl instead of freaking out about the sensations in my left temple, which are tingles over a constant odd pressure that changes only slightly when I move my jaw around. This could indicate something musculoskeletal, which would be good, but then again, there's a large vein through there that could be affected by jaw movements. If I were really rich, I could get my own CAT scan machine. I'd have to buy my own house, though. It would be too much for an apartment, and surely the neighbors would complain.

The next thing I know, Shelby's over at the other end of the bar arguing with Simon about something, and Packard's settling in next to me.

He lowers his voice. "Helmut said it was a nonstarter with the Alchemist—"

"I'll get it next time," I tell him.

"If you're having a reaction to his energy dimension—"

My whole body buzzes as I look into his eyes, breathing in his warm spicy scent. The kiss is still way too alive between us. "I'll get him."

"Helmut said you two had a quarrel over cards. Is Connor fixating on you in some way?"

"He's fixated on the fact that I'm a nurse, that's all."

"One more go at the Alchemist, but if you can't connect, that's it. I'm removing you from the case after that."

"So it's really not that important a case after all?"

"One more go," he says.

"You can't just remove me before I've done my job."

Packard fixes me with a fiery gaze. "I can do anything I want."

"So can I."

"No. You can't."

"What?"

"You spend so much time complaining about being my minion, it appears that you've forgotten that you *are*, in fact, my minion, and that you really do have to obey my orders."

My jaw drops in shock. "Well, my message to you is that if you take me off the case, I'll find the Alchemist and zing him on my own."

"No, you won't. Now that you've seen what he is, I know you won't." He rests his elbows on the bar, like we're having any old conversation. "Don't defy me, Justine. You are the minion and I'm the master. The overlord." He pauses for effect. "My mere inattention would destroy you."

My vision goes hazy with rage. "I'd welcome your inattention."

"Trust me, you wouldn't." He lowers his voice. "I'd recommend you never forget the shape you were in that night you came pounding at that door, begging for a zing."

"Well I'd recommend you never forget that Cubby is my boyfriend, so you can quit fussing over me and treating me like I'm more fragile and less capable than the others, because I'm not."

"Believe me, I'm not trying to replace Cubby. I would never want you like that."

"What's that supposed to mean?"

"Cubby just wants the parts that fits into his fake fairy-tale life."

My face goes hot. "You may be able to read people's psychological tendencies, but obviously you don't know anything about love." I use the word to hurt him. "And at least Cubby's not a parasite like you, cravenly feeding off those around him."

Packard looks at me wildly. My comment stung. It stings me to know that.

He seems to want to say something; then he rises and heads back into the kitchen and I sit there feeling awful. I hate him for lording over me like that, but I feel really awful for what I said.

Simon comes over and takes Packard's stool. His unwholesomely pale skin makes his eyes look unnaturally blue. At least he combed his hair.

"Let's get our stories straight," he says. "How long have I been your boyfriend?"

I glare toward the kitchen. "You're not my boyfriend. You're kind of . . . you're just somebody who invaded my life. *Not* a boyfriend."

"Okay. What do I do for a living?"

I sip my ouzo, trying to pull myself together. "I didn't say."

"Let's make me a professional gambler. Better to stick to the truth."

"Good idea."

Simon swirls the ice in his drink. It's stupid, but I want Simon to think I've done a good job with the Silver Widow.

"What else about me?" he asks.

"You're dangerous and intense, and she likes that. The whole point with her is that she craves intense distraction to take her mind off her skin condition. Be ready. Her skin may alarm you."

"It won't. What else?"

"I made you out to be the kind of guy who just takes over a person's mind, a person's life. I told her we only kissed once, and we shouldn't have. It's this big secret."

"Justine, if I'm your dangerous boyfriend, we've had a lot more action than one kiss."

"Well, last I told her, it was one secret kiss."

"Do I know about the other boyfriend?"

"If you count my brother, Carter, I have two other boyfriends, but you only know about the main one."

Simon smiles. "Nurse Jones. My goodness."

I shake my head. "Aggie loves that sort of thing. Anyways, she'll feel confident in taking you away from me because she's prettier."

"Is she?"

"Very much, in a luscious baby-doll way. She'll be expecting you to be bossy and controlling."

Simon narrows his eyes. "Bossy and controlling. Got it."

I take a leisurely sip of ouzo. He seems to like the way I've set him up, which makes me feel good. "The bar's set pretty high, Simon. I told her you have this dark gravitational pull on me, pulling me into things I'd never dreamed of doing. You're leading me down this path I wouldn't have chosen for myself, but there's this weird magic about you, like I feel alive around you. Even though you're sort of despicable."

He smiles. "Excellent."

"Mostly I talked about the kiss. She was very interested in the kiss."

"Do I need to know anything specific about it?"

"Just that you better be good. I told her it was mind-bendingly erotic, and there was this intense connection between us where the touch of your lips lit up—I believe the phrase I used was 'every molecule in my body' Even the touch of your fingertips—electric."

"If it was such a hot kiss, why did we stop?"

"We were interrupted."

"So this was a public place?"

"I didn't say where we were."

"Hmmm. A public place." Simon smiles in a way that makes me nervous. "A forbidden kiss."

"It's a pretty standard story," I say. "Turn on any soap opera and you find the forbidden kiss."

"You need a setting. If she asks me, I'll tell her it was a restaurant like this. What do you think about that? We could've kissed back by the booth, or in the kitchen. Maybe even in the bathroom." Simon smiles. "That would be something, wouldn't it?"

I fight to keep my face devoid of expression. "It's your story. Set it where you want." The pressure in my temple devolves into a kind of throb. Not a good sign.

"The conventional boyfriend." Simon stirs his Scotch with a swizzle stick. "How's about if we call him Cubby?"

I give him a hard look. "Don't you ever bring Cubby's name into disillusionist business."

Shelby and Enrique come by with plates of kebab hors d'oeuvres. "Join us, Justine," Shelby says.

I stand as Packard comes by with another plate; Simon stops him. "Packard," he says. "Justine told our Silver Widow quite an ingenious story for my setup. You should hear it."

"It's not ingenious," I say.

"It's fantastic," Simon says.

"I don't want to go through the story again." I point at Packard's plate. "These look good. What are they?"

Packard looks at me oddly. "Zucchini kebabs."

"She's made me out to be the dangerous love interest," Simon says. "I'm hot, intense, and charismatic—so charismatic that I make Justine do things she'd never do—"

Packard gives Simon a quizzical look.

Simon says, "I'm the source of a dark gravitational pull—"

"The Silver Widow needs distraction," I say. "That's why I made you sound like that. That's a distracting way to be—"

But Simon continues. "I'm taking over her mind, her life. It's wrong, but she secretly craves me; she feels my magic. But the best part is the description of our one stolen kiss."

I can't even look at Packard. "You need to get out more."

"She told the Silver Widow that when I kissed her, every molecule in her body—"

"Simon—," Packard interrupts.

"My touch was like electricity on her skin, the kiss—"

"Why are you telling me this?"

"Don't you find it intriguing?"

"It sounds like Justine talked you up to the target using effective details. Why are you repeating them like a titillated schoolboy?"

Simon smirks. "The entertainment value." He leaves to join the group.

How the night can get any worse, I don't know. I turn to Packard, who looks quite pleased indeed.

"Dream on," I say.

He gets this glint in his eyes. And ever so gracefully, he turns and ferries the plate of zucchini kebabs to the table of disillusionists in the far corner.

I ask the bartender for a glass of water. Let Packard think whatever he wants, I tell myself as I guzzle it down. And the temple thing is just referred tension from my jaw. Why wouldn't I have tension? It's been two weeks since I had a zing. I'll feel like a new person once I zing Aggie.

I watch Packard settle in with the gang, wishing, as I have so many times, that he hadn't deceived me so profoundly, so wantonly, wishing he hadn't stolen my freedom. He killed so much of what could've been when he did what he did.

Feeling incredibly sad, I head over for a night of feasting with my people. Packard and I ignore each other except for the few accidental moments where we catch one another's gaze, and the thrill rises until we look away and immerse ourselves back into the clinking glasses and tinking silverware and clever talk of our predatory Mongolian tribe, living it up in our hidden corner of the city, secrets in every pocket.

Chapter
Nineteen

THE SILVER WIDOW'S HOME sparkles with crystal and candlelight. The ring of polite talk and laughter rises from little groups of elegant people, and the soft, warm breeze coming through the French windows adds a magical wildness to the night.

A butler approaches us with a tray of champagne glasses.

"Got any Scotch?" Simon asks. The butler goes off. "Who the hell are all these people? I thought she was isolated."

"Help, mostly." I point to Elaine and Sasha. "The two women in the corner are stylists, and the men look like their dates. Carter and I are her pool cleaners. She mentioned she invited her lawyer. And her real estate agent."

"Dumping her real estate holdings already?" Simon says. "I haven't even started her gambling."

"She's been investing in condos. There she is." I wave.

Aggie glides across the floor in a white dress with silver sparkles. What's stunning about her garment is what's *not* there—the entire left half of her body is nude aside from the parts the law likes covered. In this way, she's effectively concealed her Osiris virus wound sites, which are concentrated on her right side, while still looking insanely sexy.

Aggie shakes her blonde curls as she nears. "Welcome!"

Simon's bored stance doesn't fool me for a second. And when I introduce them, she lowers her head and looks up at him out the top of her eyes, like a sexy little girl in trouble, and Simon holds her hand a beat too long. His suit coat's unbuttoned, and you can see the heads and tails of his dragon tattoos through his net shirt.

Aggie pulls Carter flush to her naked side and gives the four of us a tour of her house. The dreamy pulse of electronica pounds through the sound system, and I'm feeling the vibrations in my head, which is exactly where I don't want to be feeling them.

Now and then, Aggie stops to strike a pose of dissolute glamour while asking personal questions. She finds it particularly interesting that Simon likes turtles, and that Shelby washes her hair only once a week.

We get upstairs to the bedroom. I've described it to Shelby, but my description didn't prepare her for the crystal-white madness of it. We regard each other with carefully neutral expressions.

Carter looks freaked, but Simon just laughs. "Nice," Simon says to her. "Very nice."

Aggie takes this as a compliment.

After we peruse her giant closet and the guest chambers, she guides my comrades to the stairs and announces she has to borrow me. As soon as they start down, she pulls me into the office, pushes the door shut with her back, and heaves a sigh of relief. She then dissolves into a fit of scratching underneath her dress. "Do you know how hard it is to not do this down there?" she says.

"You're coping amazingly well," I say.

"I'll say. Because I can feel the filaments working their way out every second!" She directs my attention to several rows of small glass containers. "That's how many Osiris virus filaments came out of my skin yesterday." She has her dress nearly all the way off, revealing red, irritated skin and beige bandages that the intact half of the dress had covered.

I'm far more interested in her creamy pale left arm. I'm interested in coiling my fingers around it and channeling a river of fear into her. I want it. I crave it. It horrifies me, how much I crave it. What have I become?

"Don't watch me. I want you to watch this." She hops over to her computer and starts up a movie of a tweezers removing something invisible from a normal-looking patch of skin; it's taken with some sort of magnification apparatus, but still you can't see the filament.

When the clip ends she hands me a glass jar and a magnifying glass. "That's the filament you just saw."

I remove the top and search the bottom and sides with the magnifying glass. "I don't see it."

"God, you are so dense. Let me." She searches the jar herself, angling it for different light. "It's gone!" She draws away and looks at me accusingly. "It's gone!"

"I didn't take it."

"No, you didn't take it, but you did something—you probably breathed really hard and it flew out." She carries on in her usual insulting way while I stare at the place on her arm I want to zing, remembering how amazing it felt that first time in her bedroom. My hunger builds.

"What am I going to do?" Suddenly she just comes up to me and takes my hand. "Thank God you're here, Justine!"

This snaps me out of it. I can't do it. She's too pathetic. "You should get down there." I grab the doorknob. "You're missing your whole party."

We arrive downstairs, where her transformation back to normalcy is astounding. She's a personification of her own dress—an unblemished public side and a hidden crazy side.

Elaine the hairdresser comes up to say hello, and I introduce her to my friends.

"Can you believe it about Mayor Templeton?" she says. "Even the mayor, with all his bodyguards . . ."

"What about him?" I ask.

"The Brick Slinger got him. He's dead. Dead on arrival."

"That's horrible!" I say.

"And I suppose they still didn't manage to catch the guy," Carter says.

"No," Elaine says. "Can you believe it?" It really is a shock, and we commiserate about it. Sasha and two men—her and Elaine's boyfriends from what I can gather—drift over to join us, adding updates they've heard, and then Sasha and Elaine and one of the boyfriends begin to argue about whether the Brick Slinger is telekinetic.

Aggie listens with her arms crossed, stewing. "I don't think this is appropriate party conversation," she says finally. "And you know what? Templeton sucked anyway." She sends the stylists and their boyfriends to get ice and restock chips; then she drags Carter and Shelby off to meet a potential pool client, leaving Simon and me alone.

"You call that destabilized?" he asks.

"She's destabilized. You just don't see it."

He smiles over my shoulder. At her.

"What are you going to do with her?"

"Let's see." Simon places a hand on a white pillar. "I'm going to zing her; then I'm going to give her the ride of her life in that purity bedroom of hers, and then we'll head out for a whirlwind casino weekend where we'll lose obscene amounts of her money."

"You're going to have sex with her right after you zing her?"

He widens his blue eyes in fake surprise. "Oh, no! Would that be breaking one of Packard's rules? Endangering myself by giving in to the very pleasurable experience of sex with a target during glory hour? Like watching a bug on the windshield while driving too fast?" He looks me hard in the eye and laughs. "I highly recommend it."

I just stare at him, throat dry. "You could lose control."

"And perspective, too." He grins. "See, that's the difference between you and me. You won't ever give up control or move beyond your comfort zone. That's why you couldn't touch my energy dimension. Or the Alchemist's." He flips his chunky black bangs out of his eyes. "Nobody knew where your limits would be, but now we know. We might have to drop the Alchemist because of you."

I'm speechless, and flooded with shame.

"Yeah, 'cause it looks like you won't be able to hack it, and you were the key." He straightens up. "Don't feel bad. You all have targets you can't work with. Because all of you have limits. Except for me. I got rid of my limits."

"How?"

"Why should I tell you?"

Carter and Shelby are back, arm in arm.

"I do not like Silver Widow," Shelby announces.

"Tell her what?" Carter asks Simon.

"How to zing repellent targets," Simon says.

"Don't listen to him, Justine," Carter tells me. "If a target's repellent, he's repellent."

Simon smirks. "Only if you're too lazy and stupid to figure it out."

Shelby steps back.

Carter turns to him. "What was that?"

"Lazy," Simon enunciates. "And *stupid*."

Carter moves fast—ice cubes fly into the air, a glass breaks, and the next thing I know Carter has Simon pinned to the pillar, right forearm across his neck, left hand trapping his arms.

"What was that?" Carter demands.

Simon chokes out the words: "Lazy . . ."

Carter jerks him.

"Stupid . . ." Simon finishes with a raspy sound that's either laughter or coughing.

All the party is watching us now, and Simon's grunts sound less laughterlike.

Shelby smiles.

"Guys!" I say.

Carter releases him. "You're lucky Packard wants you working tonight."

Simon coughs, smiling and straightening his clothes. "Thank you."

Carter takes a chair, and Shelby settles onto his lap.

Simon leers across the room. "She's still watching us."

"There's a surprise," I say.

"Let's give her a little more to watch." Simon hangs his arm over my shoulder, thuglike. "You guys bored? Want to get out of here?"

Mysteriously, Shelby smiles, like she's just gotten great news.

"I do," Carter says.

"I do, too," I say. I'm feeling upset about the mayor, and about Midcity in general; it feels like we've crossed a new line of chaos.

"I will guarantee you," Simon says, "that if Justine would be so good as to let me kiss her, I'll have the Silver Widow shutting down this party in thirty minutes, and you can all leave."

"No thanks," I say.

Carter stands, ejecting Shelby from his lap. "That's it?"

"That's it. A kiss with Justine, eye contact, and the Silver Widow shuts down the party."

Carter crosses his arms. "The room cleared in thirty minutes? Or she starts to clear it?"

"Cleared. Timed from the start of the kiss." Simon removes his hand from my shoulder and extends it to Carter. "Five hundred bucks."

Carter takes his hand. "You're on."

"Except it's not going to happen," I say. I'm looking at the pillar. I have a feeling Simon's vision for the kiss involves parts of me pressed against it. Something alpha like that.

"Come on," Simon says. "You can have the same terms."

Shelby hooks her arm through mine. "Bet him, Justine. You will make money."

Carter says, "Do you really think Aggie will send her entire party home just from watching Simon kiss you?"

"Forget it. I've defiled my relationship with Cubby enough for one day."

"Don't be so precious," Simon says. "It's for the job."

I cross my arms.

"Okay," Simon says. "Twenty minutes, or I pay each of you five hundred dollars. But if I win, you each only pay me a hundred."

Simon stares at me—hungry, pleading. He'd do just about anything to make this bet happen.

I smile. "Okay, I'll take the bet," I tell him. "For a price."

Shelby and Carter exchange glances.

"Name it," Simon says.

"Your technique. How you can zing targets who are repellent to you when nobody else can. How'd you get rid of your limits?"

Simon shakes his head.

"Those are my terms," I say.

Simon stares down at his black boots, clompy and dirty against the white shag carpeting. *"No."*

I wonder if there's something embarrassing or intensely personal in what he does. "Help me, Simon. Help me to be effective with people like the Alchemist."

Carter grabs a champagne off a passing butler's tray. "Justine, we all have negative reactions to certain energy dimensions. We all have our limits."

"Not me," Simon says.

"So tell me," I say.

"You wouldn't be willing to go through with it. It involves losing control, and you'll never do that."

"No bet then."

Simon stares across the room at the Silver Widow, who talks excitedly with Elaine the stylist. He's craving the bet. We all see it. And we all want to hear the technique he's so reluctant to divulge.

"Clock ticks," Shelby says.

Simon frowns. "You won't appreciate it, that's all." He eyes each one of us, then looks back at Aggie.

We wait. I've always enjoyed those "downward spiral" tales of real-life corruption and dissipation you can see on cable TV—true crime stuff, rock stars gone bad. But as I stand there adding "bartering sexual favors for tips on how to be a more effective vigilante" to the list of things I now stoop to, those stories seem a whole lot less entertaining.

"Okay, okay. Deal." Simon takes a breath. "When I reach out to somebody's energy dimension, the second I sense something vile, for example . . . Wait, back up—" Thoughtful pause. "First you need a piece of understanding in place." He turns to me. "Why is my energy dimension so vile to you, Justine?" He waits. I have no answer, so he continues. "What is an energy dimension? And can it hurt you?" He pauses, looking at each of us. His whole disposition has changed with his decision to tell; for once he seems sincere. "An energy dimension can't hurt you," he says. "When you drew back in disgust from me, Justine, it wasn't to protect yourself from what's in me. You were protecting yourself from a vile, discarded, probably unknown part of yourself. That's the thing you need to understand to get my technique to work. Basic psychology one-oh-one. I'm not too horrible to you; I'm too *familiar*. You wouldn't be repulsed by me if you didn't resonate with me. Or if some disowned part of you didn't."

"Are you suggesting I resonate with the Alchemist? A rapist and a murderer? Is that what you're saying?"

Simon crosses his arms. "What happened when you touched his energy dimension?"

I think back. The feeling of a hole crawling with dark life. "I just sensed what was there and drew back. I didn't actually touch it."

"How very curious. You sensed what was there without even touching it."

"I'm not like the Alchemist."

"No, you're not a sadistic criminal, but you have things in common with the Alchemist. How else did you know what was in him? Did you touch his energy dimension before?" Simon places a cold fingertip on my chest. "You recognized it. The same thing happened when you tried to touch my energy dimension, as I knew it would. You can't recognize something you don't know."

"I believe I would recognize true love if it happened to me," Shelby says, "but it has not happened yet."

Carter says, "I like to think I'd recognize Bigfoot."

"Fuck off," Simon says. "I'm giving you my technique. My technique is valuable." He turns to me. "Have you ever gone swimming in Lake Michigan in spring? It's freezing. You dip a toe in, pull it out screaming. How do you get past that? Well, if you plunged in . . ."

"Plunge in?"

Simon smiles. "Instead of just touching it, you plunge in, hand first. When I sense a repellent energy dimension, I accept that it is only me that I feel, and that I have been to that place before. It's a mode of surrender. Throw down the walls. Let the monsters in, let the monsters out. I just surrender and plunge, with an attitude of total acceptance"—Simon places his hand upon his chest—"here." He screws up his lips and gets this distant look. *He's serious,* I think. *He's really done it.* "I love and accept it as part of me. I accept that every repellent target is me, and every vile energy dimension is my energy dimension, and I plunge. And you know when you do it right, because there's this—" He pauses, royal blue gaze into nothing. When he continues, it's in a whisper. "The otherness falls away. And you're deep inside. It's amazing."

Shelby regards him with horror.

"Spelunking, I like to call it," Simon says. "And then you burn the hole deep inside instead of on the surface. And zing the fuck out of them."

I'm stunned. "What if you can't pull out? Packard says if you go all the way inside you might not get out."

"And I'm here to tell you it's fine."

Carter squints. "You don't really go in."

"Yes, I do," Simon snaps. "I knew you wouldn't be up to it."

"That is a huge risk to take," I say.

Simon smiles. "Yes, it is."

My mouth hangs open. I've never met somebody who cares so little for his own well-being. It's here I realize that Simon probably won't live much longer. It makes me sad.

"Well?" Simon says. "You got your answer."

"Thank you, Simon. Thank you for telling."

He smiles. "And now for the entertainment portion of the evening."

I'm not eager to kiss him, but a disillusionist is good for her word. "Start the clock, Carter."

Simon looks into my eyes. "Where's Aggie?"

"Across the room," I say. "Behind you."

"Is she still watching us?"

"Yes."

He walks around and stands behind me so that we can both see the Silver Widow. He puts his hands on my shoulders and whispers into my ear. "Close your eyes, and don't open them until I tell you." I sigh and comply, and he wraps his arms around me from behind, around my stomach. "Smile, but not like you think anything's funny."

I smile, lips closed, and he kisses my cheek, just once, very lightly. "Now I'm whispering in your ear," he whispers in my ear. "Keep doing exactly what you're doing. She's watching, wondering what I could be saying to you. What could it be?"

"*That* was the big kiss?"

"I know you were probably hoping for something more involved."

"I'm just surprised," I whisper, eyes still closed.

"You've been spending too much time with Packard."

"Don't push it."

"Don't worry, baby, you're far too goody-goody to be my type," he says. "Now I'm looking up at the stairs. And now I'm looking at her. It's a good thing you can't see the way I'm looking at her. Oooh."

"You better not be too hard on her, Simon."

"Or what, ants'll eat my brain?"

"Maybe."

I hear Carter's voice, a whisper. "No, no, people. Sit back down."

My eyes are still closed. "What's happening?"

"Every single person on the couch by Aggie just stood up," Simon says. "Yes sir. Jacket going on . . ." I can feel his cheek press against my cheek, the puff of his smile.

About forty-five minutes later Carter, Shelby, and I are speeding back to town. All I want is to get home and climb into bed with my book; sometimes that takes my mind off my health enough to let me sleep. I'm determined to ride out this hypochondria episode the old-fashioned way until I zing Connor, and I most certainly will not be crawling to Packard to beg him to let me zing him in the meantime. No doubt he'd enjoy that. I surely wouldn't. I can hold out for a few more days—I'm not in the Jarvis danger zone yet.

Shelby hangs over the seat, smiling at me in the back. We all have IOUs from Simon. "Something to always remember," she says. "When Simon offers to bet, always say yes. Always yes."

"He came pretty close to winning," I say. "People were upset about the mayor—a lot of them were looking for an excuse to leave."

"Sure, maybe it looked bad for a while," Carter says, "but I knew somebody would try to stay behind. I wasn't worried, and I'll tell you why—Simon always loses. And that spelunking technique? You'd have to be insane to do that."

"What does it mean? Spelunking?" Shelby asks.

Carter says, "It's where you drop down in caves and explore."

"And sometimes you don't come back up," I say.

"Just a matter of time before it happens to Simon," Carter says. "Or worse. He thrives on loss and ruin. He's the ultimate loser."

We stop at a tollbooth; Carter hands the woman a ten and she gives him change. Just as he's pulling out, I notice a face in the sooty concrete above the little window—it's hard to tell for sure, but it looked like *the face*—the sign of Henji. "Shit," I say, staring back as the booth recedes into the distance.

"What?" Shelby asks.

I turn and give her a strong look. "I thought I saw a familiar face."

She raises her eyebrows. I nod minutely.

"See somebody you know?" Carter asks. "Need me to catch up to one of these cars?"

I shrug. "He's not the kind of guy we'd want to wave hello to," I say.

Chapter
Twenty

THE WEIRD FEELING in my temple is still there on Tuesday, and it's a struggle not to get it checked out. Having the power to zing out my fear doesn't mean I'm cured; it just means I have the unnatural ability to erase my fear, and fear is an essential part of survival. Fear is what causes people to take measures to protect and save themselves. From that point of view, I could be in more medical danger than ever before. What's more, not only are there intermittent tingles, but I've had a dull headache since Sunday, except for about fifteen minutes when I woke up this morning. That could be a really good sign or a really bad sign, depending on which medical explanation you want to go with. I keep thinking it's a bad sign. *Get through the next hour,* I keep telling myself. And then the next and the next, until tomorrow's card game where I'll zing the Alchemist.

Of course my failure to zing him at the last card game also continues to haunt me. He's dangerous and he needs to be stopped. I have to find a way to zing him. And not Simon's insane way, either.

My focus on zinging the Alchemist is so intense, it's been making me think I see him everywhere; I even think I see him disappearing around the end of the freezer aisle as I stand at the cheese counter, waiting for the cheese monger to slice me a tidbit of honey goat cheese.

"Here you go."

I take the little chunk and pop it into my mouth; it nearly melts on my tongue, all sweet and goaty. "Delicious!" It's also as expensive as gold, but what do I care? I'm a rich disillusionist. Richer than ever thanks to winning the bet with Simon the other night. I toss the cheese in my basket.

Shelby has been too busy the past few days to go back and inspect the face in the tollbooth—it's a ways out of town—but I'm eighty percent sure it was the sign of Henji. She was free today, but I'm busy helping Cubby throw the perfect dinner party. In fact, as I cheerfully informed him, I'll be handling the entire dinner aspect of it, plus cleanup. It's my way of making up for forgetting our date on Friday. He's been less talkative on the phone the past few days—a bad sign. I cannot lose him. I won't.

This dinner is a sort of "welcome to the condo" dinner for his mysterious new upstairs neighbor, possibly her boyfriend, and the couple from across the hall. I told Cubby I'd head to his place before he gets home from work to start the cooking. He loves to come home to cooking.

I rub my temple gently, just enough to relax the surrounding musculature, as I deliberate over olives at the olive bar. Eventually I settle on some briny olives as a counterpoint to the sweet cheese and crackers. For the main course I'm doing a seafood orzo with a sesame asparagus side, Moroccan salad, and several expensive bottles of Shiraz. Cubby doesn't need to know how much all this costs or how much work it will be; he just needs to enjoy the sumptuous deliciousness of it. The dress I'm planning to wear is less formal but just as sexy as the one I wore to the Silver Widow's cocktail party. I grab a tube of double chocolate chunk cookie dough— dessert, or maybe a tiny treat while I'm making the meal—and take my place in one of the annoyingly long checkout lines.

A voice behind me. "Justine?"

I spin around and nearly jump out of my shoes. The Alchemist. Standing right behind me, bright eyes and bushy pubic-hair soul patch.

"Wow," he says. "What a surprise. I didn't know you shopped here." A bag of apples dangles from his fingers.

"Connor. My goodness."

"Got yourself a big night in the works." There's something weird about the way he says this, and maybe my face shows it because he nods at my cart.

"Oh," I say. "Neighborly function." I think about trying to zing him—I have enough fear stoked for it—but I don't dare. The waves of nervousness coming off him scare me.

"Going to sheepshead tomorrow night?" he asks.

"Yeah." I smile blandly. "You?"

"I certainly am."

Awkward silence. I inspect the front of the *Midcity Eagle,* which is all about Mayor Templeton's funeral, and lower my voice. "The cashier is going slow."

"Maybe she has aplastic spindler neuroma. Ever consider that?" His tone is accusatory.

My heart's nearly pounding out of my chest because I just now realized that Connor has only one item, and the express lane is open, but he chose my line instead, then acted surprised to see me. And that wired energy coming off him. I continue my newspaper inspection, praying for the line to move. Finally I get up to the front. The cashier takes forever to ring me up.

"See ya," I say to Connor as I'm stuffing my change into my purse. The bagger repositions my crackers and things. "It's fine." I grab both bags and head off.

"Hold up!" Connor's next to me. Without his apples. "Need some help?"

"I got it." I focus on the exit. "See you tomorrow."

"I insist. You've got some heavy stuff in there."

"No thanks," I say firmly as the doors squeech open.

"Well at least let me walk you to your car. This isn't the best of neighborhoods."

I see I won't be getting rid of him.

"Well, okay then." I hand him both bags of groceries. He looks surprised. "Thanks," I say.

The point here is that my hands are free and his aren't. More to the point, one of my hands is in my purse on my stun gun. We get to my Jetta and I open the back door and stand away, watching him place the bags. It's weird, the line between politeness and protection. Am I paranoid to have my hand on my stun gun? Or am I crazy not to have zapped him by now? I'm tending toward the latter when he turns around and grips my upper arms; I feel this pinprick on my right triceps, followed by the sensation of spreading sourness.

"Hey!" I pull out my weapon, but I can't work my fingers, like they're not attached to my brain.

"Fuck!" Connor twists it out of my grasp. "Where'd you get this? Fuck, I thought it would be pepper spray." He slaps it onto the top of the Hummer next to my little car as this bright, lazy feeling engulfs me. After that, I recollect only sounds. A door clicking. The throaty pull and rip of tape.

Chapter
Twenty-one

I REGAIN CONSCIOUSNESS, if you can call it that, when I realize somebody's twisting my arm in a way it's not supposed to go. My mind is sluggish, and my eyelids feel too heavy to open, but I realize two things: I'm naked, and somebody is dressing me. And that somebody doesn't have a lot of experience with dolls. Because when you grow up dressing dolls, you understand that arms only go a certain way, and no amount of swearing or muttering will change that. This thought amuses me greatly.

I experience bouts of fuzzy awareness after that. Musty smell. Later, painful wrists. Still later, cold legs and toes.

I have no idea if these moments occur minutes or hours apart, but eventually I come to enough to actually open my eyes. I see a pine-paneled ceiling and knotty pine walls with snowshoes and rifles as decorations. I establish that I'm alone in a bedroom, but everything seems distant and pleasant. Even just staring at the ceiling is vaguely delightful. At least it is until it comes to my attention that I've been drugged by the Alchemist and tied to a bed. I tilt back my head and observe that my wrists are bound with a combination of duct tape and rope, and connected to a metal bed frame above my head. My ankles are tied together in the same fashion, and connected to the frame at the foot.

This is bad, I think, but it actually seems more surreal than bad. I lift my head, commanding myself to make serious observations. A room, dimly lit by a floor lamp. A long pine dresser and mirror across from the bed. A window above the dresser, which provides a view of a black sky with unusually bright stars. A thought comes, but I lose its trail. I relax, hoping the thought will come back. There's a sound of crunching in the next room.

Get with it! I force my mind back into pursuit of the thought, but it's difficult, like fighting my way through a pool full of lotion. Yes, dark sky with more bright stars than I usually see. I'm not near Midcity; I'm in the far suburbs, or possibly even the country. I smile, proud to have reached a conclusion, and I take a break just to lie there and float. I jerk my head up when I remember I'm missing Cubby's dinner party, and I was the one in charge of the dinner. And then it comes to me again that the Alchemist drugged me. He changed my clothes, too.

I inspect my new outfit. It's some sort of minidress, white with a red stripe around the bottom of the skirt and the sleeves. I realize here that I'm in an old-fashioned nurse's uniform, or more like nurse getup from a sexy costume shop. The thing on my head would be a nurse's hat. Is this guy kidding? It's such a fucked-up thing to do I just start laughing. I press my lips together to stop myself, but that makes me snort really loud.

What's wrong with me? I think about what Enrique said, that the Alchemist makes his own drug cocktails. Is it possible he accidentally went too heavy on some hilarity-producing ingredient? Surely this couldn't be the effect he was going for. It certainly isn't the effect I'd prefer in this situation. Of everything I have read on dealing with sexual predators, none mentioned laughter as an intelligent defense.

This is serious, I think, trying to pull myself together.

Obviously he has more in mind than a fashion makeover.

"About time." The Alchemist is in the doorway eating Ruffles. "What's so funny?"

"Nothing," I say quickly.

He narrows his eyes, twisting a rubber band around the bag for freshness; then he tosses it onto the bureau and comes over.

"Nothing at all," I whisper, trying not to laugh. The fact that I shouldn't laugh makes it downright hilarious.

"Yeah, well I'm gonna wipe that smile off your face."

I so wish he hadn't said that. I bite the inside of my lip in an effort not to crack up. My eyes are actually tearing. The Alchemist seems satisfied with this.

"My hunting cabin. What d'ya think?"

I don't trust myself to answer this question.

He smiles. "What's wrong? Don't you like being put in that outfit?"

I clear my throat and furrow my forehead. "You need to untie me."

"No can do."

I try hard to look serious. He commences, slowly, to unbutton his shirt. This is disturbing enough that my hilarity fades, and I'm just in a drug haze. I watch, dully, the way I'd imagine a starfish on the ocean floor might watch a swimmer up above. The mysterious mechanics of the world. Everything soft and unreal.

The next moment I'm disgusted with myself. *Pull it together!* I decide on a plan: I'll get my phone out of my purse and hit the panic sequence. And somehow ward Connor off until the closest disillusionist rescues me. Strongarm Francis has said he and the nearest disillusionists would come running anytime I punched in the sequence. Okay.

Next, I fix on my disillusionist training: concentrate, observe, think. I multiply the number fourteen by random factors: $14 \times 9 = 126$; $14 \times 11 = 154$; $14 \times 8 = 112$. I'm surprised how this kicks me into a mode of concentration, how my focusing power comes online like a strong, lean muscle.

Connor has stripped down to colorful nylon workout pants with pink and green tiger stripes. *The pants are not funny,* I tell myself. *They are not funny at all.* The next thing I know, he's turning a large knife in the light, seemingly fascinated by his ability to make a mirror spot move around on the wall. Thanks to the drugs, I, too, find this fascinating. Though probably not in the way he wants me to.

"Where is my purse?" I ask.

He goes to the corner of the room and lifts it high so I can see it. "This? You want this?"

Yes, I think. Yes, indeed I do.

"Or maybe you just want me to give this back to you." He pulls out my stun gun.

That would be ideal, I think.

He puts the stun gun down, and suddenly he has a hammer. I'm expecting him to smash it, but instead he pounds some nails into the wall under where the rifles hang. Is he changing the decor now? The activity seems inappropriate, given our current situation. Then he rests the stun gun on the nails under two rifles. Rifle, rifle, stun gun. He steps back and laughs at his visual joke. I laugh, too—perhaps too long and hard, because suddenly Connor's on top of me, straddling my hips, him and his crazy pants and his hunting knife. "Shut up!"

His weight makes my shoulders practically stretch out of their sockets. "I'm sorry." I reduce my laughter to snorkles, and then snuffles, and then I just hold my breath. I don't want to be laughing. I focus on the little crusties at the inner edges of his eyes.

"I'm telling you, I'll wipe that smile right off your face."

It's with a Herculean effort that I hold my breath. "I

swear, I'm trying not to laugh," I say. "God, what did you give me?"

He glares. Jolliness was clearly not the effect he was after. "What I gave you is something that worked just fine. Because you're down there, and I'm up here, and I guarantee you this—you won't be laughing when you discover what I have in store for you."

This statement baffles me, because it seems so obvious what he has in store. I try my best to look bewildered.

"You think this is funny?" He presses the tip of the big knife on the center of my chest, above the top button. It feels like a pin, piercing my skin, and everything is far away, as though I'm looking through the wrong end of a telescope.

"No! I don't think it's funny." This becomes all the more true when I notice the grime and dried blood on the blade. It's a hunting knife—the kind he would use for skinning dead animals. No doubt it's full of bacteria. And he's so heavy on me, it's hard to breathe. Is he collapsing my lungs? And what about my head? The pain in my temple is back. Shit!

Focus, I tell myself.

"First, we're going to talk about ASN," he announces.

Aplastic spindlers neuroma? He wants to talk about *aplastic spindlers neuroma*? I tilt my head and try to look serious. Focusing on the bacteria-laden knife helps me.

He continues. "They say a neurologist can tell a case of muscular weakness associated with ASN the minute an ASN patient walks through the door." I tense as he turns the knife. "Was that why you were talking about it so much at the game? Was it something about how I walk that triggered it?" He presses the knife down harder on my breastbone.

I feel a tickle of blood heading sideways over my rib cage.

"And don't you fuck with me."

I close my eyes. There's a smart way to answer, but I'm too muzzy-minded to figure it out. My stomach knots up as I realize I won't be getting to my phone.

"Are you experiencing muscle weakness?" I ask. Muscle weakness is a major sign of ASN. He would know this.

"I'm asking the questions here. Yes or no? Did something about my walking make you think of ASN?"

This must be his plan, I think. Some interaction with me as a nurse, and then rape and murder, or murder and rape. "I was just making conversation."

I can't stop thinking about that bacteria-laden knife. He's already scratched my skin with it, which is enough to transmit most any pathogen directly into my bloodstream. It comes to me that some deer carry encephalitis, which causes an acute inflammation of the brain. I can't think of a worse disease to combine with vein star syndrome. Feverishly, I picture the pathogens entering my veins. Already I feel a weird warmth in my chest under where the knife pricked. My wildly beating heart could be spreading the pathogens through my body this very moment, setting up the perfect storm of cranial maladies.

"You weren't just making conversation," he says. "I don't know what you were doing, but that wasn't conversation."

How long does it take for the virus to engage? Encephalitis starts with a headache, and probably head sensations, too, which means I won't even be able to tell if I have it.

I take a breath. This is not the time for a hypochondria freak-out. I focus, instead, on the one silver lining here: I have more than enough of the right kind of fear stoked to zing him into oblivion. But it doesn't matter, because I would need my arm free to zing him. And I can't touch his energy dimension anyway.

Connor leans forward, resting his free hand on the bed next to my rib cage. He has chosen this moment to pose a crazy, potato chip–breath question: "My feet are very sore today. Can you guess why?"

I gape at him with what hopefully looks like shock and horror. I concentrate on my legs, now prickly from sleep, and my shoulders, which are beyond pain, and the fact that a pathogen-laden knife is piercing my skin. "Hold on, okay?" I clear my throat. "My guess would be meaningless without more information."

"Fuck you! I'll tell you why, because of that stupid fucking story you told about your ASN patient, and it made me unduly aware of some muscular weakness in my ankles. So I walked on my heels all day yesterday to test it. Now my feet hurt like hell. And they're weak."

I contort my face as I attempt to wipe this image from my mind.

"But that would be natural for anybody's feet after a day like that. A person *without* ASN would have sore feet after a day like that, wouldn't they?"

I'm awash in too many possibilities of how to answer. Would a sympathetic nurse buy time? Or would a stern nurse be better? I would know the answer if I weren't so drugged up. The Alchemist presses the knife down. "It's not a symptom of ASN to have sore feet after walking on your heels, is it?"

I hold my breath.

"Because I don't have ASN, do I? And you know it."

There it is.

I close my eyes, feeling something like gratitude as the complexity flows away. The Alchemist wants what any hypochondriac wants: for the disease to be ruled out. That's his Holy Grail. It's the Holy Grail for all of us. But once I rule it out, I'm done. My Scheherezade moment, I think.

I swallow. I cannot laugh and mess this up. "How long did you walk on your heels?"

"Don't fuck with me!"

"I need to know. How long and how far?"

"No, this is a trick. I don't know why I'm even asking you. You'll say anything."

I shift under him, trying to relieve pressure from my painfully prickly right leg. "Listen here, and listen good." I'm going for stern nurse. "You can take away my freedom, you can change my outfit, but you will never, *never* take away my dedication to my profession."

He seems to be considering this. "If you fuck with me . . ."

I wait, trying my best to look stern during the long silence.

"Fine," he says. "I walked around the house on my heels for maybe an hour straight. I even made breakfast on my heels. It would cause pain the next day to anybody, right?"

I try to look thoughtful, wishing fervently he hadn't included the detail about making breakfast on his heels.

"What?" he demands. "Why are you making that face?"

"I'm sorry, nothing. You work out, right?"

He nods.

"Did you experience muscle weakness before I said that stuff at the card game?" I'm reasonably confident that he won't recall.

"I think it started before that . . . nah, it's just my imagination." He shifts his weight in a way that makes him heavier. "ASN is just my imagination."

I fight to retain my focus. "You experienced some muscle weakness and toe numbness, that's what I'm hearing."

"Shut up. I know I don't have ASN."

I'm losing him. "Do you know the difference between *perceived* muscle weakness and *clinical* weakness?"

"Don't know, and don't care."

"It'll help you in the future, as a sort of reference point. *Perceived* weakness is a rubbery feeling, and it can have good days and bad days. *Clinical* weakness comes from the muscle tissue and the nerve endings dying, and that sort of weakness doesn't have good or bad days." I'm supplying him with a negative visualization here. "The point is to learn to tell those things apart. Clinical weakness will get so bad that eventually you can't unscrew lids or even hold a glass. You say you had no problem walking on your heels . . . until the next day . . ." I look away. "Have you noticed any muscle twitching?"

"Muscle twitches can be a lot of things."

I take this as a yes. I'm getting clearer, thanks to my concentration abilities—and to that pathogenic knife. "Regular twitches are fatigue. ASN twitches are caused by dying muscle tissue. Your twitches—do they feel more like dying nerves, or more like fatigue?" The thing here is that twitches never feel like fatigue, even though that's what they are. He furrows his brow; he's worried again, but it's not enough. I need to zing him. It's here I get my brain flash. "Have you been tested for Sargasso's sign?"

He narrows his eyes. "I know I've heard of that."

"It's an abnormal toe reflex that indicates motor neuron damage. Get somebody to do it for you. It's when the small toe extends and points sideways as the ball of the foot is stimulated. This would be your indicator to rule it out."

"Sargasso's sign rules it out?"

"If the toe doesn't respond that way, yeah, we can pretty much rule out ASN."

He regards me warily; then he slides off me and sits

next to me on the bed, legs straight in front of him. I try not to show my relief as the blood flows back into my limbs. He bends forward and pokes at the ball of his right foot with a pen. "Like this?"

"You can't do it to yourself."

"You're just trying to get me to untie you."

"No, I'm telling you what's what. I'm being helpful."

"Yeah, to help yourself right out of here."

I move my limbs to get the blood back into them.

"Sargasso's test. You've performed it?"

I ignore him and practice this focus exercise Packard taught me where you retract your awareness away from everything and imagine your mind in a tiny box, and then you expand it back out. I need to have total focus here.

"What would you do?"

I keep on doing the exercise. Plus, I don't want to seem too eager to do the test.

He grabs my face by my cheeks. "Answer me!"

"Ow," I say. "Fine. I would have you lie down and relax your muscles, and I'd need one hand free to poke specific reflex points on the balls of your feet."

"You just want me to untie you."

I look at him like he's crazy—a look I perfected in high school. "One hand. What do you think I'd do? Honestly, one hand? I can barely focus thanks to your drugs, and you have the knife. But fine. Why should I give a crap? I'm sure you'll get your diagnosis soon enough."

Minutes later he's lying in bed next to me, the opposite way, angled so his head is at the far corner and his feet are near my shoulders. Three of my limbs are still attached to the bed frame, but I have a hand, and that's all I need. Now I just have to touch his repellent energy dimension.

His toenails are dreadfully long. "Hold on." I touch his right ankle.

He jerks away. "What are you doing?"

"Positioning and palpating your ankles. That would also help us rule this ASN business out." Now I'm going for stern yet motherly nurse.

"You'll be sorry if you're fucking with me." He gives me back his ankles, sitting, watching me. I grasp one and try to push out to his energy dimension, only to recoil. Damn!

I think about Simon's technique of plunging in with total acceptance.

I can't. It's too dangerous, too horrible.

Steeling myself, I push my awareness out slowly, the old way. Nausea. Repulsion. I'm running out of time, and I'm getting tired of fighting the urge to laugh.

"What are you doing?" he asks.

"You have to lie back," I manage to say. "You're using your ankle muscles to stabilize yourself, and it's obscuring your true musculature." He complies, and I move my hand to his other ankle. "Stay still. This might be good news."

"Hurry up."

"I need to position your feet."

Again I consider Simon's trick. What if I spelunked into his energy dimension and couldn't climb back out, like Packard warned? But really, what do I have to lose now?

I take a deep breath. *You've been here; you know him,* I tell myself. *Surrender!* I squeeze my eyes shut tight and let go—every muscle, every thought. I just surrender and open my heart.

And suddenly, whoosh! The otherness of him drops away; it's like the earth falls out from under me, all my points of reference gone. I'm falling into him, and it's the easiest thing in the world. I find myself surrounded by his need and fear, even shame. But it's not awful, just crowded; it's like a reunion of the old and the familiar, and I'm conscious of tears in my eyes. It's just me, all me. I get a hit of the hopelessness with which he wakes up in the morning, and the way he experiences rain and wind, and the way women upset and frighten him. I'm getting disoriented, panicky, unsure where he ends and I begin.

Burn the hole, I think, reducing my focus to an image of a fingertip deep inside him. I focus, focus, focus, and burn, and the hole opens, and this immense heat and darkness rushes out of me, on and on—there's so much of it. He stiffens as my fear floods him; I feel it around me, heating my core. I'm in him, but not of him, I realize. I have only a vague sense of which way is out, and before I get a chance to panic, I throw all my trust to my instincts and rush in that direction.

I know the instant I clear him. I'm alone again—with a breezy finger feeling and a cool, calm head—energized and peaceful at the same time. Even a little sparkly.

Connor's eyes are wide open. "What—?" he whispers, unable to formulate a question. He plops his head back. I wouldn't say he's out, more in a kind of stupor, eyes closed, breath uneven. Did the drug charge pass through the zing? I'm thinking it did, because I'm perfectly alert.

He's also relaxed his grip on the knife, but it's too far for me to reach. I don't have much time. I grip the bed sheet and jerk it toward myself, and the knife hops a little. Not helpful. Another tug jumps the knife closer. I'm rousing him, but I need that knife. I tug and pull, and once it's close enough, I stretch, nearly dislocating my shoulder to grab it.

Quickly I slice the rope that connects my hand to the bed frame and then the rope that goes from my ankles to the bar at the foot of the bed.

Just as I'm scooting off, he comes to life and grabs the end of the rope that still binds my ankles together and pulls. I try to kick him away, but he won't let go, so I roll toward him and I stab his forearm—once, then again as he grabs at me. Blood. He lets go, surprised. I scramble off the bed, hop backward. He's pulling himself up.

"Don't you move," I yell, like I'm in command. Though I'm not confident I can take him, even with a hunting blade. Especially with my feet still bound together.

He regards me with glassy eyes. Fear eyes, like an old man. He's experiencing inexplicable waves of fear—my fear—and it makes him hesitate long enough for me to grab my stun gun off the wall and pump him with enough electricity to light a carnival. He crumples onto the bed. His breathing goes jerky, then calms.

Quickly I cut the ropes off my ankles and rip the last bits of fibrous tape from my wrists. Now that I've zinged all my fear into him, I feel like a glorious giant. The urge to laugh is gone, too. I grab my phone and activate the GPS function, one eye on Connor. Now the closest disillusionist—or disillusionists—will come. Plus Strongarm Francis. I have a feeling it'll be a while.

I find Connor's rope and duct tape, and feverishly bind him up—tape, rope, and more tape, just as he did me. No use reinventing the wheel. His arm's still bleeding; I hadn't meant to hurt him so much. I bandage it expertly with a ripped piece of bed sheet and duct tape. A real nurse couldn't have done better.

I can't believe how excellent I feel for what I just went through, like I'm humming at a higher mode than usual. I wouldn't be surprised if I could fly, or lift up a car. I shouldn't feel this good, but of course I zinged out an unheard-of amount of fear and darkness.

My eyes fall on a pile of familiar-looking material. My clothes! I'm excited, but when I go over, I discover that they're in shreds, like he cut them right off me. Even my panties. Even my jeans! Creep.

I do find a costume box with the rest of the nurse's outfit inside—old-fashioned white stockings with a seam running up the back, ruffly panties, white high-heeled shoes, and even a fake stethoscope. Just like a man to ignore the accessories. I discard the stethoscope, but I put on the rest of the stuff; then I examine myself in the mirror. My long dark hair glows in the lamplight, and my eyes shine. The nurse's hat is crooked, so I unpin it, reposition it on the top of my head, and fasten it in place. Then I wet a finger and clean a blood spot off my cheek. The dress is pretty bloody, but that seems appropriate for a nurse's dress. And a nurse's dress is appropriate for the job I have to finish here. I turn to the Alchemist.

"What is it?" he asks, eyes half-open.

"What is what?" I ask.

Fear eyes. He jerks against his restraints in explosive movements, rocking the bed and the frame. If the bed collapses, he might get free. I didn't think of that when I was tied up. I grab the stun gun, but my knots seem to be holding, and eventually he stops. I go to sit on the bed next to him and he jerks around some more, trying to scare me, but I know he can't get me now.

"Tell me," he says.

"Where are we, Connor? Are we out by Branlock?" I always hear of people having hunting cabins in Branlock.

"Surrey Springs."

Surrey Springs is a rural area maybe an hour north of Midcity, maybe thirty miles from where I grew up. We played them in high school. I look over at my phone, thinking about calling Cubby or Packard, but I don't want to divert power from the GPS beacon function. Or does that not matter? I wish Francis had explained things better.

"Tell me about the Sargasso test," he says. "Was it muscle atrophy or not?"

Ominous sigh. "We'll need to run more tests to say conclusively whether it's ASN. It wouldn't be my place as a nurse to make that diagnosis."

"What diagnosis?" He jerks his arms. "Did the Sargasso's test indicate ASN?"

"It wouldn't be proper for me to say for certain." Every hypochondriac knows this is just a pernicious form of yes. He looks pale. "Don't worry," I say. "If it's ASN, there are palliative measures that can be taken."

"Palliative?"

"That's right." This is what the nurse in an old vein star article had said. I hated her for it.

"Hell if I'm going to any doctor." He pulls and jerks again. One of the ropes looks longer. Is a knot loosening?

"You understand why you need to be restrained, don't you? You tried to attack me. You need to relax."

"What if the ropes make my muscles atrophy more?"

"Atrophy is an internal process, not external." I sit up on the bed next to him and lean back against the metal bars of the frame. I have to finish destabilizing him tonight. "Connor, have you experienced any weirdness swallowing? New sensations?"

He calms down and swallows a few times, which is exactly what I wanted him to do. Most anybody will detect swallowing weirdness if they concentrate on swallowing. That's because swallowing is a bizarre, snakelike thing we do. We discuss his swallowing as only two hypochondriacs can.

"You gonna call the cops?" he asks at one point.

I shake my head. "I don't think that will be necessary. You're under enough of a sentence already." He regards me with a mixture of horror and trust. It's the way Aggie used to look at me whenever I'd tell her a new Osiris virus detail. Connor's bonded to me, thanks to the zing; he finds me inexplicably familiar because it's my fear he feels. Maybe the spelunk-zing magnified it.

He feels familiar to me, too, like a song I've heard a million times. Because I was so deep inside him.

I try not to think about what would've happened if I hadn't gotten out. Instead we discuss swallowing, and some minor aspects of ASN. Now and then he looks away from me as we talk, expression hopeless, tears pushing out from the corners of his eyes. I feel bad for him. It's monstrous, what he tried to do to me, but I understand the pain he's in now. Our conversation drops off and we sit in silence for a while. I watch the cloud-shadow of sleep pass over him, remembering how it was when I had health worries: sleep was the only time I'd forget.

When I'm sure he's out, I reach down and touch his hair. I want to get away from him, but I can't stop remembering the things I sensed when I was inside him, the ways we're alike. We're both monstrous. That's what I'm thinking as I touch his hair and watch him sleep, stunned how different yet alike we are.

A voice: "My goodness, Nurse Jones." I look up, startled. Simon's in the doorway, leaning against the frame, smiling.

No doubt I'm quite the sight in my bloody, sexy nurse's outfit, sitting on a bed next to a tied-up, taped-up target. "Oh, please." I collect my purse, my phone, and my stun gun and walk around the bed.

Simon's smile reaches deep into his dark blue eyes. He has a long face and delicate features for a man.

I grab the sleeve of his black jacket and pull him into the outer room.

"What the fuck are you wearing? You look insane," he says.

"This? This is the creepy outfit the Alchemist put me in after he kidnapped me."

Simon stops smiling. "Are you okay?"

"Yeah."

He looks at me searchingly.

"I'm okay. Nothing happened. You know, nothing like that." I give him a rundown of what did happen. "Anyway, I bet he's ready to drink with Jay now. And I need to get back to town."

"Nice work."

"Don't be impressed."

He smirks. He'll be impressed if he wants to be.

"Simon," I touch his arm. "Your spelunking trick saved me."

"You did it?"

"Yeah. Thank you for taking the time to explain that whole thing. I know you didn't want to tell, but you told it honestly."

"I can't believe you did it!"

"If I didn't, I'd be where he is right now. Worse."

"Glad to be of service." He takes out his phone. "Let's see if Jay's sober enough to drive himself out here."

The new plan is for Jay to come and untie Connor, and start the debauchery phase of destabilization.

It turns out Simon was at a casino a ways west, which is how he got to me so quickly. I take out my phone and think about calling Cubby while Simon calls Francis and Vesuvius, who are apparently racing down from the city, to tell them to turn back, and then he calls Packard with a quick A-OK.

I hit Cubby's number. No answer. It's nine-thirty—over six hours since I left the supermarket. Is he out looking for me? "Cubby," I say to his voice mail, "I'm okay. I had a slight ordeal, but I'm okay and I'm on my way back. I'm so sorry—I know you were probably worried, but I'll be back soon—" Simon holds up a finger. I sigh. "Okay, we're an hour away still." I mumble some lame sentiment about explaining everything.

I listen to two out of three *Where are you?* messages

from Cubby before my phone runs out of juice. I stare at the flashing empty battery image, unable to decide if he sounded angry or worried on that last message. "I have to get back there fast."

Simon goes into the bedroom to check my knots, and then we're off.

Chapter
Twenty-two

"HE WAS ASKING to see you," Simon tells me as we bump down a dirt road in his old white Camaro.

"Packard?"

"The Alchemist. Jay'll have him drinking for three days straight." He gives me a look. "You thought I meant Packard?"

"I didn't know who you meant."

Simon studies my face. "I heard about your lovers' quarrel."

"We're not lovers. Never were. Never will be."

He raises his eyebrows.

"Yeah, we kissed once, okay? Something I considered a mistake at the time, but when I found out the truth about what I got myself into here . . ." I shake my head. "I wish I never had to look at his face again. And I promise you, I won't be his minion for much longer, either."

Simon smirks.

"I'm serious." I hang my arm out the window, resting my fingertips on the car body, still warm from the day, even now in the evening chill. The glory of glory hour fades a little every time I think about what happened and what almost happened. "I'm getting out of this."

He looks over at me. "You sure you're okay?"

"I'm feeling a lot better than I should, considering

what I went through. It seems like I should be way more upset."

"Not necessarily. You zinged all your darkness into the Alchemist, including the trauma of being kidnapped, drugged, and manhandled. If anyone's feeling the brunt of it, it's him. And hey, you're a disillusionist now. The darkness of human nature is your territory."

"Just what I always dreamed of." I stare out the window as we turn onto a paved two-lane road. Big, bright moon. Patches of forest, patches of farm. Broken-down trucks in waist-high weeds. "Cubby's going to be so upset. He was having this dinner party, and I was making the dinner, and I need to get back there and make things right." I imagine myself in the plush coziness of Cubby's condo, warm and safe in his arms. "I have to get back there."

We drive in silence past moonlit fields and crumbly stone silos, eventually getting stuck behind an RV. Simon complains, but I'm not listening. I'm thinking about my dad, just a few towns over, holed up like a hermit. I should visit more. He can't help that he's scared.

"So how'd you like it?" he asks. "Spelunking like that?"

"Creepily intimate," I say. "Touching a person's energy dimension in order to zing them is one thing, but invading like that?"

"We're like reverse emotional vampires."

"I prefer the term *crime fighter*."

Simon snickers.

"I'm not joking," I say. "The stuff we're doing is directly helping Chief Sanchez make the city safe."

Simon turns to me. "I bet you haven't heard the big news."

"What?"

"The Brick Slinger's finished."

"Caught?"

"Dead. Just this afternoon. He was slinging bricks at a schoolyard, and Chief Sanchez was driving by. Sanchez sees what's happening and susses out who it is, and he just jumps out of his car, leaving his assistant and driver in the middle of an intersection, and chases the guy on foot. A few other guys join the chase, but the Slinger is slinging all sorts of shit back at them. The guys lose their nerve, but Sanchez keeps running and dodging. They turn into this alley, and Sanchez shoots him in the knee and the stomach. Guess Sanchez was about to read him his rights when this cinder block from way up high falls down and crushes ol' Slinger's head."

"Are you serious?"

"Obviously it was the Brick Slinger killing himself. Rather be dead than be taken in. Officially it was a freak accident, but this old woman saw the whole thing from a doorway. She's been on the news shows yakking it up."

"Wow, that is so brave," I say. "That is just so amazing. Sanchez put himself in a ton of danger to get that guy."

Simon rolls his eyes.

"And the Brick Slinger's finally off the streets."

"Most of him is," Simon says.

I give him a dirty look. "Are the kids in the schoolyard okay?"

"Little girl's in a coma."

I sigh. We drive on in silence. I'm more in awe of Chief Sanchez than ever, and I'm not feeling upset that the Brick Slinger killed himself; it would be hard to hold a guy like that in prison. He would've probably joined the ranks of Midcity Pen escapees in no time.

"Fuck, I could run faster than this," Simon says.

I stare at the back of the RV, hoping his gambling streak won't extend to trying to pass it blind.

"Hey, don't tell Packard about spelunking," Simon says. "He won't like it. He wants everybody under his thumb doing everything his way."

"You got that right," I say.

We roll by craggy trees, an abandoned shack, a little crossroads with some decrepit buildings. Beyond the crossroads stands a boarded-up gas station, looking like a lonely box in a moonlit expanse of weedy concrete. When our headlights hit the broad wall of the station, a familiar face, seemingly etched in the side, appears and disappears.

I gasp. "Holy crap! Pull over."

Simon guides the car off the road, a bit past the gas station. "Are you going to be sick?"

I instruct him to back up on the shoulder. He protests, but I insist. "A little more, stop—no, a couple feet more." And then it's visible again: the face in exquisite detail, etched so you can only see it when the headlights hit it at a certain angle. The big long beard with the upturned curl at the end, wavy curls tumbling down over his shoulders, just like on the Mongolian Delites door and the apartment building.

"Fuck!" Simon says.

I realize only now how stupid it was to let him see this.

"Fuck!" he says. "The face. Of course! Duh." He pulls into the parking lot of the ghost gas station.

"What are you doing?"

"We're going to investigate."

"We can't go in there!"

"Wanna bet?" He gets out. Reluctantly I follow. He opens the trunk, grabs a flashlight and a screwdriver. Of course he's read the highcap-watcher wikis and websites. "You know what this is, right? The fingerprint of the nemesis. Shit! All this time, I thought it was that brick pattern around Delites' windows."

How could I have been so stupid? I don't want somebody as reckless as Simon to know about Henji. "It could be dangerous," I say.

"Amazing you noticed this face at all. This is the sort of thing folks driving by every day of their lives wouldn't notice." He regards me suspiciously.

"I'm coming off glory hour," I remind him. "I just zinged the hell out of a guy while *spelunking* him. And you're wondering why I'm hyperobservant?"

He can tell I'm holding something back, but he says nothing. Up close, the exterior of the gas station appears to be encrusted with pebbles. I hold the light while he runs his hand over the indents and etches that make the face. "This face is likely a character from history or literature, or an archetype," he says.

"I think he looks Renaissance. A warrior or a king," I say.

"I think he looks like a guy with a role-playing-game fetish who never shaves or comes out of his parents' basement."

"Not at all," I say, feeling weirdly protective. "Let's get out of here."

"Are you crazy?" He heads around the back of the building, where the moon illuminates boarded-up windows and doors, all set into the pebbly walls. Behind us, a patch of weeds gives way to a tree-covered hill stretching up into the darkness.

"Hello? Anyone home?" Simon knocks on a window board.

I grab his arm. "What if somebody dangerous is trapped in here?"

"You think the nemesis has other prisoners? That's interesting." He jerks his arm out of my grip. "And all the more reason to go in. You can wait in the car or you can stay here, but you won't stop me. Packard wouldn't be keeping all these secrets about what happened and who this nemesis is if that knowledge wasn't important and valuable."

"What if you make the nemesis mad and he seals Packard away where we can't find him? What if he kills him?"

"That's a risk I'm willing to take."

"I'm not. I won't let you ruin everything." My stun gun's in my purse in the car, but Simon won't know that. I'm imagining scenarios of knocking Simon out, and tying him up and preventing him from locating Henji.

He eyes me, evaluating. Does he think I can stop him? Can I?

"Think about it," he says. "If we knew Packard's secrets, knew this nemesis, that would give us the power to make trouble for him."

I wait.

"He has a godlike control over our existences. If he even ignores us, we end up in diapers and drool-covered shirts. Don't you want to be able to push him around a little? You know you want to. Anyway, you're not going to stop me. One of us brought our weapon out here, and it wasn't you."

"You wouldn't."

He looks amused. He would. I see now I won't stop him. And he sees that I see.

He peels off his leather jacket. "Hold this." I put it around my shoulders and watch him wedge the screwdriver under a corner. "I love being a disillusionist," he says. "I'm just tired of being pushed around. Same as you."

He goes at a different corner, looking like a lanky cat burglar with his black shirt and black pants, black hair falling over his dark eyes. "Nice work on Aggie, by the way." He runs his fingers around the board. "That's some freaky skin condition, Nurse Jones."

I feel a wave of shame for what I did to her. "I'm not proud of making her feel bad."

"I'm sure it's nothing compared to how bad the mister felt, watching ants carry off bits of his brain. The state executes people for that kind of thing, and we're giving her a change of heart."

"Where is she tonight?"

"Some dinner party with people I don't know. She wanted me along, but what do I want with that? I made up an excuse, lucky for you."

"Dinner party, huh?" Out of nowhere, I get this twinge of dread in my gut. But dread is only natural for the night I'm having.

"It won't be long now—she's already running out of funds," he continues.

"Seriously, Simon, I don't want to be Packard's groveling minion, but I'll take it over being a vegetable."

"Oh, stop whining." He moves to a door, running his fingers along the boards. Finally he picks up a hunk of concrete and smashes the knob. The door swings open.

He grabs the light from me and heads in. I wait for something to fly at him. Nothing. I follow. The inside looks more like a sad, cobwebby home than a gas station. The flashlight beam illuminates a couch, a cot, tin cans. I flip on a switch. Light.

"Yow. There we go." Simon clicks off the flashlight. The place is even dingier in the brightness. "Looks like nobody's been in here for years."

My gaze falls on something white on the floor in the corner. "Simon!" I grab his sleeve and point. It's a skull, along with bones—a disordered skeleton with fabric and leather melted and crusted onto its bones. The clothes the person wore at the time of death.

"Whoa." We move closer as a unit. The corpse is male, I'm guessing, from the heavy, beat-up flight jacket. There's an old plastic airline wings pin on its fur collar,

and a bright blue chain lies limply upon the wristbones.
A bracelet. The bones aren't bleached clean like you see
in movies; they have stuff encrusted on them. And
though the linoleum floor is a light color, almost white,
the part under the skeleton is dark with stain.

"Simon, do you think he was murdered, or did he just
die?"

"Who knows?"

"Who was this? Not the nemesis, I hope. Right?
Because if the nemesis dies, Packard never leaves. Isn't
that how it goes?"

"Yup." Simon kneels down and pulls at the hand
bones.

"Simon! Stop."

He twists something off—a finger joint.

"Oh my God!"

"Hold open the door, Justine."

I give him a hard look. Doesn't he care about anything? I clomp over and fling open the door. Simon
whips the bone at the open doorway and it bounces
back, like it hit an invisible shield.

I put my hand through the opening. Nothing stops
me. "Wow," I say.

Simon tosses it again, with the same results.

"Trapped. Just like Packard." I put my hand through
again, just to make sure I can, and then this cold horror
washes over me when I realize what it means. "Simon,
Packard's not just trapped for life. He's trapped forever.
For all of eternity."

"Ouch," Simon says.

I gaze at the remains, wondering what it means on a
metaphysical level—a heaven/hell/reincarnation level.

Simon says, "Sorry about the desecration, buddy."

"That's meaningful. Can we go?" I want Simon out of
there.

"Wait." Simon riffles through a stack of mildewy

magazines. He grabs another stack. "Don't you think if you were trapped somewhere you'd keep a diary about how much you hate the person who trapped you?"

"I have to get back to Cubby."

"The faster we look through this stuff, the faster we go."

"Fine." I check in cabinets and closets and find clothes, books, and a stereopticon, a weird contraption that shows old-fashioned 3-D pictures. I glance over at the skeleton. It's so sad, this person dying alone, trapped like a neglected hamster in a cage in some family's basement. Or maybe he was killed. Simon takes a few books. When we get outside, Simon points overhead—an illegal electric hookup. That's why the lights are still on.

Finally we get on the road. I inspect the books. Lots of novels about the Old West and several books about World War II with lots of underlining and marginalia commentary, but nothing about a nemesis or a highcap. Or Henji.

"Do you think that's how Packard will end up?" I ask. "A lonely skeleton in the corner of Mongolian Delites?"

"I wouldn't underestimate Packard's resourcefulness. But now I know the fingerprint. There are more of those faces out there, and I'm going to find them, and those faces will lead me to the nemesis, and that'll be my ace up the sleeve." Then he corrects himself. "*Our* ace."

"Right."

"You want me to drive you to your place so you can change?"

"Nah." I give him Cubby's address.

"That's not the best dinner party outfit."

Dinner party. Shit. "What do you know about the dinner party Aggie's going to?"

He shrugs. "It was two other couples."

"Anything else? Was it near the Promenade?"

"Yeah." He turns to me. "Fuck. Near the Promenade."

My throat feels thick. "Cubby."

"Fuck," he says. "She's been following you."

"Hurry, Simon."

He roars through parking lots and alleys to avoid lights. I wrestle off his jacket and direct him to the end of the next block. He squeals up and points across the street at a silver car. "Ag's Jag. Need me to come up?"

I swing out the door. "I'll wave if I need you. Otherwise I'll send her down. And I need you to make her lose this condo and, you know . . ."

Simon gives me a look I recognize as absolute confidence. "I'll handle her, sister."

Chapter
Twenty-three

THE ELEVATOR takes forever to get to the fifth floor. Cubby's door's unlocked—a bad sign. I fling it open and rush in, nearly colliding with the Silver Widow near the kitchen.

"Justine!" Water splashes out of the glass in her hand. "You missed the party." She's wearing Cubby's blue robe—the one I like to wear. It looks great on her.

"Where is he?"

She smiles crookedly; she's a whole lot loopier than when I last saw her. Even her head seems unsteady on her neck. Destabilized. She eyes my bloody, sexy nurse outfit. "Somebody's been a busy bee."

"Cubby!" I head into the living room past his table full of wine bottles and dirty plates. Aggie follows. I burst into the bedroom down the hall to find Cubby pulling on his boxers somewhat unsteadily. He's tipsy.

"Well, look who finally decided to show up." He grabs his maroon button-down shirt off the floor—a shirt I always tell him he looks good in. We call it his Mr. Beaujolais shirt. I feel sick.

Aggie stalks over and wraps her arm around his waist, practically melts into him. I expect Cubby to push her away, but he doesn't.

"Cubby!"

"What?" he says. "What are you doing here, anyway?"

"What do you mean?"

"After you skip out of the dinner party—don't worry, we ordered out pizza—and after I leave messages saying don't bother to come, I don't know why you're here. That's what."

"My phone's dead."

Aggie clings on. How could I have unleashed her on him?

"Get out," I say.

Cubby pulls her closer. "Aggie's not the one who's leaving."

I pull her away from him.

"God, Justine!" She stumbles sideways, dopey smile. The tie comes undone and the robe falls open, revealing a sexy silver slip.

It's all I can do not to shake her. "He's off-limits," I warn.

"Justine! She was just in a motorcycle accident, for Chrissake."

"A motorcycle accident, huh." I get in her face. "He's off-limits."

Aggie smiles. "Too late."

I want to kill her. I can't even look at Cubby. "Out."

"But I live in the condo right upstairs, Justine."

"No, you don't."

"I own it, though."

We glare at each other. Or I glare at her while she regards me hazily. Destabilization has given her a helpless, kittenish quality—exactly the thing to bring out Cubby's savior side.

He says, "You guys know each other?"

I let her go. "Yeah."

He turns to the Silver Widow, focusing uncertainly. "Why didn't you tell me you knew Justine?"

Aggie ignores him. "It's not fair, Justine. Poor Cubby has to share you with Simon and Carter, and this is how

you behave?" She folds her arms, addresses me scoldingly. "You're not a very good sharer."

"Come here." I pull her to the window. Simon's down
there, leaning against her Jaguar, smoking a cigarette.
"He's waiting for you. He wants to see you."

"Oooh, Simon's amazing." Aggie sheds her robe and
walks across the floor in the sexy slip. Flesh-colored
bandages from her "motorcycle accident" adorn her
right arm and leg. She shimmies into a pale gray cashmere dress, getting tangled in the sleeves. How could
Cubby have slept with her?

Cubby turns to me, focusing on my nurse's outfit.
"Who's Simon?"

"Our other boyfriend," Aggie says. "Simon's got gall,
but you got a lotta honey." She looks to Cubby for a
smile and gets a frown. Now he sees that she's not right.
It nauseates me that he didn't see it before, and that he
actually slept with her.

Or maybe he did see it. Maybe that's what he saw in
me—a screwed-up, wacky girl. While Cubby's jumping
into his pants, I grab Aggie's hand and pull her out of
the bedroom and across the condo. She stumbles along
dopily. "God, Justine!"

"You will never, *ever* come back here," I hiss, low
enough so Cubby won't hear.

"I won't?"

I shove her against the front door with a thump,
muscles taut with the urge to smash her head into it,
again and again. I want to hurt her for toying with
Cubby, for exposing him to the darkness and danger of
my disillusionist world. I want to scare her, to stop her.
I'm close enough to feel the warmth of her breath on my
nose as I press my fingers onto her soft skin, alighting
upon the bright edge of her energy dimension. Without
even thinking, I call up a huge swath of fear, remembering how it was the first time with her. The exquisite

relief, and the way she crumpled under my power. I tremble with the desire to zing her now, zing all my darkness into her. Her skin is so soft, and she is such a perfectly analogous vessel. My darkness builds as she flattens herself back against the door, eyes wide with terror.

Her expression stops me. What does she see? Something in my face? I tighten my grip on her arm. What kind of monster have I become that I would zing her out of vengeance? That's what I'm doing, I realize. Is this what I am now? Is this what Packard sees in me?

I hear Cubby come up behind us.

"You stay away," I whisper. I pull her off the door with one hand, open it with the other, shove her out into the hall, and slam the door behind her. That's when I spot a shopping bag full of my stuff under the coat rack.

Cubby stands behind me. "Who's Simon?"

"A colleague."

"You need to go, too."

"You have to stay away from that woman."

He crosses his arms. "If I feel like entertaining Aggie, I will. We had some rather uncomplicated fun." He eyes my dress. "Costume party?"

I'm shocked at his bitter tone. Cubby's never bitter. And right then this wave of calm comes over me. Cubby's never bitter. But now, thanks to me, he is. I've done far more damage than Aggie has. It needs to end tonight, I think with a pang.

I push past him and head toward his office.

He follows close behind. "Justine, what are you up to?"

"You need to see this one thing and then I'll go." I sit down in front of his computer, eyes misting up so much I can barely see the screen. "Aggie's extremely dangerous, and I need you to see that." I search the *Midcity Eagle*'s archives of the summer before last. "She's crazy and a murderer, Cubby. She's somebody I interacted with on the job, and obviously she followed me to your place. And believe me, I couldn't feel more shitty about that."

"I don't need you to vet my dates."

It's hard keep my voice level when I think of him naked with her. "This one you do."

He stands beside me, arms crossed. I find the article with the courthouse steps photo. He's surprised she's been in the paper. He'll be a whole lot more surprised when he reads what for. I save the article onto his desktop.

"I don't doubt she bought the condo up there," I say. "She's fabulously wealthy, and she has investments all over. She wasn't in a motorcycle accident, though. She has a delusional skin condition. It's not real, but she believes it is, and that it's infectious. The woman has no conscience. Short version—she murdered her husband, a torture kill, but they didn't have enough to convict. You can read the article and get the specifics. Not the best bedtime reading, regarding manner of death."

He looks at me like he's having trouble focusing. This is the look he gets when something lurks beyond polite comprehension. "My God," he says.

"I'm sorry," I say. My handsome, charmed-life Cubby. I can't even look him in the eye anymore, and I can feel my face distorting from the effort not to cry. But on top of all the other shitty things I've done to him, goddamn if I'll cry in front of him. I get up from the computer. Being with me has made him bitter. It has to stop.

"Justine—"

"What?"

"Is that real blood? I'd assumed it was fake, but . . ." He touches the front of my dress, forehead furrowed. I bite my lip. "Justine, why is there blood on you? Are you hurt?" He asks this so tenderly.

"I'm fine," I whisper, still looking down.

"But you have blood on you! Something happened."

I'm not prepared for his concern, and it floods me with comfort, warms my cold edges, makes me want to grab handfuls of his Mr. Beaujolais shirt and have him hold me and say Cubby things to me and let me be in his Cubby world just one more night.

But I step back. I have to let him go. I can't bring him any more Aggies, any more bitterness. I can't hurt him anymore. "It's not real blood. This thing's just a stupid costume."

A horrible silence descends between us. The silence crushes my chest.

"You're telling me it's not real."

"That's what I'm telling you," I say.

He looks at my eyes, like he's inspecting them for the first time. Does he know I'm lying? Can he see that it's real blood?

"Just go," he says wearily. All the tenderness is gone.

I take a breath—there's so much I want to say, and nothing more to be said. There's nothing more than cold edges. I go, grabbing my bag on the way, feeling his eyes on me. I shut the door softly.

Chapter
Twenty-four

IT'S OBVIOUS from Shelby's face that she has something grim to say about my outfit, but I give her a look before she can say it. Then I walk in her door and plop down on her swirl-patterned couch. "Thank God you're here."

She sits down next to me and rests a hand on my shoulder, and that's enough for me to start crying. I give her the short version of everything, because all I really want is to get out of the nurse outfit and take a shower. After several assurances that I'm really okay, relatively speaking, she comes to life as a hostess, pulling me to the bathroom, setting the shower to the perfect temperature, and leaving me to drench myself in the hot water until I'm rubbery.

I step out to find she's laid out fluffy towels, silky pajamas, a silky Chinese robe, and even new underwear, still with the tags on, which is both thoughtful and mysterious. When I wander out to the living room, she has Burgundy poured and things set out for French sandwiches—French bread with soft cheeses and grapes and strawberries. Shelby eats a lot of French sandwiches. I don't know if she made them up or if the French really do eat them.

Drinking wine and eating a French sandwich make me feel a bit better, and I give her the creepy details about the Alchemist that I didn't feel like revealing to Simon. Though she says little, she is with me as only Shelby can be: horrified at specifics of the kidnapping, thrilled at the escape, aghast that I tried Simon's spelunking trick, and intrigued by our discovery of a skeleton at the gas station. She's also very sympathetic about Cubby. Shelby is one of those rare listeners who make you feel less alone.

I build myself another French sandwich. "I have got to get out of this," I say.

"Oh, Justine." She hates when I talk about leaving the disillusionists.

"There's got to be a way."

"There is." Meaning the Jarvis route.

"Well, that's not looking so bad right now. I've lost my relationship; I've lost my autonomy; I've lost my moral compass."

"Relationship and autonomy, yes. Moral compass, no."

"I wanted to zing Aggie out of pure vengeance."

"But you did not. You should have, I think. And you helped to take rapist from raping business. We are angels of karma, holding mirror to targets—"

"We're slaves of Packard."

"Everybody is slave of something." She downs the rest of her Burgundy.

"That doesn't really make me feel better."

"You Americans. You always want to feel better."

"Don't you want to feel better?"

"Feel better," she says with contempt, then dispatches the entire conversation with a wave. She agrees, however, that it's terrible Simon knows about the faces.

"Shelby, we have to find the other faces before he does. We have to go back to the tollbooth."

"And do what?"

"I don't know. But we can't let Simon have leverage over Packard."

"Yes, Simon is gambler born to lose. He will always go too far."

"Let's go back there."

"I want to see gas station first," Shelby says.

After a few more glasses of wine, Shelby starts feeling sorry for Packard. "Trapped man you found, he dies alone, to become jumbled skeleton, never to leave. I do not want Packard to become jumbled skeleton."

"I don't either."

"He called here before," she says. "Very worried, very upset about you and Alchemist. I told him you are fine. That you have gone to Cubby's."

"Good."

By the time the bottle's finished, we've made three plans. The first plan is that I'll crash on her couch for the night. The second plan entails picking up my car and taking a road trip north so Shelby can personally inspect the gas station. The third plan is a work in progress. It involves bringing a paintball gun to the apartment complex and splattering over the face to hide it from Simon, then inspecting the face on the tollbooth and maybe interviewing the woman inside.

The next morning, Shelby wears a black-and-red cowboy shirt and bright-green jeans and yellow cowboy boots. I throw on one of the rollerblading outfits from the bag of clothes from Cubby's—green pants with a white stripe up the side and a white top and jacket. It makes me sad to think of the happy time when I last wore it. I can't stop thinking about Cubby, and that look on his face when I lied and told him it wasn't real blood on my dress.

"We must make small stop first," she announces once we're on the road.

The stop turns out to be a cluster of one-story office-park-type buildings with tinted windows and plenty of parking. We creep up the walk and peer into a door labeled SPINAL RESOURCES FUNDRAISING CENTER and see a woman with close-cropped gray hair and big hoop earrings sitting behind a receptionist's desk.

Shelby pulls me away. "No one must see us. Come." We sneak around the side, down a slim drive between two buildings, and peer in a window. A woman with a headset working at a computer.

"What is this?"

"You will see. You will like it very much."

"Unless we get arrested."

The next few windows yield similar scenes, with about half the workers in wheelchairs. Then we get to window five, where yet another man with a headset peers into yet another computer. Big forehead, tiny nose.

"Oh my God!" I slide down under the window. "What's Foley doing in there?"

"He has become fundraiser for this charity. Do you see?"

"A fundraiser?"

"Yes," she says. "He is force for good now. He raises funds to build large and sophisticated new facility for those who are injured. Like Mandler boy he caused injuries to."

"I don't get it. It seems like he was a bum in a coffee shop two seconds ago."

"No, it is what . . . perhaps a month ago he was fully disillusioned. He was crashed and now reboots. He had change of heart. Is force for good now, Foley."

"But Shelby, do they at least know about Foley's past? How do we know he won't turn bad again?"

"Justine, did you not see him disillusioned?"

"You don't know how evil he was."

"It does not matter. He was disillusioned. You do not come back same after such a thing."

"I think these people should at least know about his past, don't you think?" I get up and head for the front.

She rushes after me. "You cannot go in!" She looks around furtively. "Foley must not see me."

I toss her the keys. "Then wait in the car. Because I'm going in. Wait—is that the name he's using? Foley?"

"Yes." She heads toward the parking lot and I go in.

The gray-haired woman at the front desk tells me Foley is head of fundraising. She raises her eyebrows. "Do you want to speak with Mr. Foley?"

"No, I want to speak *about* Mr. Foley," I say. "I have personal experience with him, and I want you to be aware of his history." The woman frowns as I continue. "I just want you to know—Foley has a track record of scamming people and . . ." I trail off here, because she's vigorously shaking her head. "It's true, I swear."

"I know, I know." She hits a few computer keys, then rolls her wheelchair nearer to where I stand. "Several people have warned us about his past," she says. "It's not necessary." She points to a colorful brochure with a line drawing of some sort of recreational-therapeutic-residential complex. "The foundation for that center will soon be poured, thanks to Ben Foley. This fundraising operation wouldn't exist if not for Ben Foley. Believe me, every dime is tracked. We all know about his past, but important friends of the project vouched for him, and he's gone on to raise more corporate and private money in a few weeks than whole teams have managed to raise over the course of years. Years! His talent . . ." She glances sideways as if to ensure he's not listening. "You might say his talent translates. People skills. Negotiation skills. We do have one worry with Ben Foley, certainly," she says. "It's that he will leave us."

"Important friends of the project vouched for him?"

She doesn't give a name. She doesn't have to. It's the

Mandlers. Their son was paralyzed. Spinal resources. It all adds up.

Back out in the parking lot I start up the car and pull out, conscious of Shelby watching me, waiting for my reaction.

"Well, there's a shocker," I say finally. And then I laugh. I don't even know why.

"He contacted Helmut for donation," she says. "That is how we found out."

"You must feel pretty good. You were on the team that disillusioned Foley."

She does one of her weary waves. "Too much butterflies and sunshine. But I am glad you saw."

You can hardly make out the face on the gas station wall in the daytime. Shelby runs her hand over the pebbly surface. "Henji," she whispers. After that I show her the interior, which looks extra sad with sunlight streaming in the door. Shelby kneels by the skeleton, motionless for a long time, almost like she's communing with it. Then she pulls a tightly rolled-up cloth out of her purse and spreads it over the remains. I'm touched that she'd thought to bring it. "I hope soul is not trapped here," she says.

"Me too," I say.

We continue Simon's search for a diary of some sort. Shelby thinks that there might be a hidden compartment somewhere, but we find nothing. We also discuss the paintball idea, though it doesn't seem quite as brilliant as it did last night when we were drunk.

On our way out we stop to gaze at the trees, and the meadow stretching out behind the gas station. It's full of yellow flowers under a candy-blue sky, all so pretty it almost looks fake.

I wonder what's worse—having this view and not being able to reach it, or the gray concrete and glass that Packard sees.

Chapter
Twenty-five

I PLUG IN my phone to charge next to Cubby's favorite blue water glass, still half-full from when he stopped by last week. Everything in my apartment reminds me of Cubby and the future I once pictured for us. If I weren't a disillusionist, I think bitterly, I'd still be with him and he would come back and drink out of this glass, and we might still have that future. I grab the glass and hurl it at a wall, and it shatters.

It's been only twenty-four hours since the Alchemist followed me out to my car, but it seems like weeks. I'm still not as traumatized as I think I ought to be. I suppose it helped to be laughing the whole time. Or maybe what Simon said is true—maybe I zinged all the trauma out. Or the other thing, that the darkness of human nature is my territory.

I take a long bath, then listen to my messages. Most of them are from Cubby last night, and my heart shrinks with each one: Cubby wondering where I am, why I'm not at the dinner party, his increasing tone of hurt and annoyance. The last one tells me not to bother coming. Clinking in the background. The Silver Widow. Three messages from Packard—one from last night, two from today, exhorting me to call him right away. I don't bother. I'll see him soon enough to give my report on the Alchemist, and to warn him about the skeleton

and the business about being in there for eternity. I
don't get the sense that he realizes it, and he deserves to
know. Just as I deserved to know what I was getting
into. Packard didn't care to warn me, but two wrongs
don't make a right.

I pull my bathrobe tight around me and step over the
glass shards in the kitchen. Maybe it was stupid to think
I even belonged in Cubby's happy life with him. Maybe
goodness really is an illusion, and reality really is just
stupid and grim. Or maybe it is just for me.

But somewhere I know this isn't true. I try to think of
things that are good and worth believing in, and I think
about Foley, and how he supposedly won't hurt anybody anymore, how he bounced back good. Thanks to
the disillusionists. Isn't that positive? And I think about
Chief Otto Sanchez, who never made excuses or gave
up on getting the Brick Slinger, and eventually he got
him. Sanchez believed; he kept moving forward. He
went after the guy when nobody else would. That's
what I have to do: just move forward. Keep believing.
There's a way to get free of Packard, and I'm going to
find it.

I knock on the Mongolian Delites door just a bit past
four, an hour and a half before the place opens for
dinner. I'm wearing brown velvet shorts with white sandals and a white cottony top with a necklace made of silver circles. In my cosmology of outfits, this is a hopeful
one.

Packard flings open the door. "Oh. Justine."

I pause on the other side of the threshold, where we
can't touch.

Packard regards me intently, black jacket hanging
crookedly over an untucked white shirt. He hasn't slept.
"People say you're all right. You're all right, right?"

"Everybody keeps asking me that, Packard. I'm fine."

"You're sure?"

"Look, of the smorgasbord of horrific things that could have happened to me, most did not. Only the minorly horrific ones. I'm here to give my report. Jay has him now."

Packard's green eyes shine with angst; he's barely listening. He opens the door farther, shirt cuff flopping free, beckoning me in. He looks distraught and piratey. In a good way. "Don't be mad. Just for a little while. Just, for this moment—"

As soon as I cross the threshold, he grabs me and pulls me to his chest; I relax into the warm, strong circle of his arms in spite of myself.

"I was so worried," he says.

Being enveloped like this, like somebody cares—it's nourishment I didn't know I needed. It's what I craved from Cubby. I was so scared for so long at the Alchemist's cabin!

I can't pull away.

"The idea of you with that monster . . ." He holds me tighter.

I rest my cheek on his bare triangle of chest, breathing in the clean, slightly spicy scent of his skin, so close I could lick it. It's almost like I'm breathing in our kiss again—breathing it into every nook of my body.

"It's not your fault. I ignored a lot of signs with him."

"Nevertheless." He releases me and looks into my eyes. "It is my fault."

"I'm okay." My pulse pounds in my ears, and I try to fumble my way back to my righteous anger. But all I can locate is our easy intimacy, and how alive he makes me feel.

"I'm going to make this work out," he says.

"Forget it. You've done enough." I take a step back.

"Since you've enslaved me, I've lost my autonomy, my morality, now my relationship."

"Cubby left you?"

"I left him. And not because I wanted to."

"Cubby could never appreciate you. He only appreciated the part of you that fit into his world."

"I wanted him, and I wanted that world. And not because I'm a misfit." I press my finger to his chest. "I'm going to be free of you soon. But I came here to tell you something, because unlike you, I believe people are entitled to all the choices and information they would want and deserve."

"When," he whispers hoarsely, "will you forgive me?"

I remove my finger, unprepared for the thud of raw emotion in his words. Part of me desperately wants to forgive him. "Maybe when you say you're sorry."

He regards me with those dazzling eyes, skin slightly flushed. Slowly, he brushes his fingertips up my arms, leaving trails of what feel like sparkles, allowing his hands to come to rest on my shoulders. My skin is way too alive wherever he touches. "You're finally free," he says.

"I used to be imprisoned by hypochondria, but now I'm imprisoned by you." I reach up and grab his wrists, pull his hands off me. "Packard, I need to tell you about something we found yesterday, and it's very bad." I struggle to be clear and objective. "You need to be serious and hear this."

"I meant, you're finally free of that relationship."

My heart beats way too fast and loud in my ears. "I'm less free than ever."

"There's more than one kind of freedom." His words contain a lewd promise that sends shivers sliding over me.

My gaze falls to his kissable lips, and down to the pale triangle of skin again.

He says, "Can you imagine, Justine, how it would feel to be with somebody who sees you completely? Who appreciates you completely?"

I place my hand over that bare triangle of chest as if to say *stay away,* but really I just want to touch him. Everywhere. It's like I'm unmoored in the middle of a surging ocean and I want to hold on to him. His eyes soften as he curls his fingers around my arms and draws me to him with a steady force that's intensely satisfying, and he kisses me hard and strong. I melt to him, lost and found all at the same time, and then my hands are on his shoulders.

Oh, God, I think, *what am I doing?* But I don't care anymore.

He cups the back of my head with both hands and pushes me against the door with a thump that's hard and good and takes my breath away, and he kisses me deeply. The firm muscle of his tongue overwhelms mine until I don't know whose mouth is whose in our mix of lips, heat, and breath. My fists fly to his hair, knuckles against his scalp, pulling him nearer until my canines bite against my tender cheeks, the cool wall flat on my back. And this crazy sense of both of us lost, unmoored . . . it's intoxicating.

Fighting my hands up under his jacket and shirt, I push my fingers into his muscular back. His cheek slides rough on my lips; his neck tastes salty. I have to devour all of him.

He breathes soft and warm against my ear, scratching his fingernails up my thighs, which makes me squeeze my pelvic muscles together into a kind of sensual wave that rises to the top of my head. This is all I want.

A new invasion, his unyielding tongue in my mouth, making me desperate to feel more of him, and I pull him and his erection closer to me, right up against the nerve bundles that seem to have multiplied between my legs. He's a rock against me, and I pulse to the movement of his tongue, or maybe he does. I'm panting to the pulse of us, on and on like an ocean.

"Oh," he says, slowing, pushing his hands through my hair. "Oh." He kisses me, fingers at the back of my head, then drags them down heavy and smooth over my shoulders and to the front of my shirt. Slowly he undoes a button, another, and then I feel one pop. I laugh softly at that, and he does, too. Gently he pushes my shirt off one shoulder. I feel the coolness of the air in the dark restaurant. With a finger, he traces the line of my bra strap down to my bra strap bulge, a little pillow of skin I'm always embarrassed of; then he runs his fingernails light as whispers over the lace that covers my nipple. I gasp; the sensation is electrifying. He knits his fingers into mine as we kiss some more; then he kisses my shoulder, and then that dreaded little pillow of skin. I open my eyes and watch as he kisses the plump side of my breast that my bra doesn't cover, and then he moves his attentions onto the lace part of my bra, drawing near to my nipple, which fills me with excited anticipation.

My eyes being open makes my mind start up again, however, and it's just about here that it hits me that he never said he's sorry. I told him I'd forgive him if he said he was sorry. And he wouldn't say it.

I stiffen and he feels it. "What?"

"You never said you were sorry. You're sorry for what you did, aren't you?"

He straightens up and releases my hands. "Please . . . ," he says softly, touching my cheek. And he *still* doesn't say it.

Everything in me starts to reverse. "Oh my God!" I

push him away. "You're not sorry for making me a
servile minion?"

He looks dazed.

I pull my shirt back over me. "It's simple. Yes or no?
Are you sorry?"

A beat. Two. Then, "No."

My breath falls out of me.

"I'm talking to you straight here," he says. "I'm not
going to say I'm sorry for a thing I'm not sorry for."

He's not even sorry. The pain of this nearly knocks me
over. I'd at least thought that he regretted it. "Thank
you, Packard," I say hoarsely, "for reminding me why
this can never happen."

I storm over to the bar area. He's not even sorry! I go
behind, pulse racing, and pour a glass of water and
drink, hoping to stave off the tears. Can I be any more
of a dupe? Kissing him, wanting to fuck him, wanting to love him, when he took control of my life from
me?

He's leaning back against the door, eyes closed.

I pour and drink another glass of water. I suppose it
was upstanding of him not to lie. Did I want him to? In
the moment, I guess. But now I'm grateful he reminded
me of who he really is, and what's really between us. It
hurts like hell, and suddenly I feel very tired.

What am I doing here? Why have I come? Then I
remember the skeleton in the gas station. The glimpse
into Packard's dark future.

He needs to know, but does it help, when you're lost
in the desert, if somebody points out the skeletons of the
people and animals who were once lost like you?

I go over to him. "You have to get out of here,
Packard."

His expression is steely, the planes of his face hard. "I
know."

"You might be in more danger than you think," I say.

"What do you mean?"

"Simon and I found something last night. Coming home from the Alchemist's, I happened to be staring out the car window and I saw a face sort of etched into the side of an abandoned gas station—a face identical to the one out there."

"A face like on the door?"

"Etched on an exterior wall. Out on 47 near Surrey Springs."

"Tell me."

I hold my water glass with both hands. It makes a kind of barrier between us. "I was staring out the window, and noticed it when our headlights hit it, and pointed it out to Simon and we decided to stop in and look around."

"And? Who was there?"

"Well, it wasn't really—"

"Who?"

"There was a body," I say. "Dead."

Packard goes still, like the actual molecules in his body have ceased to move. Finally he speaks. "Man or woman? What did the body look like?"

"I think it was a guy, but I'm not sure. The person was a skeleton. You could see he had short hair, brown maybe. When he died he was wearing a bomber jacket—it was sort of in with the bones."

Packard grabs my arms. "Brown leather? Fur collar?"

I hold my breath. It never occurred to me he might know the victim. I should've thought of that, been more sensitive. "Yes. And a little plastic airline-wings pin."

"Justine, did you see any—?" He squeezes his eyes shut. He's going to ask a question, and he doesn't want the answer. I wait. "Was he wearing any distinctive jewelry?"

"A blue metallic bracelet. Blue chain links around his wrist."

He stares at me strangely—through me, really—and lets me go.

"You knew him?"

He just stares. Then he bursts off into the middle of the dining room and overturns a table. Glass breaks. Silverware clatters. He lifts a chair and brings it down with a loud crack. Then he smashes another chair into the wall, destroying a pair of brightly painted plaster horse heads, and then he hurls it into the pagoda mirror. Shards explode out over the dining room, and still he doesn't stop. I have this impulse to do something, comfort him somehow, but when a person needs to break a lot of stuff, it's best to let them do it. I wrap my arms around myself as he casts another chair across the room, taking down the bejeweled scabbard.

I didn't expect he'd know the man. Know and love him, obviously. I feel his rage so acutely at this moment—trapped, limited, isolated from his tribe. Finally he crumples into a chair, elbows on knees, head in palms. I wander tentatively past overturned tables, chair parts, and broken glass.

"Packard," I say. "I'm so sorry."

He gazes up, face red, eyes wild and shining. "That man was my best friend in the world. A brother to me. Diesel."

I don't know what to say. I put a hand on his shoulder, and he lets me. "I am so sorry."

"He didn't deserve to die like that."

"I'm so sorry," I whisper.

He stands, shedding my comforting hand. "I want him brought here. I want to give him a proper funeral."

"You can't." I swallow. "The body can't be taken out of there."

Packard gives me a bewildered, nearly feral look, like I'm not speaking intelligibly.

I try to think how best to put it. I say, "Simon thought to move the body. But the force field . . ."

I don't need to say any more. Packard gets it. He says nothing for a very long time. Then, in a calm, flat voice, "I see."

The calm, flat voice is far more frightening than him smashing things.

Chapter
Twenty-six

TWO DAYS LATER, I run into Simon coming out of Mongolian Delites. He tells me the Silver Widow signed over the condo in Cubby's building to her lawyer.

"She's in arrears, if you know what I mean." He gives me his innocent blue-eyed look. "We're trying to make up her losses, which isn't going well, I'm afraid. Never quite goes as well as one would hope," he adds. "Come here." He pulls me down the sidewalk and into a doorway in the next building over. "Packard knows about the gas station. What else did you tell him?"

"Don't worry," I say. "Just that we saw the face and went in and found the body. And that you tried to move it and couldn't. Nothing about your quest for leverage or the fact that you whipped the guy's finger bones all over the place."

"I don't care if he knows about that."

"Go ahead and tell him, then. I'm not interested in getting between you two."

Simon seems impressed by my free-agent attitude. "Spot any more faces lately?"

"Have you?"

Simon looks at me intently. "You'd tell me if you had, right?"

"Just as you'd tell me," I say sweetly.

He looks at me for a long moment. "Glad we're clear on that."

I'm sure he's been looking; Shelby and I have absolutely got to find a way to cover the other faces.

Even though Shelby had explained to me that Henji's force field makes it so the restaurant can never be permanently altered, it's still a shock to walk back into Mongolian Delites not forty-eight hours after Packard destroyed the place and see diners casually sitting in the chairs and eating at the tables that Packard so thoroughly broke. The pagoda mirror is its old cheesy and unblemished self, hanging front and center, and the painted horse heads he smashed are intact, too, perched in their usual spots.

I head back to Packard's booth. He's wearing the blue chain bracelet formerly worn by the skeleton of Diesel. He must have sent somebody out there to get it. I feel sad for him, and obviously it shows, because Packard gives me a dark look. He's in no mood for pity. "The day this comes off is the day I strangle my nemesis with my bare hands," he says.

Over the next two weeks I prepare for an important upcoming target—a civil servant of some sort who moonlights as a crime boss; his code name is the Engineer. His most feared disease is the same as mine, vein star syndrome, which is quite convenient since I already know everything there is to know about it.

Helmut has been working on the Engineer for nearly a year, exploiting the Engineer's distress about current events—most specifically, the plight of African elephants: the way they're hunted for their tusks and how they cry when they lose a mate. Helmut and the Engineer have gone so far as to create a grade-school educational program about habitat loss.

They tell me a number of disturbing anecdotes about

the Engineer. He shot a man in the face. He cracked an informant's head in a giant vise. And he gouged out a traitor's eyes with his bare thumbs. Packard provided me with a photo of the eye-gouging victim that I deeply regret viewing. There is something profoundly disturbing about a face where the eye sockets contain nothing but bloody gristle.

In spite of all this, the Engineer assignment feels like a lucky break. Surely somebody who is involved in both the Midcity government and the criminal underworld would know something about Henji. Maybe the Engineer even knows about Packard's history with Henji. I just have to find a way to get it out of him.

My motivation for wanting to find Henji has become somewhat murky. Some days it's because I want to help Packard. Other days, it's to have an ace up my sleeve, like Simon, whom I must prevent from finding Henji. But above all, the crime wave needs to stop.

Helmut has determined that opera will be my best way to get in with the Engineer, who is apparently a fanatic and currently not on speaking terms with his usual opera companions.

"I've been building you up as a passionate neophyte," Helmut tells me during one of our endless Engineer meetings. "You've only just been introduced to the world of opera and you're crazy about it. If he thinks he can teach you about it, he'll ask you to accompany him repeatedly."

Packard says, "You'll find that the Engineer's happiest when he's the biggest know-it-all in the room."

So I listen to operas, read translated lyrics, and think up good neophyte questions to ask. I also work with Strongarm Francis to create a fake identity as a neuro nurse in a Dallas hospital. Francis has connections there, and key people are ready to vouch for me if anybody decides to check. Our big story is that I've just moved to Midcity with assistance from my Uncle Helmut, whom I'm supposedly staying with.

I continue to miss Cubby. Now and then I lurk in lobbies across from his office building, hoping to catch a glimpse of him, maybe soak up something from him. I suppose you could qualify it as stalking.

Once I see Cubby heading out to lunch with a group of workmates. I examine his body language, his face. He looks happy, but then he usually looks happy. Does he see my departure as a blessing in disguise yet? Eventually, Cubby sees every negative event as a blessing in disguise.

Already life with him seems like a distant dream.

If life with Cubby is a distant dream, then my meeting with Helmut and Packard the day before I'm to start on the Engineer is a hands-down nightmare. That's when Packard tells me the identity of the Engineer. Our murderous, eye-gouging crime boss is none other than Police Chief Otto Sanchez.

It's so outrageous, I just laugh. "Come on."

"It's true."

"No way."

"Do you know him personally?" Packard says. "I wasn't aware you knew him personally."

I say, "With some people, you can just tell."

"*You* can't tell," Packard says. "But I can."

"I won't accept it."

"He's an image to you," Packard says. "A man playing a role in the newspapers and on TV. Do you really imagine that when a man plays a hero on TV, it means he's a hero in real life?"

"Sanchez is," I say.

That's when the dossier comes out. When my heart starts pounding, I stand up from the booth where they've laid out photos of dead bodies, and Sanchez meeting with shadowy figures.

"You can show me as many photos as you want," I say. "It won't change the fact that Chief Sanchez is one of the good guys. He cares. He fights for what he believes in."

Packard looks at me wistfully. "You see that in him only because it's in you. It's called projection."

"What about him chasing down the Brick Slinger on foot? He wasn't even wearing a helmet. He could've been killed. But he went after him and he got him, and the city is safer for it. That is what a hero does. That is not what a crime boss does."

Packard sits back. "And the man was shot twice and his head was crushed by a cinder block."

"That fell from above."

"So says the lone witness. Pretty convenient, that the telekinetic would execute himself."

"Screw you."

"I'm sorry," Helmut says. "I've been working with him for months. I can't see into him the way Packard can, but it's crystal clear to me that this is a man with a dark double life. He is not what he appears to be."

"Why would he fight crime on one hand and support it on the other? It's ridiculous."

"He's controlling who gets caught," Packard says.

Helmut nods. "While the overall crime rate rises faster than ever."

"No," I say.

Packard says, "Sociopaths are brilliant at fooling people."

"Justine—" Helmut hands me a photo of Chief Sanchez in a car with a man who looks vaguely familiar. "I took this myself," he says.

I hold it, trying not to shake. "So he sits with guys in cars."

Helmut gives me another photo—the eye-gouging victim. "Hours before he was found."

I look from one photo to the other. The man in the car with Sanchez *is* the eye-gouging victim. I feel like throwing up. "Did you see Sanchez do it?"

They both just look at me.

"Just because he was in a car with him beforehand doesn't mean Sanchez did it. And I'm not going after him." I grab my purse and get out of there.

The heat out on the street makes me feel woozy and crazy. I know Sanchez only through the TV and newspaper. Still.

Footsteps behind me. Huffing and puffing. Helmut. I slow and let him catch me. We walk in silence.

"I didn't know you felt so strongly about the chief," he says after a while, wiping sweat from his eyes. "I may have pushed to warn you sooner if I'd known."

"I don't think I'm wrong about him," I say. "I don't believe he's bad."

"I understand. I didn't believe it at first, either." We pause at a light.

I turn to him. "You don't understand. I don't think I'm wrong about him."

Helmut nods.

"He's like this symbol . . ." I'm fighting not to cry. I don't trust Packard, but I've always trusted Helmut. "What convinced you? Because those photos—just because he was with the guy . . ."

"I've spent a year in his company. I've caught him in lies. I've seen him with people who later disappear. Justine, you know I have suspicions about those other cases. We both do. Questions about a larger intent on Packard's part."

I nod, feeling empty.

"I have no question as to the need to disillusion the Engineer. I guarantee you he's leading a double life. I spoke to that victim's widow. He'd been terrified of Sanchez leading up to that. I could send you to her. We'd have to be delicate, but . . ."

"The man whose eyes were gouged out was terrified of Sanchez? His widow told you that?"

Helmut nods. "I went and got the story from her afterwards. I wanted to believe in Sanchez, too, but the facts just kept piling up."

I stare at the blur of heat over the pavement. "It's too much."

"You'll see for yourself."

I study Helmut's rueful expression. I trust him. I do. And unlike Otto Sanchez, I know Helmut in person. I know he has a good heart. "You swear it, Helmut? You give your word on all this?"

Solemnly he nods. "Chief Sanchez is a man leading a double life. A life of lies. I give you my word."

"Damn it," I say.

"Come back. I'm sure Packard would let you zing him—"

"I don't need a zing. I need to be alone."

"Our assignation is tomorrow night."

"Give me a few hours," I say.

I spend my hours rollerblading, which usually makes me feel in control of things, though I don't feel much in control, and I almost pass out from the heat, too. Maybe it was childish, but I believed in Sanchez and now I feel disillusioned myself. I return to my apartment and shower. Little by little, I move from disillusioned to angry. I'm angry at Packard for the usual reasons, and angry at him and Helmut for not informing me sooner of all this.

But most of all, I'm angry at Chief Otto Sanchez. All this time, he was just another criminal? To think I was worried that Henji might go after him! It would serve Sanchez right if Henji went after him.

Three hours later I'm back at Mongolian Delites, still red-faced from my hot-weather workout and high emotions. "You two should've told me earlier who I was up against," I say. "Evil or no, you're sending me to attack somebody who's both a superstar detective and a crime boss. I could've used a few weeks to get used to the whole idea."

"I didn't want you to psych yourself out," Packard says.

Then it hits me. "Oh my God. The berets he always wears."

Packard smiles. He knows where I'm going with this.

"It's not because he's balding, or a fashion statement. It's vein star. He wears the berets for protection from bumps on the head." I sit back. "He's more extreme than I ever was."

"Your zing will devastate him," Packard says.

I find myself hoping it does. I'm as angry about Otto Sanchez's deception as I am about Packard's.

The three of us review images of his associates, paying particular attention to Sophia, Otto Sanchez's personal assistant and quasi-girlfriend.

"She'll attend the opera now and then," Helmut tells me, "but she hates it."

"Wait—dates at the opera? I'm not willing to go romantic with this guy."

"God, no!" Packard says. "Keep it on a platonic level and Otto will follow your lead. He's a bit of a Boy Scout like that."

"Boy Scout, sociopath, loves elephants . . . This guy doesn't add up."

"A wolf in sheep's clothing never adds up," Packard tells me. "He mesmerizes his victims with a fluffy, innocent exterior, right up until he rips their throats out."

"Or eyes," I say.

"This is a man who will toy with people and torture them for pleasure," Packard says. "If you think he's onto you, or if you find yourself feeling too comfortable with him, walk away."

Chapter
Twenty-seven

HELMUT AND I ASCEND the broad stone steps with a throng of glamorous people and move through the grand gilt doors of the opera house into an interior so dizzyingly lavish that I have to hook my arm in his just to keep my balance. We pass polished marble pillars and ornate statues of toga-clad women extending golden candelabras above their heads. A white marble staircase curves up and up; crystal chandeliers hang like shimmering upside-down trees from high above.

Equally dizzying are the beautiful patrons who flow around us in their gowns and tuxedoes. They are so far beyond even the fancy crowd that used to shop at Le Toile that I find it impossible to believe they dwell in Midcity.

I turn to Helmut, who looks smart in his black silk tuxedo.

He squeezes my arm. "You'll do fine."

I take a deep breath and we ascend to the third level; Helmut confers with an usher who points us toward the end of the corridor. To Chief Sanchez's opera box.

I adjust my velvet wrap around my cold, bare shoulders. My strapless black silk gown features cut obsidian beads sewn into the center of the very snug bodice, creating a darkly glittering diamond that extends from between my breasts down to my belly button, and the

skirt twists all the way to my shoes, which were beaded
to match. It is currently the most beautiful outfit I own,
which doesn't do much for my nerves. All I can think
about is that poor eyes-gouged man. I tighten my hold
on Helmut's arm, feeling like my stomach might float
clear up into my throat.

"I often feel nervous with the Engineer, too," Helmut
whispers. "Just concentrate."

"If I concentrate any harder they'll think I'm a zombie."

Helmut frowns. He's shaved a crisp line along his
cheek that's lowered his beard. It looks good. "Justine,
Otto's vulnerable to you."

"That's what they said about the Alchemist."

"And they were right, weren't they?"

The chimes sound. I take a deep breath. "If the
Alchemist had been any smarter, I'd be dead. This guy
is smarter."

"If you aren't ready, we turn back now."

"No." I close my eyes and count to five. "Okay." I
look at Helmut. "Do I look okay?"

"Ravishing."

I pat my updo, the black jeweled clip holding it in
place. "Hair?"

"Perfect."

Onward to the door. Helmut opens it, and we enter a
small ornate box that overhangs the glittering gold and
red velvet expanse of the opera house below. Chief Otto
Sanchez rises from his seat, beaming at us. He's taller
and larger than he looks on TV—well over six feet.

"Welcome, friends!" He shakes hands with Helmut,
and they clap each other's shoulders.

A redheaded woman in the corner stays calm, cool,
and seated. Sophia, the personal assistant. Clearly she
would've preferred to be alone with Otto tonight.

"Thank you again for this generous invitation, Otto.

It's such a treat, especially for my niece," Helmut says. "Justine, allow me to introduce Chief Otto Sanchez."

Chief Otto Sanchez, a.k.a. the Engineer, turns his dark, generous features to me. His elegant tuxedo matches his large velvet cap—a sort of oversized beret that should look wrong on a man. It doesn't look wrong on him.

Don't let those ridiculously foppish outfits fool you, Packard has told me. *He dresses like a poodle, but he attacks like a pit bull.*

Otto clasps my hands in two of his. I'm so nervous, I can't even pull it together enough to touch his energy dimension.

"Enchanté," he says. There's a dark, ancient elegance about him. "The niece arrives in black. In deference, perhaps, to our poor doomed heroine."

I almost choke on the doomed heroine comment. "I'm so excited," I manage to say. "I don't know if Helmut told you, Chief Sanchez, but this is my first live opera."

Otto lights up. "Your very first! Well, then, the treat is all mine." He tightens his hands around mine. "And please, call me Otto."

"Otto," I say breathlessly.

Redhead Sophia decides to join us now. "Otto adores the opera," she says. You can see swaths of creamy skin through her sexy silk-and-lace gown. Otto introduces us, and she slinks her hand from mine to Helmut's and quickly back to Otto's waist.

Otto gestures toward velvet chairs arranged around a petite marble table that holds a wine bucket, crystal stemware, and ornate dishes of nuts and figs. "Justine, Helmut." He shows where he'd have us sit, placing himself between Sophia and me. Helmut's next to me on the very end. Otto pours the wine. "A fine Brunello. Fitting, I always think, for such a performance." He seems to be directing this statement toward me, so I nod, striving to hold my hand steady as the four of us clink glasses.

The lights dim.

"Are you familiar with the story of *Tosca*?" Otto whispers.

"Only vaguely, I'm afraid."

He gives a quick overview that would be quite helpful if I didn't already know the story. The curtains part on a chapel stage set where weary fugitive Angelotti hides. The painter Cavaradossi enters and begins to sing. I sneak a look at Otto, who watches, rapt. Black velvet piping runs along the lapels of his tux, and he wears a black silk vest underneath. He really is a splendid human being, but this just makes me loathe him all the more. What is in a person's soul, to kill like that?

Between acts one and two, Otto relates tidbits about the historical basis for the villain's character. I ask him to pass me a napkin and touch his arm, grazing his energy dimension. It's cool, weighty, and not altogether unpleasant. I should have no problem zinging him. A huge relief.

I excuse myself to go to the restroom, where I duck into a stall, close my eyes, and concentrate on stoking up some fear. I don't need to use an article for it anymore; it just comes when I call—a quivering, uncomfortable mass of health anxiety that mixes with my paranoia about Otto being a great detective. And there was that doomed heroine comment, too. Is it possible he's already toying with me? I think about how, back before I knew the Engineer was Otto, I'd imagined I'd pump him for information on the Henji/Packard history. That will definitely not be happening. There is no screwing around with this one.

I emerge shaky and disoriented. Too much fear. I grasp the makeup mirror ledge and close my eyes, taking a centering breath, then another. When I open them I see Sophia, watching me from across the room. Quickly I look away, which only makes me seem nervous.

She smiles broadly and comes over. "Everything all right?"

"Yup."

Our mutual silence makes me more anxious. Quite stupidly, I say, "That's a beautiful gown."

She waits a few beats, just to let me know she doesn't trust the likes of me; then she gives me a gracious smile, followed by a thank-you, a snap of the purse, and an efficient exit. Sophia's a potential problem; she obviously polices Otto's waters more closely than Helmut understands.

"Helmut told me you worked as a nurse in neurosurgery down in Dallas," Otto says upon my return to the box. "In a research hospital."

"Yes," I say. "People were flown in from all over to get treated there." I take my seat next to him. "We did a lot of brain surgery."

"Brain surgery?" He looks at me hard, big brown eyes flecked with gold. "What kind?"

"Vascular repair, mostly. It's a very demanding area." I'm unsure how to touch him and make it seem natural, but I need to dump this fear. "Very, very demanding."

"What drew you to neurosurgery? If you don't mind my asking."

"Well, my mother died of vein star syndrome when I was thirteen, and I guess . . ." I can't believe I blurted out the truth about my mother's death like this. It shows how nervous I am. "That's all. That's why," I say quietly.

He looks at me with convincing warmth. "I'm so sorry. I didn't mean to—"

"That's okay. It's a natural question."

"Vein star syndrome is a terrible, terrible thing," he says. "I'm so sorry." He can't take his eyes from me. There's nothing worse than hearing about vein star deaths when that's your main health worry. "It must've been . . ."

I put my hand on his arm, trying not to tremble. "It's okay." I push my awareness out into my energy dimension. "She was alone when it happened; that's what gets me. Nobody to hold her hand or, you know . . ." I need more time, so I keep going. "She called the ambulance; then she called Dad"—I lower my voice—"Uncle Helmut's brother—at work, and she told him that she loved him, and for him to tell us she loved us. My brother and I were at school." I focus on burning the hole; my finger heats. "By the time the ambulance arrived, she was gone." My fear *whooshes* into him.

Otto lowers his eyes and swallows. "Jesus."

I breathe in the sweet, cool air, drenched with serenity.

He regards me with caring concern; I'm frankly impressed with his ability to cover. I wouldn't know he was consumed with vein star terror if I hadn't just channeled it into him.

"I shouldn't have gone into it like that," I say, removing my impossibly airy hand.

"No," Otto says. "Don't apologize."

The phone call part of the story isn't actually true. I lifted it from an old article. It's one of the most awful health stories I've ever come across.

Casually I turn to Helmut and ask him if he's finished his book on medieval households. Helmut knows what I need. He launches into a highly detailed explanation of something called consortial lineages while I get my post-zing euphoria under control.

"Sounds like an excellent read," Otto says from the other side of me. His stony expression tells me the zing took. I can practically feel my fear animating his. Good.

Helmut goes on about consortial lineages as I sip my wine, which tastes fantastic now that I'm glorying. Eventually I sit back, allowing Helmut and Otto to talk across me. All I have to do is enjoy the opera, and I'm sure I will, considering I've channeled every last bit of my negative emotional content into the man next to me. Just then I glance over and find Sophia eyeing me. I turn away, determined not to let her degrade my pure and perfect state of being. Instead, I contemplate the opera. I'm enchanted with the story, and full of hopes and worries for Tosca and Cavaradossi.

It doesn't even bother me when I find Otto watching me.

"I know they die at the end," I whisper, putting my hand to my chest. "Still, I hope!" I laugh, because this sums up my feeling precisely. "It's crazy. I know it doesn't turn out—you say so, the program says so—and I'm still hoping it will!"

He regards me with an air of discovery, as though he's only now realizing something about me. "I feel the same way," he whispers. "My hopes rise with Tosca's every time." The center of his upper lip is subtly bowed, like the top of a heart, I notice. They're large, classic lips. "It's never crazy to hope," he continues somewhat fervently. "Never. I'm so pleased you're enjoying it."

I'm surprised. It's unusual for somebody who's just been zinged to be interested in how other people feel. The Alchemist and the Silver Widow pretty much collapsed in on themselves. This man is a survivor, I think. He's a victor. I'm going to have to be careful.

The lights dim and he turns his attention to the stage as the curtains part. His features are somewhat exotic; his nose has an elegant curve to it, and his cheekbones are strong and proud. And then with those dark, thick waves and those classic lips, I'm sure a portrait painter would enjoy painting Chief Otto Sanchez. What's more,

there's this incredible contrast between his ornate outfit
and the sense of brute strength that radiates from him.
His strength is like a scent that calls to something deep
inside you, makes you want to put your nose to him,
makes you want to press your body to him.

I marvel at how delicate the crystal wineglass looks in
his large, intricately muscled hands. I force myself to
focus on his large thumb and imagine him plunging it
into another man's eye.

This ends my Otto appreciation session. Otto won't
come down easy, but he will come down; I'll make sure
of it. And in fact, every once in a while during this act,
he touches his head through his beret. That's a start.
Sometimes he touches the golden rail in front of us, too,
and the ledge below it, like he's communing with its
smoothness, drawing solace. Sort of an odd thing to do,
really.

The tragedy follows its heart-wrenching spin, and
finally Tosca throws herself to her death. I sit still after
it's all over, stunned. I've never seen anything so spec-
tacular and moving. The four of us rise once the clap-
ping subsides.

As if his outfit isn't outrageous enough already, the
Engineer swings a velvet cape over his shoulders. I think
about the clever and amusing things Packard will say
when I tell him about the cape, but actually Otto looks
fantastic in it. Like a villainy rogue from another era.

It's a kick to walk through the opera house lobby with
him, too, because everybody looks at him and admires
him. The four of us are waylaid down in the main lobby
by a handful of autograph seekers and people congrat-
ulating him on the capture of the Brick Slinger.
Midcity's lieutenant mayor, currently the acting mayor,
recently gave Otto a medal.

Untouchable, I think, as he scribbles on people's
opera programs. Nobody would dare cross the Engineer.

Except the disillusionists. I think again about that poor man with the gouged eyes. How do you do that to another human being?

There's some talk of the four of us going to the Engineer's private club for a nightcap, but I notice Sophia building a case for an end to the night; she and Otto argue quietly, just out of earshot, as Otto rubs his head. I know exactly what he's doing: that thing I used to do where you try to determine if the sensation you're experiencing is inside the brain, or if it's related to the musculature surrounding the scalp. If you can move the pain, that suggests it's muscular, which is what you hope.

"I don't want Sophia as an enemy," I whisper to Helmut.

Helmut looks away, replies under his breath, "Nothing to be done."

I nod.

In spite of my glorying, I do feel guilty about using Mom's condition. Talking about her reminds me of all the ways I miss her, all the things I wish I could tell her. She alone would understand how I got mixed up in all this. She would understand perfectly.

"Helmut, is the client for Sanchez the widow of the gouged-eyes man?"

"Client's anonymous."

"Here, too?"

Helmut nods. "But since this one started so long ago, I didn't feel it related to the cases we discussed before," he whispers. "You can see why the client would be anonymous—imagine the danger of an enraged Otto Sanchez."

I nod. "Right."

Sophia's back to say good-bye, and how wonderful it was to meet us, but she cannot stay. Off she walks.

Helmut touches Otto's arm and mumbles in low tones.

I watch Sophia go, green silk coat flowing under flickering candelabras. She merges with the crowd pressing through the gilded doors.

Chapter
Twenty-eight

OTTO'S CLUB, the Merovingian, is a short stroll away, and soon he and Helmut and I are ensconced in velvet furniture in a darkly paneled and leathered atmosphere drinking very old Scotch. Helmut improvises anecdotes about our extended family, one after another. I try to catch his eye because it's starting to be a lot to keep straight, but Helmut doesn't notice. He'd mentioned Otto makes him nervous. Lots of talk and details is a classic sign of nervousness. Otto, as a superstar detective, would surely get that.

Finally Helmut's phone rings, as I knew it would. He pretends to have a quick conversation, then informs us he must go.

Otto implores me to stay just a bit longer. Helmut kisses my cheek and trundles out.

Otto gives me a pointed look and holds it, like he's considering something. Then, "It won't work in the end, you know."

My mouth goes dry, and I tilt my head quizzically. "What?" I'm not safe even here, in the Merovingian, I realize. Otto could carry me out kicking and screaming and nobody would stop him.

"How can any wild species survive the coming years?" He sinks into the divan. "I don't mean to seem hopeless, but something about this project with your

uncle gets into my bones. The bleakness of it. Still, one
has to persevere."

Warily I settle back into my chair. "He's always been
dedicated."

He touches the spot on his head again, staring vacantly
across the room in the general direction of an oil painting of a man in a pince-nez.

It's a look I know well. Otto's not seeing the portrait
at all. Rather, he's focusing on the network of blood
veins under his skull. He's imagining weakened vascular
walls bulging out in the telltale star shape, like I have a
million times.

"I take him as something of a model, a mentor, somebody worth aspiring to," Otto continues. "Don't tell
him I said that. He'd be embarrassed—"

"Oh, he thinks the world of you, Otto. He is so
impressed with you."

"He shouldn't be."

"What do you mean? Of all people, Otto—even just
this week, catching that Brick Slinger . . ."

Otto nods distantly.

"Is something wrong?"

"I'm sorry. It's nothing, I'm sure."

"Do you have a headache?" I touch my head where
he's been touching.

He pulls his white bow tie loose as if he's not getting
enough air. He's panicking, and fighting not to show
it. "Of course, you *are* a nurse," he says, more to himself than to me. He undoes the studs at the top of his
shirt, and then two buttons, which affords me a better
view of his thick, solid neck and the sprinkling of dusky
hairs on his smooth chest just below. "I don't want to
alarm you, but please know that if I pass out, my pre-
cipitating symptoms were prickling sensations on a
highly localized area of my head, here"—he touches the
area—"and at times a dull pain that seems to pulse. As

a nurse, I think you can appreciate the importance of this information."

"If you pass out? Otto, what's wrong? Are your eyes sensitive to light?" This was easy. But then again, he's a perfectly analogous vessel.

"It's not a migraine."

"It's dull pain, not sharp?"

"For now. No, no, I'm fine." He leans forward and rests his elbows on his knees, supporting his face on his fingertips. "This is nothing. I simply wanted to tell you in case . . ."

"I understand," I say quickly, remembering all the times I embarrassed myself by reporting my symptoms so that they could get relayed to the medical staff once I was unconscious. "I understand. It's smart of you, Otto. Those sorts of symptoms can be troubling."

"I know what you're thinking. That it was your story about your mother. I'll confess I can be suggestible around vascular maladies." He looks up. "I hope this conversation stays within medical confidentiality."

"Of course." I move over and sit down right next to him on the divan, put a hand on his arm. I'm frightened of him and sorry for him all at the same time, like he's this dangerous wounded animal. But I have to push him further.

"I don't know why it's so intense," he says. "I've had this problem since I was a boy, but—"

"You've worried about vein star syndrome since you were a boy?"

"Since I learned what it was. Yes. A boy."

Just like me, I think. "My mother was worried about them since childhood, too."

Otto turns to me, naked horror in his eyes. "And then she actually *had* one?"

"Yes. Nobody believed her. I mean, she had all the scans. She'd go to the ER when things seemed dire, but people believed it was hypochondria. Even she came to believe it. Now there's new thinking—I probably shouldn't be telling you this . . ."

"Please, tell me. Really, Justine. Go on." He smiles warmly, like nothing's wrong.

His smile doesn't fool me; I used to do the same thing—hide my fear in order to get the maximum information from a medical professional. He's convincing. He's had plenty of practice, of course.

"Please, do go on," he says.

"Well, there's growing evidence that people can intuit their future conditions. A mind-body connection phenomenon."

Otto looks pale.

"And then there's the 'theory of negative visualization' camp. Specialists who believe that constant meditation on a specific illness can actually *cause* that illness."

He takes a labored breath.

"I'm so sorry. I hope I'm not scaring you."

"No, no! I wanted to know." He takes off his jacket, folds it over the armrest. "You're saying you know of specialists who say thinking about a disease can create it. . . ."

I nod. "Theory of negative visualization."

"Jesus." Light perspiration covers his neck, his cheekbones. His heart rate, I'm guessing, is significantly elevated.

I ask the waiter for two waters, no ice.

Otto undoes the buttons on his velvet vest; then he undoes his cuffs and rolls up his sleeves to reveal brawny, olive-skinned forearms. He's descending into a full-blown attack, the same flavor I used to get. Otto feels familiar to me on so many levels. His gaze wanders around the room, then back to me. My guess is that he's wondering whether he should try to go home now, while he's relatively ambulatory, or wait for it to pass and risk having to be helped out.

"I wonder if I need medical attention."

I stiffen. He's thinking ER already?

"Oh, Otto . . ." This is bad. If he goes, it would be logical for me to go along. And once we're there, he's sure to ask me questions about machines and hospital procedures—all the things people like us wonder about in the waiting room. And what if he introduced me to the medical professionals as a visiting nurse, and they ask me questions I can't answer? If they became suspicious of my credentials, he'd see it in their faces.

The waiter delivers the two waters.

"Thank you," I say, placing one in Otto's grip. "Drink it. Slowly."

He complies. "What do you think?"

I take the glass from him. "I think I told you a couple of terribly disturbing things."

"You were responding to my questions."

I take his hand and squeeze it. "Look at me."

He obeys, wanting me to say the magical words— why this couldn't possibly be vein star syndrome. He's so vulnerable, it's hard to picture him murdering people. All I can think of is African elephants, cool and powerful and beautiful. That's the sense I got from touching the surface of his energy dimension.

"You're okay, Otto. You do not have a vein star. Do you understand?" He needs more. "I am a highly skilled nurse," I continue. "I've seen hundreds of people with vein stars expanding, leaking, blowing out. You're not having an episode like that."

"How do you know?"

"After a while, you just know."

"How can you be sure?"

"Don't you have that? As a detective? You arrive on a crime scene and you just know?"

His gaze intensifies.

"I can't say exactly how I know; I just do. It's your color, the way you describe your symptoms, your demeanor, your energy. And wow, what a coincidence that I'd tell that disturbing story, and then that very thing happens to you. Especially"—I raise my eyebrows—"when you yourself confessed that you are suggestible in that area."

Faraway look. I'm losing him.

"Anybody would find what I told you to be disturbing."

"Not you, Justine. You grew up with unimaginable tragedy and you rose above it and turned your life toward helping others. Not toward an inane obsession with your health."

I look down, remembering the shame of it all. We have so much in common, it's difficult to keep him walled off as an enemy. "I worried about it all my life, just like you. Obsessed about it with distressing, debilitating consequences . . . Otto, I'm no different than you in this."

He searches my face.

"Honestly," I say. "In fact, in a contest for who has the most vein star health anxiety here, I would, as they say, *kick your ass.*"

Otto laughs a deep, warm laugh that makes me feel wonderful, like there's a direct line running from his laugh to something good inside me. I should probably take it as a warning. I don't.

"Believe me," I continue, "I know what it took for you to tell me your symptoms. The embarrassment versus the risk of presenting at an ER unconscious."

He closes his eyes. "Exactly. *Exactly.*" I can feel his relief as sure as I can feel his hand under mine. His eyes look even larger closed than open.

"Do let me assure you, Chief Sanchez, that being a

nurse gives you no immunity to the late-night visits to the ER. It certainly never did for me."

"The late-night visits." He opens his eyes, smiles slyly. "I always tell people I've been called out on a case."

"Convenient," I say. It's suddenly awkward that our hands have been touching for so long. I let go and take up my glass of water. "Have you ever had a positive scan?"

"No. But it's my understanding that that doesn't mean anything, considering the way the vein stars expand and contract."

"That's the special hell of it."

"But as a nurse, at least you know how to decipher the information and the spin the doctors put on it."

"Actually, no. It just adds a new layer of second-guessing and paranoia. As a nurse, I have extra information to be paranoid about."

Otto smiles. "Oh, forgive me. That is . . ." He doesn't have a word for it.

"I know."

Otto's warm smile crinkles the edges of his brown eyes. "I've never met anyone else who worries about health as I do, who suffers . . . who knows. You understand." He says this like it's this wonderful discovery. "You *know*."

"So do you." And I smile, because it *is* wonderful.

He shakes his head. "The constant longing to be free of it."

"The longing to be normal," I whisper. "A normal person for once."

"Yes. *Normal*. The quest for normal." He closes his eyes. "If only for a day."

I sigh. "And talking and smiling like everything's okay, even though you can practically feel the blood dribbling down through your cranium."

He looks at me sideways. "The silent smite."

"You named it?"

"A bit silly," he says.

"No, I like it." The truth.

"You can borrow the name if you like," he says.

"Maybe I will." I slide down next to him. "The silent smite. That's good." It's brilliant. The Engineer understands as no one else could.

"Well, *slow and silent smite* might be more accurate," he adds, "but since I use it only to myself—" He pauses, looks at me. "If you have any ideas for improving the term—"

"It's perfect as is."

"Okay, then," he says.

We say nothing for a minute or so, but it's an easy, enjoyable silence. Packard's words echo through in my mind: *If you find yourself feeling too comfortable with him, walk away.* But I don't want to walk away. This is the Chief Sanchez I always imagined. Better.

"I noticed that you spoke of it in the past tense," Otto says.

"Did I?" I'm taken aback by his powers of observation. *Had I?*

"Do you feel you're cured, Justine?"

"I wish I was cured. You don't know how badly I wish for that."

His gaze softens, brown eyes endlessly sad. "In fact, I do know," he says quietly.

"Right. Of course you do." Suddenly I hate lying to him, and I recall, with a wave of regret, how I lied to Cubby. There's a little bit of Cubby in Otto, I realize. "It never really goes away," I say. "I just move it around."

He nods.

I finish my water. I can't remember when I've felt so instantly bonded to a person. I need to walk away. It's the last thing I want to do, and the one thing I have to do. I point at a grandfather clock in the corner. "Does that thing work?"

He nods. Midnight.

I stand.

He stands, disappointment showing all over his face.

I say, "I'm sorry. I really do have to go."

"I wish you didn't. This was an enchanting encounter . . ."

Precisely why I have to leave. I hold out my hand. "It really was such a treat to spend a night at the opera with you."

Lightly, he wraps his fingers around mine. I struggle not to feel it, not to feel him. "The pleasure was all mine. Can my driver and I give you a lift home?"

"No thanks." I extract my hand from his and clutch my purse and wrap. "Thank you, though."

"Wait—what are you doing this Thursday evening?"

I freeze, except for the heartbeat in my throat. "I don't know."

"Do you mean that you don't know what you're doing? Or do you mean that you don't know if you should want to accompany me to a late-afternoon, invitation-only dress rehearsal of *Carmen,* and perhaps a bite afterwards?"

"I don't know because I'm getting over a painful, painful breakup, and if you're asking me on a romantic level, I'm sorry—"

"No, no, purely platonic. A fellow opera lover, a fellow health sufferer, but we won't talk about that. There won't be a repeat of this pathetic scene." As if to reinforce the platonic aspect, he adds, "Helmut is more than welcome to come. I'd love to have him along."

I contemplate this. "Actually, it sounds fun, Otto. I'll talk to Uncle Helmut." I thank him again and leave, trying not to smile like a lunatic all the way to the door.

Chapter
Twenty-nine

THE NEXT MORNING I stop by Mongolian Delites to give Packard my progress report, as I promised I would. He's with Carter, who greets me gruffly, then returns to scowling at the newspaper before him, opened to the big article on the special mayoral election they set for January. I can't imagine that's what got Carter so riled.

Packard barely makes eye contact with me. He's focused on Carter, too. Something's wrong.

I sit down and launch into my report about the night, minus the bonding moments. The effectiveness of my zing cheers Packard. "I definitely didn't want to risk going to the ER with Otto," I tell him. "I'd never pull it off."

"You could've pulled it off," he says.

"This guy is observant."

Carter flips a page angrily, nearly tearing it. I raise my eyebrows at Packard: *Is something up with Carter?*

Packard returns my gaze and shakes his head minutely, green eyes pale in the morning light. He's aware of Carter's state and he's on it. Packard and I are able to communicate silently more and more these days; our ragingly unhealthy attraction causes us to observe each other closely.

Packard pours me the last of the coffee and goes around to the other side of the bar to rinse out the coffeepot.

I stir some sugar into my mug. "He really is good at seeming genuine and forthright."

Packard sets a towel on the bar between us. "How do you think he got to where he is today? He's a master at it."

"I suppose."

"He probably lied to you all night."

"Right." But I know he wasn't lying about his longing to be normal, or that little name: silent smite.

"All of our targets are lying scoundrels," Packard says. "Dangerous and evil, yet thoroughly unimpressive."

"As opposed to all the dangerous and evil, yet thoroughly *impressive* people?"

Carter pipes up. "One of our old targets, Mr. Chapeau Rouge, thought he could predict the weather by smell. He tracked his forecasts against TV weathermen, and he had a consistently higher success rate."

Packard turns to Carter. "Yes, that was impressive."

Just like that, Carter's face turns red and a vein on his neck springs out. "Stop patronizing me! I think that was very goddamn impressive."

Packard places his hand on the bar in front of Carter. "You've waited too long between zings."

"Fuck you, Packard. I'll tell you if I need a zing."

I just stare at Carter. He's like an overtired kid who's too upset to sleep.

Packard leaves his hand there and turns to me. "The consequences of failure here are extreme. I wouldn't have put you in here if I didn't think you could prevail, but please, promise me you'll be careful."

"I will," I say.

Carter shoves at Packard's fingers. "Get away."

"Carter, you'll feel much better," Packard says.

"Don't fucking patronize me!" With that, Carter whips his coffee cup at the wall behind the bar; shards of mirror and ceramic rain onto the liquor bottles below. "Don't look at me like that!" He hurls another coffee cup.

I slide off my seat and back away.

"No! Justine"—Carter shows me his palms—"it's nothing to do with you."

"Why shouldn't she be scared?" Packard says. He takes a deep breath as an example for Carter, who mimics him childishly. Then Carter puts his fist to his very red forehead. Packard rounds the bar and comes to his side, wraps his arms around him, holding him tight, eyes squeezed shut like his heart's a little bit broken to see Carter suffer. I never saw it before, but it's suddenly plain—Carter's like a son to Packard.

Carter stays stiff, but he doesn't push Packard away. Finally he grabs onto Packard's arm with both hands, holding it like he wants to break it in two, but also like he's clinging to him for safety. Then he bows his head, fringe of ash-blond bangs covering his eyes. His shoulders fall. His whole body softens. Zing complete.

Carter smiles sheepishly. "Oops." I've seen lots of disillusionists zing Packard over the months, but none look as satisfied as Carter. "Man! Sorry about the mirror, Packard."

"I'm not," Packard says. "Go ahead. Have some fun."

Carter stands. "You sure?" Packard nods. Carter picks up his pack. "Want a lift home, Justine?"

I look at Packard.

"We're finished here," he says.

I pull on my jacket. "You going to be a nice driver, Carter?"

Carter nods.

"Justine. Good work," Packard says as we're leaving. "Good work."

Chapter Thirty

THERE ARE MANY factors to balance for my Thursday outfit.

It's a dress rehearsal, so that's casual. However, it's still the opera, and there's dinner after, so that's dressy. But then, it's not a date, so that swings it back to casual. But then there are Otto's many charms, which swings it to pretty, and then there's the fact that he's a dangerous killer, which swings things to casual, if not dowdy.

The outfit I wind up wearing is a blue cashmere V-neck sweater that feels like kitten fur, with huggy brown suede-textured pants and kicky brown kitten-heeled sandals. Looking in the mirror, I have to say pretty won out, yet that crucial balance between casual and dressy was achieved.

I'm not bringing Helmut along. Needless to say, I'm a bit conflicted about that.

In preparation for our outing, I study the photo of the man with the gouged eyes, trying to rekindle the fear and revulsion I had for Otto before, and how tricked I feel by him, posing as this great crime fighter.

The technique works until I actually see Otto on the opera house steps, smile as big as Texas, brown trench coat waving wild in the wind, brown beret atop luscious dark waves. He holds out a hand as I approach, and it feels like the most natural thing in the world to pop up the steps and take it. I try not to smile but fail, and my stomach lifts as he tightens his big soft fingers around mine.

I force myself to touch my purse with the other hand, to feel the outline of the stun gun. He's a sociopath, I tell myself. He's fooled you and the whole city.

I watch his face as we go in, trying to imagine him not smiling, trying to imagine his warm brown eyes cold. I picture him standing over a bound man—a double-crossing cohort, kneeling before Otto, sobbing, begging for mercy. And then Otto walks up, places his hands gently on either side of the man's head, holding it like it's a basketball, and slowly he presses his meaty thumbs right into the man's eyes, gouging them out. But they wouldn't pop out like in cartoons—the eyes would more extrude, misshapen and broken, to hang from bloody strands of ganglia and tendons. Feeling quite ill now, I imagine Otto's cruel smile as he shoves the man away, watches him stumble to the floor, writhing in agony, dying as blood and tissue seep from his eye sockets.

"This place is magical in the daylight." Otto says. "Do you see how that chandelier casts rainbows on the ceiling?"

I sigh. "Lovely."

Carmen is colorful and exciting, and I like it even more than *Tosca*. During the first intermission, Otto and I make up a silly anecdote about the man in the little side booth who opens and closes the curtains, and we laugh and laugh about it, probably more than the joke warrants; it's laughter twisted high by the excitement and pleasure of each other's company, along with a whole lot of nervousness on my part.

During the second intermission we eat grapes and build new details onto the story. Otto has a big laugh to match his big brown eyes and his big personality.

After the show he has to sign only one autograph. The

second we step out into the dark, drizzly night, a sleek black sedan appears; Otto opens the back door for me.

I get in. "Do you always get driven around?"

He settles in next to me and shuts the door. "It comes with being chief. I can't say I prefer it."

I've never known somebody with a chauffeured car, much less ridden in one myself. Otto introduces me to the driver, whose name is Jimmy. Jimmy wears a cap with a rigid brim, like a policeman, and he speeds off without being told where to go, which I find odd. We'd planned to grab a bite to eat after, but I thought we'd discuss it.

I study the locks on the doors. Are they the kind you can unlock from the inside? This is all starting to remind me of the Alchemist situation. What's more, Otto seems uncomfortable. Again I trace the outline of my stun gun through the side of my bag, wishing I'd worn it on the holster. On crime shows, they say that when you get into a car with a criminal, your survival rate plummets ninety percent. They say you're better off letting yourself be shot on the sidewalk.

"I shortchanged that man," Otto says, low so only I can hear.

"What?"

"Usually I write my motto, 'Guarding citizens from evildoers of every kind,' and then I sign my name, but I confess I wanted to get on with our night, so I just scribbled, 'Protect and serve,' with my name. And 'Protect and serve' is not even that much shorter."

"'Protect and serve' is good," I say, "because you run the police force and that's their motto."

"But people who want my autograph are looking for me to write my motto."

"I'm sure he felt your kind intent," I say, thinking how twisted all this is. It's like the Alchemist having a motto like 'To ensure the safety and happiness of ladies.'

We turn onto increasingly obscure side streets.

"Where are we going?" I ask.

"My favorite restaurant in all the world." He points out interesting features on the different buildings we pass. For a police chief/crime boss, he certainly knows a lot about architecture.

A few minutes later, we pull up between rows of vine-covered brownstones. Otto gets out and offers me his hand. I take it and find myself at the top of a long, thin stairwell that leads down to a brightly lit basement-level door below. The rusty metal sign hanging over it says CIAPPO'S. A lone candle burns in the tiny window next to it, like a secret signal.

We go down.

Ciappo's candlelit, grottolike interior is all white plaster walls and dark beams. A busy front bar and cashier area thins into a narrow dining room with tables on either side, filled with diners. Popular place. The space stretches so far back, I wonder if it doesn't go the length of the block underground. We're seated at a table next to a highly textured painting of a toga-clad woman feeding geese.

Otto takes the liberty of ordering a bottle of Prosecco and both our meals, too. Yes, the waiter very clearly approves of his selections, but still. I decide it shows Otto is a man who doesn't care what anybody else wants.

After our waiter pours the wine, Otto offers a toast to our imaginary curtain guy, and he peppers me with questions about my intentions to search for a new nursing position in Midcity. It's an easy conversation to have because I know a little bit about every area hospital.

Otto tells me the Ciappo's building was constructed over a century ago as a funeral parlor for a secret brotherhood. "The processions came through here," he says. "The services were held in the larger area up where we came in. They held them in some odd language."

"Is architectural history one of your hobbies?"

"In a manner of speaking."

Just then our first course comes: spiced breads and baby vegetables. It's so delicious that I decide I should wait until after dinner to zing him, because if he's anything like me, he'll lose his appetite once he's in an attack. And we might have to leave prematurely.

A dish of bruschetta and olives arrives next, followed by roasted artichoke hearts with cheeses, nuts, and capers. We talk and laugh and feast.

During a pause in our jolliness, Otto falls silent and puts his fingers together, just the tips, like something's wrong. I bite my lip, studying his brown beret, which is nearly the same rich chestnut shade as his hair.

"What's *your* motto, Justine?" he asks.

"I don't have one."

"Everybody needs a motto."

"I can see why you'd need one, Otto, but I'm more of an everyday person."

He laughs his wonderful laugh. "Come, come, Justine. That's the last thing you are."

I give him my most neutral expression. "What do you mean by that?"

"You know exactly what I mean. Let's think of a motto for you. Tell me, what exactly is your goal here?"

I freeze. Is he toying with me? Would a normal person say that?

I'm saved by the arrival of our next course: crepes filled with caramelized onions and chardonnay jelly.

I focus wholeheartedly on the food. "This is one of the most delicious things I've ever eaten," I say, anxiously rerunning his words. *Not an everyday person . . . What exactly is your goal here?* Why did I let myself get so comfortable?

"Do you think you're getting out of the motto discussion?"

"Honestly, Otto, what would I do with a motto?"

"A motto guides you. It's something to refer back to in times of decision and dilemma. A kind of touchstone. Everybody should have one."

"Okay, let me think." I put down my fork, resigned to playing along, whatever this is. "My goals tend to change, is the thing," I say, opting for the simple truth. "My goal used to be peace of mind, being that I was tortured by constant health worries. But later, I suppose it evolved into peace of mind within cocoonlike comfort." I'm thinking of my hoped-for life with Cubby, and I'm surprised that it's lost some of its luster. "That's not a very noble goal, is it? Just to feel serenity for once."

"It's a very human, very hopeful goal. It's my goal for the citizens I protect. But I suspect you desire more than that. Perhaps your current life purpose relates to being a nurse."

"Hmmm." I press the side of my fork into a fat section of crepe. Jelly and onions squish over the whisper-thin pastry. I bring the morsel to my mouth, savor its bright, warm sweetness, just a hint of rosemary. Am I overreacting? Maybe this is a normal conversation.

"What moved you to become a nurse? Compassion?"

I turn the question over in my mind.

He says, "Perhaps your motto could be, 'To help and heal the citizenry.' What do you think of that?"

"That doesn't really fit. That's more the goal of the medical community." I'm starting to become more interested in the motto idea now. Why not? Why shouldn't I have a motto?

Otto looks happy. He's a pretty fun date when you forget about his evil nature. He looks at me a little bit sideways. "Start with what you want. What is your heart's ideal?"

I ponder this privately. I want to be free from worrying about my health, and free from Packard, of course;

that's the main thing. And I want people to be free from fear. And in spite of my lingering reservations, I sometimes feel sort of good about being a disillusionist, especially since Foley's transformation. I like that my pathetic existence could actually have a positive effect on Midcity. I play with different words in my head, switching combinations.

"You have an idea. It's all over your face."

I put down my fork. "This will be a two-part motto." I go back over it in my mind. I want him to like it, I realize.

"Out with it."

"Okay." I take a breath and raise my hands as if to frame it in the space between us. "Promoting freedom and transformation."

He gets a serious look, seems to roll it around in his mind, to savor it. "Very interesting," he says finally. "Tell me more."

Obviously I don't tell him about being a minion of Packard, but I talk about other freedom-related aspects. Like how hypochondria, and really any disease, keeps you from being free—physically free, and free of fear, too.

He nods vigorously. He understands.

Freedom from fear of crime is a bit part of my goal, too, but I don't say that. "As for the transformation part, if I do my job well, the person I'm working with goes out better than they came in." This last works for a nurse or a disillusionist.

Again Otto is silent, and I wonder if he has a problem with that part. Then he shakes his head. "'Promoting freedom and transformation.' That is absolutely magnificent."

I grin, way bigger than I should. "You think so? Are you sure you're not just saying that?"

"No. It's simple. Genuine. Powerful." He has that

gaze of discovery again, and it makes me feel special. "Freedom and transformation—it's good for an individual, and it's something society as a whole strives for, assuming transformation is positive, which I suppose I do."

This is what I'd imagine the old Otto saying, the Otto who believes in making things better.

"I love your motto," he says.

I feel my face flash red. "Thanks, Otto. And you know what? I love having a motto. My motto could apply to any situation and any area of my life."

"As a good motto should." Otto gives me a mischievous look. "It's almost as excellent as mine."

I laugh and kick him lightly under the table. "*Almost* as excellent as yours?"

"*Almost.*"

I kick him again, and this time he's ready: he grasps my ankle and lifts it onto his knee. I catch my breath. Time slows and simmers as he slides his hand, little by little, up and under my pant leg, resting it on my bare calf, sending effervescence though my pelvis.

"Is this okay?" he asks.

It's so okay, and so not. My mind fuzzes out. "Yes," I say.

Slowly he slides his hand back, touches my foot through the spaces in my sandal. The charge between us builds, thick and humid, and his sociopathic status matters less and less. It's here I know I should walk away. For real.

His fingers move, teasingly light on my instep. He's removing my sandal. "Is this okay?"

I can't breathe, and I don't have an answer.

He holds my gaze with his. My sandal clatters to the floor, and the next thing I know, he's exploring the tenderest parts of my foot; the subtle way he moves his fingers is stunningly erotic.

"The feet are the most ignored erogenous zone in our culture," he says.

"Aah," I manage to say.

Waiters appear, plates are removed, and still he keeps my foot, like it's his own thing now. I don't want him to give it back.

More wine is poured, but I'm drunk on the feeling of the Engineer's fingers sliding slowly and wantonly around my foot, and sometimes my calf. His communication could not be clearer: *sleeping with him would be an absolutely mind-blowing experience.* At least that's what I'm getting out of it. I look around at the other diners, grateful the tablecloths hang low. This definitely isn't the sort of interaction Packard had in mind.

"So what made you think of getting a motto?" I ask this mostly to get him talking, because I need to collect myself. I remind myself that he's smarter than the Alchemist. And he has my foot. And I don't want it back.

"Oh, it's a very long story."

"Tell me," I say. "I want to know."

He gets this crooked *What the hell* smile. Then, "Just between us?"

"I give you my word."

He strokes my sole with his thumb. "Back when I was younger, I made this decision to change the course of my life. . . ."

I smile. "One of those."

"Yes," he whispers. He seems very serious suddenly. "I wanted to make something of myself, hone my skills—"

"Your crime-fighting skills?"

"In a sense. But the wisdom I sought wasn't to be found in any sort of school. So I set off trekking around the world by boat, train, camel. I visited remote villages and enclaves on every continent."

"Wow."

Otto goes on to tell a travel tale full of interesting people and shocking hardships. He keeps his hand on my foot as he speaks—a warm, live presence. He describes his eventual arrival in the remote cave region of the Vindahar mountain range where he apprenticed with a master sage.

"Are you telling me you learned about crime fighting from a master sage in a cave?"

"I learned how to better use my powers of observation, and to become more . . ." He searches for the word. "More effective. And that's where I determined my purpose in life, and my motto."

"How long did you study with him?"

He leans in slightly. "Over a decade."

I raise my eyebrows. "Gosh."

"This isn't something I publicize, you know. As far as public record goes, I was just traveling. The truth is, well, a bit exotic for people. I don't know why I'm telling you. I feel as though I know you. . . ."

The zing, I think.

"And I feel like I can count on your confidentiality."

"Of course you can," I say. "A decade in a cave and a master sage. That *could* sound a tad exotic."

"You wouldn't have recognized me when I walked out of there. I had hair to here—" He indicates a spot near his elbow. "A big, thick, long beard." He draws his hand down from his chin, completing the motion with a flourish that could only indicate a curl on the very end. My heart nearly jumps out of its socket as I picture Otto with long hair and a beard with a curl at the end. And no hat. It's a face I know well. It's *the* face. I bolt my attention to the tablecloth.

Henji.

He draws a fingernail across the tender underside of my foot, releasing a wave of shivers that sail clear through me. I think back on everything Rickie had told us. Packard and Henji as abandoned boys, living with other boys in an abandoned school. The epic battle between the two of them, and Henji leaving on a ship at the age of eleven.

"When I finally arrived at the guest house on the edge of the Moolon Basin and caught sight of myself in a steel-slab mirror, it was a shock." He laughs.

I don't.

"Justine?"

"That's such an amazing story," I effuse. Henji and Otto Sanchez, one and the same. Of course! I meet his eyes, praying my terror doesn't show. "I never knew anybody who did such a thing."

There's this weird silence.

"I can count on your confidence . . ."

"Of course. It's incredible, that's all. All the places you were, and . . . I feel like I haven't been anywhere," I say stupidly. "In fact, I haven't. Except Canada."

"Canada's somewhere."

I nod fervently. "Oh, Canada's wonderful." The more I look at him, the more obvious it is that he's the face. How could I not have seen it? I slip my foot out of his hand and locate my shoe on the floor beneath the table, manage a smile. "Could you excuse me for a moment?"

He rises. "Certainly."

I take my purse and proceed, in a stunned fog, toward the front, near where I'd spied the rest rooms. I duck into a corner near a plant and pull out my phone.

Shelby answers. A lot of talking in the background. "Where are you?" I ask.

"Delites," she says.

"Don't say it's me."

"Okay."

"Shelby—" I don't even know what to say.

"Where are you?"

"A little place called Ciappo's. Where I've been enjoying a five-course Italian meal with Henji."

"What?"

I explain to her that the Engineer is Chief Sanchez. I wasn't supposed to tell anybody, but I don't care anymore.

She laughs incredulously.

"Shelby, Sanchez is the Engineer, okay? And I'm at dinner with him, and I always thought he looked familiar, and we just had this whole conversation where he told me he went off at a young age to travel the world and he emerged from his whole wisdom-quest thing with long hair and long beard with a curl on the end, just like on the faces. And now it's so obvious—it's his nose . . . it's him. I don't know what to do. He's the face. Henji's fingerprint is his own face of ten years ago when he emerged from some cave and—"

"I am going out door right now. Give me address."

I grab a matchbook off the bar and give her the address. "It's this basement place. Easy to miss. Just walk through like you're looking for somebody and stop and say hi. See what you think; maybe I'm going crazy. I've got to get back." I look around. "Hurry."

My many years of smiling and pretending nothing is wrong while secretly freaking out—years of *silent smites,* as Otto calls them—come in handy as I take my seat across from him.

He tilts his head. "Is everything all right?"

"Oh, yes. Very much." I smile and sip some wine. And then some more. *I create and my nemesis destroys,* Packard had said.

"I'm so fascinated, Otto. You must have been quite young when you set off."

"I was just a boy," he says.

"So the world was your classroom."

"Yes," he says.

I cajole him into telling me more and he complies, describing how he lived on bark and roots, carrying out impossible trials set for him by the master sage. Keeping him talking is the best way to handle him right now.

"The experience helped to expand my sense of what's possible in a life." Otto settles back, wine in hand. "I came back and joined the force, worked up to detective. My first case was of a homicide connected to a diamond necklace." He proceeds to tell a story full of surprising turns and red herrings, and he tells it enchantingly.

As he talks, I think about how a highcap with structural powers can supposedly get impressions of significant things that happened in and around a structure. Pretty handy for a detective. I think about what he told me about the secret history of the restaurant, his fascination with architecture, the way he rubbed the ledge at the opera house, as if to soothe and orient himself.

A plate of pineapple, cherries, and chocolates appears, along with Amaretto coffees. And then Shelby walks up. "Justine!"

Seeing her is such a relief I almost jump up and hug her. Otto stands and I introduce them. Shelby explains she was supposed to meet a date up in front some time ago. "I believe he will not come. I believe he did not want to know me after all."

Otto invites her to join us for dessert. He's insistent, even. It makes him seem like a normal and thoughtful date.

Shelby declines. "I no longer feel social."

"Maybe it was a misunderstanding," I say.

"It was not misunderstanding." She eyes me significantly. "Is exactly as it appears, I think. Please. I did not mean to disturb your dinner."

I stand. "Shelby, let me walk you out. Do you mind, Otto?"

"Of course not." He rises again.

I drape a consoling arm over her shoulders as we go.

"Give him beard and long hair and he is face, yes," she whispers. "Is Henji."

"No wonder Helmut thought Otto was leading a double life. Not only is he a police chief and crime boss, he's a highcap with highcap enemies stashed all over the city. One of the most powerful men in the city is a high-cap madman!"

"Who can kill with his thoughts. Who works with revisionist."

I think about the old woman who witnessed the Brick Slinger's suicide. Was she revised? "Why wouldn't Packard tell us who we were up against?" I say.

We stop by the front door, just under the candle-in-the-window display.

Shelby looks at me hard. "Perhaps because of what will happen if you fail, Justine. If you are frightened, your chance of failure, it is too great. If you knew your target was Henji . . . this case gambles with all our lives, but most especially yours."

"Because if he figures it out . . ."

"You die," Shelby says. "And that is best-case scenario."

"Great."

"Worst he kills or hides Packard, and then we all become like Jarvis." She gets this stunned look on her face. "Is it possible that our usefulness has always been for this? That we exist only to disillusion Henji and thus free Packard? That all cases before were buildup to Henji?"

It takes a while for me to digest the outrageousness of it all. "Oh my God—the Silver Widow and the Alchemist, they were just tests, practice runs—that's what he meant by *phase*. He'd been keeping them in the hopper, waiting for somebody like me to come along; that's why they appeared when they did. I once even asked him, why not disillusion his nemesis? And Packard said if we knew him, we wouldn't dream of it."

"He is right in that. There is too much danger."

"That is so Packard. How could he?"

"Packard would do anything to be free."

"It would work, though. A disillusioned Henji would free his prisoners. Maybe the crime wave would end."

"But Justine, you cannot be expected to destabilize Henji now that you know. I think when you did not know, you had far better chance. You cannot continue." Shelby seizes my arm. "I will let you out of your word. We will go now to Packard. We will tell him we know Henji is Otto, that it is too much. The stakes in this, they are too high."

It's like the whole world's spinning upside down. "It would work. It's not a bad plan."

She tightens her grip on my arm. "You cannot. . . ."

It's here that I come back to my motto: "Promoting freedom and transformation." I take a deep breath. "I can. I will."

"No, Justine."

"Henji deserves to be disillusioned. Packard deserves to be free." I remove her hands from my arm. I feel new. Shaky, but new. "I promote freedom and transformation."

Shelby furrows her brow. "You what?"

"Never mind," I say.

"You are not scared?"

"I'm terrified. And Henji has this ability to make himself so likeable—he lulls you into this sense of enchantment. But he's vulnerable to me. I'm going to destabilize the hell out of him. Maybe this is the way through, the way we all get free. Shelby, promise me one thing—if I disappear, no matter how sure you are that I'm dead—"

"I will find you. I will not let you die alone."

"Even if you think you saw me die."

"I will find you."

"I have to get back. He's going to wonder." We kiss cheeks good-bye.

I rejoin Otto.

"Sorry to leave you so long," I say. I'm looking at the beret. The beret is the key. The beret has to come off.

"You were being a friend. That poor girl."

"She's a very tragic person." I tell him about her rough Volovian childhood.

"I find her very impressive," Otto says. "In matters of the heart, people are rarely inclined to go with the evidence."

I nod, wondering if he's toying with me. He seems nervous, and I'm hoping this keeps him from noticing how nervous I am. I pop a pineapple chunk into my mouth.

He folds a foil wrapper from a chocolate into a tiny little triangle; then he unfolds it and folds it again. "I don't want this night to end," he says suddenly. "I want to bring you to my home."

My stomach tightens. I knew this was coming, but now that it's here, I don't know if I can handle it. I don't know if I can handle him.

"Please, I'm not expecting anything," he continues. "I want to show you my night garden, and we could just look at the stars. You could leave anytime. My car and driver would be at your disposal." He reaches across the table and covers the back of my hand with his. "You said you don't want any pressure, that you just went through a difficult breakup, and I respect that. And maybe I've been too forward tonight—you can tell me so—but—"

"A night garden?"

He smiles.

Chapter
Thirty-one

CHAUFFEUR JIMMY DROPS US OFF in front of a majestic stone building on the lakeshore, at the edge of the most fabulous area of downtown, not far from the opera house. Otto leads me into a lobby that looks like a fancy hotel atrium, past a guard in a bright red uniform, and into a shiny silver cylindrical elevator. The doors squeak shut. Otto puts a key in the panel and up we go. The next thing I know, we're walking out into the living room of Otto's ornate top-floor penthouse. Bright, blocky, comfortable-looking furniture and rugs provide splashes of color, but the amazing thing is the woodwork. Nearly every wooden surface—walls, pillars, doors—is carved with elaborate patterns and scenes of leaves, creatures, even faces. The woodwork is so intricate, I can't believe it was wrought by human hands. And then it occurs to me that it wasn't. It was Otto doing his structural interface.

As soon as he leaves to get us sparkling waters, I examine the carving next to the bookshelves, run my fingers over a nature scene with deer and rabbits. Did Otto tell the wood to do this? Did these beautiful designs come from his mind? Then I'm drawn to his books. Lots of adventure and detective novels, and books with titles in an alphabet I don't recognize.

And then he's strolling across the colorful rug toward

me, jacket off, tie loosened, a magnificent beast in his magical habitat. He hands me one of the crystal glasses. Bubbly water with lemon slices.

"You like to read?" he asks.

"I love to."

He regards his books in somber silence. "Sometimes I wish I could spend the entire day with my nose in a book. Just let the world drop away." He sounds so sad, I don't know what to say. Does he regret the evil path he's chosen?

I follow him out a sliding door onto an expansive rooftop terrace that's surrounded by big rectangular stone planters bursting with tangles of exotic plants, leaves big as bicycle wheels. A table and chairs are arranged under a canopy, and there is also a sauna hut and, beyond that, a sunken soaking pool. And all around, incredible views—the dark expanse of Lake Michigan on one side, downtown on the other. You can even see the tangle from here, like a sculpture of circling lights.

I draw near a planter to smell a cluster of purple blooms. "They're lovely, Otto. These are all night flowers?"

"More or less." Otto comes over and draws my attention to a pair of red bell-shaped flowers. "These are crepuscular more than nocturnal," he says. "Dusk and dawn flowers. And this—" He indicates a large gray bloom, like a cosmic tulip. I lean in to smell it, but he pulls me back. "No. It might think you're a mosquito. It eats mosquitoes and moths."

"A carnivorous flower?"

"If you consider bugs to be meat, then yes." He moves his hand along my shoulder. He's discovered the fuzzy kitten softness of my sweater.

"If I was a flower," I say, "I would think of bugs as meat."

He looks at me strangely, and I get this awful feeling he suspects something. I have to move fast. I have to destabilize him thoroughly. I have to get that beret off.

He turns back to his flowers but he keeps his hand on my shoulder. It feels nice. "Gardening is a great solace. I have to confess, doing that elephant project with your uncle has been so deeply distressing to me, I don't know what I'd do if I couldn't come out here at the end of the day and care for these living things."

I give in to the urge to tilt my head so that my cheek touches the back of his hand. It's easy to fake an attraction to him. Mainly because there's no faking involved.

"What happens to these plants in winter?"

"The roof is retractable." He gestures toward where it comes out, then brings his hand down on my hair, touching it, smoothing it.

I close my eyes. Whereas my attraction to Packard is fiery excitement—unpredictable and even chaotic—my attraction to Otto is cool and lush, full of order and depth. And so luxurious. I drink in the cool feel of him.

"You are so beautiful," he whispers, and I hear a soft clink. He's set his glass on a ledge. He takes my glass from my hand, and when I look up and meet his earnest brown eyes, it's like a shot down through me.

He smooths my hair some more, arranging it to splay around my shoulders, and then he kisses me, feathery light, lips soft and cool and lemony, and I explore the contours of his shoulders. He takes this as license to kiss me even more fervently, hand on my soft sweater, and then he kisses my cheekbone, my eyelid, even a handful of my hair, like it's this precious substance. "Oh, Justine." He draws back with an almost drugged look in his big brown eyes and pushes a long dark strand of his own hair away from his cheekbone. "I know you said you didn't want to start something—"

I touch his sandpapery jaw. "Let me officially retract

that. But that doesn't mean, you know—" He nods. "It does mean, though . . ." I stop here. I have no idea what I mean.

He kisses me again; he feels good—too good. It's the way our lips fit, the press of my chest against his, the intoxicating scent of his neck. We pull closer, and I feel him with the tenderest part of my stomach. We move together warmly and smoothly, as if our bodies already know one another.

I'm trembling, I realize—not with fright, but with desire. I need to zing him before my will disintegrates. I need to zing him hard, or glory hour will be a major problem.

I pull myself together enough to ask, "Is that a soaking pool over there?" My thought here is that people don't swim with their hats on. I need that hat off.

"It is," he whispers.

"Got a suit for me?"

"Come on." He leads me by the hand to the sauna, which includes a cedar-smelling dressing room with a number of men's and women's suits hanging on pegs.

As soon as I'm alone in there I work on reminding myself that Otto is a killer who robbed Packard of almost a decade of his life. I cannot fail here.

I select an orange bikini whose parts are connected by gold rings. Not the raciest thing there—that would be the thong bikini—but certainly not the dowdiest. As soon as I have it on, I close my eyes and call up the fear. My pulse speeds as it builds. I'm light, jittery, dangerously keyed-up.

The still-warm stone surface feels good on my bare feet as I stroll out, looking all around. And then I spot the Engineer, waiting in the pool.

With his hat on.

I stop. I needed that hat off! Okay, I tell myself, it's okay. This only shows how important the hat is to his well-being. Once it's off, he'll be more vulnerable than I ever imagined. It'll take more than a dip in the soaking pool to get it off, that's all. Possibly a lot more.

Blood *whooshes* in my ears as I continue toward him. Otto watches me approach, full of sensual gravity. And then he hoists himself up to sit on the side. I catch my breath, gazing at his olive skin, shining wet in the moonlight. Drips travel down his chest and stomach to dark swim trunks. The full deliciousness of him over-whelms me, and the notion that I can and will touch that wet, moonlit skin makes my stomach go springy.

Packard's voice rings in my head: *Just walk away.* I proceed.

"Watch out!" Otto points at my feet, and I look down just in time to avoid tripping over the corner of a lounge chair.

"Oh!" I step carefully around it, eyeing the ground. I deposit my stuff on the fat, white cushions of the divan and go over to Otto, who gazes up, wet and magnifi-cent. "How's the water?"

"Perfect," he says.

Concentrate, I tell myself, dipping in my toe. The pool seems almost carved into the stone floor, with interest-ing steps and angles, and it's covered in a mosaic of small brown tiles, some with a luminescent sheen. I sit down by him on the edge and slowly ease myself into the hot water next to his fabulously thick calves. "Ah." I settle onto an underwater ledge-seat. The heat feels wonderful after the chill of the air.

The Engineer slides down next to me, still with his hat on, and I touch his warm, solid chest, just because I can. He leans his head back on the stepped edge and takes a deep breath, gazing up into the night, letting me touch him.

"You are such a surprise," I say.

He smiles. "Did Helmut give you a negative report of some sort?"

"No. Just a surprise of a person."

He scoops up a handful of water and drizzles it over my dry shoulders. I wish so badly I could concentrate on having an enjoyable time with him instead of what I'm about to do. I wish so badly that he wasn't evil. He touches my thigh and slides his other hand around my waist. "Come here," he says, gliding me onto his lap.

I don't have to zing him right away. That's my thought as I enjoy myself on his lap in the warm water. Why not zing him later? I lean back against him and stare up at the stars as he kisses my neck and snakes his hands around my waist, resting them near my belly button.

We relax together. It's nice just to relax.

"Just one thing I don't understand," he says, in an odd tone. "Why did you call her so suddenly?"

"What?"

"In the restaurant. You called your friend Shelby after I told you the story about my apprenticeship in Vindahar."

My stomach drops clear through me. "What makes you think I called her?"

"I'm a detective, Justine. I know what a chance meeting looks like. I can tell when people are playacting." He tightens his hold on my stomach, and I can hear the smile in his voice, lips to my ear: "I know when people are posing as something other than they are. I know when they're nervous. And I know when they're hiding things. The timing of the call is the only part I can't figure out."

The *only* part? I fight to keep from stiffening, or worse, jerking away from him. I'm thankful he can't see my face, but he surely feels my heart, which is beating with enough force to fly me into orbit.

"The police chief," I say coolly, "needs a vacation." Why did I think I could fool a superstar detective and crime boss? Now he knows I'm up to something. Just as he knew the man with the gouged eyes was up to something.

"The police chief is never on vacation," Otto says. "Truly, Justine, of all the anecdotes about my life, the story of my apprenticeship is . . ." *Relatively undisturbing,* I think. *Surprisingly free of gore.* Lazily, he slides his thumb in circles around my belly button. "So tell me, why did you jump up and call her?"

It's here I get clear on what I'm dealing with. He knows I'm an enemy, but he doesn't know what kind. If he knew, he wouldn't let me touch him. I have to zing him profoundly, deeply, and immediately—it's my only hope. "Sometimes girls call their friends, Otto."

"But why right then, and with such urgency? Tell me, Justine." And then, "You know, I do have ways of making you talk."

I feel sick. I never imagined I'd hear this line and have it not be a joke. He even says it humorously, as people will, and he seems to expect some reaction. *He loves to toy with his prey,* Packard said. Otto's certainly having fun now. No, make that Henji.

Praying he doesn't sense my terror, I turn, straddle his lap, and give him a hard look. Casually, I say, "It was when I knew."

I'd meant to throw him off balance with this comment, make him think I know something he should be worried about. Instead he smiles broadly, brown eyes lit with pleasure. Why did I think I was any match for this man?

Arrogantly, he whispers, "I knew the minute I met you."

I think back to the way he looked at me—that air of discovery. He knew I was an enemy from the first. What I don't understand is why he's letting this go on, why he hasn't turned on me. Then again, where could I go? I'm literally in his clutches.

I focus fuzzily on what I once knew: Otto is a hypochondriac who is vulnerable to me. I am here to zing him. I have to get the hat off. And it will take every single one of my big guns to do it. I slide my fingers over his cheeks, gazing into his gold-flecked brown eyes. I touch his hair, close my fingers around a lock on either side of his head. It's strange—I've lived with terror as my companion for so long that it hardly affects my intense desire for him. Maybe it's even heightening it. I breathe in the scent of his skin in the moist night air, struck dumb with a mix of fear and arousal. And just like that I kiss him.

I half think he'll stop me, but instead he makes a rumbly sound and pulls me close. His hands slide heavily on my neck, my shoulders, my arms. My world is so simple suddenly. His skin, warm and wet under my fingertips, and the exciting sensation of his erection through my swimsuit. My entire being sighs into him, curling around his deliciously cucumbery cock like it's my new center of gravity.

Vaguely, it comes to me that I'm spinning out of control. *Focus!* I think. *You have one chance of getting out of this.*

With my awareness I push onto the surface of his energy dimension. It's easy to find. But it's not enough to touch it; I have to make this devastating. So I loosen my hold and I plunge in, as Simon taught me, accepting Otto's energy dimension as my own, letting the otherness fall away. I breathe, conscious of my pulse, his pulse. Finally I feel it: the vertiginous *whoosh* where the walls of my individuality blow out and I'm sinking fast and deep, drenched in his cool masculinity.

I've only ever been deep in the Alchemist, and that was bewildering and frightening. This is the opposite.

Otto is unexpectedly lush and orderly inside. I get this hit of honesty and sincerity as I move my awareness deeper. I slide along his skin, inside and outside him. I don't know where I stop and where he starts.

His thighs tense, and he makes a rough throaty sound as he pushes his hands under my bathing suit top, rolls his thumbs over my nipples, sending shivers through me, and then I feel the shivers go through him and then come back to me, back to him, like we're inside the same feeling. Maybe we are.

"Oh," he gasps. "I've never felt like this." This swell of potency overwhelms me, and somehow I know it's coming from him. Is this what it's like for a guy, being exuberantly hard, wanting to fuck? I want to fuck, that's for sure.

The desire builds between us, and every new way he touches me satisfies and stokes it higher, and I laugh and Otto smiles through a kiss, like we're both lost in the mirrors reflecting back and forth in an erotic infinity tunnel.

He slides his hands against the tender skin of my bottom—I enjoy the magnificent pulse of male potency as he pushes my suit bottom off. A few swishes of water and both our suits are off. I can tell he wants to switch and be on top but I can't let him. I need his head by the pool edge. I'm not lost yet.

"I have never felt so on fire. It's like I'm being consumed," he says, taking my nipple into his mouth, a light touch of teeth. I gasp; the sensation flying between us is too much. His chest is warm and solid, and I grip his shoulders. He scratches my thighs, long drags up and down, as I slide against his hard length between my legs. The combination of his fingernails and his cock are slowly disabling my mind. I need to get going; get his hat off and zing him to Neverland. I feel like a praying mantis.

I reach down and grasp the hard length of him, and he grabs my hips and enters me. The inside-out pressure of just his tip in me makes my senses reel; I come down on him slowly, exquisitely, letting him fill me, all fat and wonderful. Slowly I slide down on him, again, and then again, as the urgency builds.

I sink lower in his energy dimension—it's criminal, how deep I am in him—and it adds a mad intimacy to the sex I wasn't ready for. I feel him inside me, and I feel me from inside him, the slick squeeze of me when I grip my pelvis, and I'm exuberant with the urge to fuck further and deeper and feel more of his lushness.

Otto seems positively inebriated. He kisses me and I move on him slowly—maddeningly, perfectly slowly, getting my senses back.

I have to do it. I settle my hand onto the damp wool cap. I pull away and create a sensory distraction by biting his earlobe and tightening my pelvic muscles around him. He inhales sharply as I slip the hat off.

Slowly I coax his head up above the hard corner of the pool, up and up into a kiss, supporting us with my knee on the underwater shelf, burning the hole between us all the while, deep inside us. And then I pretend to slip, smashing his head backward onto the tile edge—not enough to knock him out, but a strong, surprisingly loud clunk at the exact moment I release a fierce stream of fear into his deepest core.

Otto stops moving and opens his eyes—wide. Panic drains his face. "Did I just hit my head?" He pulls out of me, bringing his hand to his head. "My hat! Did I just hit my head without my hat on?"

I move away, looking hazy. Like I don't get it. I do feel sort of hazy.

He grabs my shoulders. "Justine, this is important. Did I hit my head just now? Did you hear a smack?"

"Otto, I wasn't really paying attention." I kneel on the ledge next to him. "Are you okay?"

He stares past me, eyes shining with fear. He swallows. "It's happening." He hoists himself out of the water and onto the side. "It's happening." He seems to have forgotten all about my status as enemy.

I clamber out and wrap a big, fluffy towel around his shoulders, then tuck one around me. Cautiously, I kneel next to him on the side of the pool. I'm off-kilter from the abrupt halt of our sexual energy, even though it was my doing. Part of me wants badly to get back to it. Actually lots of me does. I'm glorying.

"This cannot be happening," he says softly, more to himself than to me.

"Is this a vein star issue?"

"It's not a vein star issue. It's a *vein star*. I'm more vulnerable to them than I let on to you the other night, and it's critical I protect my head. I'm sorry. It's not your fault. It's just, hitting my head with my hat off is the worst possible thing that can happen. I know it may seem silly to you, putting so much stock in the protective qualities of a simple beret. But I just . . . I—"

"No, no, Otto, I understand. I do."

"Maybe I should go to the ER. But once it's leaking it's too late, of course." He looks at me quickly. "I know it's true. My God!" He touches the place again. "The worst possible thing."

"Hey," I say, rubbing his back, hating what I did to him. But he's Henji, the dangerous madman, and I have to push him even further. "Can you get up? I want you all the way out of the hot water, even your legs."

"Oh, right, right. Thinning the blood." He's so distracted, so pliable.

"Shhh, you're okay," I say.

He stands and tucks the towel around his waist, and we settle together onto the cushiony divan.

"Now take a deep breath."

He complies. I can't stand the desperation in his face. It's what I wanted, but now I feel terrible. And that just makes me like him all the more. My hands find their way to his shoulders. I squeeze, knead, gazing at his earlobe, thinking about taking it into my mouth. I want to take everything into my mouth. I want to taste and feel him completely. I want to twine my limbs to his; I want to open for him, be penetrated utterly by him, to live and die in our ecstatic union. . . .

Shit! Glory hour. I remove my hands and straighten up. "Pinpoint pain?"

"I wouldn't characterize it as pinpoint."

"Otto, an impact like that doesn't necessarily cause a vein star to rupture. I agree it is dangerous, but it doesn't have to cause a bleedout in all cases." The trick here will be to appear to comfort him, but not actually comfort him. And then get the hell away.

"Bleedout," he mumbles.

"Not one hundred percent of the time."

"For me, the least impact is dangerous. The problem is that I have more cranial pressure than most people."

I place a hand on his strong, bare back, taking care to keep my touch clinical instead of sexual. "Extra cranial pressure? I've never heard of that. Do you mean high blood pressure?"

"Something else entirely." He turns to me. "I'm sorry." He gestures toward the pool. "That was terrible, but at the same time, I felt—I don't want to embarrass you, but I felt so connected to you. I wanted to never stop—" He winces, touches his head.

I spy his hat in the pool on a shallow ledge. I get it, wring it out, and hand it to him, wondering again if I was reading him wrong. Oh, God, I so want to be wrong. And I'm dizzy with desire.

"Thanks." He pulls his hat gently over his head. "I

wanted to know everything about you," he continues. "I wanted to see you live out that motto of yours. My God, how can it be that I'm dying the moment I've met you?"

"You're not dying." I'm breathlessly unsure what to do with the other part of the comment. I wrap a comforting arm around him; I want to wrap my whole self around him, to tell him the fear is fake, that it came from me. "You're not dying. I've seen dying people." I brush a dark lock of hair from his strong jaw, tuck it behind his ear. "You are not dying, Otto." He doesn't need to think he's dying this exact moment to be weak and destabilized.

"There are some things you don't understand, Justine. Please, know that the connection I just felt with you, the connection I've been feeling ever since that first night, it's given me a taste of something beyond what I knew, and that means so much to me. I never expected it."

I have this horrible thought: what if Otto actually has vein star risk factors? "Otto—"

"I know I must sound melodramatic."

"What's going on, Otto? What's the cranial pressure? I need to know. Do you have special risk factors or preconditions?" The night flowers stir in the balmy breeze as I rub my palm in a circle on his back. The moment stretches long. He closes his eyes.

I'm really worried now. The fact that he's been frightened of the disease since boyhood certainly doesn't make him immune to it. It is potentially hereditary, after all! And now I've destabilized him with fear. "Otto, tell me!" His silence panics me. What if he has it? What have I done?

"All I can say, Justine, is that I do extra things with my mind. I carry out certain mental processes that cause cranial strain."

"What does that mean?"

He shakes his head. "Extra brain activity, that's all."

I breathe a sigh of relief. I'm getting the picture now: he's hooked his highcap status to his hypochondria, like it makes him especially susceptible. I'd do the same thing in his place. "I can't help you if you don't tell me," I say sternly. He wants to open up to me; I can feel it. And I really want him to. It'll be easier to destabilize him if I can talk about his status as a highcap. "Consider it nurse-patient privilege."

He shakes his head.

"I know you're not talking about doing lots of cross-word puzzles, Otto. Extra cranial pressure? You know what that makes me think?"

He's silent. I feel his anxiety deepen as I fight the inappropriate urge to pull him back into the pool. "Let me suggest a hypothetical situation," I say. "Let's say some-body is a highcap."

He looks at me guardedly. He doesn't deny it. He wants me to continue. I do.

"Many medical professionals, myself among them, accept it as fact that some people have increased mental capacity that give rise to certain abilities. It sounds like that's what you're getting at. So let's say that person believes exercising his power makes him vulnerable to vein stars. Of course he can't exactly tell a doctor because of his position in society."

He watches me—debating, it seems. And then he says, "A person in that situation would lose everything, no matter what good he'd done." A pause, then, "How would you advise this person?"

"I'd need to know more."

"God help me. I barely even know you."

"You know me."

He takes a deep breath. "I have what's called a gift for structural interface."

"I'm familiar with that." I repeat a bit of the knowledge I've gathered. It seems to comfort Otto that I know so much.

"Most people consider us flakes, delusionals, or evil mutants with dangerous powers. One highcap can lift objects with his mind, another can invade dreams, or perhaps has partial psychic gifts. I can interface with structure." He watches my face, worried, I guess, that I'll find all this repellent. I'm just shocked he's telling me. But of course he feels inexplicably bonded to me. I spelunked him; I was inside him. All my fear is still in him. So of course he feels like we're close.

I find myself wishing it was more than that. I touch a soft, damp lock of hair.

He continues, "What regular humans don't yet understand is how fantastically dangerous highcaps can be when they turn violent. When enough go violent at once, they threaten the very fabric of society. Human prisons simply aren't built for highcaps. Most escapes you hear about are criminal highcaps." He touches his head. "Which brings me to my risk factor. I've been using my powers of structural interface to seal violent highcaps away from each other and from society. You could say, Justine, that I'm single-handedly holding a population of dangerous criminals at bay with my mind. Maintaining the number of force fields I am, it's straining the integrity of my blood vessels, I'm sure of it. I can feel it!"

"You seal away violent highcaps?"

"I keep them in apartments, warehouses, coat-check stalls, wherever I feel they won't be a threat. What do you think? Wouldn't that aggravate a vein star?"

I can't breathe. "Is it always dangerous highcaps that you imprison? Because they hurt people?"

"Of course. I have no choice, Justine. At first I sealed up the major underworld crime bosses who were undermining law and order. But in the past few years, a new, truly violent crop of highcap criminals has emerged, and I've had to seal up so many, I can barely keep track. Do you know what the crime wave would be like if I wasn't doing this? The one doing all the brick kills? Highcap telekinetic. I sealed him up in an old warehouse."

"I thought he killed himself."

"No. Sophia made the witness remember it that way. She's a revisionist—"

"Sophia? Your assistant?"

"I shouldn't have told you that. Please—"

"Don't worry."

Silence. He regrets telling me about Sophia; I really have weakened him. "The problem is, I'd always seen this as a short-term solution, but now I can barely hold them all. I'm nearing a kind of tipping point. If I seal up any more, there's a chance I'll lose my control of all the force fields and they'd vanish, freeing my prisoners all at once. But the violence is mounting. At this point I can only seal in the most dangerous ones. As police chief, it's up to me to keep the citizenry safe. So I seal up another highcap, then another. It seems like exactly the thing that could cause a vein star blowout, wouldn't you agree?"

"How long have you been doing this?"

"Do you think that's significant?"

"Very."

"A little over eight years."

"And you started with just a few? The underworld bosses?"

"One. And his lieutenant. That solved the problem until the violent ones came along. Now I'm keeping so many in different places, sometimes I feel like it's ripping my head apart."

Packard, I think. And Diesel. I swallow. It's like my entire universe got flipped when I wasn't looking. Or is this an elaborate trick?

He says, "If I were to die, Justine, all those highcaps would be sealed in forever. A mass death sentence, and that's not fair. They are my people, after all. I set up various systems and helpers to get food and water deliveries to them, but I don't always know if that works out, and if I died . . . God, what kind of monster am I to pass these sentences? But if I had some sort of breakdown, or if I dissolved my force fields voluntarily to relieve vascular pressure and save my own life, I guarantee you that this city would descend into an uncontrollable bloodbath. There are too many of them pent up for too long, and all so angry. My brothers and sisters on the force would not survive the carnage."

The pain in his brown eyes is deep as the night. I see him and I feel him so strongly.

"My motto is to guard the citizens from evildoers of every kind, and I'll die doing it, even if my soul is damned to hell for bringing all those highcaps down with me. Please give me your word of honor, Justine, that after I die, you won't reveal my secret."

I'm stunned. "Of course not," I whisper. I think about the pictures of Otto in disguises, shadowy meetings. Is this what it was? Otto maintaining his personal penal system? What about the man with the gouged eyes? But then, why would a man with Otto's powers of force fields need to use his thumbs to kill? Or a vise? And if he's such a brutal killer, why put himself out to imprison anybody?

"It's easy to say you'll die for a thing, Justine, but it's not easy when you're facing that death. In moments of weakness, I think, Why not just release them and fight them all over again? Because I don't want to die." He touches my cheek, and my pulse pounds. "Especially not now."

I'm filled with crazy, huge emotions, and I don't know if I can trust them. Is he toying with me? Is this the truth? I wish suddenly I could put the world into a holding pattern, just freeze everybody and everything until I figure out who is lying. Is it Otto or Packard? I think back on my impressions when I was spelunking him—I'd sensed order, honesty, sincerity. Can I trust that?

"Is that why you traveled the world? To learn how to seal criminals?"

"Not at first. As a boy, I used my powers in dark, dark ways. My trek around the world, it was really about running from myself. If I could've shed my entire being—as a snake sheds his skin—I would've. My mentor helped me to stop running, to turn my powers to good."

I stare at him stupidly.

"You must agree I'm doomed or you would've said something."

Right there and then, I decide to pull Otto out of the attack. I need time. I can always put him in later. I tighten my towel around me and grasp his biceps, looking him square in the eyes. "No, I don't agree. Listen to me, Otto—you do not have a vein star leak or significant expansion, and do you know how I know?"

"You *don't* agree?"

"Number one, lack of pinpoint pain. Your only pain is your bump, right? And that's not pinpoint."

"Well—"

"Right or wrong?"

He furrows his brow. "It's sort of pinpoint."

I shake my head. "*Sort of* means it's not. Two, your color. You have good healthy color. If you had been bleeding internally since you bumped your head, you'd be pale. Three—I do recall your telling me you've been frightened of vein stars since boyhood. You had a fear of vein stars then, but you weren't holding prisoners at that time. As a former detective, tell me, doesn't a cause usually *precede* the thing it causes, rather than coming after?"

"I don't know. . . ."

"Who's the nurse here?"

"You are."

"That's right. And here's the most important thing for you to understand: veins are the plumbing. Mental energy is the electricity. It's not the same system. You can have all the electrical overload in the world and it won't affect your plumbing." I don't have any scientific or medical proof for what I just said, but it seems like it would be true.

The relief that spreads over his face is incredible. "Are you sure of that?"

"Think about it."

"I guess, but . . ." He looks away, falls silent.

"Stop it! I know what you're doing. You're analyzing the sensations in your head." I sit on his lap and grip his shoulders. *Concentrate!* I think. "Otto, if you focus on your head, you'll just cause sensation." He's not hearing me; he's too charged up with my fear. "Look, let's talk about something else. I need to understand more about these guys you sealed up. How can you be sure they deserved it? Is it possible you sealed up some that were harmless?"

Otto shakes his head. "I'm always sure."

"You can actually seal them away with your mind?"

"It's not as though I can do it remotely. I have to be there in person to create the force field. And I have to brand it, in a way, to set it. Though I could release them all remotely." He snaps his fingers. "Just like that, if I decided to."

Or if you were disillusioned, I think. "I don't understand this brand thing."

"The brand sets it. The brand is of my visage from when I was in Vindahar."

"Your visage? Like a picture of you?"

"It appears wherever I seal somebody. Me with the beard, the hair . . ."

This is what I needed, but I have to be very careful. I look away, as though something is coming to me. "Oh my God. That one restaurant—that Mongolian place. That door. Is that you? That door?"

He smiles. He's a little bit proud of it all, I realize, behind everything else. Every master wants an audience. "My first. The brands got less elaborate after that."

I bite my lip, trying to get my expression under control. "Do you have a dangerous one in there?"

"He was the original highcap boss. A diabolically gifted leader."

"So he's, like, the worst of all?"

"In a scenario where I released control and set my criminals free, this one would eventually rise to the top and lead them."

"And he's a killer?"

Otto laughs bitterly. "He controls the killers. I've known him since boyhood. We were friends once, struggling to survive, but things went out of control. There was so much I didn't understand—I was quite young, really, though that's no excuse. We fought, but I wasn't strong enough . . ."

"Why did you fight?"

Otto shakes his head. "I don't talk about that."

Neither does Packard.

"My point is that when I returned from Vindahar and discovered he was a far more devious criminal than when I left, I gave him a chance to turn his life around. When he refused, I put him away. This man is the only one of my prisoners who knows it's me who trapped him. He deserved that much." He looks down at his knees. "In another life, he could have made a brilliant psychologist. I left him with access to regular humans, hoping he'd use his gifts in a positive way. Back then, I had certain notions about reform."

"And?"

"Who knows? I've been meaning to check for years, but I've become so overwhelmed with the task of keeping the citizens safe and beating back the crime wave I haven't gotten to it. Honestly, I'm lucky at this point just to get through the day without—" He pauses, tilts his head as though he hears something.

This all has the very upsetting feel of truth. Am I unwittingly working to release Packard along with hordes of violent criminals? Or is Otto toying with me as Packard warned he would? Could Otto be that sophisticated?

"Justine!" He moves his head from side to side. "It's gone!"

"What?"

"The pain, the sensation. I'm still aware of an unsettling knot of fear, but that's it." He clutches my arms. "You got me out of it."

And I could put you right back in, I think, but I just nod. Otto tests his head some more.

I stand, tighten the towel around my chest, and wander off to a nearby flower bed, as if I'm drawn to examine some blooms. One of these men is lying, and either way, I'm in trouble. If Packard's lying and he really is this criminal, that's a problem because my sanity and my life depend on zinging, which depends on Packard. All the disillusionists' lives depend on Packard. Not to mention the pain of so huge a betrayal.

If Otto's the one who is lying, it means he's been toying with me, and that he knows exactly what I'm up to. It means everything he said about his deep connection to me isn't real. It also means I'll probably wind up like Packard. Or Diesel.

A plane flies overhead like a big lazy star. I'm tempted

to believe Otto, but then again, everything he said is all just words. And anybody can say words.

I jump—a hand on my shoulder. I didn't even hear him come up.

He removes it. "I'm sorry, Justine. I didn't mean to startle you. Are you all right?"

"It's overwhelming, that's all." I stare at the flowers, the city lights beyond, longing for the hand back. *Glory hour.* I have to get out of here. "I'm fine."

"No, you're not. I wasn't thinking about how frightening this might be to you as a citizen." His breath is warm on the top of my head.

"That's okay," I say, ragged with his sudden nearness. He caresses my hair, trails his fingers down my neck to my shoulders. The night colors swim in my vision. "I don't know what to think, that's all," I say, vaguely aware that I should do some sort of mathematical exercise so as not to plunge deeper into a state of sensual insanity.

Otto wraps his big arms around me from behind and says, "You don't have to think at all. Let me do the thinking." He tightens his hold, a warm, strong circle; I hook my fingers to his forearms. "Nothing's going to happen," he says. "The criminals can't escape tonight. I don't have a vein star, and I'm going to figure something out about my prisoners. A superior solution." He moves around to face me, stands between me and the flowers and the night sky. Dimly, I marvel at his power over fear—I shot so much of it into him. "I trusted you. Now you need to trust me," he says. "Nothing bad is going to happen to you, I promise."

I stare at his chest, wanting to believe that. The truth is that bad things will happen to me no matter who is lying.

He touches my cheek. "I'll take care of everything."

I look up, and that thing happens again where his

smiling makes me smile. I have as much resolve as a kitten now.

With a sudden movement, he scoops me up, holds me aloft. I laugh, startled at the sensation of lightness, of the world having fallen out from under me, of Otto's warmth and goodness.

"Let me take care of everything," he says.

I wrap my arms around his neck as he carries me across the patio.

His kisses me as he pushes backward through the door. Maybe he's lying; maybe he's not. None of it matters. I'm glorying in the Engineer's arms.

Deep inside his penthouse he lowers me onto the bed and pulls my towel knot free, and I just let him, and I let him look at me, craving his touch. There's no going back now. He sits next to me and draws an excruciatingly slow finger along the outer curve of my breast. The sensation of his finger becomes more important than bloodbaths and gouged eyes and everything else in the universe.

"Please." I take hold of his hair, pulling him to me for a kiss, careful not to disturb his hat. I have never wanted somebody so desperately in my life.

He draws away to kiss a line of kisses down over my ribs to my belly. "I am going to slowly and carefully and deliberately consume every bit of you." The way he kisses my belly button feels indecent, and I gasp. "I am going to make love to every last inch of you." A kiss on the tickly skin below my belly button. "I am going to enjoy you slowly and thoroughly."

"Okay," I whisper—a stupid answer to a statement that doesn't require an answer, but I'm distracted by his hand over my thigh, and then the sensation of fingers between my legs. I can practically feel the ridges of his fingerprints as he explores across wet and excruciatingly sensitive skin. Then, slowly, one finger then two slide inside me.

He moves down, watches me watch him, fingers slow and lazy, and then I feel his warm tongue on me. It's like I can feel every tiny taste bud. I gasp as he pushes my legs farther apart. My mind shrinks to the slow drag of his tongue . . . nothing matters but the feeling. I'm a quivery jellyfish, helpless under him. On and on he goes; it's like he's devolving me into a single-celled organism that lives on air and feeling. The world outside gets even smaller; I lose touch with everything as sensation builds and bursts over me in a wonderful wave, leaving me floating, breathless.

When I get myself back, I say, "Gosh," thinking I may have made some sounds. Hopefully in the range of normal sounds, and not, like, critter sounds.

He looms over me; luscious hair shadowing his face, and there's a primitive look to his eyes that frightens and excites me. Otto isn't thinking about sounds; he's thinking about fucking.

"I am going to take you," he says, "slow and hard."

"Do." I love that he says that; it's old-fashioned and a little bit dirty. I so want to be taken by Otto right now.

He opens the bedside drawer.

"What are you doing?"

"Trying to be bit more responsible this time around." He lifts out a condom and unwraps it with leisurely, elegant movements. I run my hand up his solid thigh, feeling like I might die without him touching me everywhere. He rolls it onto himself slowly. Then he stands, like a magnificent bull.

"Are you enjoying making me wait?"

He gives me a sly look. "Yes." Then he lowers himself slowly, still with that look, kisses my neck, and I gasp as he pushes into me, slow and thick. I close my eyes, starry-headed from the sensation.

"Oh, God," he says. I arch up to meet him and he grabs my thighs, stilling them. "Slow," he says. "And hard."

Jesus, I think. The way he moves, I feel everything. I push my palms over his chest, exploring, grasping. We fall into a deep, delicious rhythm.

Later, the slow thing goes out the window, and even the hard thing goes. Our fucking follows its own wonderfully raunchy storyline, full of twists and turns, and sweat rolling down arms and chests, and a little bit of teeth.

Sex during glory hour—Simon was right. The bug on the windshield is everything. We spend the next hour speeding off the cliff.

Chapter
Thirty-two

I WAKE UP EARLY and just lie beside Otto, watching him sleep and feeling so very close to him. I want to touch him, but I don't want to wake him. I'm far too confused. I keep remembering Diesel's skeleton. He died helpless and alone. I also picture Diesel's metallic-blue bracelet jangling around Packard's wrist as Packard strangles Otto to death. And Packard instigating a bloodbath. And Otto gouging out a man's eyes. The mind-boggling enormity of Packard's betrayal if Otto turns out to be right.

I think back to what it was like spelunking Otto's energy dimension, the order and goodness. Can I trust that? Was it the actual truth of him, or a small, buried part of a sociopathic whole?

I need answers.

Quietly I creep out of bed and make my way to the terrace. My clothes are on the divan where I left them. I pull on my bra and my fuzzy sweater and suedelike pants. The sun rises over the lake, beaming brightness through the sky. It would be so lovely to sit out here and have our morning coffee. Or lunch. Or a lovely dinner. I get the exciting thought that the patio is the perfect place to wear the silver bikini and cover-up the Silver Widow gave me. And then I wonder what planet I'm thinking of. Otto and I can never be together.

Back inside I find a piece of paper, write XOXO on it, and stick it in the corner of the mirror. Then I get out of there.

People and cars zip up and down the street in front of Otto's building; this is an early-rising, high-achieving part of town. I look around for a cab. And then I see her. Sophia. She's crossing the street with two coffees and a bakery bag. I wander slowly away from the building's entrance, willing myself to blend into the surroundings, but it's too late.

"*Nurse* Justine!" She says this with a flourish. Is she mocking me? "Speak of the devil."

"You were talking about me?"

A humorous light plays across Sophia's features. "Why not? It's such an honor to have met such a remarkable nurse."

I nod, stomach in throat. "How are you?"

"Oh, I'm very good, thank you." She raises her eyebrows. "Very good." And she turns and enters Otto's building, leaving me with a very paranoid feeling.

I arrange to meet Shelby downtown; she's temping as a secretary for her latest target, Lady Brazil. I wait for her in the bagel shop on the ground floor of Lady Brazil's office building, and I barely recognize her in a prim gray suit, her hair in a bun.

She eyes me as she buys a bagel at the counter, warning look on her face; I'd better not laugh at her.

I'm not in the mood for laughing, and neither is she once I tell her what happened. Feverishly, we dissect everything Otto said, and everything Packard ever said, trying to divine the truth. The notion that we might be dupes in a scheme to unravel the fabric of society upsets her.

"Packard would not allow it," she says again and again. "He could not." Shelby has experience with unraveled situations.

My phone rings. "Packard." I turn it off.

Shelby frowns. "I believe he would do anything to be free, but he is not wicked. He would never allow blood-bath. You will see Sanchez is bigger danger than Packard."

"I can't believe he'd gouge out people's eyes and crack heads and all that."

Shelby sniffs. "You saw photos, did you not? Helmut believes, too. Do not forget, Justine, Helmut spent much more time with Otto Sanchez than you did."

"But he didn't figure out Otto is the nemesis, did he? All he knew was that Otto led a double life, and that he was with people who later disappeared. That supports either story—Otto as good guy or Otto as evil." And always I go back to the spelunk. I wish I knew if I could trust it. And us together—the way we felt. "Otto didn't feel evil inside. I'm going to find answers, and if he's truly struggling to keep the city safe, no way am I desta-bilizing him. I won't let him be disillusioned."

"What do you mean? You will warn him?"

"I don't know, but I can't let an innocent man be dis-illusioned. And can you imagine a horde of Rickies being set free?"

"Justine! You always want to have choice, but there is no choice. To warn Otto is to hurt Packard, and that is to hurt all of us. This is what Simon wanted to have, this power. And we were frightened he would use it, do you remember? And now you would use it? Justine, if you warned Otto, he would punish Packard and we would perish." She clutches my arm, waits for me to look at her. When I do she says, "We would die."

"He wouldn't let us die."

"You cannot say that. You do not know. Think, Justine. You have zinged Otto twice, and you zinged him as you made love!" She widens her eyes. "If he knew this, he would hate you as he hates Packard. He would punish you, too. And Helmut. His dear friend Helmut, performing psychological attacks for months as they wept for elephants."

I feel cold as I consider the enormity of our crimes against Otto. She's right. I slide down in my seat, thinking back to last night on his rooftop. *I knew the minute I met you,* he'd said. I'd thought it was a threat, but it was a declaration of feeling. And it wasn't about binding to me from the zing. He felt that way about me before the zing. He opened himself to me and I attacked him. What have I done?

"We had this connection, Shelby. We could've—"

"Been happy together?" she sneers. "Do not torture yourself with such illusion." She looks at Foley's watch. "I am late. I must meet Lady Brazil." She looks back up. "There is nothing for you with Otto. You have lost nothing. You have no choices."

Chapter
Thirty-three

I ARRIVE at Mongolian Delites just as the lunch shift is leaving. Ling calls to me to hold the door; her hands are full of papers, the bank deposit pouch and other manager items. "Something's up with Packard. He's in such a fantastic mood. Can you lock up behind me?"

"Sure."

She leaves, and I flip the bolt. A hush falls over the place, but there's nothing hushed about my mood as I stalk toward the booth.

Packard looks up from his book and smiles. Of course he's feeling fine. He thinks he's closer than ever to getting out. The final phase of his master plan is rolling right along.

Was rolling right along.

I slide in across from him, wondering, for the first time, where home is for him. It occurs to me that I haven't thought this through. Why have I come?

"What could be wrong, Justine, on this glorious day?" he asks. "You look beautiful. I have no doubt you've come from yet another triumph. . . ." He pauses, skin creamy and flawless, one of the effects of no sunshine. "He doesn't suspect, does he?"

"No."

"Well then." He sits back. "Tell all."

"You want me to tell all? The way you've told all?" I glare at him. "Like about Henji?"

The happiness drains from his face.

I lean in. "Imagine my surprise when I discovered Otto is *not* a ruthless killer running a criminal organization after all. It seems Otto is not only your nemesis, but a man who has dedicated his life to protecting innocent citizens." I hold up a hand, warning him not to speak. "And imagine my surprise, also, that my actions to disillusion Otto will result in hordes of dangerous highcaps running free."

Packard laughs. "Oh, Justine, this is what I was warning you about. He's toying with you. Do you see how good he is? How he's turned you around—"

"Stop. Don't insult me. No wonder you were so desperate for me and my vein star paranoia! I was perfect for going after Otto. It was always about Otto. You were just using me. And laughing all the way."

"I never laugh about you."

"Oh, stop. And all that talk about Otto being a sociopath and a wolf in sheep's clothing? God, I am so sick of you deceiving me! And what about those photos? Otto gouging out that man's eyes with his own hands and cracking a guy's head in a giant vise and all the rest? You cooked it up, right? No more lies. No more."

Packard contemplates me grimly. Finally he says, "No, Otto didn't do those things."

My breath goes still. "Then how'd you get the gouged-eyes photo? It had to be taken right after—"

His brow tightens. He's guessed my thoughts. "Oh, Justine, you know me at least that well. Do you really think I could do that to a person?"

I look down. If nothing else, I know him at least that well. "Maybe not that."

"Believe me, Otto *was* responsible for that. It might

not have been his thumbs in the man's eyes, but it was his fault all the same. By sealing that man up, he made him helpless and vulnerable to various enemies. Look at Diesel. Lord knows who else has died in those makeshift prisons of his."

I stare at the Korean painting on the wall. The brush-stroke legs of the horse.

"You said Otto doesn't suspect," he says. "Did you mean it? He really doesn't know?"

"Not yet."

"How could you have extracted so much information from him without his knowing?"

"It wasn't easy."

He smiles his beautiful, evil smile. "Oh, you are good."

"Stop it."

"I won't ever stop." He takes my hand and squeezes it, then pulls it to his soft, warm lips. Otto may be depth and order and harmony, but Packard is heat and the wild unpredictability of life. He feels me feel him. He thinks he can use the hot coil of our chemistry to pull me back to his side. "Justine—"

I pull my hand away. "How could you put me in this situation? I want you to be free, but to unleash a bunch of violent criminals for a bloodbath? To disillusion an innocent man?"

"Otto's hardly innocent. And nobody's unleashing a bloodbath."

"You obviously don't know about the new crop of ultraviolent highcaps."

"I would control those people. I would help them find outlets for their destructive impulses. Do you forget what I am? The violence is Otto's fault. If he hadn't sealed me up, you wouldn't turn on the news and see the hurtling bricks, collapsing bridges, and sleepwalking killers. It's Otto's fault—all of it. I kept order in the underworld. By sealing me up, Otto created anarchy. Did I run a criminal organization? Maybe I did. But the streets were safe when I was in charge."

It all starts to make a fuzzy kind of sense. "Eight years ago."

Packard looks at me hard. "He sealed me up, and it sparked the crime wave. When I ran my organization, this city was a safer, cleaner, better place. I was creating something magnificent before Otto destroyed it. When I get out, I'll restore sanity to the highcap world, and that will improve every strata of life. We'll make things better for people, and we'll have everything we want—you and me and all the disillusionists. I wouldn't allow there to be a bloodbath."

"Oh yeah?" I will myself not to cry. "The way you lied to me, and used me, and betrayed me . . . it feels like a bloodbath in me. Inside me."

Softly, he says, "I know." He looks away. "Justine, I have to be free."

"And the hell with everyone else?"

I walk off into the empty dining room, wrap my fingers over a chair back. I think about Packard free, walking in the sunshine. In spite of everything, I want that for him. Am I an idiot for still caring about him? I can't help it. I want it for him, but the price is too high.

I sense him drawing near, but I don't turn around. I picture the scene Rickie described—Packard stepping out of a shiny car with his gang, mighty and free in the fresh air.

"Think, Justine, what it could mean," he says. "The whole city would be free from the grip of fear." His hands close on my shoulders. "I know how it must've been for you these past years, seeing the people around you feeling so much fear. How it would remind you of where you came from."

My heart hitches in my chest. Goddamn him and his insight.

"Only I can make it happen."

"As if you care about how the people of Midcity feel. Even criminals having their changes of heart. You don't even give a shit—that was just a convenient side effect."

"Side effect or not, we were making a difference. Freeing me will make a bigger, far more profound difference."

I shut my eyes, feeling the fire of his passion and his crazy ideas. For one wild moment, I imagine all of us happy together, and Midcity free from fear. I wrap my arms around myself as if that will counteract the feeling and turn to Packard. "What about Otto?"

"You don't know him, Justine."

"I didn't know him when he was Henji. Is that what you mean?"

"What did he tell you about that?"

"About when you were boys living in the abandoned school? About why he leveled it?"

He studies my eyes. "Henji wouldn't talk about that. Somebody else gave you that." He waits. He's right, of course. It was Rickie who told me.

"Is that Henji's real name?"

He considers the question. "No. I gave him that name. Back when he came to live with us boys. *Henji*'s short for *Stonehenge*. His ability to manipulate structure with force fields was fascinating to us. But you have to understand, Henji—the man you know as Otto—has no imagination. He's a lover of rules who sees only black and white. Look what he's created by mindlessly enforcing laws—he's part of a machine that crushes the creative impulse. We're so much more. You have vision, imagination. When I think of the inspired maneuvering it must have taken to zing Otto twice and extract all the information without him having any idea—God, the ingeniousness of it!"

He slides his fingers down to my forearms. I'm softening and melting the way I always do when he touches me. "You're part of this family. Otto has certain enchantments, but he's a drone. He'll try to make you over into a mindless doll the way Cubby did, accepting only the part of you that fits into his unimaginative life."

I plant a hand in his chest and shove, sending him back a step. "I wanted that life and I still do."

"You used to, but you're beyond it now. That's why I make you feel good and wild and free—because this is what your heart wants; this is where your home is." He comes closer. "You know it's true. And I say to you, Justine, let's be wild and free. Let's blaze right up into the stratosphere."

This is Packard at his most glorious, and what I've always relished about him. I put my hand to his pale cheek and he takes it and holds it, gazing at me hard, all hot, handsome heat. "I have to be free."

"I want you to be free, Packard." I see the smile starting in his eyes, and then I take my hand from him. "But I won't let you destroy any more lives. I don't care what you're offering. And I won't disillusion Otto. I won't let you hurt him. I'm telling you—"

"Justine, I know he must seem safe and strong to you, and he leads the type of upstanding life you were always shut out of, but you can't let him mesmerize you. You're bigger than that. And he shares your brand of hypochondria—I'm sure Otto could feel like your soul mate in a certain light, but you have to see through to the man."

It occurs to me here that Otto does seem like my soul mate.

Packard has gone pale. "No," he whispers.

He's guessed of course. About Otto and me. Maybe all of it.

"What?" I protest. "You lied to me and sent me after him specifically because you knew that we'd connect, because all you truly care about in life is getting free. And now you're upset because what? We connect? And now you want me to believe that falling for Otto is just part of what a screwed-up misfit I am? I am so done with your psycho-whammy."

Packard just stares. He's frozen on the outside, but there's an earthquake in him. The look in his eyes gives it away.

I don't know why I feel like I betrayed him, but I do. I still feel this crazy connection to him. I need to break from his gaze, but I can't. "I don't know why you're so upset when you're the one who betrayed me," I say stupidly. "Over and over and over. And lied and lied."

"I saved your life."

"Only to send me to risk it with Otto. You're just using us. It stops here."

This is where he turns; the change is nearly palpable— a certain set to his jaw, a lifelessness in his eyes. It makes my heart hurt. "You will zing him again. And then you will zing him again. Whatever it takes to destabilize him, and then you will connect Otto with Vesuvius."

I shudder at the thought of Vesuvius ripping apart Otto's self-esteem. "Or what?"

"You know what." His voice is steady, dispassionate. "If you reveal or otherwise destroy my plan out of some infatuation with that foppish drone, I'll end up imprisoned somewhere far worse than this. And do you really think Otto would allow me to see my disillusionists again? No. Which means you and all your friends end up drooling vegetables on your way to slow, ignoble deaths. And if you simply refuse, Justine, I'll find another way to go after Otto, and you alone will be cut off, and you alone will face that end."

"You wouldn't."

His eyes burn with emotion—what emotion, I can't tell. For once, I can't read him.

"I am the master, and you are the minion. And I need to be free."

The horrible silence that settles between us makes words seem irrelevant.

"You will zing Otto as many times as it takes, and you—"

"Yeah, yeah, yeah." I turn and beeline back to the booth and pull my purse off the seat, conscious of him watching me, conscious, suddenly, that Packard has every reason in the world to hate me, let me die, even kill me. I could destroy years of work and his best hope for freedom. Our eyes meet as I pass him on the way to the door, but he doesn't move.

I get out of there and walk forever, barely conscious of where I'm going. There's just this awful churning feeling inside me.

I think about my disillusionist friends and allies. How could I allow them to end up like poor Jarvis? Or for Otto to be destroyed? And would Packard really cut me off?

Packard's betrayal hurts like hell—more than I could ever imagine. I'd felt so close to him all these months, in spite of what he did. The feeling between us was an alive thing, like nothing I'd ever known. And he was just using me the whole time?

It hurts like hell. And my motto, "Promoting freedom and transformation," proves to be no help whatsoever.

I walk in the sunshine, wondering if Packard's heart is beating as wildly as mine.

Chapter
Thirty-four

I SHOULDN'T ANSWER my phone when I see it's Otto calling the next morning, but this crazy part of me just wants to hear his voice and have a sweet, excited conversation with him and pretend he's my new boyfriend.

"Justine, hello!"

The smile in his voice makes me smile. "Hello, Otto."

"What are you doing this very minute?"

"I'm drinking coffee and thinking about making oatmeal. What are you doing?"

"That's not important."

"Are you saying that what Midcity's chief of police is doing is less important than oatmeal?" I tease.

"Did you start it yet?"

"No."

"Good. Come down to the station and have breakfast here. In my office. I'll have something brought in."

"Oh, Otto, I practically just got out of bed."

"Justine, I have to see you. It's important." Is there something different about his voice? Or does the idea of going to the station just bother me? "I'm dispatching my car."

"What's so urgent?"

"You'll see."

"Is it something urgent on the salacious side?"

He just laughs.

I would have preferred an answer on that, but I have this idea that maybe I can have one last nice time with him and pretend, like I used to with Cubby, that we really can be together. I know it's pretend now. Aspirational. Otto will hate me no matter what I do. "Okay," I say, "but I can't stay long." I give him my address.

I rush into my bedroom and put on a fabulous red knit wraparound shirt that ties on the side. The wraparound gives the effect of a V-neck, with just a bit of a plunge. I jump into my black jeans and put on my black sandals and silver hoop earrings and pop down to the street. The first chill of fall is in the air. I consider going up for different shoes and a jacket, but then Otto's car pulls up. Did it get here kind of fast? Was it waiting down the street?

Jimmy jumps out and opens the back door.

"Hey, Jimmy."

"Good morning," he says.

It's weird to ride back there alone, like I'm this important person, but I know it would be weird for Jimmy if I rode in the front. Riding along, looking at the back of Jimmy's head, his policeman-like cap, my paranoia about Sophia's mocking comment rekindles. I've been so caught up in the threat from Packard, what about the threat from Otto? What if Sophia discovered I'm not a nurse and told Otto? If you dig hard enough, you can pierce any fake identity. And what if they got my phone records somehow? I've certainly placed my share of calls to Mongolian Delites. I watch the signs and storefronts flash by the window. Would Otto investigate me, and then lure me to the station like this? No, surely he'd be straightforward, as he is in all things. But what if Packard's right, that I don't really know Otto? Briefly I imagine asking Jimmy to pull over, like maybe I want something at a store, and then ditching him. But where would I go? Mongolian Delites?

"You really got to my place fast," I say. "Is there a fire at the station they need my help in dousing?"

Jimmy smiles. "I should hope not, miss."

Jimmy's smile calms me. Surely he'd know if I was being driven to my doom, and if nothing else, he wouldn't smile so readily. And Otto was happy and excited; I heard it in his voice. And if a problem comes up, I'll handle it. In the end, he's vulnerable to me, just like the Alchemist. I sit back, hating myself for thinking that.

Police headquarters is a tall building of polished gray stone, one in a forest of stately municipal structures. Security guards flank the door, and two others attend the metal detectors.

"Are you Justine Jones?" One of guards asks as I walk through. I nod, and she clambers down from her chair. She's a middle-aged woman who reminds me vaguely of my mother. She walks me to the elevator and explains how to get to the Sanchez office suite. That's what she calls it.

I follow her directions, and soon I'm on the eighteenth floor knocking on a door bearing the number 1882 painted in thick black letters on wavy rain glass.

Otto opens it, and without a word he wraps his arms around me and sweeps me up into a kiss. I laugh, partly from relief, as he turns and shuts the door with his foot.

"Welcome!" He puts me down.

"Hello." I touch his tie, taken anew by his dusky gorgeousness, and gaze into his deep brown eyes. I decide that part of what I love about his eyes are his eyebrows—rich, dark smudges that match the rich locks flowing out below his black beret. He's wearing a smart outfit, too: a black jacket cut long in the old-time style, with a fine white shirt underneath. Really, it's impossible to consume his handsomeness in one glance. It's like an endless feast, course after delectable course. "Hello," I say again, softly.

"You"—he gives me an accusing look—"are a scoundrel."

My stomach flips as I assemble a calm and pleasant expression. "I don't understand."

"I was so very disappointed. . . ." He pauses and regards me thoughtfully, and I have this sense he's seeing into me somehow. He reaches into his back pocket and pulls out a square of paper, which he unfolds slowly and then displays to me. *XOXO.* "A note? I wanted to wake up with you yesterday. Come."

We leave what seems to be his waiting area, full of chairs and books and a small desk in the corner—Sophia's?—and go through another door into a large, long, wood-paneled room.

"Fancy," I say, walking around the perimeter of the space like I'm exploring, but really, I'm buying time; my heart is racing off the "scoundrel" comment and the way he looked at me. It really did seem like he was seeing something wrong.

Otto's inner office is adorned with plaques, framed certificates, and photos of Otto with various officials and newscasters. On the far end there's an enormous wood desk in a kind of ornate cave of bookshelves and old lamps. On the near end, a window looks out onto the buildings across the street. I peer down at the car tops; then I inspect some photos and run my fingers over a beveled glass cabinet that encloses a wet bar. A room service–type cart, laden with juice, coffee, and delicious-looking pastries, stands by the wall opposite a plush brown couch. I'm far too nervous to eat. It was a mistake to come.

Just then Otto locks the door.

I stiffen. "So what was so urgent?"

He comes over and pours coffee. "Cream?"

"A splash."

"Scone?"

"Maybe later." I smile. "I'm just curious about the urgency of this meeting."

He hands me my coffee and settles onto the couch, clopping his boots up on the coffee table, which is lit with a sliver of sun. "Is something wrong, Justine?"

"No. Well, I got some troubling news about a friend recently, that's all."

"Ah. Troubling news about a friend. A friend in trouble."

"Excuse me?"

He pats the cushion next to him. "I wonder if you might be concealing the true source of your anxiety from me. Come, sit." And he smiles his big warm smile.

"Is this an interrogation, Otto?"

"Should it be?"

My anxiety crosses over to adrenaline. I go to him, half sit next to him, curling a knee under me. I lay my arm on the soft couch back. "Are you always this suspicious?"

"Only when I know I'm being lied to."

I sip my coffee and set it down, trying not to show the jolt. "What do you mean?" I'm waiting for him to say more, and he's waiting for me to say more. The master interrogator. I look over at the door. The locked door.

"She glances toward the exit," he says. "Never a good sign. At least not for the subject."

"What?"

"Police maxim. When an interrogation subject looks at the exit, it means she feels cornered."

"I do feel cornered. I haven't even had my breakfast yet, and all these questions. I don't know what this is." I stand, feeling shaky. I go over to the cart and take a scone and a napkin. I break off a corner and stuff it in my mouth, staring out the window, back against the wall, physically and metaphorically.

Cherry almond. Delicious, of course. Eating calms me. "I tell you I have disturbing news about a friend and you're not satisfied with that?"

He laughs his warm laugh. "My my my."

My my my? What does that mean?

He stands, and I wait stupidly, partial scone in hand, unable to breathe, as he crosses the space between us. I fight not to gaze longingly at that exit. My goose bumps are now on full alert.

He looks at me straight—too close, too intimate. My blood races as he takes the scone from me, puts it down, and knits his fingers into mine. And then he presses the backs of my hands up to the wall and kisses my cheek, nuzzles my neck. And God help me, it feels fantastic.

"I know, Justine," he mumbles into my neck, "and it's okay." And then he kisses me harder, presses into me, and I move against him, wantonly soaking up his body as the line between fear and arousal disintegrates completely.

"It doesn't matter," he says.

I pull myself back to my senses. Maybe he knows something, but he can't know everything or he wouldn't be touching me. "I thought you would be upset," I whisper.

"I don't like that you lied, but I know why you did it." He unties my shirt. "Why should I care that you're not a nurse?"

Okay, I think, trying not to show the enormous relief I'm feeling. *Okay.*

"I don't care about any of it, because when you're away from me, I just wish you were here." He kneels, kissing my bare stomach. "I hated it that you weren't there yesterday morning, and all my calls went to your voice mail."

I stroke his hair, stunned. This is why I've gotten away
with so much: he wants to believe the best of me. Just
like I wanted to believe the best of Packard. And Otto
will ignore his instincts and fool himself into it. The
rush of relief intoxicates me almost as much as his sandpapery whiskers on my belly, and the way he's undoing
my jeans, fingers like smart spiders. My adrenaline
transmogrifies into ninety-nine percent pure delicious
lust.

He yanks open my belt and undoes my fly. "None of
that changes our connection. None of it." He shoves my
panties and jeans down around my ankles, and I stomp
out of them. He pulls me to his conveniently large
couch, and I sit on his lap. I'm all the way naked, and
he's barely out of his clothes. I go to work unbuttoning
his shirt, and then I just start laughing. I can't stop. I
press my hands to my face. "I'm sorry, I don't know
why I'm laughing."

"You feel relieved." The trust in his gaze breaks my
heart a little, so I close my eyes, just enjoy the drag of
his hand on my face. He trails his palm from my neck
down my chest, to my stomach, my thigh. "I just don't
care," he says again. The way he says it, it's like he's surprised at himself. "I don't care."

If he knew anything, he'd care. He'd run as far as he
could, because I really ought to zing him again. That
makes me incredibly sad, and suddenly I want to feel his
weight on me, and for him to blot out everything. I
stretch out next to him, and move my way under him.
"Please," I say. "Don't wait. Don't stop. Don't hold
back, just—" I pull him over me. "Please."

Being the master detective that he is, he requires no
further clues. And suddenly he has freed himself from
his pants, or at least free enough to produce a condom
and get it onto himself. He hooks an arm around my

thigh, pushing it up as he enters into me with a force that jars my mind loose of the snarl of guilt and worry.

I gasp and cling onto him, pulling him ever closer. I have this crazy desire to gather up more of him, gather all his muscles and skin and goodness and pull him into me.

He kisses me and bears into me and slides his hands up the tender underside of my arms, up over my head, thrusting, and I just drink him up. And when I close my eyes, I see only darkness, and feel only his solid presence. He comes some time after me, with an exuberant grunt that dissolves into panting. I'm loose and fabulously fluid in his arms.

Afterward I lie by his side, squished onto the couch with him, enjoying a catatonic feeling as I watch him watch the ceiling. I love being so dizzily connected to him, but it's more than the physical connection; it's like I'm connected to his breath, earnest and heavy, and to the rich tones of his voice, and the order and goodness I felt when I spelunked him—one of the many things I've done to him that he would hate me for. I want to stay forever, just like this.

"I want you to know, Justine," Otto says, "though I had suspicions about your being a nurse, I never had you investigated. I never wanted that. I felt confident you would tell me if there was something to tell. Sophia, however, ignored my explicit instructions and pursued connections in Dallas. I came very close to firing her. Instead I put her on a week's leave. A cooling-off period for us both."

"I'm sorry I lied, Otto."

"Don't apologize. My God, you've brought so much understanding to me. Let me bring some to you, because I understand—I do—how people with our affliction can become obsessed with medical professionals. Citizens often assume I have medical training as a law enforcement official, and I frequently allow them to think it. I sometimes give out medical advice I have no business dispensing."

I nod, realizing if I'm serious about saving myself and my friends, this is my opportunity to zing him. He's completely vulnerable to me now.

But I can't do it. I won't. The thought makes me sick.

I sit up and kneel next to his legs. His pants are around one foot, but he still has his black socks on. I draw an invisible line down from his right knee, along the indent of his calf muscle, to his right big toe under his sock, thinking about the consequences of not zinging him. Of course, if Packard made good on his threat to shut me out, I'd end up like Jarvis. And eventually Packard would find a new way to go at Otto anyhow. Even if people would be safer with Packard free, how could I not warn Otto? But that would spell death for my fellow disillusionists. And me.

I button the bottom button of Otto's shirt. "Look at you, all rumply and sheriffy," I say.

"Look at you, all naked and gorgeous."

I fumble with the next button up, feeling faint. Vegetablehood and a slow ignoble death for all the disillusionists? Including me? That can't be my choice. Shelby was right: I don't have a choice.

I lean over to kiss his cheek, pausing to breathe in his scent, which contains the slightest hint of autumn leaves; then I straighten up and place my hands on his chest, all pillowy muscles and warm olive skin. His heart beats fierce and steady under my fingers as I close my eyes and call up my fear, picturing the photo of the Hofstader's victim in France, just before her diagnosis: *"I thought I'd leave the clinic that day with a prescription and some free time to shop. Instead I spent the afternoon getting my head shaved for surgery."* I let myself float free into the fear at the edge of my awareness.

This is why Packard insists we belong together, I think. We both have this hateful ability to hurt people to get what we want. Otto's skin is warm under my palms. Now all I have to do is dip in and graze his energy dimension. Complete the connection. Simple.

But I can't do it.

I pull my hands away from him and fling open my eyes. Slowly I smooth the dusky whispers of hair on Otto's chest. I should, I could, and I can't.

"What dark thoughts, my sweet?"

"Nothing." Again I take up the project of buttoning his shirt, slower and shakier this time, heart *whooshing* in my ears. All that stoked fear with no place to go.

"He would understand, Justine. If you told him the truth, he would understand."

I hold my breath. "Who?"

"Helmut. You ought to tell Helmut you're not a nurse. He'd be proud of you either way. It would make no difference to him. He has such a generous heart."

"I want to come clean," I whisper. "So badly." I leave him laid out on the couch and cross the room to get my clothes. I latch up my pink bra and tie my shirt around me.

"You can tell him."

"It would cause too much harm." I pull on my pink underpants and black jeans.

"That's crazy."

I look across the room at him, try to be cold and clinical. He's a target, and I should've zinged him. Now I have to start over again. I go over and sit by him, place my hands on his chest. "I'm so sorry," I whisper, "so sorry." I try to connect, but my mind is a muddle. I still can't do it. I shut my eyes tight against the tears. Everything is lost now. There's no way out.

"Hey, hey," Otto sits up and pulls me to him.

I'm trying not to cry. "Otto—" I swallow hard, lips on his shoulder. "All I ever wanted was to be normal. It's the only thing I was trying to do."

"I know. I understand."

"I wanted to be free from fear. I want it for everybody. I do."

"We both want that. That's one of the reasons I feel the way I do about you." He strokes my hair. "We're together now. We're not alone anymore, and that changes everything. At least, for me it does." He pulls away, looks at me straight. I regard him blankly, catch a flash of embarrassment before he recovers and smiles. "Anyway, I have a surprise for you." He reassembles his outfit, buttoning and buckling.

I'm too shaky to handle another surprise, and maybe he sees that on my face. "A good surprise," he adds. He strolls over to his desk and picks up a golden envelope. "Would I be remiss in assuming you own a formal dress?"

"What?"

He comes around to the front of his desk. "I want you to accompany me to the Mandler-Foley Spinal Resources charity ball tonight."

I gape at him, feeling like I'm in one of those dreams where random parts of your life merge together. Here is Otto inviting me to a ball that bears the name of Shady Ben Foley and his victims, the Mandlers. "What . . . ?" I begin feebly.

He seems amused. "It's only a first annual, but it's shaping up to be the social event of the season, and it supports a good cause. Most importantly, this fellow Ben Foley is something of a law-enforcement success story. It's critical that I, as head of Midcity law enforcement, put in an appearance."

I stand up. I don't get it.

"I know this is late notice. I usually escort Sophia to

these official functions, but due to our falling out . . . Anyway, if I'd known you back then, I would've asked you. What do you think?"

My stoked fear mixes with my confusion, making me quite light-headed. "A law-enforcement *success story*?"

"Indeed. Ben Foley is one of our most dazzling law-enforcement triumphs. He's a con artist we've arrested numerous times, but we could never quite make the charges stick. It seems we finally got through to him, because he's turned his life around. Mr. Foley realized crime doesn't pay, so to speak, and has become an asset to the community. A reform story that's all too rare. A truly enlightened society, of course, makes reform its goal. I might like to speak on that at the ball if I get a chance."

Otto's explanation does not help my bewilderment. "*You* reformed him?"

"Not personally. It seems to have been a combination of steady police work, arrests, warnings, and lectures from my officers. We do occasionally get through to some of them."

It strikes me as both outrageous and wonderfully hopeful that Otto thinks Foley might have been affected by lectures from police officers. I don't know if I should laugh or cry. Here I am, paralyzed, unable to save myself, my friends. And Otto invites me to a ball for Foley. Nothing makes sense anymore.

He sits back down on the couch. I stand above him and I look down into his eyes, and I realize one thing: Otto makes sense. I felt goodness in him. I felt his desire to make things right, and that desire is my desire. I had a good feeling about him even as a face on the door. I know his heart. It's a shock to think that.

"What do you say?"

Shelby and Packard said Otto would punish us all. But I was in him; I know him. My gut says to tell Otto the truth. To trust, to believe. There's a third option where nobody has to die, and the road there runs through trusting Otto. He wants what I want.

I take a breath. "That's not why he turned good, Otto."

Otto tilts his head.

"Ben Foley isn't a law-enforcement success story. He was disillusioned."

"By his life of crime."

"No, he was disillusioned by disillusionists." I pause. There's no way back now. "He was professionally disillusioned. For money."

Otto laughs. "Justine, the disillusionists don't really exist. That's a myth."

I soak up the warm glow of his adoration, knowing it may be the last time.

"No, they're real. I'm telling you, the Mandlers paid to have Foley disillusioned. They took out a hit on him—not on his life, but on his psychological status. Basically, Foley was broken down, psychologically, by professionals who do that work for money. Who very much exist."

Otto crosses his legs. "It's simply not logical that anybody would have that kind of control over another's well-being. There's certainly no highcap power like that."

"A disillusionist has a different kind of power from a highcap. A disillusionist draws power from being emotionally messed up."

I kneel in front of him and look up to find his handsome features softened. It has to be okay for him to hate me. I never had him anyway.

"Otto, disillusionists are screwed-up neurotics who channel their overload of crazy emotional energy into others. It's a kind of physics. A kind of energy physics. In a sense, disillusionists crash and reboot people."

He looks at me sideways. Smile gone.

"Foley was disillusioned, and the Mandlers would probably confirm it," I continue, "if you asked them in confidence. They felt terrible afterwards."

Otto narrows his eyes. "I have to say, I was taken aback by how readily they embraced the man who destroyed their son."

"It was pity that made them do it. You'd be surprised, Otto, how healing it can be for the victims to see their victimizers broken. To see their humanity."

He's silent for some time. I can see his mind working. My insides tighten as Otto settles a pained gaze on me. "It seems I should've investigated you after all."

There's this moment here when all I can think is, *What am I doing?* But what I'm doing is trusting and believing and going forward.

Otto peers down at me, repeats my words: "'Channel their overload of crazy emotional energy.' Justine, back at my club, I asked you how you'd overcome your health fears, and you said they never go away, that you just move them around. I often returned to that, wondering, *how does she do that?*"

I bite my lip. I wasn't ready for him to put it together so fast. I'd wanted to tell it at my own pace. I need to stop him. "Well, see, Otto—"

"You channel it into people." His olive skin's gone ashen. "Jesus, the vein star. The fake nurse. You channeled it into me. My God—"

"It's not as if—"

He's got my wrists. "You were attacking me all along?"

"No—"

He stands, pulling me up with him, eyes blank with horror. "You made me feel all of that . . ." He tightens his grip. "You filled me with fear, and with such overwhelming joy, too. And our connection—" He lets me go with a look of revulsion.

I stumble backward. "That wasn't part of it, I swear."

"Just a gratuitous twist of the knife?" He sees me as a monster now.

"No, Otto—"

He doesn't hear. "Well played, well played. Incredible—" He's looking back and forth, little eye movements that show a brain at work. And then he laughs the angry kind of laugh that hurts to hear when you care about the person. "Only one man on this planet could recognize the exquisite damage you could do to me. Only one man would come up with an organization dedicated to performing *psychological hits*, of all things . . ." He's trembling. "Even now, Justine, even now—Jesus . . ." He stares out the window. "Uncle Helmut, too. I'm not ashamed of all that despair. And then you came and filled me with unbelievable joy and passion. And terror, of course. I thought I was losing my mind, and I didn't care." He faces me now, eyes shining, lids angular with pain. "Brava. Are you with him?"

"What?"

"Of course you are. I can practically smell Sterling Packard on you now."

"No, hold on. I'm not with him like *that*."

"So it is Packard." He shakes his head. "The way you made me feel . . . and then you attacked me!" He walks around to the other side of his desk and extracts handcuffs from a drawer. "I am going to round up Helmut and everybody in your organization and I am going to seal you all up so far and wide . . ."

"You can't."

His gaze is cold now. "When it comes to maintaining law and order, there's very little I can't or won't do. You can't begin to imagine how I hate to be kept in the dark."

My pulse races; my stoked fear is spiraling dangerously high. Frantically I look at the door. Locked. Like

I'd escape anyway. Out the window, the blue and yellow Midcity flag flaps angrily on a flagpole.

Otto comes across the room to me, calm exterior. We're both masters at that. My mind races over my friends and Packard, and I cross my arms. "You'll kill us like you killed Diesel." I wait. "You remember Diesel?"

He stops in front of me. "I didn't kill Diesel. He's sealed up."

"His skeleton is sealed up. He died alone and helpless in a boarded-up gas station out in the middle of nowhere. Because of you. That qualifies as you killing him."

Otto seems to have a hard time comprehending this. "Diesel's dead?"

"I saw his bones myself. You're a one-man legal system and executioner."

"I never meant for Diesel . . ."

"To die? Well, you killed him all the same. You're a killer, same as the Brick Slinger."

"I had a neighbor set up to help Diesel. I had an account paid up for his food—"

"And the man who ended up with the gouged-out eyes? You rendered him helpless by locking him up." Otto doesn't deny it. I continue. "They died because you've got too many people imprisoned. And if you lose control and let them all escape at once, and that blood-bath really happens? Then a lot of civilians will die. What I told you here today saved you and countless civilians."

He fingers the cuffs; he seems so angry I'm not sure if he's going to follow my thinking. What have I done?

"Otto, what if all these highcaps you have stashed all over the place, what if there was a way to reform them?"

Silence.

"What if they were disillusioned, and they came out the other side like Foley? Reformed?"

He shakes his head. "No."

"Packard has something you need—a method of reform that works on humans and highcaps alike. You have a prison overpopulation problem. You need us. If we disillusioned your ultraviolent highcaps, most of them could be freed. It would relieve all the pressure on you."

"We know how deeply you care about that."

"You need Packard to lead the disillusionists and get the highcaps back under control, and for that Packard needs to be free."

"Do you have any idea what Packard's capable of?"

"Has he ever killed anybody? Even out of neglect?"

The look on Otto's face hurts my heart.

"Don't you think he's served his time? You said he's not one of the violent ones."

"You don't know what happened."

"Maybe that's why I see things clearly. I'm responding to reality here, and you know what I'm seeing? I'm seeing you making your history with Packard more important than your motto. To protect the citizenry—"

"Don't you dare use my motto on me!"

"The citizenry is kept safer by your enlisting Packard to reform the highcaps instead of struggling to keep them sealed up. You've reached capacity. This is your best option. I know you see it. And he'd control the highcaps. Nobody deserves to live in fear."

I hold my breath, hating the way he looks at me now; his brown eyes shine with hurt. "You attacked me even as we made love for the first time." His disdain feels like a knife.

"I didn't know. I thought you were a murdering crime boss. We believed you'd gouged that man's eyes out with your thumbs, Otto. We had these horrible photos . . ."

I stop here. It's just as twisted that I'd sleep with a man who'd do that.

He stares at his still-untied shoes.

I say, "Packard would do anything to be free."

"I'm sure he would." He looks up at me coldly; we regard each other silently across what feels like an endless tundra. Then he asks, "Are you going to come with me voluntarily, or do I need to use these?"

"Where are we going?"

He shakes his head. "Answer the question."

"We both know you don't need those."

He drops the handcuffs in his jacket pocket and leads the way out of his office and down the hall, walking just a little too fast, like part of him wants to lose me and the other part wants to make things hard on me. In the elevator he watches the lit buttons count down from eighteen, and I watch his face; my faith in my leap of faith descends with every floor.

He grips my upper arm hard, too hard, as he marches me straight through the bright lobby and out to his limo down the block.

He said he felt overwhelming joy. So had I. I feel sick for what I've lost.

Jimmy starts to get out, but Otto signals for him to stay in the driver's seat. He opens the back door for me himself.

I get in and slide over to make a place for him and look up, waiting, hoping. But he just stands there. The dark look he gives me sends chills through me. And then he slams the door.

He walks around and gets in the front seat next to Jimmy. And I start wondering here if I'm riding with Chief Sanchez or Henji.

Chapter
Thirty-five

OTTO POUNDS on Mongolian Delites' door, and then he runs his hand over the face, tracing the elegantly curved nose that matches his. I think it's a good sign we're here, and not in some storeroom out in Branlock or something. He's thinking about the offer. I may have lost him, but at least I was right about him.

It's still morning, two hours before lunch. Carter opens up and looks back and forth from Otto to me. "What's up?"

I stammer, unsure where to begin. My left temple is starting to throb in a way it never has before.

"I'm here to see Sterling Packard," Otto says.

"It's okay," I say.

Carter lets us in. "What's going on?"

"Is he in the booth or the kitchen?" I ask.

"Kitchen," Carter says.

I take his arm. "Let's go get him." I pull him away from Otto, leading him around some tables to the bar area where Shelby, Helmut, and Simon sit.

Helmut nods at Otto, who stayed near the door, keeping his distance from me, from Helmut. From all of us. "What's he doing here?" Helmut asks under his breath.

Simon says, "You're pals with Chief Sanchez?"

"Look closer," I say. "Add hair and a beard."

Simon exhales loudly. "The face. Shit, Justine—" He grabs my shoulder. "The nemesis. It's him."

Helmut pales. "I'm getting Packard."

I feel Carter stiffen against my arm. "Sanchez is the nemesis?"

"Carter, be calm."

Carter jerks away from my grip. "You're telling me Sanchez is the nemesis?"

Simon stands up from his barstool. "This oughta be interesting."

I grab for him, but it's too late: Carter's across the room, and in a flash he attacks Otto, all fury and speed.

I run over. "Stop it!" I grab Carter's shirt, but it rips. Otto's recovered from the surprise of the attack enough by this time to be hitting back. I step back, flinching with every smack, thwack, and grunt. They're in a full-on guy fight. Otto's got height and mass and power, but Carter has speed and a whole lot of rage. I grab for Carter's arm, but it's like grabbing a moving fan blade. Things are too out of control; it's like the fight is a blinded beast, thrashing wildly around the room. Just like that they're on the floor, rolling, pushing at each other's necks and faces.

The next thing I know, Packard piles on. He pulls Carter off Otto and back a few steps, arms around the thrashing Carter, encircling him, mumbling into his bloody hair. Otto grabs his beret, which came off during the fight, and puts it on. The way he touches the back of his head, I'm guessing he sustained a blow there.

"What do you want?" Packard says, still holding Carter, who redoubles his struggle. With a jerk, Packard tightens on him. "Stop it," he whispers loudly.

"I want to make a deal with you," Otto says. One of his cheeks is tomato red.

Packard glares at him. "Will it bring Diesel back?"

Otto doesn't answer.

"Then I'm not interested."

Carter's calmed down, finally. Packard lets him go with a warning look, and they both straighten. Blood runs down from Carter's eyebrow, and there's a red circle on the side of his mouth.

"It's open," Otto says suddenly.

Packard shoots his gaze to the door, regarding it with fear and longing, like it's this live thing and not just a slab of wood.

"I lifted the field because I need your help, Sterling."

I'm surprised. If Packard decided to let Carter kill Otto now, wouldn't the field stay off? Is this some show of submission? Repentance? A bargaining salvo? How fast can Otto reknit the force field? He'd have to get to the wall. Or can he interface from the floor?

"I'm sorry about Diesel," Otto continues. "I know how you loved him."

"Don't ever say his name again."

Otto moves closer to Packard. "The door stays open if you help me. I need you to help me keep the city safe."

"I'd put a bullet in my head before I help you do what you do."

"I'm not asking you for that. I want you to do what *you* do. I want you to reform my current prisoners the way you reformed Benjamin Foley."

Packard tears his attention away from the door and regards me with a subtle smile in his eyes; then he closes them, thinking.

Otto continues. "And the violent humans and high-caps I haven't grabbed yet. Quietly, of course."

"So our upstanding Chief Sanchez wants to set up a shadow arm of the law." Packard turns to Otto. "No thanks. I'll stay where I am and wait for you to crack."

"I won't crack."

"I think you will," Packard says. "What's more, seeing the crime wave unfold and knowing it's all due to *your* foolishness has been one of my greatest pleasures in life. It wouldn't have happened if you'd left me alone."

"I was cutting the head off the snake."

"And you created a mindless monster. I told you that would happen, and you didn't listen."

I half expect Otto to argue here, but he doesn't. It's clear, suddenly, how he climbed so high: he's as goal-oriented as Packard.

"And now I'm making you an offer," Otto says. "I need you to disillusion and reform them."

"I will never disillusion the people who trusted me and followed me. All they ever needed was a leader. I'll die in a hole before I betray them."

"It's the new ones I need you for. The ones you never knew, never met, never led." Otto touches his vein star spot again. "The ones I need you to reform were never your people."

"How many highcaps are you holding, Otto? A dozen?"

Otto says nothing.

"Three dozen?" A pulse of a smile passes over Packard's lips. "More?"

"I want you to disillusion the violent highcaps I have sealed in, then disillusion the people who are problems on the outside—humans we can't convict, other violent highcaps."

Packard crosses his arms. "I won't be your employee."

They regard each other calmly. And just steps away, the door is open to Packard. I can't believe he doesn't run right out.

"You'd be an independent operator."

Packard's tone is cool, almost careless. "No thanks."

"What do you want?"

"What I had."

Otto shakes his head. The room feels strangely still. Simon grins hungrily. Shelby comes over and takes my arm, and with a wave of gratitude I pull her close. Otto says, "I can't bring him back."

"He was innocent."

Otto presses his lips together. Pain. Packard understands just how to wound him. It makes me wonder about this secret past of theirs.

"Here's the offer, Sterling. Disillusion and reboot whoever I direct you to, in a timely manner, and you're free to lead life as you please. Just stay under the radar of the police and out of the media."

Packard says nothing.

"I need citizens to stop feeling frightened. Beyond that, stay out of my way and I'll stay out of yours."

"If I didn't know better, old friend, I'd say you were running for office."

"I'm here to keep the citizens safe from evildoers of all kinds," Otto says.

"Right," Packard says.

"Is that a no?"

Packard's silent. It's not a no.

"Will you give your word of honor on this?" Otto says. "As long as you disillusion who I need you to disillusion, you remain free."

"I won't do it indefinitely," Packard says. "There has to be an end."

They negotiate. There will be a list. The issue of pay for us comes up.

Shelby frowns. "Secret police," she whispers to me.

I turn to her, voice low. "You don't like this? You don't want to do it?"

"I did not say that. Vigilante, secret police. Is much the same."

Otto comes to Packard hand outstretched. The two

men eye each other; then Packard takes it and they shake.

Packard glares at the door, but it's a glare that hides a smile. He sucks in his lips, as if to swallow his happiness. It's done.

And then Carter pushes both doors wide open to the late-morning light, holds them open to a scene of stone buildings, signposts, light poles, and trees growing from iron circles in the sidewalk. A car drives by, momentarily blotting out the parallelogram of sunshine on the street. Packard gazes out with an expression that looks something like grief. Shelby offers him her arm.

"No," he whispers. "Let me." He crosses the space to the door in a few steps, slows as he passes over the threshold, and pauses on the outer stoop.

I hear the slightest intake of breath as Helmut comes up next to me, hands clasped tight together against his belly. We all draw slowly toward the door, not wanting to crowd Packard. But during a lull in the traffic, Packard wanders into the street. We move out onto the stoop and sidewalk, unsure what to do. The parallelogram of sunshine in the far lane glows and sparkles on the pavement, and that's where Packard kneels, lifting his face upward.

The traffic light changes, and the cars approach. "Shit." Carter goes out there, followed by Helmut. They wave and direct the oncoming cars into a different lane to avoid Packard, who kneels still, bathed in light, oblivious to the honking, eyes closed in what I can only describe as a look of bliss.

Shelby puts her hand over her heart. "He wanted only to feel sun on skin. Eight years." She glares at Otto, who leans in the dark corner of the restaurant doorway, holding a bloody towel to his eye. I'm guessing he's a lot more worried about a vein star than his eye; after all, his hat came off during the fight. He may even be enduring a silent smite. I have this urge to touch him, to help him, but obviously that won't be happening.

Shelby leaves us and crosses the street to join Packard, Helmut, and Carter, who are laughing, now—happy, infectious laughter. The cars honk and avoid them. I suppose the drivers think they're crazy.

Simon turns a wary eye toward Otto—his new boss, in effect. "Well then," he says.

Otto simply nods; I wonder if he hears the note of challenge.

Simon, too, abandons Otto and me for the jolly fun in the street, taking up a place just apart from the knot of disillusionists.

I wonder how long it will take them to realize I gambled their lives. Have I lost them, too?

I'm awkwardly aware it's just Otto and me in the doorway. Like a beggar, I soak up these last seconds of being near him.

They start off down the sidewalk—Packard, Shelby, Carter, Helmut. Simon follows at a few paces—with them, yet not. Packard glances back at us briefly, glowing with lust and life.

"The citizenry should be safer, at least," Otto says.

The citizenry. I miss him already. "Yeah."

"Where do you think they're going?" Otto removes the towel from his face and sets it on the ledge. There's a bright red blotch on the outer edge of his eye.

I only have to consider this for a moment. "The beach. Probably Mexico."

We watch in somber silence.

"I'm sorry," I say.

He regards me strangely. What is there to say? I could remind him I likely saved his life and the lives of others. But that's not the issue. I turn to go.

"Wait." A hand, heavy on my shoulder, urging me back. I turn. He looks troubled, even a little bit desperate; I can't tell if he wants to arrest me or kiss me. The pathetic truth is, I would welcome either.

"When you—? Was it—?" He stops. He can't find the question.

I can find the question. "Was it easy?" A horrible silence unfolds around my words. "You trusted me and opened yourself to me. God, I always felt so happy to be with you. But I attacked you at your most vulnerable—twice." I wrap my own arms around me. "I went against my feelings about you and lied to you and hurt you to achieve my mission. Was it easy? How could I? Is that what you're wondering?"

His eyes shine with pain. "Yes," he whispers.

"No. It was *not* easy. And yes, it hurt like hell—hurts still. But . . . how could I? I guess I just could. That's what I'm capable of." I won't lie to him. "And if I thought innocent lives were at stake, including my own, would I do it again?"

He regards me sharply.

"I would," I say.

His nostrils move minutely; he seems almost to breathe in my answer, weighing it, maybe battling it inside himself.

My stomach does this queasy flop. "I can't tell you how awful it is to know I invaded you with my fear and darkness."

"I thought I was going into overload. I felt crazy. My head . . ."

"I'm so sorry. I know you can never forget it."

"I can't."

There's this long silence. I glance up the street to find my disillusionist gang has disappeared from view. This makes me feel unaccountably sad.

"But I would've done it," he says. "In your shoes, I would've done the same."

I search his face, waiting for the *but*.

"I understand perfectly why you did it. But the fact remains you did it to me."

I nod.

"Still, I find myself at such a loss."

"A loss?" I echo stupidly.

He touches his chest. "More a conflict." I'm thinking a conflict might be good, but it's not the kind of thing you say to a person.

"You tried to destroy me, but you also gave me the means to destroy you. You believed."

I'm so grateful, I actually feel like crying. I try my best to get a grip. "Of course I did." I try not to smile as I touch his lapel. "Of course."

He reaches out to me, and my heart leaps as he takes my hand and pulls me to him. "God help me," he says, and he kisses me, long and strong, like his whole heart is pouring into it. He feels so good; I hold him to me, drinking in his lips, his arms, his warmth.

He pulls away as abruptly as he started, regards me with a baffled look. "You never answered my question," he says.

I try and focus. "What question?" I don't know if I can answer any more questions.

"Are you free for the ball tonight?"

I regard him dimly. Is he really asking?

He weaves his warm fingers into mine. "I want you with me."

"You do?"

"I need time to repair, to trust. I can't—"

Have sex with me again, he means. "It's okay." I try not to smile quite as hugely and wildly as my heart wants. "I would love to accompany you more than anything."

He holds my gaze and pulls my hand to his mouth, kisses my palm without taking his eyes from mine. It's shockingly intimate—even more intimate than the kiss. "Good."

Ever so lightly, I raise a finger to touch his left cheekbone, ragingly red. "Are you okay?"

He knows what I mean. "Yes."

"But look at you. This will be a terrible bruise."

He gets a mischievous look. "I know."

"Hey!" Ling's ambling up the street with Spruggie the cook, and they both seem shocked. At first I think it's because Chief Sanchez is there, but then I realize they're actually looking past us, at the door. I turn. There are recessed panels where the face once was. "What's with the new door?" Ling runs a hand over it.

"A change," I say. "And Packard's taking some time off."

This surprises her more than the door. "Packard?"

"Can you manage the place, Ling, until he comes back?"

"Of course," Ling says.

"Packard never takes time off," Spruggie says, pulling open the new door. They go in.

"Packard'll never set foot in there again," Otto says under his breath.

Chapter
Thirty-six

I DON'T KNOW what I expected from the Mandler-Foley ball, but certainly not a genuine, full-blast ball. To me, a ball is an event from another time and place, most probably a fictional one. As we walk through the two-story door of the majestic Van Horner Place, however, and follow the lobby master up the elegant steps, passing under the arch and into the upper level of the cavernous ballroom, joining a number of stunning guests in the receiving line, it comes to me that this is, in fact, a ball. How can it be, I wonder, that people have been giving and attending balls without the general populace knowing?

I link my arm in Otto's as we wend toward the front of the line on the grand balcony. I'm wearing the beautiful brown velvet gown I bought for the Silver Widow's cocktail party, with a silver wrap and silvery jewelry to match the silver sparkles around the neck and waist. But I could have a gown encrusted with diamonds and I wouldn't outshine Otto.

Injuries usually ruin a man's appearance. Cuts and bruises around the mouth can make a guy look like he's frowning, or maybe a messy eater. Poorly placed swelling can evoke defects of various kinds, and many black eyes look downright monstrous as they color and swell.

Otto's injuries, on the other hand, only heighten his dashing good looks. The redness on his left cheekbone has turned into a midnight-blue bruise that emphasizes the sculpted beauty of his face and the mahogany richness of his eyes and hair. The brilliant red gash above his right eyebrow balances out the bruise; taken together with the white butterfly bandage, it creates a contrapuntal echo to the red satin sash set diagonally over his white shirt. His black suit is cut long, and a golden dress badge gleams upon his breast. He also wears a black beret, of course. I can't stop looking at him, can't stop smiling at him. I can't believe I'm with him.

As we draw closer to the front I get a view over the banister of the cavernous ballroom below, and my heart stops. It's lit by soft sconces that make the sparklestone walls glint; the white alabaster floor, already filled with beautiful revelers, appears to glow. Colorful banners are draped from the ceiling, many featuring the blue-and-yellow Midcity flag, and a string quartet plays softly in a far, dark corner.

When we get to the front of the line, we're announced by a jowly man with a booming voice: "Police Chief Otto Sanchez and Ms. Justine Jones." They way he says it makes my name sound special. Otto squeezes my hand as we move to the side, where reporters question him about his injuries.

"Keeping the citizens safe from evildoers has its occasional hazards," Otto says as the camera flashes go off.

Somebody touches my arm. "Excuse me—"

I turn, and there he is: large forehead, too-small nose, thinning gray hair. Foley. His suit is plain and brown, like you'd see at an office. But it's his eyes that shock me. They don't have that predatory "peering out" quality anymore. They're warmer, somehow. Engaged.

"I know I could never apologize enough," Foley says, "but I am deeply sorry. Your father was desperate to keep you and your brother out of harm's way, and I took advantage of that. I took advantage of his love for you."

I just stare at him, bewildered by my impulse to cry. "Thank you, Foley," I say, grasping his hand. "I really appreciate your saying that to me."

Then Foley is drawn by the reporters to pose with Otto and the Mandlers, who don't recognize me, luckily. Otto speaks on the subject of an enlightened society reforming criminals rather than avenging crimes. Everybody carries on as if Otto and the police had everything to do with Foley's reform, and Otto allows this. Then Otto deflects a question about his running for mayor. If he were running, of course, this situation couldn't be more perfect.

Finally we're released from the interviewers and well-wishers to descend the curved stone staircase. "So was Packard right, Otto? You want to be mayor?"

"My secret status as a highcap makes it complicated and risky. Though it does give me certain advantages."

"So Packard was right."

"Sterling Packard is rarely wrong about people. It's what makes him valuable—and dangerous."

Not an answer. I take it as a yes. "They all think it was *you* behind Foley's big turnaround."

"They need to think it was me," he says. "And Sterling needs them to think that, too. If people knew about what you and your friends were up to, you wouldn't be so effective."

As we near the bottom of the staircase, Otto greets a well-wisher, and I'm thinking about Cubby for some reason. I'd wanted to change and reform for Cubby, but I'm glad I didn't. Packard changed me against my will, supposedly for my own good as well as his. I still don't know if I can forgive him for that, but Otto likes me for who I am.

The music switches to a waltz, and the revelers begin to glide around the floor. Just then I look back up at Foley; I can't get over how different he is. Essentially different. But even though he's law-abiding and productive and maybe even happy now, something about it seems not quite right. Or am I just thinking too much? For some reason, my thoughts go back to Jordan the Therapist's riddle: *When is good not good?* Something about it nudges at the edge of my mind. Am I missing something?

"Justine?"

I break out of my reverie to find Otto in front of me, palm outstretched. "A dance, my dear?"

Gently I place my hand onto his and gaze into his earnest brown eyes. He pulls me out to the floor and we move as one, and suddenly everything seems okay.

Chapter
Thirty-seven

TEN DAYS LATER, I head into the cracked-mirror-decorated lobby of Rickie's scary apartment building all by myself. Shelby is ill from Mexico. She'd exhorted me to wait, but I'd managed to find a group of ants, including what I believe to be a queen, at a construction site near my building, and it seemed cruel to keep them in the jar forever. Plus, now that I've been there, the place doesn't seem that scary.

I trudge up the back stairs over the bundles and past a few dazed people and knock on Rickie's door.

She opens up and her eyes grow big. "What are you doing here?"

"I have your stuff."

She looks out at the hall behind me. Her lacy tank top is pink today, and her jeans are held up by a pink belt. "I told you to stay away."

"It's safe, I promise. And I wanted you to have this." I put my shopping bag down and push it over the threshold with my foot. Rickie pulls out the jar. The ants scramble around on the leafy twigs in there. She's already set up the farm, I notice. "The big one's the queen."

"I think I know that."

I don't say anything about what's happened. Packard is going around assessing Otto's prisoners, at least the ones who aren't mass murderers, and deciding which ones can be freed right away—released into his custody, so to speak—and which need to be disillusioned first.

"Thanks," she says.

"It sucks to be trapped." I watch her put the other stuff on the couch. Batteries. Three bottles of tequila.

"I never thought I'd be so bored that I'd want an ant farm," she says. "Fuck, it's all I could think about since you left. Pathetic." She looks up. "You can come in."

"Will I regret it?"

"Will I?" Then an expression of astonishment comes over her face.

I spin around and there he is, smiling behind me, holes in his jeans, hair in his eyes, and a blue shirt so faded it's almost white.

He looks at her for a few moments, assessing her emotional structure. You can always tell when he's doing that. Or at least I can. I haven't seen him since he walked away from Mongolian Delites. He's sunburnt. And he seems taller.

He strolls in. "You ready for that job, Rickie?"

Movement out of the corner of my eye—the giant horse book levitates off the coffee table.

"Shit!" I back up as it flies across the room and embeds itself in the wall like an overfed throwing star.

Packard arches an eyebrow. "You need more than that to be on my crew. Being on my crew means you can't use your power just because you feel like it. You use it in the line of duty only. Being on my crew means when you feel angry, you settle things with words. It means a vow of total self-control."

"I can do it. I'm ready!" Rickie says.

"Are you? This is a serious vow that you cannot break. I want you to spend this night deciding whether you can really give your word of honor, because once you give it, you can't go back. I can't have you drawing negative attention to yourself or my crew. Or me."

Rickie's nodding vigorously. "You're alive."

"You'll be let out tomorrow," Packard continues.

She brightens. "You'll let me out tomorrow? I don't understand. What about Henji?"

"You don't have to worry about him. Listen, I'll send Chief Sanchez over to check on you when the force field lifts."

An ugly look passes over Rickie's face.

Packard points at her. "In some ways, this will be your first challenge. Can you be polite to him when he comes to see you?"

Rickie's mouth hangs open. "Does Chief Sanchez work for you now?"

Packard waits a beat. "I didn't hear an answer."

Rickie apparently takes this as confirmation that Otto does, in fact, work for Packard. And that Packard is somehow engineering her freedom. "You're on," she says. "Absolute kindness to Mr. Sanchez. Thank you."

She thinks Packard's letting her out. I think back on how Otto took credit for Foley's reform. It's amusing, the way Packard and Otto both take credit for everything.

Packard places a card on the coffee table. "Call my man Francis when you're ready to get to work, and he'll come get you and set you up with a temporary place."

I pick up the jar of ants. "I guess you don't need these guys anymore."

"Hell, no!"

I say good-bye to Rickie and accompany Packard to the elevators. "You know, you shouldn't ride the elevators here."

He pushes the button. "It's a new day."

"Did you know I was here?"

"Shelby called. She didn't want you to come alone. And I wanted to get straight with you."

There's this silence between us that contains everything.

"I want to get straight with you, too," I say simply.
Then the elevator arrives. We get in and doors snap
shut; a caged bulb above casts a dim glow. "Frankly,
Packard, I don't know whether to apologize to you or
slap you in the face."

"Don't apologize to me, Justine." The elevator jerks
and descends.

"Does that mean you want the slap?"

He gives me a long look. "I might enjoy the slap."

"Oh, stop," I say, annoyed, like my face isn't all red.
"Packard, I know I took a chance with you and everyone else, bringing Otto on board and everything. I need
you to know, I never wanted you destroyed. I would
never want that—"

He smiles.

"What?"

"It so amusing, how little self-understanding you have."

"What does that mean?"

"How little you see of your own integrity. I knew
what I was playing with." He squints. "I knew if I
tricked you, that you could be my strongest ally or my
most destructive enemy."

"I hope I'm neither."

"The night's still young." The brightness fades from
his face, and he looks at me the way he does when he
has something important to say. "We belong together,
Justine. I know you felt it before you got so angry. You
won't ignore the truth of us forever, and you will come
to me as more than a disillusionist."

"Packard—"

He flings up a hand. "I'm done. Except to thank you
for effecting an alternative to my plan that was actually
superior in some ways. Astonishing as that may be."

I smile. Good old Packard.

"In *some* ways," he repeats.

"You really think Rickie can control herself? Because I'm telling you, she's pretty aggressive."

"You forget what I alone can see. She just needs a sense that she's heading toward something. . . ." He breaks off, thoughtful for some time. The doors slide open. "I'm finding that about a third of Otto's prisoners are fit to emerge now; the rest we'll need to disillusion. I have an easy one for you this week. A telepath with a thing about airborne pathogens."

"How do I fool a telepath?"

"I've got a guy who can show you how."

We stroll through the lobby and out into the courtyard of weeds pushing up through shattered concrete.

"What will she do? Rickie?"

"Muscle. I'll put her under Francis. She's a very powerful telekinetic."

I raise my eyebrows. "You need a lot of muscle?"

"A shadow arm of the law requires muscle, Justine. Or to be more precise, a shadow arm of Otto. That was the essence of our agreement. I'm free as long as we disillusion who he says to. We're putting him in power, you and me. All of us. Otto will run for mayor, and he *will* win. This couldn't have worked out better for him."

"I think it worked out well for you, too."

He gives me a look I can't quite read.

I smile. "Come on." I lead him to a mass of weeds where metal fence meets sidewalk; I kneel, unscrew the lid of the jar, and tip it into the sandy dirt.

Packard crouches down and pulls some weeds aside so I can aim the ants into good, rich dirt. It's at that moment I notice he's still wearing the blue metal bracelet, the one from Diesel's body. The bracelet he swore never to remove until he had vengeance. He looks up, green eyes brilliant in the sunshine. He saw me staring at it. He knows what I'm thinking.

"Don't worry. Staying out of Otto's way includes not killing him. As long as he stays out of my way. You can go ahead and report that back to your new boyfriend."

"Don't, Packard."

"You chose wrong, Justine."

"I chose to promote freedom and transformation."

He tilts his head. "Is that a motto?"

"You should get a motto, too, Packard."

"A motto is a pathetic substitute for an opinion." He stands and extends his hand down to help me up and I take it. "Justine," he whispers, pulling me up, letting go.

"Packard," I say.

He pulls dark sunglasses from his pocket and puts them on, then heads down the sidewalk all cool. I hear a car engine start up, and I see Carter and Helmut parked a little ways down in a shiny blue boat of an old convertible, just like the one Rickie described. I wave to them as Packard hops into the passenger side, and then they're off.

I watch them for a block, and then another, all the way until they're obscured by the cross traffic. Up above on the building there's Otto's face, etched into the fourth-floor wall, watching out over the citizens and the city like a griffin, all keen eyes and sharp talons.

I screw the lid back on the empty jar and head home.